"Horror-fantasy epic is a difficult beat to hit—but Christopher Golden's sprawling saga of vampires, demons, and dark sorcery is nothing less."
—Mike Carey, author of the Felix Castor novels

—Jonathan Maberry, author of *The King of Plagues*

Praise for *Of Saints and Shadows* . . .

"Golden's book is the template for a score of books that have been published in the years since its publication. Many of those books have been bestsellers. Reading *Of Saints and Shadows* again, I was amazed how many elements now familiar in the vampire and thriller genres appeared in *Saints* first. Golden's imagination and expert plotting wove these elements into a startlingly original book, as exciting to read now as it was when it first appeared on the rack."
—Charlaine Harris, #1 *New York Times* bestselling author of *Dead in the Family*

. . . and for the Peter Octavian novels

"A delightfully different take on vampires . . . sure to stand out in the current crop of urban fantasy."
—Kelley Armstrong, #1 *New York Times* bestselling author of *Waking the Witch*

"Christopher Golden has reinvented the vampire myth into nonstop action, suspense, and fascinating dark fantasy. [He's] an imaginative and prodigious talent who never lets genre boundaries hold him back."
—Douglas Clegg, author of the Vampyricon trilogy

The Shadow Saga

Of Saints and Shadows
(July 2010)

Angel Souls and Devil Hearts
(October 2010)

Of Masques and Martyrs
(December 2010)

The Gathering Dark
(February 2011)

Waking Nightmares
(May 2011)

ABOUT THE AUTHOR

CHRISTOPHER GOLDEN is the award-winning, bestselling author of such novels as *The Myth Hunters*, *Wildwood Road*, *The Boys Are Back in Town*, *The Ferryman*, *Strangewood*, and the Peter Octavian series. He has also written books for teens and young adults, including *Poison Ink*, *Soulless*, and the upcoming *The Secret Journeys of Jack London*, co-authored with Tim Lebbon. A lifelong fan of the "team-up," Golden frequently collaborates with other writers on books, comics, and scripts. He co-wrote the lavishly illustrated novel *Baltimore, or, The Steadfast Tin Soldier and the Vampire* with Mike Mignola, and the comic book series spin-off. With Tim Lebbon, he has co-written four novels in the Hidden Cities series, the latest of which, *The Shadow Men*, hits in 2011. With Thomas E. Sniegoski, he is the co-author of the book series *OutCast* and *The Menagerie*, as well as comic book miniseries such as *Talent*, currently in development as a feature film. With Amber Benson, Golden co-created the online animated series *Ghosts of Albion* and co-wrote the book series of the same name.

As an editor, he has worked on the short story anthologies *The New Dead* and *British Invasion*, among others, and has also written and co-written comic books, video games, screenplays, and a network television pilot. The author is also known for his many media tie-in works, including novels, comics, and video games, in the worlds of *Buffy the Vampire Slayer*, *Hellboy*, *Angel*, and *X-Men*, among others.

Golden was born and raised in Massachusetts, where he still lives with his family. His original novels have been published in more than fourteen languages in countries around the world. Please visit him at www.christophergolden.com

WAKING NIGHTMARES

Christopher
Golden

SIMON &
SCHUSTER

London · New York · Sydney · Toronto

ISBN 978-1-84737-791-3

Typeset by M Rules
Printed in the UK by CPI Mackays, Chatham ME5 8TD

*This book is respectfully dedicated to all of the
fantastic friends and readers who simply would not
stop asking when Octavian would return.
I hope you enjoy this homecoming as much as I have.*

Acknowledgments

Enormous thanks to my wonderful editor, Ginjer Buchanan, who has always left a light burning in the window for Peter. Thanks to everyone on the Ace team, to Tom Sniegoski for the morning chats, and to Tim Lebbon, Amber Benson, and Ashleigh Bergh for keeping me in line. Most of all, my endless love and thanks to my wife, Connie, and our crazy kids, Nicholas, Daniel, and Lily Grace.

Octavian climbed out of the professor's car, hoping they had come to this grimy corner of Montreal on a fool's errand, that there would be no monsters tonight. Fighting monsters took time—magic or spirits or demons even longer—and he had promised to return to The Red Door before Nikki took the stage tonight. *Don't make me break my promise*, he had warned the professor. The man had nodded anxiously and tried to reassure him, but Octavian did not feel reassured.

He stood on the sidewalk in the golden light of the setting sun and looked up at the windows of the third-floor apartment. They were dirty, like everything else in this neighborhood, and the glint of the waning daylight only made the glass opaque and almost sinister.

"So this girl is a student of yours?" Octavian asked.

The professor slammed his car door and thumbed the button on his keychain that made the car chirp, its doors locking automatically. He looked even more pale and nervous than usual.

"Last year," the professor said. "We've stayed close."

Octavian raised an eyebrow but did not comment. Derek Tremblay had been a professor at McGill University in Montreal for a dozen years. A decade before that, he'd gone to visit friends at Boston College and—after a drug-fueled rave—woken up to find one of those friends dead and himself under arrest for murder. In those days, before the world knew the truth about shadows and vampires and demons, Octavian had been a private investigator in Boston. Helping people like Derek Tremblay, back before he was Professor Tremblay, had been Octavian's way of trying to make up for the hideous things he had done in his first few centuries as a shadow . . . as a vampire.

"A lot of students in this neighborhood?" Octavian asked, glancing around at the bicycles chained to lampposts, the posters for music events plastered on the bus station, and the old VW bus parked at the corner. Across the street was a coffeehouse, its open door pumping music. Two grungy-looking guys came out as he watched, both carrying skateboards.

"Who else would live here?" the professor asked.

Octavian smiled thinly. There were millions of people who would weep with joy if offered the opportunity to live here, but he knew what the professor meant. There was certainly a Bohemian air in the neighborhood, which spread for several blocks, not far from the university. The Red Door—the music club where Octavian's girlfriend, Nikki Wydra, was playing tonight—was only a few blocks away. They'd been to The Red Door, or La Porte Rouge, before, and the clientele would fit right in on this street. They were Boho twenty- and thirty-somethings with a passion for coffee, music, peace, and the environment. Octavian figured as long as people like them existed, there was still hope for the world.

Most visitors thought Montreal could be divided into two basic areas: the tourist-friendly Old Town, with its European architecture, cobblestoned streets, and eclectic shops, and the rest of the city, which was much more metropolitan and modern. But it would be too simple to split Montreal between the distant past and the vibrant future, especially when neighborhoods like this one, stuck in the 1960s, still thrived. Vidscreens might show news and advertisements 24/7 in the subway, the underground malls, and bus stations in the city's business centers, but such technology might as well not even exist here.

So it surprised Octavian all the more when the professor used his own key to open the apartment building's front door. Tremblay caught himself, but too late. As he pushed the door open and pocketed his keys, he glanced guiltily at Octavian.

"You said you were close," Octavian said.

The professor nodded. "Yeah."

Neither man needed to elaborate. If the professor had a sexual relationship with one of his students, that was an issue for the university. Their reason for being here tonight—if the professor and his young girlfriend were right—concerned Octavian much more. Enough to take time away from Nikki to accompany Tremblay on this errand, despite the distance he had been feeling in their relationship of late.

The foyer smelled of mold and piss. Someone had painted the walls within the past few years but had just slathered the latex on top of the old, peeling paint without doing much scraping. If not for the cat on the stairs and the mail stacked on a table just inside the door, the place would have seemed abandoned.

Cooking smells wafted from the closed door to the first-floor apartment. Octavian nodded for the professor to lead the way and they started up the stairs.

The professor had his key to the girl's apartment building, on the same ring as his car keys and the key to his own place. He unlocked the apartment door, swung it open, and stepped inside.

"Viviane?" he said quietly.

Octavian followed him into the apartment and the professor shut the door. The day had been warm for September, and the air in the apartment was musty and close. Not quite stifling, but it must have been almost unbearable earlier in the day. No air moved. No breeze. The place was closed up tight. If the professor hadn't told him the girl was home, he would have thought the apartment was empty.

The professor pocketed his keys and ventured into a small living room full of mismatched furniture. Based on the décor and the overall tidiness of the place, it was clearly an apartment without a permanent male presence. Chinese paper lanterns hung from the ceiling above the sofa. A light hummed in the galley kitchen, as though the bulb might burn out at any moment.

"Viviane?" the professor said, a bit louder now, as he started toward the short hall that led deeper into the apartment.

Octavian resisted the urge to check the time on his cell phone. Nikki would be doing sound check right now. He had hours before she went on stage. Plenty of time for whatever darkness lay ahead.

A door clicked softly open down the hall. The professor halted, letting his young girlfriend come to him. Viviane emerged from the shadowed hallway tentatively at first, but when she saw Octavian, her expression turned hopeful.

"Hey," the professor said, reaching for her hand.

Viviane let him pull her into a quick embrace but barely seemed aware of his kiss. She wore a McGill sweatshirt and pajama pants and looked as if she hadn't showered in days. The dark circles under her eyes, visible despite the deep chocolate hue of her skin, suggested she hadn't slept in at least as long.

"Is this him?" she asked.

Octavian nodded. "I'm him."

Viviane smiled, and suddenly she didn't look so weary. But then the smile faded as she remembered what awaited them in the other room.

"Thank you for coming," she said, approaching him and holding out her hand. "I'm Viviane Chenot."

"Peter Octavian," he replied, shaking her hand. "And it's no trouble. I'm in Montreal for a few days anyway."

Viviane was nodding. "That's how Derek tracked you down. He saw on Nikki Wydra's Twitter that she was playing at La Porte Rouge tonight—"

"I explained it all to him," the professor interrupted.

"Yeah," Viviane said, nodding. "Sorry. Of course you did."

Octavian always thought it was interesting when people referred to Nikki by her first and last name, but that was her public identity. She wasn't a celebrity by any means, but to people who liked the kind of music she played, she was famous enough. And to them, she was *Nikki Wydra*. Names of famous people were like that; they held weight. And that was indeed how the professor had known Octavian would be in Montreal tonight and had tracked him down—through Nikki's Twitter page. Octavian hadn't seen Derek Tremblay in more than twenty years, but the professor knew what Octavian had been up to in that time. A lot of people did.

"It's no trouble," Octavian said, trying to soothe the girl.

It was not quite a lie. Nikki had not been entirely pleased with his leaving her to meet Tremblay, but neither was she selfish enough to have attempted to stop him. Her career had become more and more important to her. The time they spent apart had grown more frequent thanks to her music and to his work. Whenever unexplained super-natural phenomena appeared, he would get a phone call. Sometimes he had to get involved. When the two of them were alone together, without the pressures of the outside world, it was easy for her to forget that he was supernatural, and for him to forget that she was not—that she was ordinary and mortal and could not imagine some of the things he had seen and lived.

So it was no trouble for him to meet with Tremblay today. He was in Montreal, after all. But it certainly did nothing to heal the rift that he felt beginning to grow between himself and Nikki. He loved her, but of late he had begun to wonder if that was enough.

"I'm happy to help, if I can," Octavian continued. "Derek and I go back a long way."

The professor smiled awkwardly. "I knew Peter before he came out as a vampire," he said, and then he glanced quickly at Octavian. "Sorry. A shadow. No offense."

Octavian waved it away, though it did make him tense, being called a vampire. The world had learned the truth of their existence years before, thanks to live news coverage of a bloody battle in Venice between shadows—the blood-drinking shapeshifters who were the source of the world's vampire legends—and a rogue sect of Vatican sor-cerers who'd murdered the pope and launched a crusade to exterminate all shadows, whether good or evil. The world was still feeling the after-shocks both of that revelation and of the events that followed. The Roman Catholic Church had splintered and was severely weakened. Shadows lived peacefully, side by side with humanity, but there were still some who embraced the word *vampire* and all of the savagery it entailed, and those creatures were hunted by human and shadow alike.

"No offense taken," Octavian said. "Though you know I'm not one of them anymore."

Viviane nodded. "I read that somewhere. How does that work, exactly? How do you stop being a vam—I mean, a shadow?"

Octavian thought about answering, considered telling her about the thousand years he'd spent in Hell learning magic, and the metamorphosis that had evolved him from shadow to human mage. But then he remembered why he had come.

"It's a long story," he said, remembering how much trouble people had understanding how he could have spent a thousand years in Hell while only five years had passed in the human world. *Infernal physics* was enough of an answer for someone used to dealing with the supernatural, but just another conundrum for a regular citizen. "Another time, maybe."

Guilt and sadness washed over Viviane's face, as though she had been trying just for a moment to forget her troubles and knew she couldn't put them off any longer.

"Sure," she said. She glanced at the professor and then back at Octavian. "He's in my bedroom."

Octavian gestured for Viviane to lead the way, and at last she did, walking down the hall as if she wished she were anywhere else. When she reached for the bedroom doorknob, her hand trembled. She pushed the door open and stood aside to let them enter first.

"Jesus," the professor said, wrinkling his nose. "What's that smell?"

Octavian had caught it as well, earthy and damp, like a hothouse full of dying flowers. Both bedroom windows were open, but the warm breeze did nothing to diminish the aroma. And unless Viviane had a wilting, rotten garden hidden underneath her bed, there could be no doubt about the source of the smell.

A young guy lay sprawled on the bed, legs tangled in the sheets like he'd been sleeping off a bad drunk or ugly nightmares. His arms were flung wide and his head lolled to one side, a thin stream of yellowish drool trailing from one corner of his mouth. His throat rattled with every exhalation and his neck looked swollen, and for a second, Octavian thought of plague . . . he'd seen more than his share of such sickness since his childhood, but that had been centuries ago. And there were no welts or sores or even the sort of inflammation that might suggest plague. The sight of the young man and his constricted breathing reminded him of hideous memories, but this was no plague.

Still, even if the professor hadn't already said so, Octavian would have known at first glance that this was no ordinary flu or infection. The smell offered the first clue. The man's complexion provided the second. No healthy human being had flesh of that particular hue—not so much a jaundiced yellow as a slight greenish tint.

"His name is Michael, you said?" Octavian asked, glancing at the professor.

"Michael," Viviane confirmed from just inside the open bedroom door. She hung back, arms crossed, fretting and tense as though she might flee. "He hates being called Mike."

Octavian nodded. "Michael it is, then. How long has he been like this?"

"Two days that we know of," the professor said.

"The sink was leaking," Viviane said, her voice cracking with emotion, her gaze haunted, as though she blamed herself for her brother's condition. "The landlord kept promising to fix it, but he never showed up, so Michael came over to take care of it. He didn't . . . well, I mean, he wasn't . . . green. Just a little pale. But he didn't look well and he kept coughing and he was short of breath and he seemed a little weird—"

"Weird how?"

Viviane shrugged. "Like he'd been smoking something, y'know?"

Octavian nodded and moved closer. Something was strange about the unconscious man's arms and legs, his body hair. Bending to take a closer look, Octavian saw that amid the hair were tiny growths that looked almost like sprigs of something growing there. Something green.

"He thought he was getting a cold or something," Viviane went on. "I told him to come in here and lie down and when I checked on him a little while later, I couldn't wake him up."

He investigated the man's hands. Similar sprigs grew from beneath his fingernails. Unsettling as these things were, the most troubling of Michael's afflictions were the tiny leaves visible in his right ear and both nostrils. Octavian cursed inwardly, wondering how much time had elapsed since he had gotten in the car with the professor, and how much time he had before Nikki took the stage at The Red Door.

"It's awful," the professor said.

Octavian shot him a hard look. Of course it was awful. Did he think Viviane needed him to confirm that her brother going catatonic and growing twigs and tiny leaves out of his orifices and pores was something other than a joyous event? Asshole.

With what he hoped was a comforting glance toward Viviane, Octavian turned back to her brother. The thick rattle of his breathing turned into a choking noise, and Michael twitched several times before he began breathing through his nose and relaxed again. The rattle hadn't vanished, but lessened.

Octavian reached for his face. Gently, he pulled back one of Michael's eyelids. Tiny plant roots had grown across the eyeball like the miniature wiring on an old computer circuit board.

"Oh, my God," Viviane whispered.

Octavian glanced at her. "His eyes weren't like that before?"

"I didn't look at his eyes," she said. "But check his throat. I thought . . . I wanted to see if I could clear his breathing or do something to help him, so I got a little flashlight and had a look. I would've taken him to the hospital, or called an ambulance, but once I saw that, I knew there was nothing a doctor could do for him. When Derek said he knew you . . . Please tell me you can help him?"

Her smile was brittle, as though she were teetering on the brink of hysteria.

Octavian did not answer. Conjecture would not help Viviane or her brother at this point. Instead, he worked Michael's mouth open, massaging the muscles of the lower jaw to get it wider. A dark mass was visible just inside, and at first Octavian thought the man's tongue had swollen. The smell that wafted out of Michael's throat was much worse than the rest of the room—moist and filled with rot.

He glanced around, grabbed the slim flashlight from the nightstand, clicked it on, and shone its beam into Michael Chenot's throat. The mass had seemed more solid in the dark, but now Octavian could make out the tiny leaves and green and brown strands that made up the mossy clump growing there.

"Have you ever seen anything like this before?" the professor asked.

"Not exactly like it, no," Octavian admitted, stepping away from the bed.

"What *is* it?" Viviane asked. "How does something like this happen?"

Octavian narrowed his eyes, studying the man in the bed. "Things like this *don't* just happen. It could be a curse. It could be that Michael was attacked by something or someone . . . an earthwitch, maybe."

"What the hell is an earthwitch?" the professor asked.

"Usually benevolent, actually," Octavian replied.

"But can you help him? Can you get it out of him?" Viviane pleaded.

"I can try," Octavian said. Somehow that did not assuage Viviane's fear for her brother, but he had not come to take away her fear. He'd come to help, if he could. "Do you know what kind of plant this is?"

The professor glanced away. Obviously he had some ideas. Viviane only frowned and shook her head.

"It's cannabis," Octavian said. "Marijuana."

Viviane stared at him and gave a soft chuckle of horrified disbelief. "Pot? Michael's got pot growing inside him?"

"Does he smoke regularly?" Octavian asked.

Her eyes began to glaze over with confusion, as though she were looking inward for an answer.

"Yeah," she said. "Plenty."

"Where does he get it?"

At that, Viviane gave a sickly laugh. "Get it? They grow it. Michael and his housemates. They've got a whole crop in the basement of their place. Heat lamps and everything."

"Have you heard from any of the housemates since Michael came over here the other day?"

Viviane shook her head.

Octavian glanced at the professor, then back to his girlfriend.

"Give me the address," he told her.

"Okay. But . . . can you get this stuff out of him? Derek said you . . . that you knew magic."

She said the last word as though it embarrassed her. Octavian figured it probably did. Not the word itself, but the suggestion that she might believe it to be more than a word. A lot of people felt that way about magic, right up until they needed it.

"I'm going to check out the house," Octavian said. "Try to get to the bottom of this. If I can, that might cure him. But if it doesn't, I know an earthwitch who probably can."

"But you said you thought an earthwitch might have done this!" Viviane said.

Octavian took a last glance at her brother.

"Time to find out."

Michael Chenot lived in a three-story brownstone with a faded blue awning over the door and a peaked roof with a little walk-out balcony. According to his sister, there were three apartments in the building, all occupied by McGill students. Michael and three friends lived on the first floor, which gave them the best access to the basement, but the students in the other apartments didn't complain about their little pot farm as long as they were able to share in the spoils once in a while.

Octavian had learned all of this from Viviane before leaving her place. Now he and the professor stood outside Michael Chenot's brownstone, studying the dark windows and quiet façade. The place seemed almost abandoned. One of the first-floor windows had a crack in it. A strange moss grew from beneath the window frames on the ground level.

"You've been here before?" Octavian asked.

The professor clicked the tab on his key fob and his hybrid chirped, doors locking.

"Never inside," he said. "I've dropped Viviane off a couple of times, but never met her brother."

Octavian looked down at the weeds growing up between the cracks in the sidewalk and the concrete pathway leading up to the front door of the brownstone.

"She didn't want her brother to know she was sleeping with her teacher," he said.

"Why is this relevant?" the professor asked.

Octavian glanced at him, saw the pain in his eyes, and softened. "It's not, Derek. Sorry. It would've been helpful if you knew the internal layout of the place, that's all. Since you don't, I'm going to ask you to stay outside."

For a moment, the professor looked relieved, but then he frowned in irritation. "I'm not exactly frail, Peter. I can take care of myself."

"No doubt," Octavian agreed. "But you're human. Okay, technically so am I. But unless you're secretly a mage and have real sorcery at your command, then whatever happened to the people in that building is probably going to happen to you the second you set foot inside."

The professor looked as though he might argue further, but then he glanced at that strangely silent house and said nothing more. Of course it was impossible to know if there was activity inside a building simply by looking at it, but Octavian had a sense for such things. The place felt *still*. As if it waited, holding its breath.

"There's nothing I can do?" the professor asked after a moment.

"If I don't come out in ten minutes, call my cell. If I don't answer, go over to The Red Door and tell Nikki what happened."

The professor nodded and went back to his car, leaning against the door. Octavian bent to study the weeds growing in the sidewalk cracks. There were small leaves with a very familiar shape. He stood and started up the front walk, noticing the ragged grass in the small yard and the tiny plants that had begun to grow.

Cannabis plants grew like vines inside the door frame, poking out in fringes along the top and bottom. Viviane had given Octavian the keys to her brother's place, but the knob was crusted over with a strange moss, the lock bursting with a bristly marijuana bud. The key wouldn't be any use to him at all. He held out a hand and nearly cast a spell that would have burned away the plant growth, then considered another that would have caused it to age and rot, but he worried about the building and the people within it. Instead, he settled for brute force, launching a hard kick at the door.

It barely shuddered.

Force was still the answer, but he needed more than he could muster with a kick. A thousand years in Hell had given him time to become a true mage, so intertwined with magic that he wielded it by instinct and reflex. With a gesture, he cast a concussive spell, causing the doorknob itself to explode. The door blew open with a loud ripping noise as tightly latticed tendrils of plant matter tore away from the frame. Where the doorknob had been was a smoking hole in the wood, and the door hung at an angle from its shattered frame, but the spiderweb of pot plants that filled the foyer would not let it fall.

The plants grew up through the floorboards and from cracks they had forced through the walls. They hung from the light fixture overhead and had woven together in a hanging mesh, a cannabis jungle. The house was filled with the same aroma of damp decay that had come off Michael Chenot, but another smell lingered beneath it—one Octavian knew all too well. This was a different kind of rot. He smelled death in that house, and a moment later, he saw the source.

He could see the body through the curtain of marijuana plants. The girl lay on the stairs, halfway up to the second floor. *Or halfway down,* Octavian thought, and realized that made more sense. He grabbed a fistful of plants and tore them away, ripping himself a path toward the bottom of the stairs. Moving nearer, he could see down the short corridor to the left, where the door to the first-floor apartment—the one Michael Chenot shared with his friends—stood partway open.

The door to the basement was farther back, set into the wall beneath the stairs. The door was closed, but so many pot vines had pushed through between door and frame that the wood had cracked and warped. In some places, it seemed as though cannabis plants were growing right out of the cellar door, and now that he looked more closely, he saw that the same was true of the floor, and the banister at the bottom of the stairs.

The dead girl was sprawled on the stairs, face first, hands outstretched as though she had not only been crawling, but dragging herself toward the foyer . . . toward the front door. Marijuana stalks and leaves and buds had burst through her dead flesh. The thickest and strongest of the plants grew up out of the back of her skull, but whether it had taken root there or grown up through the stairs and then through her brain, Octavian couldn't tell. Her vital fluids had dribbled down the stairs and puddled at the bottom, but were dry now.

She had been pretty, once upon a time.

"Jesus," a voice said.

Octavian turned to see that the professor had followed him up to the door.

"What are you doing, Derek? I told you to stay back."

But Octavian knew. He'd seen the naked curiosity in the professor's eyes before, usually on people who ended up dead.

"I just . . ." the professor said. He shrugged, trying to look penitent and failing. "This is awful. But it looks like whatever happened here, it's over." He covered his face with his hands, peering out over the tops of his fingers. "This is like a nightmare."

"Enough of that. It's real enough. And it's not over."

That troubled the professor. He furrowed his brow. "It's not?"

"The plants are still growing. They're thriving."

"Is it magic?" the professor asked, taking a nervous step back, looking at the plants fringing the frame of the broken front door. "Witchcraft?"

Octavian shook his head, tearing away more of the cannabis web, moving toward the open door to the first-floor apartment. "I've only ever met one earthwitch capable of something like this. But if one of them had done this, she'd have moved on by now. Whatever did this, it's still here. Can't you feel it?"

"Do you think they're all dead?"

"That," Octavian said, "or they wish they were."

"So . . . what is it?" the professor asked, his voice barely a whisper. He'd moved back several paces from the door, looking as though he might be starting to understand how stupid he'd been to come up after being warned off.

"A wood god, maybe. Some kind of forest spirit, for sure. It must have slipped through."

"Are you fucking kidding me?"

Octavian shot him a hard look that sent him scampering back down the front walk to wait by his car, the way he should have from the beginning. A wood god wasn't something he would joke about, but to the professor he knew it must seem almost ridiculously fanciful. Octavian would never understand the human mind's reluctance to believe in the extraordinary even after learning how common extraordinary things were. In a world where vampires and demons existed, why was it so hard to believe in forest spirits and goblins?

From the days of its founding, the Roman Catholic Church had spent nearly two thousand years driving unnatural things, creatures of darkness that preyed on humanity, out of the world. The Vatican trained sorcerers to wall off this reality from others, to keep those creatures out. The accumulated knowledge of those sorcerers, passed down from the time of Christ, had been kept in a book called *The Gospel of Shadows*. But that sect of sorcerers had been corrupted, and eventually destroyed, and the church had fallen into disarray. Splinters of the church still existed, but without the central power that Rome had represented, and *The Gospel of Shadows* had been lost to them.

No one was keeping the monsters out anymore. They were slow to realize that the barriers between worlds were deteriorating, but once in a while, something slipped through. Considering the role he'd played in the destruction of the church and the loss of the book, Octavian did what he could to combat whatever dark forces slipped through. But monstrous incursions into this world had become more and more common. He couldn't be everywhere.

For tonight, however, he found himself in the right place at the right time.

No, he chided himself, the moment the thought crossed his mind. *Not the right time. Too late for the girl on the stairs.* Too late, he figured, for everyone who lived in this house, except perhaps—if he worked quickly—for Michael Chenot. And if he didn't stop this here, how many others would die? Somehow the entity, whatever it was, had gotten into the cannabis growing in the basement here. But now that it had spread out into the yard, where grass and weeds grew, its influence would touch those things as well. Plants and trees, all over Montreal. And who knew where it would end.

The time for hesitation had passed. If he tried to tear his way through the jungle inside that house in search of someone who might still be clinging to life, he might be hours, and Michael would end up like the girl on the stairs. Even if he found someone alive, the first step in trying to save them would be to kill the thing growing inside them.

Octavian took a step forward and felt his shoe catch on something. He looked down to see the plants that had started to curl around his ankles.

"Enough." He reached out his left hand and grabbed a fistful of the cannabis lattice. With his right, he began to sketch at the air with contorted fingers, muttering a few words in a guttural tongue that had been old before Babylon. It was not death magic—Octavian feared the consequences of wielding death—but the outcome was the same.

The plants began to turn brown and then to wither, dying all around him. The lattice jungle of cannabis wilted and drooped and decayed so badly that it started to fall apart. *Dust to dust,* Octavian thought. That was the nature of the spell he'd cast, speeding up the process of entropy, hurrying something toward its natural corruption.

The effect spread, plants dying and withering all through the foyer and hall, and up the stairs. He watched the dead girl on the steps a moment, hoping that it would affect only the plants that had taken root in her and not her own dead flesh. If the spell jumped from the cannabis to her, it might do the same to the others in the building, and if any of them had a chance of survival, that would be the end of them. But he'd had no other choice. Doing nothing would have killed them just as surely.

Octavian moved down the hall, brushing away the dry, rotted remains of the cannabis web with ease. He went to the open door of Michael Chenot's apartment and pushed it open the rest of the way, looking inside. A dead man sat on the sofa, almost as though he had died watching the television. If not for the pallor of his skin and the wilting plants growing where his eyes ought to have been, he might almost have been alive.

The entropy spell spread. Octavian moved deeper into the apartment. He would have to confront the wood god before he left, but he wanted to see if anyone was still alive.

The floorboards creaked underfoot, but then the walls seemed to do the same. Plaster flakes drifted down from the ceiling. He glanced at the walls and saw that the paint had begun to yellow and peel. A crack spread slowly from the upper corner of the door frame.

"Shit." The cannabis had so completely infiltrated the house that it had become a part of it. The entropy spell was eating away at the building itself. It wasn't going to be safe in here for much longer.

He ran, darting through rooms. Two other bodies, long past hope. But there were the upstairs apartments to think of.

Octavian raced back into the hallway, hearing the creak and moan and crack of the brownstone's structural integrity beginning to crumble. Dried, desiccated pot plants gave way like spiderwebs as he ran for the stairs. But he hadn't made it halfway up to the second floor before a scream of grief and fury rose from beneath the building.

From the cellar.

Green shoots erupted between floorboards, and then the boards themselves splintered. The dust of desiccated pot plants sprayed across the foyer. Octavian took a step back, raising his hands, and his fingers contorted into claws as he cast a spell to solidify the air into a defensive shield in front of him.

The green shoots twined together, branches and leaves and flowers growing off them with a fluid grace, sculpting a figure. Vines crawled along the floor, anchoring it there, spinning a new sort of web. From the budding figure, she bloomed, unfolding herself and standing up to her full height, nearly two feet taller than Octavian. Her hair was golden corn silk, spilling down her back, and her body pulsed with some semblance of breath. The wood god had a female form, lithe and strangely erotic, and Octavian thought of a thousand fairy tales, and the men who had been lured into the forest to find fleeting bliss and enduring regret.

Her mouth opened, dewy sap stringing between her newborn lips.

"You've hurt me," the wood god said.

Octavian made a fist of his right hand, summoning a raging flame. Entropy had not worked on her, but fire might. All he needed was a moment to distract her so that he could work a banishment spell and drive her from this reality.

"You don't belong here," he told her.

"*I don't belong?*" she said, sneering. "*It's you who are the abomination here. You and your accursed* civilization!*"*

She lunged at him, fingers hooked into thorny claws, ready to flay his flesh from his bones. Octavian lifted a hand, a sphere of fire burning around his fist.

Which was when the floor gave way, entropy crumbling it away beneath his feet.

Fuck.

Nikki Wydra took the stage at The Red Door with a smile on her face, but it felt like a mask. The applause filled the room, blanketing her in welcoming energy and the happy aura of people who were, in that moment, exactly where they wanted to be. She let it wash over her, taking strength from it as she always did. With a nod toward the band—a handful of Montreal musicians she'd played with the last time she'd come through town—she launched into "Not Enough to Exist" and a cheer went up from the audience. People started to move to the music and some to dance. It was the right choice, a track off her second album that had never found its way onto the radio but had taken off online and quickly become a favorite among her fans.

She tried to focus, feeling that she owed these people that much. They had put up their hard-earned cash for this show, and she wanted to make it worth their while, to connect with them. The set list had been cultivated with care. She pruned it every show, adding and subtracting, playing the best and most popular of her own songs, plus a few of her favorites from other artists. Sarah McLachlan's "Ice Cream" didn't always go over as well as she wanted, but she played it for herself, not for them. For them, she did "Cantankerous Bitch," from her first album—she'd come to hate that song, but God they loved it.

Finishing up the opener, she scanned the audience. On the last note, the hooting and cheering began. She said something appreciative into the microphone, then repeated it in French, but wasn't really paying attention. She smiled, but her gaze slipped across the faces, searching for the only one that really mattered. With a glance into the wings, she sought him backstage, but there was still no sign of Peter.

Nikki figured most girlfriends would have been pissed if their guy didn't show up when he promised, especially for something like this. And with the too-long silences and unspoken pressures that had been putting a strain on them over the past year, even Peter couldn't have blamed her. They had a lot of things they needed to sort out.

But she wasn't angry; she was worried. Peter Octavian wasn't the sort of man who broke his word without a damn good reason, and for him, a damn good reason probably had sharp claws.

Where are you, Peter? she thought, peering out at the crowd. Some of the faces she saw looked restless, and she realized that she must look a little lost on the stage.

"Cantankerous Bitch!" someone called from backstage, off to her left.

She turned and saw him there, tall and lanky, that laconic gunfighter stance, and relief flooded through her. He wore a mischievous grin, and no wonder—shouting for a song he knew she hated—but he looked a wreck. His shirt was spattered with what could only be bloodstains and there were scratches all over his face, along with what looked like soot smudges. His night had not gone well so far, but he was there and in one piece. God, she loved him. Whatever distance there was between them, she wanted to erase it.

With a throaty laugh, she turned back to the audience and grinned. This time, the smile was real.

"My boyfriend wants me to play 'Cantankerous Bitch,' " she said.

The audience erupted with clamorous applause and shouts for the song.

"You think he's trying to tell me something?" Nikki asked her audience, who answered with whistles and hoots.

They started to chant—"Bitch! Bitch! Bitch!"

Nikki laughed and shook her head. The song was supposed to come later in the set, but for once, she *wanted* to play it. She turned to the band and signaled them, nodding. A stagehand ran out and traded her electric guitar for the acoustic she'd opened with, and she hammered out the first, crashing chord.

The crowd sang along.

When she'd hit the last note, she ran to the wings, whipping off her electric. The applause raged, but she could spare a few seconds while she swapped guitars again. She ran into Peter's arms, smiling, and shook him.

"Where the hell were you? You scared the shit out of me!"

His gray eyes brightening, he smiled the lopsided grin that had first made her want him. "You know the expression 'Let sleeping gods lie'?"

Nikki frowned. "It's 'dogs.'"

"The rule works the same either way," Peter said, speaking up to be heard over the crowd. "I'll explain later. Get back out there."

Then he kissed her, and Nikki pressed her body against his, thinking about washing all of that blood and soot off him later tonight. How he could make her so frightened, make her laugh, frustrate the hell out of her, and make her want him all at the same time, she would never understand.

They kissed deeply, the bristly stubble on his face scraping her skin, inspiring her to kiss him all the harder.

She pulled back, narrowing her eyes, finally figuring out the taste and smell of him, and at last noticing how bloodshot his eyes had become.

"Holy shit," she said. "Are you *high*?"

Octavian laughed and pushed her away. "Go. I'll tell you all about it over a late dinner."

Staring at him in amused disbelief, she backed away. "I can't wait."

Nikki took her acoustic from the stagehand who held it out for her, slung it over her shoulder, and ran back onstage, basking in the cheers of her audience. That was life with Peter Octavian—always fighting against the darkness, and finding their way back into the light.

2

Amber Morrissey knew a lot of girls on campus who didn't care if they showed up to class looking like crap. Her best friend, Tami, had been known to roll out of bed, pull on a battered pair of out-of-date Uggs, brush her teeth, and go to class in whatever clothes and whatever condition she'd been in the night before. Pajama pants or stained sweats, a tangled nest of hair, a faded T-shirt . . . in warmer weather, when she couldn't cover up with a sweatshirt, Tami would spare the extra seconds to put on a bra. Amber called it "junkie-hooker chic."

No one liked getting up for an early class, but Amber couldn't go out without putting at least the minimum effort into her appearance. This morning she'd showered, pushed her coppery red hair back with a clip, and pulled on a clean, fitted cream top and a pair of jeans. She never managed even the slightest touch of makeup this early in the morning, but her face would have to do.

As she walked along one of the tree-lined paths on Hawthorne University's main academic quadrangle, she inhaled deeply of the September air. It had been warm yesterday, but now it felt more like mid-September—no longer summer, but not quite autumn yet. The morning felt good, though she would never have admitted it. She took a sip of her coffee, and all was right with the world.

Hawthorne had not been her first choice of colleges. She loved her family, but going to the university in her hometown felt a lot like settling. There was no question that it was a great school, and it was the best of the universities to which she had been accepted. But for the first couple of years, it had almost felt as if she were still in high school. Too many of her childhood friends had not gone to college at all, or were attending the community college in Jameson, just a couple of towns away.

Then, this past summer, she had spent a month in a study-abroad program in Talloires, France, and had barely seen any of her old friends before she'd left or after she had returned. Now she only ever heard from them if they got in touch on Facebook. She didn't want to leave them behind completely—they would always mean something to her—but she was starting her junior year in college, and she had a new life, with new friends, and a future to start living.

"Morning, Amber," a voice said.

She glanced over to see Ben Draper cutting across the grass to join up with her. He was a sweet guy whose tufted mess of hair, big hands, and goofy grin always made her think of him as a sort of giant puppy-boy. Amber always wanted to hug him, but she had a feeling that Ben hoped there were other things she wanted from him as well.

"Hey, Ben."

"You forgot my coffee again, I see," he joked.

Amber feigned regret. "I'd give you mine but, y'know, cooties."

Ben grinned. He teased her about bringing him coffee nearly every time they had this class together. She was never without a cup, and happily endured the envious gazes of others in the class who hadn't had the foresight to fortify themselves with caffeine before trudging onto the quad.

"No one should have to get up this early on a Wednesday morning," Ben said, falling in beside her as they approached Baker Hall, where the history department was headquartered.

"It's almost nine a.m.," Amber said. "Most people with regular jobs are already at them."

"I know," Ben replied. "Obviously I need to be independently wealthy, so I can sleep as late as I want."

Amber nodded, letting the sarcasm flow. "Yeah. So many history majors become independently wealthy."

He laughed and bumped her as they went up the front steps into the old brick academic building.

"Hey! Watch the coffee," she warned him.

Properly chided, Ben stood aside and let her precede him through the inner door. Baker Hall had a musty, old-book smell that never went away, but Amber loved it. It was one of the oldest buildings on the Hawthorne campus, and she knew if she had the opportunity to search its closets and basements and eaves, she would probably find generations of history of the students and professors who had passed through these halls.

"All right," Ben whispered, taking a breath. "Ninety minutes of Professor Varick. I can make it."

"Stop. He's not that bad," Amber said.

Ben rolled his eyes. They had this argument at least once a week. Professor Miles Varick had a reputation for being acerbic, impatient, unsympathetic, and overall a merciless bastard. But he also had a reputation as a fantastic lecturer, from whom a great deal could be learned by a student willing to pay attention. Amber had found all of those things to be true. Professor Varick began his Byzantine History lecture at precisely 8:50 a.m., the scheduled class time, and he took his time, investing the stories of Byzantium with suspense and humor and a vibrancy that dusty books could rarely muster. When he finished his lecture, he would glance up, breaking the spell he had cast over the class, and the second hand would be ticking toward the final moments of the period.

Varick's Byzantine History was the one class Amber never minded waking up for.

She drained the last of her coffee and dumped it the trash bin outside the women's bathroom. Ben waited for her, then gestured for her to enter the classroom before him.

"Go on. He likes you. Maybe he won't notice me."

"I'm not sure he likes anyone," Amber whispered. "But he likes people who take his classes seriously."

"How could you take them any other way?" Ben said.

Smiling, Amber preceded him into the room. More than half the class had already arrived. Professor Varick perched on the edge of the desk at the front of the classroom, leafing through a thick leather-bound volume with ragged-edged pages like a priest searching for just the right prayer. The priestly analogy was one that popped up in Amber's mind frequently. Something about Miles Varick's lean shape and stern countenance brought her back to her Catholic school days. The man had haunted blue eyes and graying hair cropped close, likely so that he could pay as little attention to it as possible.

As Amber and Ben found a pair of seats by the tall, drafty windows, bathed in the warm morning sunlight, Professor Varick glanced at the clock on the wall and then confirmed the time with a glance at his watch. Stragglers hurried through the door. Professor Varick set the leather book on the corner of the desk and picked up his lecture note-book. Some teachers used laptops to aid them during lectures, but Amber thought Professor Varick would be using paper notebooks for as long as he had students to teach.

A Middle Eastern girl darted into the classroom—Amber thought her name was Priya, but the semester was only a couple of weeks old and she didn't know everyone in the class yet. The girl went up to Professor Varick and muttered something, practically under her breath.

Professor Varick gave her an irked look. "I'm not your father. Go if you need to. Class begins in"—he glanced at the clock again—"about a minute and a half."

For a second, Amber thought the girl would argue, but she seemed to think better of it and hustled from the room, making a beeline for the women's bathroom down the hall. Professor Varick did not try to hide his disdain, though whether it was because the girl had bothered to ask permission to go to the bathroom or because she would now miss the beginning of his lecture, Amber didn't know.

He made his way to the lectern and opened his notebook, glancing casually at the clock. The second hand ticked away the last thirty seconds and then 8:50 rolled around.

"Today," Professor Varick began, "we're going to discuss the strange dynamic of the relationship between the Eastern Roman Empire—the core of Byzantium—and the Huns, beginning with the

ascent to the throne of Emperor Theodosius II in a.d. 408, at the age
of seven. Theodosius II, also called 'the Calligrapher,' built upon the
achievements of his predecessors in several ways you will want and
need to remember, but in order to firmly lodge him into your brain, I
will first tell you the story of how he paid Attila the Hun not to kick
his ass."

A ripple of laughter went through the room.

Professor Varick smiled thinly, letting them enjoy their own amuse-
ment for a moment. Amber understood that it was all choreographed;
it was a show to him, and one he had performed many times over. But
that was what she appreciated the most about Professor Varick—his
showmanship. It was what made his lectures so memorable, and memorable lectures were invaluable when it came time for midterms and
finals.

"If any of you did the reading, you might be able to tell me who
served as regent for the child emperor," he said, surveying the room
with a dismissive glance, a challenge. "Anyone?"

Amber waited to see if anyone else would answer, then raised a ten-
tative hand.

"Miss Morrissey?" Professor Varick said.

"It's a trick question, Professor."

"Is it? Would I do that?" he asked, arching an eyebrow.

"Constantly," Amber said, and the class rewarded her with a cas-
cade of chuckles. "There were two regents before Theodosius was old
enough to rule. I don't remember the first guy's name, but the second
regent was his older sister."

Professor Varick frowned, always surprised when his students actually did their homework.

"Not bad, Amber. It may be that some of you aren't complete air-
heads after all," Professor Varick said, turning to write the name
Pulcheria on the board. "Much like 'Augustus' for Octavian in Rome,
they called her Augusta. Probably because her actual name sounded
like some kind of sexually transmitted disease. Or maybe as a sign of
respect. I'll let you all logic that one out."

The whole class scribbled in their notebooks. Amber wrote

Pulcheria = Augusta and kept her pen flying, trying to keep up with the stories of ancient Byzantium. As she wrote, her hand began to tremble, and she frowned at the strange markings on the page where she knew she had written words. Her writing had become a trail of swoops and scratches.

She frowned, blinking, and looked up at Professor Varick, who was gesturing to the class, almost acting out the lecture. But Amber couldn't hear him anymore, just a muffled drone, as though she had her ear pressed against the wall, desperately trying to eavesdrop on a conversation in the next room.

The aftertaste of her morning coffee turned bitter on her tongue.

"Professor?" someone slurred. And maybe it had been her, because now blurred faces were starting to turn her way.

Her arms flailed and her legs shot out as she began to shake violently. Her chair toppled over and she hit her head on the floor, a murmur of warped monster voices around her. Her whole body jittered, her teeth clacking together, and she tasted blood in her mouth, coppery and warm.

. . . and she stands on the beach, her feet sinking into the sand as the surf foams and ripples around her ankles. She feels a moment of peace before it is shattered. The golden sunset darkens too quickly, the sky turning bruise-purple, indigo clouds beginning to gather, low-hanging and pregnant with brutal storm. It is as though the storm and the angry night chase the sun out of the sky, drowning it in the ocean on the horizon.

"Why?" she asks, though there is no one to answer, and she isn't even certain of the meaning of the question.

Car horns blare and tires screech and she tenses, waiting for the crash that must follow, but instead that scream turns into another . . . a human scream. She glances up the beach and finds that she is standing in the center of Hawthorne, though the tiny waves still ripple around her and the street is still giving way beneath her feet like sand. Glass shatters and there are more screams as it begins to rain.

Hot rain. The drops are painful, searing her flesh.

Dark things flit in the storm. A man and woman—she knows their faces but not their names—run down the street, water splashing around them. Their terror is carved upon their faces, and suddenly they have a child with them, a little girl with a long ponytail who is crying—Amber can see her tears, even in the rain. The little girl's mouth is open, but her little-girl screams are drowned out by other shrieking, like the whistle of fireworks just before they explode, but so much louder and filled with such anguish that at last Amber screams, too.

The Reaper stands in the street, swirling from nothing to solidity as though sculpted from and by the storm. Black ribbons of fabric whip in the wind and hot rain, dragging against its body so that she can see it is anything but human. Its limbs and torso are thin as iron piping, and the wind wails as it passes through the gaps where its eyes should be. Yet it turns and looks at her, and there is a kind of ice-blue light that gleams deep down in those pits like distant stars. In each of its hands it holds a thin, curved blade, black as pitch but gleaming in the rain.

It moves through the air as though it is spilling from one world into another. Ribbons of torn clothing flutter from its stick-body. Sickles slash the air and it has fallen upon the family, cutting the woman and her husband and her child, but it isn't blood that splashes out of them. It is light. It is laughter. It is spirit.

And the rain pelts down, and screams echo along the streets of Hawthorne, and the hateful storm sags lower, smothering, and there are so many more Reapers in the sky, riding the winds like murderous ravens, like ancient witches . . . like Death.

Amber only screams. The hot rain is burning her skin, eating flesh and muscle, heading for bone. The sky splits, the clouds peeling back like the edges of a wound, and something is born from the labial folds of that storm. She can see infinite stars like Reaper's eyes in the night sky beyond that split.

In the street stands a woman, bathed in the light of those stars. But she is not a woman at all. She is wrapped in gauzy veils that do nothing to hide her three sets of heavy breasts. Her long arms end in talons as sharp and savage as the Reaper's blades, but entirely her own. Her hair is indigo fire, burning cold, and her flesh the blue of drowned children. Light and shadow play across her face, showing beauty and grotesquerie in zoetrope flashes.

The Reapers flock to her, moths to a terrible flame, their sickles gone. Their hands are filled, instead, with the viscera of their victims, and with it they begin to paint their goddess's flesh the bright crimson of human suffering, and the goddess shivers with arousal.

The whistle of the wind through the Reapers' empty eyes grows suddenly loud and Amber spins to see one of them spilling through the air toward her. At last, she stops screaming. She can only stare at this death that comes for her.

The rain turns cold.

"No," a silken voice says. "Not her."

Amber turns to stare at the goddess, and finds the old one looking back at her. Knowing her. And this time her scream destroys her own voice.

She knows *me.*

Desk chairs scraped the floor as students got up. People swore and muttered, whipping out cell phones. Some of them were calling for help, but others were catching the girl's seizure on video.

For a few seconds, Miles Varick could only stare at the flailing, bucking student sprawled on the floor. In his years of teaching, he'd had classes disrupted before—by rude boys, feuding girls, snoring sleepers, ringing cell phones, and once even by the police there to make an arrest—but never anything like this. *Is this some kind of joke?* he wanted to ask. But then his thoughts and vision both cleared and he saw that it was Amber Morrissey there on the floor, twitching hard enough that her skull kept knocking on the linoleum, and he knew it wasn't a joke. Not from Amber. She wasn't that kind of student.

"Son of a bitch," he muttered, and rushed from the lectern, knocking his notebook to the ground. Miles strode toward the students who had begun crowding around her. "Back away. Give her space, you idiots!"

Most of them scrambled away as though burned. Only Ben Draper did not flinch at Miles's approach. The kid hovered around Amber in alarm and confusion, looking like he wanted to do something but clueless as to what.

"Did someone call 911?" Miles snapped.

A chorus of replies assured him that help was on the way. He spent his days grappling with an internal debate over whether he loved his students for their potential or hated them for their lack of interest. But suddenly they weren't his students anymore, and he felt a momentary pang of regret for calling them idiots.

He dropped to his knees and pulled her head into his lap to keep her from slamming it against the floor. A light froth bubbled at her lips, and he tried to remember training from years before that would have told him whether he needed to do something to keep her from choking on her tongue.

"Mr. Draper," he snapped at Ben, "hold her legs, please. Let's try to keep her from breaking anything."

But even as Ben knelt to help, Amber went rigid, frozen in place. Her hands clenched into fists and the muscles in her neck stood out. Her eyes had rolled up to the whites, but now she blinked and then stared at the ceiling as though something terrifying hung above her.

Amber started talking, muttering in a tiny, frightened, little-girl voice—the same three words over and over, although Miles had to bend closer to make them out.

"She knows me. She knows me. She knows me . . ."

And then it stopped. Amber sagged in his lap, eyelids fluttering closed. Her breathing steadied and the rigidity went out of her. The seizure had passed.

"Jesus," Ben said, looking up at Miles. "What the hell was that?"

"Duh," one of the students said. "She's epileptic, dumbass."

Miles ignored him. If Amber Morrissey had epilepsy, it was the first he'd heard of it. Not that students always shared such information with the administration or their professors, but over the years he'd had a number of students with diabetes or epilepsy who did share that news, just in case of a situation like this.

"Amber?" he ventured, gently sliding her head from his lap and kneeling beside her instead. He took her hand. "Amber?"

"I don't think you should move her, Professor," Ben said.

"I'm not moving her," Miles replied. He bit his tongue on the rest of his intended reply. What he wanted was to make sure the girl wasn't going to lapse into a coma, and that the seizure hadn't caused brain damage—or the other way around. He was pretty sure that an aneurysm or tumor could cause seizures.

Amber let out a long, shuddering breath, and Miles tensed, afraid she would start to seize again. She coughed, and then one of her hands floated up to wipe spittle away from her mouth.

"She's coming around," a girl said softly, just over Miles's shoulder, crowding him.

He hated to be crowded. His mother had called it a kind of claustrophobia when he was a child, his teachers said he had antisocial tendencies, and his ex-wife had said he didn't like people getting too close because he was a coldhearted bastard. Most days, Miles thought they had probably all been equally correct.

"Go away," he said, looking up.

His students looked back, wondering who he was talking to. He scanned the room, trying to get it through their beer-soaked and college-sex-addled brains that he meant all of them.

"Go. Class is over. EMTs are on the way. Read chapter four and take notes. Refer to the syllabus for themes. I'll make up for lost time on Friday, so missing that class would be a spectacularly bad idea."

Some of them started to leave immediately, reaching for books or bags or backpacks. Others looked worriedly at Amber, who had begun to blink and look around like Dorothy stepping out of her black-and-white farmhouse into full-color Oz.

"Is she—" a girl named Yasmin began.

"Miss Joyce, I've got it from here. You're all dismissed."

The edge in his voice—the cold steel of it—shut her up. At last they had all begun to retreat. Even Ben Draper, with his poet's eyes and football neck, had reluctantly started to back away.

"You can remain, Mr. Draper," Miles said.

Ben seemed relieved. Miles didn't have the heart to tell him that he hadn't asked the kid to remain because he needed help or wanted company, but because the university had rules about the conditions under which faculty could be alone with students. They didn't want anyone suing, saying they'd been groped or worse.

As the last of the stragglers departed, leaving only the three of them, Amber let out another long breath and gave her head a little shake, wincing in pain.

"Damn, that hurts," she said. Eyes narrowed, the sunlight washing through the windows too bright for her, she focused on Miles. "Professor Varick? What happened?"

Miles leaned against a desk. "Maybe you can tell us. You had a seizure. Just fell out of your chair and started shaking."

"You scared the crap out of the whole class," Ben added.

Amber tried to sit up, but couldn't quite manage it. She reached a hand up to touch the back of her head, pushing her fingers through that coppery red hair. Miles stared, worried that she'd find blood there, but she only winced with pain and stopped probing. No blood; that was a good sign, at least.

"Don't try to move. Some of the other students called 911. Wait for an EMT to look you over. We'll wait with you," Miles told her.

"Okay," Amber agreed. But he could see she wanted to get up and get out of there. She had a faraway look in her eyes, her brow furrowed with unease.

"I always see you with coffee," Miles said. "Sometimes if you don't eat enough but overindulge in caffeine . . . do you drink those energy drinks, too?"

"Not really," she said. "I mean, I have. But usually it's just coffee."

"You said something," Ben added. "When you were coming around."

Amber frowned. "What did I say?"

"I couldn't make it out," Ben said. "Professor Varick was closer."

Miles wanted to snap at him. Whatever had been going on in Amber's mind during her seizure, it had really upset her. Why bring that up?

"It was just mumbling," he said. "Were you having a bad dream or something?"

Amber hesitated, gnawing on her lower lip a moment. She would not look either of them in the eye.

"Yeah. It had to be a dream, right?"

Miles arched an eyebrow. A dream, as opposed to what?

"It was a bad one?" Ben asked.

"The worst," she said. "There was a storm. And these things were coming down from the storm and . . . and killing people. Cutting them. And the rain—"

A crackle of static interrupted them. They all looked toward the door, and a second later the EMTs were bustling into the room, hurrying over to Amber and asking questions, and the conversation about what she had seen during her seizure was over. Miles wanted to know more, but he stood back and let the professionals do their job.

"Anything I can do for you, Professor?" Ben asked, shuffling over beside him.

Miles kept his gaze on Amber and the EMTs. "Get her to cut back on her caffeine," he said.

But he knew that whatever had caused this, it wasn't coffee. He only hoped it wasn't anything truly serious. Students like Amber made it easier for him to put up with the morons. The class would be far less interesting without her. Although today she had made it a little too interesting for his tastes. The girl was lucky she hadn't cracked her head open.

As the EMTs checked her vitals, Miles remembered the fear on her face just before the seizure ended, and the way she had stared at the ceiling, rigid with terror. He wondered if she would turn out to have a tumor after all. That might have caused her to hallucinate.

Otherwise, it had been one hell of a nightmare.

Tommy Dunne sat in the shade of the little cabin of his father's thirty-two-foot Boston Whaler, nudging the throttle now and again to make sure she didn't drift too much. Days like today, when he knew a lot of his friends from high school were sitting in a college classroom somewhere, he relished being out there on the water, the sky so blue and the salt breeze off the Atlantic still warm. But now that the nights had begun to cool down and he knew fall was not far off, he had started thinking about what it would be like to be out here night and day as fall turned to early winter, and he'd begun to have second thoughts about his decision to skip college.

All through high school, Tommy had spent summers working with his father, Norm Dunne. By night, they prowled the waters off Salem, Beverly, and Hawthorne, cast-netting for squid, and by day they netted as many bunkers—what they called menhaden, an otherwise useless bait fish—as possible. Norm Dunne sold most of the squid to local restaurants, and the rest of it went with the bunkers to Tommy's uncle Paul's bait shop. Tommy's mother had died in a car accident when he was nine years old. His father had been out with a few women in the years since, but never dated anyone seriously, which maybe explained why Norm and Paul still referred to each other as brothers-in-law, though the woman who had been the link between them had been dead going on ten years.

Uncle Paul had encouraged Tommy to go to college. His dad had taken a more neutral stance. If Tommy wanted to go, that was fine by him, but if his son preferred to become a fisherman like his father, Norm made no effort to hide how pleased and proud that would make him. Uncle Paul didn't want this life for Tommy—a life of hard work for little reward, when some years slim margins could turn into big losses. *My sister wouldn't have wanted her boy to ever go hungry,* Tommy had once heard Uncle Paul say, in a conversation he was sure he hadn't been meant to hear. Tommy's dad had been furious. *Have I ever let my son go hungry?* he had shouted.

There'd been beer involved. There always was.

Tommy had loved the summers he had spent working the nets with his father. Days and nights on the water. Money in his pocket on his days off. And there had been no shortage of girls. Being a fisherman during those summers earned him a great tan, lean muscles, and an aura of maturity that other guys in his high school just couldn't pull off.

But now that he looked ahead to a lifetime of this work, not just beautiful summers but cold, dismal falls and winters, it gave him pause. His father was forty-three and still in decent shape, but he'd started to have problems with his back and his right shoulder, and Tommy had a hard time picturing himself doing this work without his dad. Would he really want to be out here on his own?

Fuck, no.

So he had pretty much decided this would be it. One year off from school. Next fall, he would go to college. Now he just had to figure out how he was going to tell his father.

Tommy heard a splash and then his dad called his name. He jumped up and ran to the port side, where he'd tied off the net. Norm Dunne bobbed in the water, his unruly thatch of salt-and-pepper hair plastered to his skull. Despite his age, his work had kept him in damn good shape. If not for the scar on the left side of his face, he'd have been a pretty good-looking guy.

"Did you get it unsnagged?" Tommy asked.

His dad grinned. "Not exactly."

"Then what are you smiling about?"

"You'll see," Norm replied.

Tommy stepped back while his father grabbed hold of the rail and hoisted himself up and over, spilling into the boat. He scrambled to his feet and reached for the net.

"Gimme a hand, punk," he said.

Norm had a dozen affectionate nicknames for his son. *Punk* was only one of them. Some people thought Norm was trying to echo Clint Eastwood, and that was fine with Tommy. He would never admit to anyone that it came from his toddler days, when his mom had called him Punkin. Dead mother or not, sappy shit like that could haunt a guy forever if his friends got wind of it. His father knew it, too, and had never breathed a word.

"What was it, Dad?" Tommy asked, moving next to his father and grabbing the line to help him pull up the net.

His father didn't answer. Tommy wondered what he'd found down there that would make him so weirdly happy. He thought of Gregg

McKeown, a friend of his father's who had found an old cannon while scuba diving and spent the last three years recovering bits and pieces of a sunken Spanish galleon. Surely they hadn't found something like that; they were much too close to shore. If there was a shipwreck here, someone would have found it already.

Then again, the net had snagged on something. Tommy had cast it himself. It had gone down just as it was supposed to, ballooning like a parachute as the weights around it dragged the edges down. Cast-netters weren't supposed to drag the bottom, and that hadn't been his intention, but a lot of times the weights hit bottom before the net could be drawn taut, cinching it closed around whatever had been caught inside. They'd caught it on something, that was for sure.

Tommy and his father hauled on the line, but the resistance was still there.

"Dad, it's still caught."

Norm gave him that lopsided grin, the scar tugging at the left side of his face. "It's not caught. We've just got something heavy in the net."

Tommy knew that look. His father had always enjoyed secrets and surprises, and he had one now. *Okay, Dad,* he thought. *It's your net.*

They pulled, muscles straining. Tommy felt the sun baking the back of his neck. The water seemed so quiet, a silence broken only by their grunting efforts and the radio that played low in the small cabin. They swayed, keeping their balance as the boat rocked on the gentle waves.

"Jesus, Dad," Tommy said through gritted teeth. "Is it a friggin' anchor?"

They heaved, dragging it up, and then the net was there. Whatever weighted it down was still in the water. The Dunne men thrust their hands into the mesh of the net to get a better grip and pulled even harder. It came out of the water like a cork from a bottle, the splash of its emergence like a sigh. They staggered back, both men swearing, and Tommy nearly fell. He felt certain his father had been wrong. It had to have been caught on something, because it had weighed

hundreds of pounds a second ago, and now the dark shape inside the
net was a hell of a lot lighter than their usual catch.

It clanked to the deck, and Tommy frowned, peering at it. His father
peeled the net away, and at last he could see what it was they had
dredged up from the bottom.

An iron box, maybe eighteen inches long and nine high. Once upon
a time it had had leather strapping, but now only the tiniest vestiges of
that remained. The lid of the chest had a sort of trapezoidal shape, and
two heavy locks kept it sealed up tight. The construction was strong
but crude enough that the box had to be hundreds of years old. The
iron should have been pitted and corroded by salt, but it seemed
strangely smooth.

Tommy glanced over to see his father watching him expectantly.

"Come on, Dad," he said. "Tell me you don't think this is some
kind of pirate treasure. That shit only happens in *The Goonies*."

"It doesn't need to be treasure to be worth a fortune to us, bud,"
Norm replied. "You've gotta ask yourself how it got here."

They stood back and stared at the chest, the net spread out around
it like discarded wrapping paper on Christmas morning. *Is that what
this is?* Tommy thought. *A gift?*

"You're thinking of Gregg McKeown," he said.

Norm nodded, his smile gone. His thoughts had turned serious as
he regarded the trunk. "If we can establish that this thing came from
a wreck, we could make a claim and . . ."

Tommy looked at him. "Dad?"

"Don't want to get ahead of myself," Norm said, heading for the
cabin. He opened a hatch and tugged out his toolbox. "Let's see what's
in this thing before we get too excited. Could be nothing."

"Are you sure that's a good idea?" Tommy asked as his father knelt
by the iron chest and retrieved a hammer and a big screwdriver from
the toolbox. "I mean, what if the box itself is valuable, y'know? Or,
like, they can learn something about what ship it came from because
of the locks or whatever?"

Norm faltered with the flat of the screwdriver already propped
against the hasp of the lock. He looked at his son.

"Sometimes I forget how smart you are, punk," he said, rubbing the back of his right hand—the hand that gripped the hammer—across the stubble on his chin. "You could be right."

A few seconds ticked by. Tommy almost felt guilty for taking his fun away.

"Screw it, Dad," he said. "You know you want to see what's inside."

Norm laughed, nodding. "Damn straight."

He set the screwdriver against the hasp again, raised the hammer, and struck the back of the screwdriver's handle. On the third blow, the hasp of the lock broke off. The second lock took only one hit to snap off.

Norm set aside his tools and reached for the box, raising the lid and looking inside.

He froze. The way he crouched, Tommy couldn't see his face.

"Dad? Come on. Don't keep me in suspense."

But his father didn't move. The boat rocked and Norm managed to maintain his balance, but otherwise he seemed almost to have turned to stone.

"Dad?" Tommy ventured again.

He moved up next to his father, but the second he saw Norm's face he stopped short. His features were contorted with terrible emotion, as though he might be about to scream in fear or collapse in tears.

"What is it, Dad?" Tommy asked, dropping to his knees.

He put a hand on his father's shoulder and shook him. "Dad!"

When Tommy shook him again, his father let go of the box's lid and it slammed down. Norm collapsed onto the deck and began to shake, arms and legs flailing, eyes wide and staring at something Tommy could not see.

Then he started to scream.

Fear flowed into Tommy, the terror of loss. "No, Dad, stop," he said, grabbing hold of his father's shoulders and pinning him to the deck, trying to trap his arms. He wanted to join in the screaming, help-lessness seizing him in its grasp. Ever since his mother's death he had lived in private terror of losing his father as well.

"Dad!" he shouted. "Look at me!"

Tommy slapped his father's face, then immediately felt ashamed and afraid it had been the wrong thing to do. He lay down on the fishing net beside his father and gathered the man into his arms, wrapped himself around those jittering arms and legs and trapped them, refusing to allow them to move.

"Stop it! Look at me! Norman Dunne, look at me, God damn it!"

Tommy screamed his father's name, letting all of his fear out in one burst. When he stopped, the wind carrying his voice away across the waves, his father had gone still. Norm's eyes were still wide, but they had focus again, staring at Tommy.

"Do you see the shadows, Tom?"

"What? What shadows?"

Tommy glanced around. The only shadows were in the small cabin. Otherwise they were in full sunlight. But his father's eyes kept darting back and forth, anxiously peering at things in his peripheral vision that Tommy couldn't see.

"The corners are dark," Norm Dunne said, like a little boy talking about monsters under his bed. "The shadows are cracks, and they keep trying to slip through."

That was when Tommy knew that he couldn't help his father. Either Norm would come to his senses on his own, or he would need someone who could figure out what had happened to him—some kind of aneurysm or something. Had to be, the way he was babbling.

"Okay, Dad," Tommy said. "Just sit tight, okay? I'm going to bring us home."

He stood, trying to fight the emotions welling up inside him as he watched his father turning and flinching away from things Tommy couldn't see.

"I'll get us home," he said, pulling out his cell phone as he headed for the cabin.

As he passed the iron box, he stopped and stared down at it. Aneurysm, he thought. Something like that. It couldn't have anything to do with the stupid box. The timing had to be coincidence. But still . . .

Tommy crouched down, just as his father had, and opened the lid.

He stared into the chest. "You've gotta be shitting me."

Inside the iron box were a small pile of old scrolls. How they had remained dry under the water, how the old chest had remained sealed airtight for who knew how long, he had no idea. But it was just paper, and there was nothing frightening about a bunch of paper. Nothing that would send his father over the edge.

He let the lid slam shut again.

Just paper.

3

Summerfields Orchard occupied acres of rolling hillside in a small valley just north of Brattleboro, Vermont. The huge red barn on the property had been transformed into a marketplace, where shoppers could buy the fresh fruits and vegetables grown at the farm, along with a huge variety of other products, including both dessert pies and chicken pot pies, homemade apple cider, handcrafted goods, and the ever-popular cider donuts, cranked out by the dozens every day, and the hundreds on weekends.

During the summer they were busy with corn and had festivals during which employees grilled corn outdoors for visitors. Children romped in the play area and climbed all over the enormous wooden pirate ship that stood, apropos of nothing, in one of the front fields. But once school started up again the orchard was always quiet on weekdays, visited mostly by older folks and young mothers with pre-school children. When apple-picking season got under way—and well toward Halloween, with the pumpkin harvest in full swing—the week-ends were wonderful, happy, smiling chaos.

Come Saturday, there would be live outdoor music and children running amok in the hay maze. Parents and kids alike rode the hay wagon up to the top of the hill, filled bags with apples they'd picked themselves, and then trudged back down, laden with fruit. People lined up at the windows at the back of the barn to buy cider and donuts without even having to go inside.

In all her life, Keomany Shaw had never met a group of people who worked as hard as the owners and employees at Summerfields. The two women who owned the place, Tori Osborne and Cat Hein, were the kind of married couple that other couples envied. They fought, but they never went to bed angry, and whatever conflicts arose, neither of them ever seemed to worry that they would erode the foundations of the relationship. Keomany wished she could find someone—man or woman—who would give her life the peace and harmony that Tori and Cat gave each other. She admired the women, and all of the Summerfields employees, for the sincerity of their efforts.

Keomany lived among them, but as much as she tried to help out where she could, she also lived apart from them. Unlike the rest of the people who worked at the orchard and farm, she had her own business on the grounds. When Keomany's original shop had been destroyed, along with her entire hometown, Tori and Cat had given her an entire corner of the big red barn and hung a sign from the ceiling—*Sweet Somethings: Confections by Keomany Shaw*. She had tried to argue with their generosity, but they insisted, and at last she had relented, not only because she did not want to seem ungracious, but because they were her friends, and she couldn't imagine anywhere else she wanted to be.

Summerfields had become her home. She had her own bedroom in the big house far across the fields from the barn. Tori and Cat usually had one or two other friends and employees living with them at any given time—it was simply their nature—but Keomany had become a permanent resident. At first they had taken nothing in return for the gifts they had given her, but in time, as Sweet Somethings had grown more and more successful, they had agreed to a percentage of her profits in exchange for the space her shop took up in the barn. But that was where they drew the line. They would not allow her to pay rent for her room in their house, and so she paid them back in other ways, by taking turns shopping or fixing meals, and by helping out at the orchard or on the farm whenever she had free time.

In the handful of years since she had come to live with them, Summerfields had only become more popular. Vermont was one of the most progressive states in the Union, and Keomany had never run into anyone who seemed at all troubled by the fact that the two women who owned the place were lesbians. She had often wondered, though, if people would be quite so accepting if they knew that Tori and Cat— and Keomany herself—were also witches. They practiced earthcraft, not traditional witchcraft, but she doubted most people would see the difference, especially given how fearful some people had become in the years since the existence of vampires and demons and magic had been revealed to the world.

So, although they didn't really go out of their way to keep their beliefs and practices a secret, they also didn't broadcast it.

Which was how Keomany came to find herself walking alone up the hill through rows of apple trees on that Wednesday morning. So many people favored the sweeter apples, but Keomany loved a good Granny Smith. She tugged one off a branch as she passed and took a bite, savoring the slightly sour flavor.

At the top of the hill, on the western end of the orchard, far from the most frequently trodden rows, Tori and Cat had ordered a section of the land staked off from the rest. Yellow caution tape was strung from one stake to the next, making that section of the orchard look like a police crime scene. Dozens of witches would be visiting for the equinox. Added to the Summerfields employees—all witches, though most in faith only—there would be nearly one hundred people gathering on this small patch of the orchard that day. Summerfields would be closed to the public for a "private party."

The preparations were already under way. Blessings had been spoken and spells cast. Ribbons surrounded the trunks of trees on the edges of the clearing that had been set aside for the celebration. There would be prayers and rituals at dawn and dusk, and music and dancing at intervals during the day. The entire day would be filled with celebrations of the equinox, or Harvest Home. They would celebrate nature's bounty and honor the passing of the growing season. It was a time to give thanks for the fruits of the earth and of their labor, to look back on the year that was ending and forward to the future. There would be wine and cider, some of which would be poured at the foot of each tree in the ring around the clearing.

The clearing itself had been partially prepared already, but Tori and Cat had asked Keomany to complete the preparation and purification in a way that only she could. The two of them had some skill with earthcraft and some innate power, but nothing on the level of the magic that Keomany had discovered within herself. Of them all, only she could perform the desired purification.

The soil in the clearing had been turned and most of the yellowing grass raked out, as though in preparation for a garden. This section of the orchard was kept as free of pesticides as possible, but still the soil had trace chemicals that traveled through groundwater. The celebration of the equinox called for purification. For many, this would be symbolic purity, but Keomany wished for something better.

From somewhere far off, she heard a woman calling after her child. She turned her face toward the sun and closed her eyes, arms outthrust, apple still clutched in her hand, and let its warmth fill her and flow through her. She felt it in her bones and relished it, even as she enjoyed the sound of the autumn breeze rustling through the apple trees. The scent of the rotting, fermenting apples already fallen mixed with the sweet smell of those still hanging from the branches, and this was the smell of life, and of the earth.

Contented, she opened her eyes and walked to the center of the clearing, her shoes making impressions in the freshly turned soil. Closing her eyes again, she faced eastward and whispered blessings to the air and earth, then turned and repeated the blessings facing west, then again south, and finally north.

As she spoke, the wind rose around her, buffeting her gently with breezes both warm and cold. The air caressed her, her silken black hair whipping around her face, and she breathed deeply. She felt Gaea, the earth mother, the goddess, there with her. At all times, Keomany felt a small buzzing in her mind, a warm shiver in her flesh, a power that lay mostly dormant within her, but that connected her to Gaea. She could summon that magic at will. It connected her to the elements, to all of nature, and she had called the wind that surrounded her now.

She opened her arms and let that magic flow from her, down into the ground. The soil began to shift and the clearing to tremble as the chemical impurities in that patch of land were destroyed or rendered inert as if they had been burned away. Grass began to spring up from the soil, growing quickly. She could hear the wind singing from the blades and could feel the grass underfoot and brushing against her legs.

Keomany took a bite of the apple, opened her eyes, and dropped it to the ground. She stepped back to watch as the seeds inside the fruit sent shoots down into the soil. In the space between eye blinks, a finger-length sprig emerged. Smiling, feeling the harmony of earth magic, she moved farther away to give it room to grow, and as she looked on, the sprig stretched upward with a whisper of life, branches forming, leaves growing, blossoms appearing and then flowering into being as gleaming, green, Granny Smith apples. The tree—nine or ten feet tall now—seemed almost to sigh and settle its roots more deeply, and then the wind subsided and only the smallest breeze remained to gently sway its branches. With its leaves turned toward the sun, this newborn fruit of the earth thrived.

During the celebration there would be at least one apple for each of those in attendance—Keomany would make certain of it. They would partake together, and in years to come, other trees would grow from this one, and so the purity of the earth and the peace of Gaea would continue to spread through Summerfields and to all of those who ate of this tree, and those that would grow from its seeds.

"Blessed—" Keomany began to say.

The pain made her cry out, surging up through the magical umbilical that tethered her to the goddess. It made her muscles contract and her legs give way, and she fell in the newly grown grass. Spikes hammered into her skull and the shadows cast by the trees at the edges of the clearing reached knife-blade fingers for her, forcing her to close her eyes. But she couldn't hide from the pain, or the nausea that roiled in her gut, or the images that rose in her mind of waves crashing against a pier, of unnatural things scuttling onto the shore, and of dark mist flowing through the streets of a small town, swallowing it up.

The mist enveloped her, pain and darkness suffocating her, and she sank down into herself and oblivion claimed her.

For a time, Keomany knew nothing. The darkness coalesced, eddying around her as though she lay in some midnight tide pool, pain subsiding and her breathing returning to normal.

A voice whispered her name. For just a moment, she thought it might be the goddess herself. Then, as consciousness returned, she winced away from the brightness of the sun. Slowly, she opened her eyes to slits, and saw Tori Osborne looking down at her, beautiful ebony face framed by ropes of beaded hair.

"Hey," Tori said gently. "Anybody home in there?"

Keomany groaned. The pain in her head had gone, but the moment she tried to move, it returned.

"What happened to you?" Tori asked.

It took Keomany a moment, but then the memory flooded back into her mind. Whatever connection Gaea had created to link her to that place, she still felt it. The goddess had cried out as the taint of evil had touched that town and began to spread. Keomany had felt her anguish, and she knew the name of that town.

She tried to speak, but her voice was a rasp.

"Hang on," Tori said, turning to the others who had gathered around her in the clearing by the new apple tree. She reached out toward them, and the orchard manager, scruffy Patrick, handed Tori a bottle of water.

Tori helped Keomany prop herself up and handed her the bottle. Keomany winced at the pain in her head, but the water tasted wonderful. She wondered how long she had been out there under the sun before someone had wondered why she had been gone so long and come looking for her.

"Goddess, is she all right?" a familiar voice called.

They all turned to see Tori's wife, the tall, curvy Cat Hein, come hurrying into the clearing. Cat fell to her knees beside Tori, and now both women were doting over her. Keomany managed a smile, more for them than for herself.

"Are you okay? What happened?" Cat asked.

Keomany took another sip of water, then nodded to her friends. "I'm all right. Help me up. I've got to get to the house. I need the phone."

They steadied her as she rose to her feet.

"What's going on, Keomany?" Tori asked. "Who do you have to call?"

Keomany started away from the new tree, toward the house on the other side of the orchard.

"Octavian," she said, glancing back at them. "And I'll need someone to watch my shop. I'm going to be going away for a little while."

The coffee Viviane Chenot had brewed could have doubled as a rust remover, but Octavian didn't mind. He liked it strong, and if it was also bitter, he didn't mind, and he never tried to subdue the flavor with sugar. Nikki had no such hesitations. She smiled as she dumped three heaping teaspoons of sugar into her coffee, and even then he knew she only drank it to be polite.

They sat around the little table in the dining area just outside Viviane's galley kitchen. Perhaps the change could be attributed to a new lightness of spirit for Viviane herself, but the place seemed brighter to Octavian, the colors of the paintings and even the flowers on the table more vivid.

"I can't thank you enough for what you did," Viviane said.

"I'm only glad I was in time," Octavian replied.

Viviane's lover and former professor, Derek Tremblay, raised his coffee cup in a toast.

"Don't be modest," the professor said. "You've earned yourself a certain notoriety, Peter, but a lot of people think you're some kind of charlatan. I thank God that you're not."

Nikki reached out and touched Octavian's face, pushing her fingers back through his hair. "He *is* something, isn't he?"

Octavian rolled his eyes, not because he minded public displays of affection but because he had never been comfortable with lavish praise, not even from the woman he loved.

"All right, rock star," he teased.

Nikki bristled. She always argued that her music wasn't technically "rock." When they were sparring like this, it never failed to get a rise out of her. It felt good to be playful with her. Much of the tension that had been growing between them had abated, though he feared that soon enough, like the tide, it would roll back in again.

Nikki did not offer a retort, and he knew why. Ever since Viviane had opened the door to let them into the apartment, the girl had been alternately staring at Nikki and sneaking glances at her. She hadn't made it to superstardom, and would be happy if it never came to that, but there was no denying that Nikki had attained a certain amount of fame. Viviane Chenot was having difficulty adjusting to having a celebrity sitting at her table, drinking her coffee.

"How's your brother doing, anyway?" Nikki asked.

Viviane smiled at her. "Amazingly well. When he woke up this morning, his vision was a little blurry, and I'm going to take him to see a doctor if it doesn't clear by tomorrow. Otherwise . . ." She frowned, shrugging. "His throat is sore and kind of hoarse. I'm not sure if it will ever go back to normal, but honestly, if that's the worst of it, he'll adjust. Everyone else is . . . well, they're gone forever. And I've still got my brother."

Her eyes welled with emotion. Octavian shifted in his chair, a bit uncomfortable.

Nikki laid a gentle hand on Viviane's arm. "He was lucky to have you. If you had just brought him to a doctor and waited for them to realize they had no idea how to help him, he'd never have survived."

Viviane smiled, then glanced lovingly at the professor. "It's Derek, really. When I told him . . . he was the one who suggested calling Mr. Octavian. I was totally out of my mind—just didn't know what to do."

She grabbed the professor's hand and tugged him toward her for a tender kiss. Octavian caught Nikki watching them and smiled at her. Tough as she pretended to be, Nikki had a profoundly romantic heart. She met his gaze, and a moment of sweet silence passed between them. Once, it had been this way all the time.

"We should go," Nikki said, as much to him as to Viviane and Derek. "Let you guys get on with your lives. I'm sure you've had to let a lot of important things fall into chaos this week. You'll need to catch up."

Viviane nodded, squeezing Derek's hand. "After something like this, your definition of what's 'important' changes."

She rose from the table, and they all followed suit.

"Thank you so much," Derek said, shaking Octavian's hand, and then Nikki's.

"I'm happy I could help," Octavian said, as he and Nikki put on their coats.

"Hang on," Viviane said. "Before you go, let me just have a quick look and see if Michael is awake. I know he'll want to thank you himself."

Octavian glanced at Nikki, who nodded. Her next show was in Portland, Maine, on Friday, so they had two days to make their way down into the States. No rush at all. They waited while Viviane went down the hall and checked on Michael, but now that they'd said their goodbyes it felt strange to linger.

A musical trilling sound defused the awkwardness. Octavian had left his cell phone on its factory-set ring tone, but still it took him a moment to realize the noise came from the pocket of his jacket. Nikki looked at him expectantly—usually it was her cell phone that rang incessantly. Only a handful of people even had Octavian's cell number.

"Hello?" he said, pressing the slim black phone to his ear.

As he listened to the voice on the other end of the line, he saw Nikki watching him and already he felt the distance between them returning, so much sooner than he had expected. He felt a twinge of guilt knowing he would be drawn away for a time, and resented the feeling.

Viviane rejoined them. "Sorry, guys. He's still . . ." she began, before she realized Octavian was on the phone and let her words trail off.

"All right," Octavian said. "I'll call you from the road and give you an ETA."

He ended the call and tucked his phone into his jeans. The interior of the small apartment seemed to have dimmed, as though clouds had begun to gather outside.

"What's going on?" Nikki asked, making a visible effort to hide her disappointment.

Octavian glanced at Viviane and Derek but then returned his attention to Nikki, the others in the room forgotten.

"That was Keomany," he said. "There's trouble."

What more could he say? She knew that there were certain kinds of trouble he was better at handling than anyone else in the world, and that his conscience would never allow him to refuse to help. Nor would she want him to refuse, if only for the sake of her own conscience.

Her gaze full of regret, she nodded and reached for his hands.

"I've toured on my own plenty of times."

"You don't have to go on your own," Octavian offered. "The label will send a minder or an assistant or something."

Nikki arched an eyebrow. "I'd rather be on my own than have a babysitter from the label." The corners of her mouth lifted in a coquettish smile, a game attempt to dispel the renewed hesitation between them. "I'm a big girl. I can handle myself."

"I know you can," Octavian said.

"I could come with you. Cancel a few dates," Nikki offered.

But Octavian shook his head. "No. I know how you feel about letting people down when they've paid good money to see you. I'm only going as far as Massachusetts. Keomany and I will get this thing sorted out, and then I'll catch up with you, wherever you are."

Nikki kissed him. "You'd better."

Octavian glanced at the professor. "Derek, can you run me to the airport? I need a rental car."

"Sure," the professor said, he and Viviane looking at them with concern. "Just tell me when you want to go."

Octavian turned back to Nikki. "It needs to be now."

"It's that bad?" she asked, worry creasing her forehead for the first time.

Octavian kissed her, caressing her cheek, wondering how many days it would be before he saw her again.

"I guess I'll find out when I get there."

All Amber wanted was to go home. She smiled and nodded at the nurse but barely listened to the woman. From the moment Dr. Millet had given her a clean bill of health, she had been champing at the bit. All of her life, she had hated hospitals. At age six, she had broken her leg, and she could still remember the hellish discomfort of the hospital bed and the stink of human rot that lay just below the smell of disinfectant they used to try to hide it. But the worst part of being hospitalized had not been the injury or the treatment—it had been the sensation of being trapped there, on that awful bed, surrounded by the sick and the dying.

So she forced herself to smile and she signed the paperwork for her release, and she took the piece of paper the nurse had printed up giving her nutritional advice on how to avoid doing the kind of damage to her body that might lead to a seizure. They were giving her a piece of paper instead of drugs because they had spent five hours trying to figure out what had caused her morning to turn to shit, and they'd come up empty.

"Just call us if you don't feel well, or if you're concerned about anything at all," the nurse said.

Kind of hard to make a call if I'm spazzing out on the floor, she thought. But she smiled and nodded some more, and managed to thank the woman.

Amber had been holding her cell phone in her hand, ignoring the buzz of new texts coming in because she didn't want to be rude to the nurse. Now, as the woman ushered her out of the examination room and pointed her toward the exit, she glanced down at her messages. Two new ones, both from her best friend, Tami Nguyen.

What time can u meet tonite? read the first message. Tami had followed seconds later with *Is he really still waiting for u?*

Tami had been fretting dramatically over Amber's health ever since Amber had first texted her that she was being taken to the hospital. But the second Amber had told her that the doctor thought she had just been dehydrated and possibly overcaffeinated, Tami had moved on to her more traditional concerns—partying.

The doc said to rest tonite, she texted, which was halfway to a lie, in the sense that the doctor had actually given her that instruction, but Amber would never have obeyed it if she really wanted to go and get drunk with Tami. More and more, of late, she had found herself losing interest in such things. She still had nearly two years left of college, but partying had lost its appeal the day she had turned twenty-one. Not that she had ever been nearly as into it as Tami. The girl had her charms, and Amber adored her, but she was a self-proclaimed drunken slut. There was real heart and intelligence and wisdom underneath the party-girl exterior, but over the past six months or so, Amber had been having to dig deeper and deeper to find that part of her friend, and it saddened her.

Loser, Tami texted her.

I know. How can u stand me?

So is he still there or what?

Amber clutched the phone in her hand and shifted her pocketbook from one shoulder to the other as she went out into the emergency room's waiting area. She spotted Ben Draper immediately. He was reading a paperback book but seemed to sense her attention and glanced over to see her looking at him. Instantly, he jumped up from his chair and hurried toward her, his eyes hopeful.

Yep, she texted.

Wow. He so wants you.

Doesn't everyone?

I do, Tami joked. *Right now.*

Rain check. TTYL.

Amber silenced her phone and dropped it into her pocketbook, zipping it up as Ben approached.

"Hey," Ben said, searching her eyes. "Are you okay? You *look* okay."

"Yeah. I mean, they think so. But ohmygod, Ben, you didn't have to wait all this time. You've been here all day."

"Not all day," he said, smiling. "Besides, it's fine. I told Professor Varick I'd go with you, and when you said you didn't want anyone to call your parents, I figured you'd need someone around to drive you back to campus to get your car. Anyway, I ate lunch and picked up this book at the gift shop." He held it up like a prize he'd won. "Plus I was texting people. The time went by. Mostly I was just worried about you."

A strange warmth spread through Amber. She had liked Ben from the very first time they'd met, appreciated his sweetness and sincerity, but there had never been a spark between them, at least not for her. She had told herself he was *too* sweet, and too earnest. But now she looked at him and thought she saw, just for a moment, the man he was evolving into. She thought about the guys she usually ended up hanging out with when she partied with Tami, and she felt like she had just stumbled upon a universal truth—none of those guys were going to evolve into the kind of man she envisioned as part of her future.

Maybe sweet could be sexy.

"Thank you so much for waiting," she said, and kissed Ben on the cheek. His clothes were rumpled and his hair its usual mess after hours in the waiting room, but that disarray—his Ben-ness—suddenly seemed more than cute.

Amber laughed, ending a moment she knew they both had felt go on too long.

"What's funny?" Ben asked.

"Me," she said, forcing herself not to look him in the eye. "I must have hit my head pretty hard."

As soon as she said it, she realized he would understand. Of course he would. Ben wasn't stupid. He must have sensed something between them in that moment. How could he take that comment as anything but an insult? A dismissal?

She looked up and saw the hurt in his eyes before he smiled to mask it.

"You banged it a bunch of times," he said. "Did the doctor say if you have a concussion?"

Amber almost apologized—the words were on her lips—but then she would have had to explain aloud what she was apologizing for, and it would just get incredibly awkward. If Ben was willing to let it go, she wouldn't argue.

"Actually, he said it was amazing I *don't* have one," she said, smiling and putting a hand to her temple. "I do feel kind of weird, though. Not myself, y'know?"

Would that work? Would he understand what she was trying to say?

Amber did like Ben, and maybe—despite Tami's teasing—she had felt a spark here today, after all the time they'd known each other. But it had already been a long day and she was tired. Now wasn't the time to act on emotions she might not still have when she woke up in the morning.

"Hey, you've had a traumatic day," Ben said.

She rubbed his arm, smiling. "Thank you, again."

For letting me off the hook, she thought. *Today's just not the day.*

"No problem," Ben said. "Now, come on. Let's get you back to campus so you can get your car, and you can figure out how you're going to explain today to your family."

Amber rolled her eyes as they walked toward the door.

"God, you had to remind me? My mother will be grilling me about it. But it's all right. Mostly, I just didn't want to talk to them until I knew what was wrong with me. I didn't want them worrying until I found out if there was something to really worry about. My Gran especially. I love her, y'know, but she torments my mother about the way she's raising me."

Ben laughed. He had met Gran before and knew exactly what Amber was talking about.

"I'd invite myself over for some of your mother's cooking, but I don't think I want to be around there tonight."

Amber smiled. "It'll be all right. If I know my mother, she'll keep the whole thing a secret from Gran. She doesn't want to hear a lecture any more than I do."

Gran had strong opinions about what was appropriate for a young woman, especially where wardrobe was concerned. It didn't help that she spoke only a little English, even after all of her years in the United States. Gran—her mother's grandmother—had been born in Italy, and everything about her was still "old world." But Amber loved the ninety-four-year-old woman and indulged her as much as she could.

"Maybe another night, though," Amber said, glancing at Ben. "Next week?"

He seemed to pause, as though to decide if he should read anything into the invitation. They'd known each other since the first week of classes, freshman year, but for the first time there was this odd dance going on between them. Amber knew it was dangerous—that it could threaten their friendship—but she liked it.

"Sounds good," Ben said.

The doors shushed aside and the cool, late-afternoon breeze swept in, tousling Amber's hair.

"Cool," she replied, linking arms with him as she marched him out onto the sidewalk. "Onward, then. To my car, driver! With a Starbucks stop on the way!"

"I don't think so," Ben said as they headed for the parking lot. "Professor Varick said all the caffeine you drink might have caused your seizure. Did you ask the doctor about that?"

Amber could have said no and been telling the truth. She hadn't asked, but the doctor who treated her had brought it up as a possible explanation.

"I don't even drink that much coffee," she said. "Only in the morning. Usually. They're just saying that because it's convenient when you don't have any real answers."

"Maybe you should stick with that story," Ben suggested. "If you tell your family the doctors don't know what caused it—"

"Oh, crap. You're right. They'll haunt me every second."

Ben dislodged his arm from hers and fished out his keys. "I'll stop on the way if you promise to get decaf."

"Deal!" she said happily.

But her smile turned to concern when she spotted the figure leaning against the building ahead. Blond and tan, a Red Sox T-shirt stretched across his muscular chest, Tommy Dunne looked as unhappy as she had ever seen him. He took a long drag on a cigarette and blew out the smoke, radiating anger.

"Tommy?" Amber said.

The kid looked up, and in that anger, she saw that he wasn't a kid anymore. He had been two years behind her in school, and their backgrounds were completely different, but he had dated her friend Alyss for a few months during his freshman year, and she had always enjoyed talking to him. Tommy Dunne had turned out to be pretty soulful for a pot-smoking skate punk.

"Amber," he said. "Hey."

"What are you doing here?" she asked. "Is everything all right?"

He took another drag and let the smoke come out with his words.

"My dad. We were out in the boat today and he had some kind of . . ." He hesitated, then shrugged. "Fuck if I know, really. The nurse kept using the word *episode*, like that really means anything. Now they're saying he had a minor heart attack, but that's not all that's wrong with him. He's not really talking."

Amber stared at him. "Oh, my God. I'm so sorry," she said, thinking maybe what had really happened to Norm Dunne was a stroke, and what a shame that was. The man was so young. "Is there anything I can do? Anything you need, from the house?"

Tommy's expression softened, showing the sadness and worry underneath.

"I'm good. Thanks," he said. "But it's wicked nice of you to offer."

"You have my cell?" Amber asked.

Tommy didn't, so she gave it to him and he keyed it into his phone.

"Call me if there's anything I can do. If your dad's going to be in a while, my mom will want to make you some meals, at least."

The suggestion that his father might not be released from the hospital that day seemed to trouble him deeply.

"Thanks," he said, "but I'm sure he'll be coming home tonight. Or tomorrow, at the latest."

"I'm sure he will," Amber said, because it was the sort of thing one said.

She touched Tommy's arm and he thanked her, and then she and Ben set off for the parking lot again. When she glanced back, she saw Tommy flick his cigarette onto the sidewalk and hurry back into the hospital.

"Poor guy," she said.

"How do you know him?"

"An old friend," Amber told him. "It's a small town. We're all old friends around here."

But as they drove back to campus, those words rang hollow. Small patches of chaos had erupted all over town. Somehow, the entire system of traffic lights in Hawthorne had malfunctioned at once, so that every single one of them had turned green simultaneously, causing dozens of accidents.

Police cars were everywhere, some cops directing traffic while others took statements and broke up arguments. As Ben drove carefully through the intersection of Franklin Street and Harbor Road, Amber watched a screaming woman slap a man across the face. She thought she recognized the woman as a pharmacist down at the Rite Aid. One stupid malfunction, and Hawthorne had started to unravel.

All in all, it had been a crazy day.

No matter how many times Tami asked, she was definitely staying in tonight.

4

Herbie's Beachside Diner opened its doors in the spring of 1957 and had been a landmark in Hawthorne ever since—more than fifty years of serving legendary breakfasts, passable burgers and fried clams, thick ice cream frappés, and possibly the world's greatest onion rings. Herbie Barbour had passed away in '99, leaving the business to his grandson, whom most people called Little Joe, and since the fire in '01 and the relocation to Sandpiper Road, it wasn't technically "beachside" anymore, but its reputation remained, mostly thanks to Little Joe Barbour's skill in the kitchen.

Little Joe had never been on a motorcycle in his entire life, unless he counted the little dirt bike his cousin Ronnie had owned when they were teenagers. But he knew that to the untrained eye, he looked an awful lot like a biker. Six and a half feet tall, barrel chested and bearded, he cut an imposing figure, and though he spent most of his time back in the kitchen, if local kids or just-passing-throughs started acting up in the diner, just an unamused glance through the serving window was usually enough to settle things down. Little Joe was unlikely to break anyone in half, but he most certainly looked capable of it, and he used that imposing presence to keep the peace when necessary.

Most of the time, though, people were too busy enjoying their food to raise any ruckus.

Which was why he frowned deeply that Wednesday afternoon when he heard shouting from the front of the diner. He had burgers and some chicken on the grill, clams and fries and rings all frying, and his kitchen help—Anthony and Bonita—were too busy with salads and sides and desserts to take over for him. He didn't have time for distractions. Still, this was his place of business, and he couldn't ignore it, so he flipped a couple of burgers, turned down the burner, and moved to peer through the serving window, over the tops of a couple of sandwiches Bonita had plated and left there, ready for pickup. One of the sandwiches smelled funny, and he wrinkled his nose and looked down at them, thinking that, actually, maybe both of them smelled funny.

"It's not just the coffee," a voice barked out in the dining area. "Yeah, the cream you brought me is fuckin' curdled, but that ain't it. This chicken salad tastes like shit. The mayonnaise is spoiled."

Little Joe didn't recognize the guy raising the ruckus, but he sized him up quickly. Short . . . graying . . . uptight. The guy's wife looked embarrassed to be seen with him, and Little Joe saw their whole lives in that tiny sliver of a moment. She was trying hard, but they barely knew how to communicate anymore. They were married but couldn't stand each other. Given the arrogant whininess of the guy, he sided with the wife immediately.

But he could read their dynamic well enough to tell that the husband would be paying the bill, so as long as the guy didn't abuse anyone, Little Joe had to make sure he was treated like any other customer—and that meant fresh food and coffee with cream that hadn't gone sour. Fortunately, Felicia was waiting on him, and though she wouldn't take any crap, she also knew how Little Joe felt about the food they served. *It might not be good for you,* Herbie Barbour had been fond of saying in the old days, *but I guarantee it'll taste good.*

"Sorry about that, honey," Felicia told the man, putting on a sweetly mystified expression. "Never had that happen before. But we'll get you squared away. They'll make up a fresh batch of chicken salad, too."

"I'll pass," the angry little man said. "Let me have a chicken Caesar salad instead. That should be safe enough."

Little Joe thought he caught Felicia smiling, but things were starting to sizzle too loudly on the grill and he didn't want to create more disgruntled customers by burning a bunch of dinners. He went to work, scraping and flipping and spicing, dousing some chopped-up chicken with teriyaki sauce. Quick as he could, he started plating some of the meals. Anthony appeared at his side to help out, the skinny little Honduran kid snatching order tickets off the line and supplementing Little Joe's burgers and chicken with fries or rings. He added two huge orders of clams and started loading it all up onto the shelf of the serving window.

"Cassie! Order up!" Anthony called. "Brian! Order up!"

Bonita muttered something behind them, at the sandwich station. Little Joe didn't catch it at first, but then she swore.

"Boss, you better come look at this," she said.

"Just a second," Little Joe said. He wiped his arm across his forehead to dry the sheen of sweat that had begun to build up there. Then he reached up to spin the rack above the grill where the wait staff clipped the order tickets and snatched the next order down. Western omelet and hash browns. Herbie's Beachside Diner had been offering breakfast all day long for more than half a century, but Little Joe had never understood people who ate pancakes or omelets at dinnertime.

"Boss?" Anthony said.

His tone made Little Joe frown. The kid bent over to peer through the serving window. Little Joe could hear more voices raised out in the dining room, and he wondered if the little Napoleon out there was still bitching about the meal he'd already sent back.

"Just a second," he repeated. He'd fallen a bit behind and now had to catch up in order to keep everything running smoothly. He wiped his hands on his food-stained apron and opened the fridge under the counter to his right, pulled out three eggs—fingers splayed like he might start juggling them—and banged the fridge shut with his knee.

He kept a section of the grill dedicated to breakfast foods. The last thing he'd cooked, maybe half an hour before, had been pancakes, but he always kept the heat on low so he wouldn't have to start with a cold surface. He turned the burner up higher on that section of the grill, dropped a pad of butter in the center, and cracked the first egg—one-handed, the way his granddad had taught him when Little Joe was only nine.

The smell snapped his head back.

"Jesus!" he said, wrinkling his nose at the stench.

The egg had gone bad. Working quickly, he scraped it off the grill into the trash, put a dash of water on the surface and scoured it for a second or two, then cracked another egg, with the same disgusting result.

"What the hell?" he said, turning to glare at the fridge under the counter as though it had offended him. Which it had. The thing had to be broken if all of these eggs were rotten.

"Boss!" Bonita snapped.

As Little Joe turned to look at her, the door to the kitchen banged open. Felicia stood there, propping the door open with her curvaceous behind, blond hair tied back in an unruly ponytail. She looked skittish, trapped halfway between pissed off and worried.

"Joe, we've got a problem," Felicia said.

From the serving window, Anthony gave a humorless laugh. "More than one."

Little Joe looked over and saw two of the waitresses bent over and peering into the kitchen through the serving window, looking confused and nervous.

"The milk's gone sour," Felicia said. "Cream, too. Ginny made frappés and they're awful. And the sandwiches . . . the mayo in the tuna and the chicken salad has gone bad. It's all spoiled."

"Get some more from the fridge," Anthony said.

"We tried that. It's all bad. All the dairy we've got in-house is spoiled. All of it," Felicia explained.

Little Joe frowned, then turned to look at the rotten egg burning on the grill. The smell made him want to gag, and he hurried to scrape it into the trash. He couldn't imagine how something like this was possible. Sabotage? That made no sense. There weren't a lot of diners competing for his trade in Hawthorne. And how could they have worked it, anyway? Twenty minutes ago, all that milk and mayo had been just fine. And he'd used eggs from that same dozen to make pancakes.

"What do we do, boss?" Bonita asked, coming up behind Anthony.

Little Joe glanced around at his employees, all of them looking to him for an answer.

"Tell them," he said. "Tell the customers. Anything dairy, we can't serve right now. If people walk out, there's nothing we can do about that. Anthony, I want to check every container in the place—milk, cream cheese, mayo, anything dairy—"

"But mayonnaise isn't dairy," Anthony said.

"The base is eggs, dimwit," Bonita snapped.

"That ain't helping, Bonnie," Little Joe chided her. He looked around at the others. "We'll check all the food, and we'll check the fridges and freezers. I'll handle it, okay? Just get back to work. And for God's sake, when you're telling the customers about it, *smile*."

His team went into action. Crisis mode. Some nights, when they were short-staffed or there'd been a big ball game or something, the place could get pretty chaotic. Every one of them had worked in crisis mode before. They would do all right. But that didn't solve the mystery of how an entire restaurant full of dairy products could be perfectly fine one moment and spoiled the next. Something like that didn't just happen. There had to be a cause. Scientists might come up with some bullshit explanation, like a change in atmospheric pressure. But he couldn't help thinking of old folk tales he'd read about meat or milk spoiling when the devil passed by.

Stupid, he thought. *Get that crap out of your head.*

Little Joe got back to work. But he shuddered a little, just the same.

Amber fiddled with the car radio, but every time she thought she had found a station, it would start to buzz with static, the voices or the music crackling in and out.

"Your radio's crap," she told Ben.

"Or something's causing interference," he said. "They're putting a new cell tower on Admiral's Hill. If this keeps up, people are going to be pissed."

Amber stared at the radio for a second but knew it was useless to keep running up and down the dial. She had wanted local news more than music, but they were almost at Starbucks now, and then Ben would be dropping her off near where she'd left her car parked on campus, and then she'd be going home. If there was something to report, she'd find the news on TV or online.

"Here's another one," he said, tapping the brake.

"Damn," Amber said. "What the hell is wrong with people today?"

She hit the button for her window, and it whirred downward. Tucking her hair behind her ears, she poked her head out and stared at a Ford F-150 pickup and a rusty old Audi sedan that had collided. The testosterone-boosted pickup had a dented front end and a shattered headlight, while the gray Audi had been mangled by the impact. The crash had smashed its windshield and accordioned its hood. A huge smear of the Ford's red paint scarred the Audi's crumpled front end.

"Check out the PT Cruiser," Ben said, pointing out the window on his side.

Amber glanced past him and saw a ruined purple PT Cruiser being hauled up onto a flatbed tow truck. The whole side of the car had been caved in. Apparently there had been at least three cars involved in this accident, but it was the fourth time in the three miles since they'd left the hospital that they had seen recent wreckage. The police were at some of the accident scenes, but not all of them. Amber had been searching the radio for some news, something that would suggest a reason for the accidents.

"So weird," Ben said.

Amber nodded. "It's like there's just bad luck in the air or something."

"Had to be some kind of malfunction with the stoplights or something," Ben muttered, mostly to himself. It wasn't the first time he had said it, and Amber had the strange feeling he was mostly trying to persuade himself.

"All of them at once?" Amber asked.

Ben scratched at the stubble on his chin. "I guess," he said. And then he smiled mischievously. "Wouldn't want to be the guy in charge of this stuff. His ass is fired, as of right now."

"Or at least in time for the next newscast, so the mayor has a scapegoat."

They turned onto Eastwind Avenue, a tree-lined street that had once been home to fish markets and dive bars but—over the course of the past twenty years—had been the locus for Hawthorne's twenty-first-century gentrification. The façades of the shops and restaurants were pristine and relatively uniform. Victorian-style lampposts had been installed up and down the street. There were a couple of other expensive restaurants in Hawthorne, near the marina, but the rest of the town's fine-dining establishments were on this particular three-block stretch of Eastwind Avenue. Most of them were places where Amber could rarely afford to eat, but she had been to the Sea Glass twice during high school and loved it. Of course, it wasn't all fine dining on Eastwind Avenue. College students and twenty-somethings packed Pedro Diego's pretty much every night for authentic Mexican cuisine and a long list of specialty margaritas. Neo-hippie high schoolers frequented the Troubadour, a café where members of the staff performed four or five songs an hour.

Not every storefront window was a restaurant, of course. Eastwind Avenue boasted a florist shop, an especially snooty bookstore, a handful of clothing boutiques, and a jeweler's. But for Amber, the best reason to drive down Eastwind was the green-and-white sign that hung at the intersection with Church Street, the beacon of the Starbucks logo. As weird as this day had been, a good cup of coffee would make everything better. She could practically taste mocha latte on her tongue.

"Remember," Ben said as he pulled up to the curb across the street from Starbucks. "No caffeine."

"Really?" She gave him sad eyes.

"You promised."

"It's been a crisis kind of day," she said. "A girl can't be held responsible—"

"No caffeine," he repeated.

"Cruel, cruel man." She popped the door and climbed out. "Thank God for chocolate."

Ben followed her across the street, but Amber's focus was on the cars moving up and down Eastwind Avenue. All the accidents they'd seen on the drive over had made her wary. If people were driving crazy today, she didn't want to end up as a bloody hood ornament.

As she approached the door to Starbucks, a pair of fortyish women—fit and fashionably dressed—were exiting. One, an athletic blonde, held the door for her and Ben.

"I'm hearing at least thirty accidents, maybe more," the blonde said to her friend. "Someone's going to get sued."

Amber paused, taking the weight of the door from her. "Are you talking about the car accidents today?"

The woman nodded, eyes lighting up with interest. "Yes. It's crazy, isn't it? How does something like that happen?"

"What *did* happen?" Ben asked. "We saw a few of them on our way here, but do you know what caused them all?"

The blonde gestured inside. "There was a policeman here a few minutes ago who said something went wrong with the system that controls the traffic lights. They all went green simultaneously. None of the drivers are to blame, but I'm sure their insurance companies are going to come after the city. The mayor's lucky no one was killed."

Her friend started talking to her again, and then the women were drifting away.

"Thanks," Amber said, but they were barely paying attention to her and Ben now.

"Told you. Malfunction," Ben said.

But Amber still felt uneasy. Malfunction or not, it was a strange day. And it only became stranger as they walked into Starbucks. Her gaze had taken in the short line and started to turn toward the menu board when she heard someone make a gagging noise at the table to her right. She turned just in time to see a paunchy businessman—his laptop open in front of him—make a pinched, disgusted face and spit a mouthful of coffee back into his cup.

"What the hell?" the man said, staring sourly at his drink.

Before Amber could comment to Ben, the man's behavior rippled through the place. Others made similar faces, some swallowing a gulp of something awful and some spitting it into their cups or into napkins.

One teenage girl, standing in front of the pickup counter, turned and spurted some kind of frozen coffee drink into the trash can.

"This is disgusting," the man next to Amber and Ben said, rising from his chair.

They stood back as the complaints began, people marching up to the counter to explain that the milk or cream in their drinks had gone sour. A man who had just received his coffee from the pickup counter called over the noise of grumbling customers to say that the cream in the dispenser there had become completely curdled.

"Looks like cottage cheese over here," he said.

The girl who'd been taking orders and was now taking the brunt of most of the complaints looked like a deer in the headlights. She was rescued by another barista, a huge bear of a man with his reddish hair tied back into a ponytail. He lifted his big hands in a calming gesture.

"All right, folks. Please settle down. We'll get fresh cream and milk out there in just a minute, and we'll be more than happy to set you all up with replacements for your drinks."

A beautiful girl with caramel skin came over with an open container of milk and whispered something in the burly man's ear. Amber knew from his expression that it wasn't good news.

"You're shitting me," he said, frowning as he took the milk container from the girl.

He took a whiff of the open container and made a face, holding it away from him. With all of the customers looking on, he turned and dumped the milk into the sink. It came out in sludgy chunks and he let the container fall into the sink.

"Change of plans," he said, looking back at his customers. "People who don't like black coffee may need to get refunds."

Amber turned to Ben and fixed him with a glare. "Are you still going to try to tell me this isn't a weird day?"

Before he could reply, a loud thump echoed through Starbucks, silencing the complaining masses. Something had hit the plate glass window at the front of the store. Everyone in the place seemed to be on pause, looking expectantly at that window, but there was no one outside and no indication of the source of the noise—just gray skies and a light sprinkle of rain. People started to turn away, but Amber took a step nearer the front door.

Something dark struck the plate glass and she jerked back, startled.

"Okay, this day is officially weird," Ben said.

"Ya think?" Amber snapped.

The window had a long crack in it now, and she worried that further impacts might shatter it. But curiosity drew her forward. She thought she knew what she had seen but wanted confirmation. Others followed her, moving toward the front of the store. Through the glass, she could see two dead birds on the sidewalk outside—one a crow, and one a fat seagull.

"Over there," Ben said, pointing to the left, up Eastwind Avenue. "There are more."

And there were. Amber counted at least a dozen dead birds on the sidewalks on either side of the street. An old Volkswagen Jetta parked right in front of Starbucks had a dead pigeon on its hood, nestled in a fresh dent.

A muffled thump reached them, and Amber glanced over at the façade of Holland's Flowers, watching a dead gull drop to the ground. The front window of the florist shop had a spiderweb of cracks in it. One more blow and it would shatter.

"What is this?" someone whispered behind her.

"The fucking End Times, or something," another voice muttered.

Amber ignored them. She leaned forward and craned her neck, looking up into the cloudy sky. The light drizzle continued to fall. Against the gray storm clouds, hundreds of dark, winged figures flew in circles. Then some of them started to dive.

"Back up," Ben said, pulling her a few feet away from the window. Stumbling, she almost shrugged him off before she realized he meant to protect her in case another bird hit the window and smashed it.

"Jesus, look at that!" said the businessman who'd been the first to complain about his coffee.

But they were already looking. Amber watched in silent amazement as birds began to rain down on Eastwind Avenue. Sparrows, crows, gulls, and pigeons dove from the sky, darting with unrelenting speed into the rain-slicked windows of the restaurants and shops all up and down the street. The front window of the Scarlet Letter Bookshop imploded with a crash they could hear half a block away at Starbucks, even with the door closed. Birds hit parked cars, cracking windshields. For thirty or forty seconds it went on and on, hundreds of birds flying straight into windows and walls and cars.

"They're aiming," Amber muttered to herself.

"What?" Ben asked, whispering so that only she could hear.

Wide-eyed, she looked at him. "None of them are hitting the street. Did you notice that? Yeah, they fall on the ground when they die, but it isn't just some fucked-up bird suicide. It's like they're pissed off and they're attacking."

"That's ridiculous," Ben said, shaking his head, ready to argue.

"Is it?" Amber asked.

Ben peered back out the window. Whatever he had been about to say, he swallowed the words, unsure.

The big redheaded barista stood in front of the doors to the store. He bent and looked up at the sky. "I think it's stopping."

Amber could have told him that. The avian assault slowed. A final gull swooped down, headed right for the front window of Starbucks, and then—even as they scrambled back to avoid shattering glass—it banked to the left, flapped its wings, and soared skyward once more, attack aborted.

The people inside Starbucks held their breath for ten or twelve long seconds before they began to wonder aloud if it was really over, and safe to go outside.

"Ben," Amber said, taking his hand to get his attention. "Please take me to my home."

"I thought you wanted to go back to campus and get your car."

"I'll get my dad to drive me later. Right now I just want to see my family."

She'd lost interest in coffee.

*

As Octavian drove along the rutted road that led past the sign for Summerfields Orchard, the willow trees overhead seemed to lean in toward his car, although whether they welcomed him or meant to keep him away, he did not know. It might have been entirely his imagination, but with a sprawling farm and orchard owned and staffed by earthwitches, it seemed entirely likely that the willows would respond to the witches' intentions, conscious or not. Cat Hein and her wife would not be happy to see him; that much he knew. They looked at him as a danger to Keomany, and Octavian could not deny it. Whenever he and Keomany were together, it seemed there were dark and perilous events afoot.

One of these days, he thought as he turned into the Summerfields parking lot, *I'm going to have to come here just to buy apples.*

He piloted the silver Lexus he'd rented in Montreal across the yellow grass and dried mud of the field Summerfields used for most of its parking. It was after six o'clock now, and he assumed that the handful of cars still in the lot must belong to employees. On the far side of the lot, he turned into the narrow path that led to the enormous farmhouse where Keomany lived with her employers. Dust rose behind the Lexus, turning into a swirling cloud in his rearview mirror.

As he pulled up in front of the farmhouse, the dust cloud billowing around the car once he came to a stop, the front door swung open and Keomany came out onto the front steps, a big black shoulder bag and a lavender backpack her only luggage for their trip. A beautiful woman, Keomany had a gorgeous smile, but she wasn't smiling today.

She didn't even give him a chance to get out of the car. Pulling open the back door, she tossed her bags in. The rich, earthen scents of the farm and the sweet, slightly decaying smell of the orchard blew in on the breeze that swirled into the car.

"Do you need to use the bathroom or anything?" she asked, before shutting the rear passenger door and then opening up the front.

"I'm fine," Octavian told her as she slid into the passenger seat and yanked the door closed.

"Good. Let's get going, then."

"Tori and Cat don't want to come out and say hello before we go?"

Keomany shot him an impatient glance. "Tori and Cat don't like you."

Octavian laughed and feigned offense as he put the car into gear. "You'd think saving a woman's life would earn you a little affection."

"Cat appreciates that you saved her life," Keomany said. "But that doesn't make her like you any better. Maybe she's just envious of how easily magic comes to you."

Octavian grinned again, but this time he did it to hide the anger that flickered through him in that moment. He had a command of magic that Cat Hein could barely conceive of, but he had paid for that knowledge with centuries of torment in Hell.

"So, do you have a better fix on our destination?" Octavian asked, bluntly changing the subject.

Keomany nodded, reaching back to grab her backpack. From a side pocket, she drew a map of New England, which she unfolded to reveal a spot that had been circled in purple marker.

"Hawthorne, Massachusetts," she said.

"And what's in Hawthorne, Massachusetts?" Octavian asked.

"I honestly don't know," Keomany replied, tucking her silken black hair behind her ears. Her soft, brown eyes were full of fear. "But it's something old and dangerous. The natural order of things is unraveling in Hawthorne, and whatever is causing the chaos is growing stronger."

Octavian pushed a little harder on the accelerator. Keomany turned on the car radio and starting punching buttons until she found something she liked—a tinny, edgy bit of rock that sounded like it would only be played on the local college radio station. Now that they were on their way, she seemed to lighten up a bit.

"It's good to see you, Peter," Keomany said.

"Always good to see you, Keomany."

"Nikki didn't want to come with you?"

Octavian smiled. "It's sad. She was so disappointed not to be able to join us. It's been months since something evil tried to eat her. She sends her best, though."

Keomany smiled archly. She traced her finger along the map, following the route they would take to Hawthorne, and then glanced out the window at the dimming sky.

"No sign of a storm," she said.

"Was there supposed to be?"

"No. But I have a feeling that will change as we get closer."

"So, Hawthorne?" Peter said. "You really have no idea what we're going to be driving into the middle of?"

"I told you. Chaos."

"You can't be more specific than that?"

Keomany rolled her eyes and started scanning radio stations again.

"That's why they call it chaos."

Norman Dunne groaned in his sleep, furrowed his brow, and reached out his right hand in search of his alarm clock. Half conscious, he tapped the nightstand and extended his probing fingers farther, bumping a plastic water glass, which tumbled off the table and spilled its contents onto the linoleum floor.

"Come on," he muttered, his voice a dry rasp.

The alarm emitted loud, rapid-fire beeps, irritating as hell, and after several more seconds of this, he opened his eyes into slits, glancing to his right in search of the offending clock.

Awareness flooded back into him. He felt the IV tube in his left arm tug as he shifted in bed, saw the chair against the wall and the tray table with its plastic bedpan and the white cable wrapped around the metal side rail of the bed—with which he could call the nurse—and he remembered it all. Out on the boat, fishing with Tommy, dragging up that old trunk in the net, opening it, and then the pain in his chest. A heart attack at his age!

"Shit," he whispered, sadness sweeping over him.

But that irritating alarm kept going, and as he came more fully awake, he realized that he could hear others echoing up and down the tiled hospital corridor. A sickly yellow light came from two units set into the ceiling of his room, but it took him a moment to understand that these were emergency lights. The alarm came from the machine that had been monitoring his vital signs earlier in the day. It was no longer attached to him now—the nurse had disconnected it when she had last checked on him—but it had yet to be removed from the room. Now the contraption beeped and flashed. He figured it had a battery backup, and that the lights in the ceiling meant there was a fail-safe system so that people on other machines—the kind that kept you breathing, or your heart beating—wouldn't die just because the wind had blown down a power line. In fact, any moment . . .

Even as the thought crossed his mind, the lights popped on, electricity in the hospital switching over to backup generators. He exhaled, relaxing the tension that had gripped him without his even being aware of it. The machine beside him was not keeping him alive, or even monitoring his vital signs anymore, but it had still unnerved him to think the hospital's systems might go down.

People rushed by in the corridor, no one even pausing long enough to poke their head in to see him. Not that Norm minded. After a day or two of observation, they would send him home with instructions about changing his diet and adding exercise to his life, not to mention prescription drugs to cut his cholesterol. His heart attack had knocked him on his ass, but the docs had told him already that it didn't seem to have done any significant damage. He needed rest and a new lifestyle, and there were lots of other people in the hospital whose condition required more attention. Norm didn't mind at all. He just wanted to go back to sleep.

First, though, he needed to take care of other needs.

Careful not to tangle up his IV tube, he climbed out of bed and shuffled to the bathroom, wheeling the stand that held the IV bag along beside him. When he hit the switch, the bathroom light flickered on, and he caught sight of himself in the mirror and shuddered. Damn, he looked like death warmed over.

"Hello, handsome," he sneered at himself. "Shit, you're an old man."

Still weak, but breathing without the same ache that had been in his chest earlier in the day, he shut the door and lifted the toilet seat. He sighed with pleasure as he let out a stream of urine, and shivered a bit as a chill went through him.

As he stepped out of the bathroom, hands still wet from washing, he went to click off the light and then changed his mind. He'd leave the bathroom light on to guide him if he should need to get up again, and shut off the other lights in the room instead. He wheeled the IV stand along with him as he closed the door, leaving it only slightly ajar, and then switched the lights off. Enough illumination leaked in from the corridor and from the half-open bathroom door to light his way back to bed.

Weak but content to be alive—feeling as though he had been given the gift of second chances—he made his way back toward the bed. The lights on the dormant monitor glowed steadily, and he wondered why no one had taken it away yet. He supposed they would remove it when they needed it for someone else.

As he reached the bed, he thought he saw movement out of the corner of his eye and turned toward the window. In the darkened room, his eyes had adjusted enough that he could see a figure silhouetted against the darkness, framed by the rain that pelted the glass. Something twitched, flicking side to side like an eel moving through water, but above it, set into an oil-black patch of nothing, a quartet of sickly golden eyes peered in at him.

"Jesus Christ," Norm whispered, staring.

The thing unfurled from the fourth-floor window like a flag and took the wind, vanishing with a flutter. Muttering under his breath, Norm hurried across the room. Part of him believed it must have been an owl—maybe two owls. Or bats. A voice at the back of his mind was already telling him to forget it, trying to persuade him that he had hallucinated, that there had been nothing there at all.

"What the hell was that?" he whispered. *And what if it bites your face off?*

The thought almost made him laugh. As he approached the window, he managed an uneasy chuckle. He should go back to bed, maybe call someone to have a look. But he had never been a coward, not even as a boy, and he wouldn't start being afraid of things outside his window in the dark now that he was a grown man. Mortality might have come knocking on his door today, but Norm Dunne wasn't going to let that turn him into some kind of pussy.

He pressed his forehead to the glass and looked out into the dark. He could see the edge of the parking lot off to the right, its lampposts partially dimmed by rain and a fog that had begun to rise. The rest of his view consisted of the rocky hill behind the hospital and the woods at the high edge of the property.

"You're off your nut," he muttered to himself.

Norm moved around, looking left and right, and then tilted his head to peer up at the stormy night sky.

Black figures darted back and forth in the churning clouds. They were hard to discern through the rain, but he counted at least four black silhouettes moving high up in the dark. They seemed to ride the wind, undulating as though draped in robes, circling like carrion birds in search of a feast.

Norm staggered away from the window. He wanted to fall back into bed and hide himself, but instead he wheeled his IV stand back across the room and snapped on the lights. His heart hammered in his chest, racing too fast, and a fresh ripple of fear went through him. He held a hand over the spot as he trudged back toward the bed and lay down.

His son, Tommy, had gone home for the night. The urge to call him and ask him to come back, to spend the night in the hospital room with his old man, was almost overwhelming. But Norm would not give in to that temptation. How could he admit to his boy that he was frightened— that something, maybe Death come calling, ready to collect him—had scared him so badly that he didn't want to be alone? He couldn't.

Just birds, he told himself. *Too big to be bats. They were crows, you stupid son of a bitch.*

Norman Dunne lay in bed and stared at the window, feeling smaller than he had in his whole adult life. *There's nothing in the dark that isn't there in the light,* his mother had always told him, back when he was a boy.

He wondered if she had lied.

5

Amber lay stretched out on the sofa in the TV room, cell phone clutched in her hand as if it were some talisman she thought would protect her from the storm. The floor lamp behind the sofa cast a wan golden light that did not do much to relieve the gloom that seemed to seep into the house from the stormy night outside. Her Gran lay asleep in her chair in the corner—which was where she could be found nearly all of the time that she wasn't in bed—and a tiny trickle of drool wetted the corner of the old woman's mouth. She might as well have been alone, and it wasn't a night for being on her own.

She could have gone into the basement and visited her father, who was trying to get some exercise on the treadmill down there, or into the kitchen, where her middle-school-teacher mom was correcting science tests, but laziness beat out loneliness tonight. She just wanted to stay there on the sofa, huddled away from the storm, trying not to think about the bizarre mass bird suicide from earlier in the day, or the vision she'd had during her seizure in Professor Varick's class. Besides, as long as she could text, she wouldn't be completely lonely.

The volume on the TV was turned up too high. Normally it would have bothered her, but tonight it canceled out some of the noise of the storm—the punishing rain that pounded on the roof and windows, and the occasional drumroll of thunder. But though she watched the tele-vision, she wasn't really paying attention. Her great-grandmother had a love of idiot comedy, everything from the Three Stooges to Will Ferrell and beyond, and could often be heard chuckling to herself as she watched them, even though Amber was sure she understood very little of the English-language dialogue. Tonight she had flipped channels until she'd found a moderately amusing and truly idiotic Jim Carrey movie from years ago, and then promptly fallen asleep.

What is the Jim Carrey movie where he has stupid hair? she texted to her best friend, Tami.

Her eyelids fluttered sleepily and the TV screen began to blur, but then her phone vibrated with the incoming text.

Isn't that all of them? Tami had replied.

Amber sent back a ☺ and a moment later, the phone vibrated again. The message was from Ben. *You seemed pretty shaken up earlier. You okay now?*

An image of Ben swam into her mind, the way he'd looked when she had first had her seizure that morning, and she felt the urge to kiss him. If he had been there beside her on the sofa, she would have done that and more. Her attraction to him seemed to come and go, but at the moment, it was very much present.

You're sweet, she texted. *I'm good. Bored, which must mean I'm okay.*

I have a cure for boredom, he wrote.

Scrabble? she asked.

Not the game I had in mind.

Amber hesitated before replying. How much did she want to encourage him? Knowing how fickle she was when it came to Ben, shouldn't she draw a line? Probably, she should.

She grinned as she typed. *Hmm. Something to ponder. Rain check for tonight, though. It's late and nasty out and I'm already under the covers.*

Cute. In your jammies?

Who said anything about jammies?

A long pause before the reply came. *Tease.*

Girls are evil. Didn't anyone ever tell you? Now she was grinning so broadly it hurt her face, and the flirtation had stirred something deep inside her. Maybe she wasn't just teasing Ben after all.

Some lessons I prefer to learn on my own, Ben replied.

Maybe I'll let you buy me coffee tomorrow. ☺

Great. Let's just pray for no kamikaze crows.

Amber shuddered, a ripple of unease passing through her. Her smile faded. Flirting had ceased to be fun.

Talk to you in the a.m., she texted.

OK. Night.

With her Gran snoring softly in her chair, Amber settled deeper into the sofa and let her brain drift into autopilot as she watched television. God, what a stupid movie. She clutched her cell phone to her chest the way she had seen some old ladies hold their rosary beads and let her mind empty of all of the tension of the day. But it didn't stay empty for long. Memories and images kept slipping back in, and her brow furrowed with thoughts of her collapse in Professor Varick's classroom, and then the creepy insanity at Starbucks, what Ben called the "kamikaze crows," though it had been more than just crows.

She had a flash of memory from the hospital—she hated lying on those gurney beds; they were so damned uncomfortable—and then an image of Tommy Dunne rose in her mind. *Poor guy,* she thought. They weren't exactly close, not these days, but she had always been fond of Tommy, and she felt badly that she hadn't spared him another thought after she had run into him earlier and learned that his father had had a heart attack. Norm Dunne usually looked in need of sleep or a drink or both, but he had also had a pleasant wave and a smile for Amber, and not in a creepy, ogling way.

Scanning through her cell phone contacts list, she found that she didn't have Tommy's number. That didn't surprise her, considering how long it had been since they'd talked. But then she remembered they were friends on Facebook and quickly used her phone to get online and access his page, where she found the number easily, and sent him a text.

Hey. I hope your dad's doing better. Let me know if you need any-thing.

Jim Carrey's antics unraveled on screen as she waited for a reply, but she received none. Soon her eyelids began to droop again, the yearning for sleep making her thoughts muzzy and slow, and she felt her head begin to fall forward. She bobbed several times, her breathing matching the cadence of her great-grandmother's snores, and then she closed her eyes, phone still held tightly to her chest.

. . . and she is standing in the hot rain again, Hawthorne burning with green fire all around her. The flames do not char. Instead the glass in the windows melts and runs and the brick crumbles and the wood warps and begins to grow sprigs and then branches, roots pushing down into the ground. Thorns appear. From inside those now windowless, malleable structures, people scream in the voices of birds. She sees a middle-aged couple and their young daughter through a second-story window, their mouths open, emitting the shrieks of murdered gulls.

The hot rain sears her flesh, but she does not try to find a place to hide. Her skin blisters and peels and the fat underneath runs like candle wax, but she is moving, searching. Running. Around a corner she staggers to a halt. Hundreds of people are in Melville Park, up to their waists in the floodwaters, in hot rain. Chaos has erupted. They are drowning one another. They are murdering one another. They are fucking one another. Some are trying to drown themselves, even as others look toward the bell tower of the abandoned Methodist church, reaching into the sky as though a lifeline will be thrown that will hoist them out of the anarchy, out of the blood and death and bestial rutting.

Amber walks among them like a ghost, untouched in the flesh but wounded in the heart. She looks up to see what has caused them to reach toward the sky with such hope, such elation, and a wave of sickness passes through her. She retches and falls to her knees, the floodwaters sucking at her. The water up to her shoulders, scouring her naked flesh until it is raw and pitted and bone has begun to show through, she stares at the clock tower.

The goddess clings to the face of the clock, insectlike. Her three pairs of breasts dangle, full of poison milk that trickles out and mixes with the rain. The indigo flames of her hair whip around her face in the storm. Her black lips peel back from her rows of jagged teeth in a lascivious grin. She is terrible and beautiful and repulsive all at once, and when she begins to chant, it is the sound of drums beaten in prayer and in bloody, barbaric victory. An ancient sound.

The goddess points a gore-encrusted talon into the crowd, and the darkness of the bell tower unfurls, shadows taking shape. The Reapers spring from their perches even as others fly down out of the storm, and she cannot decide if what flutters around them is fabric or skin, black ribbons of nothing that move of their own accord. Their limbs are sticks, bone piping. They are scarecrow things, clutching the curved blades with which they do the bidding of their goddess.

The Reapers sweep down into the crowd and begin their harvest, slashing and tearing, cutting the worshippers open to reveal a golden light within. The light streams into the Reapers and they consume it greedily, then jet back toward the clock tower to feed the goddess. She opens her thighs and her mouth and the Reapers pour the stolen light into her.

A man rises from the waters, somehow above the crowd. He stands atop the flood, a scroll open in his hands, and he begins to read. The goddess and her servants and her worshippers all fall silent, as though chaos itself is taking a breath, and then the goddess screams and leaps from the church, falling toward the man with the scroll, trailing poisonous mother's milk and indigo fire in her wake.

Amber feels the water rising. She weeps and cries out. Something moves under the water, touching her, and she hears it whisper in her ear.

Navalica, *it whispers.*

And she turns to find the Reapers all around her, eyes lit with ghostly blue, carapace faces brittle and blank, sharp proboscises probing the air, all pointing toward their goddess, their anticipation palpable. They gaze at their goddess, stroking the small scythes in their hands.

One of them caresses her beneath the water, its probing touch cold as ice. But then her skin feels brittle and stiff and she glances down. It's difficult to see through the dark water and so she raises her hand, lifts it to her face, and instead sees the black, bony claws of a Reaper.

Amber shakes her head, backing away from the killers, the Harvesters, who have now all begun to whisper the same thing.

Navalica.

Amber finds she cannot breathe. But it is not the water suffocating her. Shaking, she reaches brittle shell fingers up to touch her face and finds a carapace there, a stingerlike proboscis, the face of a Reaper.

She screams, and her voice is a shriek. Another dying gull.

Navalica.

Amber jerked awake, heart pounding in her chest. Her cell phone flew from her hands and landed on the floor as she held her hands in front of her eyes. In the light from the television, she saw that they were ordinary hands. Woman hands. *Her* hands. Foolish as she knew it was, she touched her face, felt the familiar contours there, and wanted to weep with relief.

"What the hell?" she whispered, sitting up quickly, afraid of what she would see inside her mind if she fell back to sleep.

She sat on the edge of the sofa and tried to sort out what she'd seen in her dream, knowing it hadn't really been a dream. There were too many elements that she had also seen in her vision, which came back to her now much more clearly than it had earlier in the day. Falling asleep had triggered something in her mind. Even as she considered this, the memory of this new dream vision began to blur.

"Jesus," she whispered.

Her Gran snored loudly just then and Amber flinched, startled. Then she laughed softly, amused by her own skittishness. Gran continued snoring, but more softly. The rain pounded the roof and the wind made the house creak. For a moment, Amber wondered why her parents hadn't woken her and Gran and ushered them both off to bed, and then she looked at the television and saw that the same stupid movie was on. She felt like she'd been asleep for hours, but it had been only minutes. A quick look at her phone and she discovered the time. 10:27 p.m.

Navalica, she thought.

Then she remembered the man in her vision. The one reading the scroll.

She knew him.

Professor Miles Varick.

Amber held her cell phone in her hand, stroking the screen with her thumb, worried about the lateness of the hour but far more worried about her own sanity. She glanced at Gran, at the peace on the old woman's face, and envied her.

A scratch on the window behind the TV made her jump. Her heart raced again, though she knew it had to be the ash tree out there, branches swaying in the wind. It had to be, because bone-thin Reapers with scythes would have just crashed through the glass and torn her apart.

Funny, she chided herself. But even though she thought her fears were absurd, she didn't go any nearer to that window.

Instead, she found Professor Varick's number in her contacts list and hit the *send* button. The rain drummed on the roof as she listened to the ringing on the other end of the line. Though Gran was in the room with her, and her parents were both presumably still awake elsewhere in the house, Amber felt more alone than ever.

Miles Varick stood in his mother's kitchen, rinsing out coffee cups and wiping crumbs off the table. He washed the cups—and the small plates they had used to share the cappuccino cheesecake he had brought her—and put them away. Over the past few years, Toni Varick's vision had been deteriorating rapidly. She could still see the shapes of things, but her vision was blurry and indistinct on the best days. At seventy-one, she knew a number of people who had begun to lose their sight or had had surgery to correct problems with their vision. But she refused to talk about blindness, or to accept that there would come a time in the not-so-distant future when even blurry and indistinct would seem like a fond memory, bad eyesight a luxury.

Though she was stubborn, Miles had been starting to edge his mother slowly into a mental place where she would be willing to accept help. Every Wednesday night, and on the occasional Sunday, he would visit and read to her. Toni loved books, but even the large print gave her trouble now. She resorted to audiobooks most of the time, but often enough there were things she wanted to read that weren't available in that format. Given her insistence on doing things for herself, it said a great deal about her love of reading that she would never fight him over these times, pretending that they were just mother-son bonding opportunities, and that she could have read for herself if she wanted to do so. Miles let her go on pretending.

She drew the line at Scrabble, though. For as long as he could remember, it had been her favorite board game, but in order to play she would have to rely on him to read the spaces on the board that indicated multiple letter or word scores, and sometimes she had difficulty making out the letters on the tiles. He had bought a Braille Scrabble game, and his mother had sniffed at it like a child at strange vegetables.

"I'll let you know when I need the blind people version, Miles," she had said.

But he doubted she ever would.

So he read to her—right now they were halfway through a Clive Cussler adventure—and they played chess. Toni could feel the pieces to make sure she knew which one she was moving, but she had to bend down and stare at the board as if concentrating very hard to have any idea where the other pieces were. Miles didn't let her win as often as he could have, but he played poorly on purpose. His mother had raised him on her own from the time he was four years old, making a living as a high school teacher in Hawthorne. Those years had made her tough and proud, and he never wanted to take those things away from her.

He dried the last of the cups and put it into the cabinet in the corner. He had to be careful to put everything away precisely where it belonged so that his mother could find it when she needed it. At some point, she was going to need more help than having her son over to read to her once or twice a week. Fortunately, she'd at least had the good sense to give up her driver's license. She had friends who would take her on any errands she needed to do, and Miles helped out when he could. Her life would have been much simpler if she would agree to sell her house and move in with him, but she wouldn't hear of it. Miles would leave it alone for now, but not for long.

He stepped back, took another look around the kitchen, and pronounced it clean. Sliding the chairs up to the table, he picked up the chess set and carried it into the living room, returning it to its usual place on an end table to await their next game. From somewhere in the house he heard water running and knew that his mother was getting cleaned up for bed. He had sent her off, insisting that he would clean up for her. She had agreed reluctantly, claiming that she allowed it only because she was so tired. Miles didn't challenge her. Toni could hold on to the strength she had for a little longer.

Patting his pockets to make sure he had his keys, he grabbed his light brown canvas jacket from the back of a chair and slid it on. He just needed to say good night and let his mother know he was leaving, and then he could head home. His first class in the morning wasn't until half past nine, but he wanted to relax a bit before bed, and he knew his mother needed her rest.

"Mom?" he began, not sure if she could hear him over the running water. She must have been brushing her teeth or maybe washing her face.

He was about to call for her again when a strange sound disturbed him. The rain had been a constant hard patter on the windows and the roof, but this was different, almost like something being dragged across the shingle siding outside the house. Miles frowned and started toward the window. He peered out, forehead pressed against the glass, but couldn't see anything but darkness and rain and the glow of a streetlight.

His cell phone buzzed, making him jump.

"Dumbass," he muttered, pulling out the phone and looking at it. The number wasn't one he recognized, but at 10:30 on a weeknight, he figured it must be important, so he answered. "Hello?"

"Professor Varick?"

"Yes?"

"It's... I'm sorry for calling so late, Professor. It's Amber Morrissey."

Miles glanced out the window again, but the sound had not returned. "Amber? Are you all right?"

The girl had had a seizure in his classroom that morning, and now she was calling him after hours. His thoughts raced with a hundred variations on the terrible news he was sure she must be about to deliver. He had been getting sleepy, but now he felt fully awake.

"I'm not sure, honestly," Amber replied.

Miles sat down, rubbing one hand on the leg of his jeans, barely aware of how often he needed that friction to soothe his nerves. Hints of his childhood OCD slipping through.

"What did the doctors say today?"

"It's not that," Amber said. "It's just . . . Well, it's been a wicked strange day, Professor."

Not that? Miles thought. *Then why are you calling me, Amber?* He hoped it wasn't some kind of teacher crush. A situation had developed several years previously with a lovestruck, delusional student, and he didn't want to deal with that kind of stress again.

"Maybe you should elaborate on that, Amber. Are you talking about the stuff I saw on the news? The traffic lights and the animals going crazy?"

"The birds, you mean?"

"Not just birds. Dogs and cats, too, according to Ed Harding on Channel Five. Probably other animals, as well, but we only see the domestic ones, and the birds, of course."

"I didn't know that," Amber said, thoughtful.

"I suspect there's some kind of atmospheric disturbance. The animals could be reacting to the storm. There are all kinds of stories about that kind of thing. But that wasn't what you were calling about."

"No."

"So what do you mean, 'wicked strange'?" Miles asked.

"Okay, this morning? When I had that seizure?" she said, as if he might have forgotten the sight of a beautiful girl spasming on the classroom floor.

"Yes?"

"I had what I guess you'd call a vision," she said, and in her tone he could tell that she had begun to wish she had never called. "It was awful. Like a nightmare, but not. I forgot a lot of it. It was kind of vague in my head, maybe because I was just focused on the seizure and the hospital, y'know?"

"Okay," Miles said, encouraging without interrupting.

"Well, I just had another one."

"Another seizure?"

"A vision," she said. "Shit, this is all coming out wrong. I sound crazy. But screw it, there's no real way to tell you any of this without sounding crazy. I just thought . . . you know history and mythology and all of that, and you were in the . . ."

Miles sat down on his mother's coffee table. The sound of water running had ceased and he figured she had already gotten into bed and turned on the news.

"Amber? What was I in?"

"Never mind. The point is, you were the first person who came to mind. Maybe I'm going a little crazy, but it doesn't feel like that. It feels like I'm really seeing something, like I'm tapped into a signal that's broadcasting from somewhere, weird as that is."

Miles rubbed at his eyes. "Look, Amber, can we talk about this tomorrow?"

"Please, Professor. I've got to get this stuff out of my head. It's awful. I'm hoping you can tell me if you've ever heard of anything like what I've seen."

He sighed. "Okay. Shoot."

So Miles listened while Amber told him about chaos and suffering in Hawthorne, about things she called Reapers who ripped the life out of people, and about a goddess with blue skin, razors for fingers, blue-black fire for hair, six breasts, and a face that shifted from beautiful to monstrous with every blink of the eye.

"They kept saying this word. *Navalica.* I think it might be her name."

Something creaked upstairs. He barely noticed, enrapt by Amber's visions. If they were invented, that would be interesting in its own right, but if she had really experienced these scenes as true visions—or even as dreams—they were fascinating.

"And you're sure you've never seen a picture of this 'goddess' before?" he asked.

"Positive. She reminds me of something out of Hindu mythology, but it's not that. She's not anything I've seen before, and the things that are her servants, or whatever . . . I don't know what that is about. I just . . ."

Her voice got very small.

"I'm afraid to close my eyes, Professor. Afraid to go to sleep."

Miles took a deep breath and let it out, thinking. As he did, he heard that scrape against the side of the house again, but this time from higher up on the shingles outside. He stood up and went to the window, looking out as he spoke.

"I wish I could help you with the sleep thing, Amber, but I don't know what to do about that. I guess a doctor or a therapist could prescribe something to help you sleep, but you don't even know if you'll have another of these things."

"I know," she said. "It's gonna be a long night, but I'll feel better in the morning. Stupid, but in the daylight, I won't be so freaked out."

The wind gusted, rattling the windows, and he heard a sound from the roof. Cursing silently, he wondered if the storm had started pulling off roof shingles or siding. Maybe that was what he'd been hearing.

"Listen, Amber, I'm sorry but I need to go," he said. "But I'll tell you what. Tomorrow morning, I'll do some research into your goddess. Maybe I can dig something up."

"That would be amazing," Amber replied, her relief carrying through the phone signal. "I don't want to be channeling some ancestral memory, or something totally bizarre like that, but it'd be better than the whole thing being a hallucination."

"You never know," Miles told her. "With the things we've learned in the past decade or so . . . nothing would surprise me now. It's a weird world."

"You can say that again."

They said their goodbyes and hung up. Miles slipped his cell phone into his pocket, thinking about Amber Morrissey's seizure and her visions. The occult had always been a particular obsession with him. Most historians tended to look down their noses at his enthusiasm for the study of such esoterica, preferring more generalized research into ancient theology, but Miles had always found it fascinating. In the modern world as redefined by the existence of vampires and magic, his store of knowledge had become decidedly more valuable.

In centuries past, Amber would have been accused of witchcraft and burned at the stake. Ages earlier than that, she might have been called a saint. But these were different times and the world had its eyes wide open. There were things in the shadows; humanity knew that for a fact. But the line between saints and shadows was badly blurred.

Miles went to the stairs, ascending quietly in case his mother had already fallen asleep. He wanted to say good night, but he didn't want to wake her. As he approached her room, he heard the creak of old bedsprings and frowned, wondering what she might be up to. At least she was still awake, and he could talk to her before he left.

"I've got to get going—" he began, as he turned into her room.

The scene unfolding upon his mother's bed staggered him, knocking him back so hard that he had to grab the door frame to steady himself. Miles shook his head, his body beginning to shake, exhaling nonsense words, trying to deny what he saw.

A nightmare.

A man—*not a man, a creature, a thing*—crouched over his mother atop her bed. Coal black and skeletal, its face a dully gleaming helmet, a horseshoe crab with its tail darting out as if it were the creature's tongue, the thing held his mother up and jerked her around like a marionette.

The bed creaked under her shifting weight, but the thing had no solidity, did not even make an impression in the bedspread as it tore at her. Miles opened his mouth and screamed for his mother. As the thing twisted to look at him, eyes like seeping blue mist, he realized that it was not holding his mother up with its hands. It wielded twin blades, curved like scythes—

Dear God, just like Amber said.

—and the thing had one of those blades thrust through his mother's sternum, hoisted up like a fresh kill at the slaughterhouse. The other scythe slashed and dug into her abdomen, impossibly deep, so deep that it should have punched right through her back but did not.

No blood. How can there be no blood?

He blinked, breaking through his shock. The thing—Amber called them Reapers—ripped something out of his mother, then, a squirming thing of shifting color, like liquid light.

"Get off her," Miles growled, shaking off the momentary paralysis of shock and fear. "Get the fuck off her!"

Sickened, mad with anguish, he charged at the thing and threw himself across the bed. It darted away, light as air, flying for the wall. He scrambled over his mother's prone form—*dead, she's dead!*—and lunged for it, but his fingers caught nothing. He crashed into the wall and fell to the ground. A painting of Victorian ladies fell off the wall, and the glass in the frame shattered.

"No," Miles whispered. "No, no."

He stood up, head ringing from smashing it against the wall. One of his fingers had jammed and might be broken, but he was only dimly aware of the pain. He glanced around the room, thinking it might still be there, but the wraith had gone. On the wall where it had passed through was a dusting of black. He ran his finger over it, and it stained his skin. Rubbing it between thumb and forefinger, he found it reminded him of soot.

Shaking, he squeezed his eyes closed, turned toward his mother's bed, and opened them. A sigh of grief escaped his lips, and he staggered toward her and fell to his knees beside the bed.

"Mom?" he ventured.

No blood, he thought again. The sheets were not splashed with crimson. Hope insinuated itself into his heart, a false friend. For when he looked at her more closely, he knew that though he saw no blood, nor even any wounds—somehow the scythes had passed through her without cutting muscles or flesh—his mother was dead. Her body remained still, no sign of a breath. Her eyes were closed but they did not move beneath the lids. In life, she had sometimes been stern or frustrated, but more often had worn a smile. In death, she wore a mask of utter sadness that broke his heart.

Miles held her hand, felt for a pulse, and found what he expected—nothing. He slid to the floor, holding on to her, and the tears began.

"What was it, Mom?" he whispered, leaning his face against the hanging bedspread. He pushed up closer to the bed, staring at the sooty smudge on the wall, fearful it might return.

"What the hell was that thing?"

Amber. Somehow, she had known the creature existed. She'd had a vision.

Miles stood. He placed his mother's arms gently across her chest and then sat beside her, reaching for the phone on the bedside table. He would need to speak with Amber about her visions—warnings, really; they must be—but right now, he had to call for help. The police. They would bring the coroner. Someone had to take care of his mother.

His mother.

He shuddered, wiping at his tears as he mumbled something to the 911 operator. After he hung up the phone, he lay down beside her to wait, and he wondered about the diaphanous butterfly of softly colored light that the thing had torn out of her, like a baby from her womb. Miles didn't want to think about that thing, what it might have been, and where the creature had taken it, because if he let himself contemplate that, he feared he would go mad with anguish.

He didn't want to think about her soul.

6

Octavian could feel the air pressure change as he drove through Salem. The meteorologist on the radio talked excitedly about the rapid and unexpected change in the local weather, explaining it away with the classic pass-the-buck of generations of New England forecasters: "If you don't like the weather in New England, just wait a minute." But Octavian could hear the confused edge in the woman's voice; she had no idea where the storm had come from and didn't like that at all. Maybe she felt incompetent, or maybe she was just afraid that global climate change had finally made her occupation obsolete.

"Everything is so unsettled," Keomany said, bending to look out her rain-slicked window. "And I can feel it spreading. It's still mostly in Hawthorne. The town is filling up with chaos like it's a bowl, but the storm is only the start. Eventually, the bowl's going to overflow and the chaos is going to spill out like a dam bursting."

Octavian held the steering wheel with both hands. The wipers were at full speed, and still it was difficult to see through the rain.

"How long?" he asked.

Keomany didn't reply at first. He glanced over and saw that she had her eyes closed, trying to get a sense of how badly the natural elements had been disrupted, or perhaps communing with Gaea herself. In the golden glow of the dashboard lights, with her almost regal Asian features, she had the air of a goddess herself. Octavian had always known she was attractive—anyone with eyes could see it—but he felt a new, keener awareness of her now. She really was lovely. But they were friends, nothing more, and he loved Nikki, so he forced himself to focus.

"Kem?" Octavian prodded. "How long before it overflows?"

She opened her eyes, frowning with uncertainty. "Two or three days, I think. Not much more." She looked at him. "And maybe less."

Octavian turned off the radio. There was nothing the meteorologist could tell them. They were in the thick of the storm now. The rain had started as a light drizzle while they were driving south on Interstate 95, and hadn't been much worse than that when they had turned north at the junction with 128. But while they were threading their way east toward the coast and into Salem, it had begun to rain in earnest, and now that they were working their way up toward Hawthorne, it beat down on the car as though a new deluge might be underway.

The GPS on the dashboard instructed him to turn right in two hundred feet. Octavian complied, and soon they were wending their way along Route 116, which would turn into Hester Street when they crossed the town line into Hawthorne.

The wind gusted hard enough to sway the car, and Octavian tightened his grip on the wheel. Strangely enough, the rain diminished slightly, enough so that he could click the wipers down to their ordinary speed, and they shushed the rain off the windshield so that when they approached the *ENTERING HAWTHORNE* sign, he could see it clearly.

"Turn left in one hundred feet," the GPS instructed. "Reverse direction."

Octavian frowned and glanced at the gadget. The screen showed white and green and red threads to illustrate the street plan of Hawthorne. The red arrow noted their current position as well as the course the GPS wanted them to take. A left. Another left. Essentially a U-turn.

"Why is it—" Keomany asked.

"Turn left now, Yancey Road. Reverse direction," the GPS demanded, its electronic voice somehow more brittle.

The Hawthorne sign lay ahead. Octavian slowed a bit as they approached it. The headlights picked out glossy black spray paint on the sign. Beneath *ENTERING HAWTHORNE* someone had written, *NOW GO AWAY*. The GPS seemed to agree.

"Reverse direction," it insisted.

They rolled across the town line, and the GPS screen blinked off. Octavian glanced at it, then at Keomany, but neither of them spoke. They didn't need directions anymore. They were driving right into the heart of chaos.

As an experiment, he pulled out his cell phone. It hadn't turned itself off and the window showed two bars for a signal. He had spoken to Nikki only an hour before, but he tried dialing her again. At first it seemed the call would go through, but then the screen blinked, two words popping up. *CALL FAILED*.

He glanced at Keomany. "Try yours."

She did, with the same result. "Too much interference."

Octavian popped the GPS off the dash and tossed it into the backseat. They would have to find their own way from this point on.

Hester Street banked eastward, where it merged with Shore Road, the picturesque stretch of two-lane that ran between deep woods on one side and rocky coastline on the other. Octavian had once been to Plum Island, which was several towns to the north, and been surprised at the expanses of marsh and the cottages and shacks that separated the stilted vacation homes out toward the beach. Hawthorne had none of that. There were huge, modern homes tucked away in the woods on the left and the occasional smaller home—probably 1950s in origin— on the right, high enough above the usual water line that no one had ever thought to put them on stilts.

Hands steady on the wheel, Octavian bent to get a better look out the windshield, then to glance past Keomany, out her window. In the rain it was hard to tell, but the tide seemed to be out quite a ways. Keomany kept silent, watching the darkened homes as they passed, but peering even more closely at those with lights burning inside, looking for signs of the chaos that she had felt from so far away.

The woods on the left were flanked by sidewalk now and broken by streets named after presidents and types of trees. They were broad avenues, lined with Federal Colonials and Victorians that had originally been inhabited by ship's captains and well-to-do merchants more than a century before. Octavian thought they must be nearing the center of town.

Another quarter mile or so, and Shore Road dipped down, the rocky coast giving way to actual beach. There were shops and restaurants on the left and a boardwalk on the right, just along the water, illuminated by streetlights fashioned to look like Victorian gas lamps.

"Pull over," Keomany said, her voice a hushed rasp.

"What is it?" Octavian asked, hitting the brake and gliding the car up to the curb.

Keomany got out and slammed the door. Octavian killed the engine and followed, pocketing the keys as he hurried around the front of the car, buffeted by wind and rain. She was already onto the boardwalk, and he quickened his pace so that when she started down a concrete ramp toward the sand, they were side by side.

"Listen," she said, wiping rain from her face.

He did. At first, all he heard was the howling of the wind and the patter of rain on top of the metal roof of the sun shelter they'd just left behind on the boardwalk. Then he realized that he wasn't listening for a sound, but the absence of one.

As they stepped onto the sand and walked out onto the beach, Octavian focused. Straining, he could just hear the sound of distant surf. The tide was out, as he had already suspected. But as they kept walking on the soft, damp sand, leaving the illumination cast by the gas lamps behind, he peered into the night and the storm and realized that he could not see the ocean. His shoe splashed in a puddle made by the rain—or maybe left behind by the receding water—but they kept walking, and kept walking.

"There," Keomany said, squinting against the rain.

Her black hair was plastered to her now, and Octavian felt the dampness soaking through his clothes. But he ignored the rain, picking up the pace. Keomany hurried to keep up with him. The sound of the surf grew louder, and at last they could see the white foam rippling on the sand ahead, hundreds of yards from the shore.

Octavian stopped and looked back. He could see more of the town from here, the docks that had once been for fishermen but had been turned into a small warren of boutiques and cafés for the tourists who visited Hawthorne three seasons of the year. Farther inland, the land rose a bit, and he could see the buildings that composed Hawthorne's original downtown, including a church with a white steeple bell tower and what he presumed was the city hall, with its clock tower the dark twin of the church.

He turned back toward the water. Keomany stood beside him, staring, shaking her head.

"How does this happen?" Octavian asked. "It's like before a tsunami, the tide pulling out before the . . ."

He trailed off, turning to stare at Keomany.

"It's not that," she said. "I don't think there's a wave coming. I would feel that. It's as if the ocean has withdrawn, like it's holding its breath."

Octavian allowed himself another moment to stare at the surf, and then he turned back toward the boardwalk and the car. Maybe no tsunami was imminent, but the people of Hawthorne were in grave danger, nevertheless.

"There's something here," Keomany said.

Octavian glanced around, hands coming up, magical static crackling quietly at his fingertips. "An enemy something?"

"Yes and no," she replied. She had her eyes closed and her head tilted back like a dog scenting the wind. The rain pelted her face, dripping from her chin and nose and pooling in her eyes. "The chaos . . . I think it started here. Like a bomb going off, somehow, and what we're seeing is the fallout from that. It's an ancient thing, so old it doesn't have any place in the world anymore—"

"Something else that's found its way back in because the church's wards are breaking down," Octavian said.

"Most likely," Keomany agreed. "But it's strange. It's as though what I'm feeling is the echo of a burst of chaos magic, not the source of the magic."

"Can you track it to the source?"

Keomany cocked her head. "Did you miss the part where it's *chaos* magic?"

"Worth a shot," Octavian said. "Let's get out of the rain."

"Please, let's," Keomany replied.

They started back up the sand toward the boardwalk. Octavian looked around warily. Nothing could be trusted now, not in the middle of a chaos storm. He glanced left and right and then left again, and then he narrowed his gaze.

"Now what?" Keomany asked.

"Something's moving over there."

They headed toward the movement, a dark slithering along the sand. Once again Octavian lifted his hands and woke the magic inside him. He could feel it surging through him like an electrical charge, and his fingers and palms prickled with the magic as though they ached to unleash it.

"Are they crabs?" Keomany asked as they moved closer to the parade of creatures sliding along the sand.

A few more steps and she could have answered her own question. They were indeed crabs, but not the sort likely to end up on a dinner plate. A line of horseshoe crabs extended from the distant, receded surf all the way up to the rocky seawall below the boardwalk. In the dark and the rain, their strange shells made them look like moving rocks, their tails leaving narrow trails in the sand behind them.

"All right," Keomany said. "Now this is just getting fucking weird."

Octavian laughed and pushed his hands through his hair, shedding rainwater.

"*Now* it's getting weird?"

"You know what I mean," she said, as they walked back to the ramp and started up to the boardwalk.

"Considering the circumstances under which we met, I'd have thought your definition of *weird* would be a little more discriminating," Octavian said, thinking back on the bizarre events that had first brought them into contact with one another, when a demon from a parallel world had begun stealing towns and cities from this one, shifting them from one reality to the next.

"Point taken," Keomany replied. "But you know how this sort of thing works. If we don't get this thing squared away quickly, the crap with the Tatterdemalion could end up looking like a minor tremor of weirdness in comparison."

Octavian frowned, tugging his keys out of his pocket. He hoped Keomany was wrong. They'd had a lot more help against the Tatterdemalion. Now it was just the two of them. They had to get to the bottom of this quickly and restore order. If chaos erupted completely and started spilling outward, the effects would only snowball, picking up speed and strength. Octavian might be the most powerful mortal sorcerer in the world, but he was still only one man.

Two days, more or less, Keomany had said. Two days of chaos.

Keomany sat in the passenger seat, listening to the rain and feeling the rumble of the engine and the road beneath the tires. She looked through the rain-slicked windshield at the main area of the town ahead, the church steeple and the clock tower facing each other over the tops of the other buildings. She closed her eyes, tuning it all out, sifting through the things she could feel, what she could sense of Hawthorne. It had occurred to her that she should tell Octavian that she could no longer feel the presence of Gaea here, that in the rain and the air and the ground beneath them, she felt only the unnatural. She would tell him, of course. But first she wanted to try to break through whatever had tainted Hawthorne, to reach beyond that unnatural poisoning of the town. Gaea was there. She had to be. Go deep enough into the earth or far enough into the sky or out to sea, and Keomany would be able to touch her again.

Closing her eyes, she let the earth magic inside her reach out and touch the ground beneath them. Under the paved road she found a sewer and in the sewer, weeds that grew through cracks in stone and concrete. With a gentle pressure from her mind, she reached out to those weeds and gave them the smallest encouragement, just to see if she could touch the elements without Gaea's influence. The weeds grew larger, proliferating violently, shooting cracks through the walls and making chunks of concrete cave into the sewage.

Keomany exhaled. The car rolled on, leaving the underground damage behind. Eyes still closed, she reached out and touched the rain, drew sigils on the leather seat with her right hand and soundlessly moved her lips, feeling the magic course through her, connecting her to the sky.

Even before she opened her eyes, she knew the storm had lessened. Her earthcraft was unpredictable here, the tether between herself and Gaea corrupted, but she still had magic. The elements would still respond to her, and that was good. Without that power, Octavian would feel the need to protect her. She would be a liability.

He clicked the windshield wipers down to intermittent and glanced over at her.

"Did you do that?" he asked.

Keomany glanced at him. "Yes."

"But you can't stop the storm completely?"

Even as he asked, the rain picked up again and wind buffeted the car hard enough that he had to grip the wheel tighter, as if the storm were angry at her for tampering with it.

"Not even for long, apparently," Keomany said.

Octavian took that in, nodded gravely, and kept driving. Keomany wished she had his confidence. She had endured horrifying things, encountered demons and vampires and had her hometown destroyed, most of the people she had known her entire life murdered. The darkest time of her life, and yet it had also given her the greatest gift she had ever received—a full understanding of her capacity as an earthwitch. Somehow she had found a courage within herself during that time that had endured, but that did not mean she was not afraid now.

The chaos swirling through Hawthorne made her so uneasy that she felt ill. The thought of it springing from some enemy, some ancient evil driven from the world centuries ago but now returned, terrified her. Yet Gaea had faith in her, and so did Octavian. He had lived so much longer than she had, so many lifetimes, in so many guises, and faced so many horrors, that he marched in without fear. He had been to Hell and back, literally. Someone had to step in and do something about order unraveling in Hawthorne, and if it was just the two of them, Octavian did not mind. A part of him must be afraid—only a fool would not have been—but he refused to be hindered by it.

Keomany took inspiration from that, and from Gaea. This town had become a wound in the heart of the world, and she had to help heal it.

As Octavian turned up the street that went through the center of town, Keomany surveyed the façades of stores and inns and bars. They passed a lawyer's office and a proud old stone bank building and the office of the *Hawthorne Letter*, which she assumed was the local newspaper. An empty storefront had once been a video store, a relic of the past. Another had been converted into a campaign office for someone named Castiglione, who was running for mayor. She had seen a smattering of political signs as they drove in.

The dashboard clock read 11:39 p.m. Thanks to the storm and the lateness of the hour the street was largely deserted, save for people exiting bars and hurrying for their cars. They drove by a two-story post office building and something caught her eye, movement on the roof. Keomany turned to look over her shoulder just in time to see a dark figure dart out of sight. She craned her neck, looking up at the roofs of the other buildings they passed.

"What are you looking for?" Octavian asked.

"Not sure."

But she kept scanning. Movement overhead made her crane farther and she saw something diving through the clouds above, emerging long enough to be momentarily silhouetted against the storm by the lights of Hawthorne and then lost in the morass again.

"There's something up there," she said.

Octavian bent over the steering wheel, trying to peer up into the clouds.

"I don't see anything," he said after a moment, his eyes gleaming in the glow of the dash.

"You're driving. Trust me," she said.

"I do. Want me to pull over?"

Keomany considered it, but they were both soaked to the skin from standing out on the beach in the rain.

"Let's keep driving. Go slowly. Maybe we can follow one of them. We need to figure out what they are, and that's more your area than it is mine. I know elemental magic. You're more intimate with demons."

Octavian hesitated a second, bending over the steering wheel to look up at the sky again. "I don't like the sound of that."

"Bad word choice, maybe," Keomany said.

"I forgive you. Find me something to catch. Something I can get answers from."

As Octavian slowed the car, she peered out the window again, searching for some sign of the black things that were lurking in the storm that had come to Hawthorne. Half a block later, as they neared the park at the center of town where City Hall and the old white church faced one another like opposing armies, she spotted another of the things. It clung to the brick exterior of an apartment building that had an ice cream shop on the first floor. Like some kind of skeletal salamander, it stuck to the bricks, looking down upon the people who were coming out of a trendy Thai restaurant, having drunk their way to last call at the bar inside. Umbrellas blossomed from their hands, buying them a few moments to exchange farewells.

"You'd better stop after all," she said.

Octavian pulled the car to the curb by a parking meter. Keomany got out quickly and turned to get a better look at the dark shape clinging to the building, but it had vanished.

"What've you got?" Octavian asked, shutting his door and clicking his key ring so that the lock chirped.

Frustrated, Keomany moved into the street, searching to see if the thing had moved. What did she have? Nothing but soaking-wet clothes. The rain felt strangely warm, which was unnerving, and her clothes were sticking to her in uncomfortable places.

"Come on," she said to herself. "Where did you go?"

A burst of laughter drew her attention back to the group of revelers saying good night in front of the Thai restaurant. She looked over, pushing her wet hair out of her eyes, and watched a blond woman huddled arm in arm beneath an umbrella with an older black man. The couple made their way along the sidewalk to a silver Jaguar. The man took out his keys and the car beeped, lights flashing as it unlocked. He went to open the door for his companion.

"Kem, what did you see?" Octavian prodded her. "We're getting soaked out here."

Keomany was about to look away when the man went down hard. His wife let out a squeal of alarm even as he shouted, cursing, and Keomany heard the question in his tone. She took a single step in their direction before the man started to scream. His wife shrieked his name as he reached for her, his arms flailing as something dragged him underneath the Jaguar.

Octavian bolted past her, running for the car. Keomany raced after him, the only sound now the screaming of the blond woman and the wet clap of their heels on the sidewalk. The others who'd come out of the Thai place with them were calling, hurrying toward the Jaguar as well, but Octavian got there first.

"What is it?" the blonde cried, turning to Octavian even as she backed away from the car. She made no effort to help her husband, shying as far from the car as conscience would allow. "Help him, please!"

Octavian threw himself onto the sidewalk, reaching beneath the car.

"Roland!" the blond screamed. "Roland!"

Keomany reached the driver's side of the Jaguar and followed Octavian's lead. She went down on her knees first, then forced herself to ignore the rain-slick pavement and the puddle beneath her, going down on her belly and peering into the darkness under the car, calling for Roland.

A hand thrust out from beneath the car and Keomany grabbed for it, in time only to catch a handful of Roland's jacket sleeve. He jerked back and forth, hard enough to drag her several inches, her own hand tugged under the car.

"Something's under there with him!" Octavian snapped.

Now she saw it moving, a shadow thing made of coal-black ribbons.

"Keomany, get back," Octavian said. "I'm moving the car."

Just before she released Roland's sleeve, Keomany felt the man go still. The only movement was a twitching from the ministrations of the thing under there with him. Something slashed out from beneath the car, black and gleaming, and cut through her wrist. She pulled away and staggered to her feet in time to see Octavian stand, clawing at the air with his fingers contorted, a golden light crackling around his hands in spheres of magic.

"Out of the way!" Octavian shouted at her.

Only then did she realize that he didn't intend to lift the car.

Keomany jumped aside, cradling her arm against her. There was no cut, but her hand felt numb and swollen, though it looked completely normal. As she stared at it, she saw a black figure, a wraithlike oily smoke, slip from beneath the car and dart up into the stormy sky, clutching a squirming blob of soft, colorful light in its hands. The people who'd been with Roland in the restaurant saw it, too, pointing and muttering and wondering.

Octavian thrust out his hands and a blast of golden-red light slammed into the Jaguar, blowing it across the street, where it rolled onto its roof and crashed into a parked SUV. Car alarms wailed, but the others in the street were silenced, staring at Octavian in awe. All save for the blond woman, who ran to her husband and knelt by him on the wet pavement. She did not touch him, though. Only stared.

For a few seconds, Keomany only stared as well. Then she went to join Octavian on the sidewalk. No one rushed to checked Roland's pulse; there was no point. What remained of the powerfully built man was a withered husk, as though he had been dead for months.

"What happened to him?" one of Roland's friends demanded.

Octavian shot him a regretful look. "I don't know. But we're going to find out."

The blond woman, Roland's wife, looked up at Keomany and Octavian with an expression of such sorrow that Keomany could not meet her eyes.

"How did you do that? What are *you*?" she asked.

"Just people," Keomany told her, wondering what the thing had done to Roland, and what it had done to her hand. "People who want to help."

*

Octavian took Keomany's arm and hurried her into the shelter of a dress boutique's awning, a couple of stores away.

"What exactly did you see?" he said, examining her hand and keeping his voice low enough that they would never hear him over the wind and rain. "What are we dealing with?"

The wail of a police siren filled the air. Blue lights danced off the downtown façades as a patrol car came skidding around a corner. Someone had called 911.

"Some kind of specter? I don't know," she said. "I saw something on a roof, and then another in the air. I told you to pull over because I saw one sticking to the side of a building. I think it's the one that got that guy."

She gestured toward the dead man, whose wife still knelt, weeping and bereft, at his side. The police car stopped and two cops climbed out and started toward her, both of them looking around warily, one with his hand on his service weapon. They looked skittish, like this wasn't the first crisis they'd encountered today. Octavian figured they'd been trying to figure out all day why their picturesque little town was falling apart.

"What do you think is wrong with my hand?" she asked.

Octavian frowned. "I don't get a sense you've been poisoned in any way. The numbness may be just a reaction to contact with it. But I'm going to do a purge spell on you tonight to make absolutely certain."

"No way," Keomany said. "I've seen how those work. I'll sleep for hours. This chaos effect is only going to get worse. You'll need me."

"You said two or three days. I'll need you more in the morning than I do tonight."

She flexed her hand. "It's feeling a little better already."

He could see she was lying. "We'll talk about this when we check into the hotel. Now back to whatever that was. There's nothing else you can tell me?"

"Remember the things that served the Tatterdemalion?" Keomany asked.

Octavian's insides went cold. "Do you think it's back?"

"No," she said. "At least, I don't think so. This doesn't feel the same. The circumstances aren't the same. Hawthorne isn't cut off from the rest of the world. And the Tatterdemalion was about possession, not about chaos. This is not theft, it's like . . . an eruption. An infection. These things are part of it, but I don't know what they are. You're the one who knows demons and all of that."

"Okay," he replied. "But are these things the source of the chaos, or just a symptom?"

Keomany considered it, then gave a small shrug. He didn't blame her. Earthcraft didn't really work that way, not even for Keomany, who was more in tune with nature than any earthwitch he had ever encountered. Gaea had touched her personally, had spoken to her directly, in some way that Octavian knew he would never understand. If Gaea really was nature itself, some spirit that embodied the entire planet . . . that was a level of power and spirituality that he had never encountered. In history, many cultures had believed that all life was connected, that the planet had a singular life force shared by all living things. What Keomany had sensed was a disruption in that life force, in nature. Something had corrupted a part of the order of the world. It might be beyond her craft to be able to pinpoint the nature of the bits of chaos they encountered. But they had to find the source of the chaos and put a stop to it.

"All right," he said. "The cops are going to want to talk to us. Let's make it quick."

"You used magic to toss a car across the street," Keomany said. "They're going to want to do more than talk."

"We don't have time for that," Octavian said, looking past her toward the police. "If they try to detain us, I'll cast a . . ."

His words trailed off. Beyond the grieving woman kneeling by her dead love, beyond the friends clustered under their umbrellas bearing witness, beyond the policemen and their car with its swirling blue lights, he saw a new light.

"Something's burning," he said.

Firelight bloomed in the sky, making orange and black shadows on the storm clouds. Back the way they had come, near the beach, a fire had broken out. Keomany turned to look at it and the cops and others noticed them staring east, toward the water, and they all glanced that way as well.

"God damn it," one of the cops said. "What the fuck is *this*, now?"

Octavian nudged Keomany toward the car, and they hurried toward it. The older of the two cops, a graying guy who moved like an ex-soldier, turned and saw them.

"Where do you two think you're going?" he asked.

Octavian made a fist, feeling the magic surge through him, just in case he needed it.

"To have a look at the fire," he said. "One of you want to come along? There could be people in trouble."

"That's the fire department's job," the former military man said, his chin high, all about protocol and authority.

"Minutes could mean lives lost," Keomany said. "There are things happening in this town none of us understand, Officer. We just want to help."

The cop studied them, but only for a second. Octavian saw the thought process in his eyes. The officer wondered if they were trouble, but then decided that if they were, he was more than capable of dealing with them.

"Tony," he said, turning to his young partner, a twenty-something guy who looked like he'd been in one too many bar fights and wouldn't hesitate to start another. "Call in the . . ." He seemed about to use some kind of dismissive word for the dead man, then glanced at Roland's weeping widow. "Cover the body and then call this in. They'll send backup and someone from the coroner's office."

Octavian didn't have the heart to tell him that an examination of the crime scene wasn't going to turn up any evidence that made sense to anyone.

"Let's go," the cop said, walking over to the car.

Octavian climbed into the front seat of his car. Keomany seemed about to offer the passenger seat to the cop, but he opened the back door and slid in without hesitation.

"What a Godforsaken night," the cop said.

Octavian agreed, but did not respond. He started up the car. As he pulled away from the curb and did a U-turn, he glanced at the people out in the rain with their umbrellas, watching as Tony the cop covered Roland's withered corpse with a plastic tarp from the trunk of the police car, like they had skipped straight from death to funeral with nothing in between.

"Now that we're all cozy, in out of the rain," the graying cop said, "why don't you tell me who you are and what brings you to Hawthorne."

Octavian glanced in the rearview mirror, then over at Keomany. He often ran into people who recognized his face or name. To some he was famous, and to others notorious. It troubled him more to be celebrated than to be despised, because the people who hated him had clear motives. They were easy to understand. They hated vampires or the supernatural in general, or they thought that his magic meant he was in league with Satan and ought to be burned at the stake, or worse. The people who loved, or even worshipped, him were harder to understand. Some were simply open-minded and understood that he only wanted to help, but others admired him for the same reasons the narrow-minded hated him . . . because he had once been a killer and a blood-drinker, a warrior. Or because he wielded magic, and they hungered for some of that power for themselves.

When people didn't know him, that could make things easier, or it could make things harder.

"My name is Peter Octavian," he said, glancing in the rearview mirror again. "My friend is Keomany Shaw. You have some dangerous magic happening in your town. Keomany . . . sometimes she can sense that sort of thing. We're here to help."

"Dangerous *magic*?" the cop asked, practically sneering.

Octavian nodded. "You don't believe in magic?"

"Not much choice, the way the world is these days," the cop said, his disapproval evident. "But I don't have to like it."

"No, you don't," Octavian agreed.

The cop laughed. "As long as we're agreed on that. On the other hand, after a day like today, I'll take help where I can get it."

Neither Octavian nor Keomany replied.

Octavian drove them down to Shore Road and turned left, and they saw the burning building instantly. Some kind of music club, complete with old-fashioned marquee. People were helping each other across the street toward the boardwalk along the beach. Some were bleeding and others were coughing from the smoke that poured out of the front doors of the club. Flames had engulfed the upper floor and burst through the windows. Broken glass littered the street. The rain hissed as it touched the flames. But Octavian's focus was on the fire itself, which burned a sickly orange but had within it threads of greenish flame that were not found in nature.

"Son of a bitch," the cop muttered. "It's just getting worse, isn't it?"

"What's your name, officer?" Keomany asked.

"Jim Connelly."

"You may not like magic, Officer Connelly," Octavian said, "but we can help if you'll let us."

Octavian pulled the car to the curb and killed the engine.

"Fuck, yeah," Connelly said as he popped the door and jumped out. "Help away."

The three of them hurried toward the confused crowd, many of whom were still spilling from the burning club. The smoke mixed with the rain and made it hard to breathe. Wet ash made the pavement slippery.

A black girl ran up to them, grabbing Officer Connelly by the arm.

"Oh, thank God," she said, frantic, her face smeared with soot and tears. "My friend Makayla . . . she's still in there. You've gotta get her out. Those fucking crazy people are going to burn to death in there, and they're not going to let her out. Help her!"

"What crazy people?" Officer Connelly asked. "Did someone start the fire?"

The girl threw up her hands. "I don't know. It just . . . we were dancing. Everyone was dancing and it was totally amazing. Then it got out of control. People started fighting, like really just beating the shit out of each other. The fire started during the fight, back at the bar, all the alcohol went up so fast, but they kept fighting. One guy . . . oh, God, one guy clawed this other crazy bastard's eye out. And they started to look like . . . their teeth were all sharp and they just looked wild, like animals. And they're not coming out. They're still fighting! Makayla got beaten up. I don't know if she's conscious. She's going to die if you don't help her!"

Octavian touched Officer Connelly's arm. "We've got this."

Connelly looked at him in surprise. "You sure?"

"Just remember we're on your side," Keomany told him.

Octavian started toward the club, weaving through the people still staggering out. Keomany joined him, and they heard Connelly on his police radio, calling in to report the fire and the violence. Already they could hear fire trucks screaming in the distance.

"Be careful!" the girl called to them. "They went totally nuts. They'll kill you."

"We'll be all right," Keomany called back to her.

"Just watch out," the girl said. "It's not just the crazy people. The vampire's still in there, too."

Octavian stopped short and turned back to stare at the girl.

"What vampire?"

7

The patients in the psych unit at Hawthorne Union Hospital were having a long night, which meant that for the staff, it was going to feel like an eternity. Dr. Jenny O'Neil hated stormy nights almost as much as she hated the full moon. There were those who attempted to dismiss the effect that the lunar cycle had on psychiatric patients, but as far as she was concerned, they were idiots who had never had to spend the night in a hospital psych unit when the moon was full. Lightning storms had a similar effect, though not as pronounced.

Tonight, though . . . it was worse than any full moon. Tonight the patients were going bugfuck crazy.

"Marlon, help me out," Jenny said, beckoning to the chief orderly, a devastatingly handsome man with milk chocolate skin.

"What do you need, Dr. O'Neil?" Marlon asked as he joined her at the nurses' station.

The chief orderly stood six foot six. His nose had been broken more than once, and showed it, but that imperfection only made him more attractive. Jenny had to pretend she didn't notice. But she had to pretend a lot of things to get through a day on this job, the first of which was that the potentially violent patients didn't scare the crap out of her. Jenny knew how to fight. You didn't grow up in a house with the neighborhood's notorious O'Neil brothers—all older than her—and not learn how to defend yourself. Add to that the self-defense classes that she had taken in the early years of her residency in psychiatric medicine, and Jenny had become capable of taking care of herself. But at five foot two and a hundred and ten pounds soaking wet, she still appreciated having monstrously powerful orderlies around to back her up when things got out of hand.

Tonight, for instance.

"We need to take precautions," Jenny said. "This place is sounding like some Victorian asylum tonight, and I don't want us losing control. We need to get on top of it now."

Marlon nodded firmly. He didn't give her the patronizing smile some of the orderlies did, looking like they wanted to pat her on the head like she was a little girl. Those guys inevitably ended up learning that they could get hurt on the job if they didn't take her seriously. But Marlon had been on the unit for six years, and had seen a few things. At thirty-four, Jenny might be nearly a decade younger, but he respected her both as his superior and as a formidable woman, and if he caught any of the other orderlies doing any less, he made their lives miserable. Every day she wanted to kiss him for it, but never would.

Besides, you'd need a ladder, she thought, as always. The joke helped keep her focused on the job.

"Elissa, let's have the patient roster," Jenny called to the nurse in charge of the station for the shift.

Mid-forties, with a burnt blond dye job, Elissa had been a psych nurse for twenty years. Nothing surprised her and nothing scared her, and Jenny admired that. She needed that kind of no-nonsense attitude, especially on a night like tonight. It was a good team. No matter how out of control the patients got, she thought they would make it through until morning without any major trouble.

Elissa handed her a clipboard with a listing of all of the patients currently on the unit, their diagnosis, current status, and medication schedule. All of that was on computer, and some of the doctors carried around the small pad computers to keep track of it all, but Jenny liked having something to write on, something she could tack to the wall at the nurses' station if necessary. Something concrete. Any medical instructions or comments would end up in the electronic file anyway, courtesy of Elissa, but Jenny liked paper, especially when she wanted them all to put their heads together.

Thunder boomed outside, loud enough that they could hear it even in the corridor. *Hear it?* Jenny thought. *I can* feel *it.* The rumble lingered for several seconds, and Jenny smiled at Elissa and Marlon.

"I hate storms like this," the nurse said, looking uneasy.

"Me, too," Jenny said. Since childhood, thunderstorms had sent her scurrying under her covers or into the arms of her father. But her father had died of an aneurysm two years ago, and there were no covers for her here at the hospital. Only patients who were far more troubled by the storm than she was.

"Walk with me," she said, holding the clipboard and coming out from behind the nurses' station.

Marlon and Elissa flanked her and the trio headed deeper into the secure wing of the hospital's third-floor psychiatric unit. There were two rooms outside the secure area, one of them currently occupied by a fifteen-year-old girl with a penchant for cutting herself. She'd had another incident this morning, this one especially bloody, and though she seemed rational now, she needed close supervision.

"The Langan girl hasn't shown any reaction to the storm, but I want a bed check every half hour," Jenny said quietly, glancing at Elissa. "No need to disturb her, but make sure she hasn't gotten her hands on anything sharp, and that she's doing all right."

"Of course," Elissa said.

"Marlon," Jenny went on, "I know one of your guys has gone through the room, but I'd like you to go through it yourself. It's a weird night and I don't want to take any chances."

"I'm on it," Marlon replied.

The second room outside the secure area was empty tonight, but only because its occupant—a woman who had been pulling out and eating her own hair—had been moved inside the secure unit. She had seemed stable enough until nightfall, when she had relapsed in dramatic fashion, tearing out her hair in clumps and trying to choke it down. If a nurse hadn't interrupted her, she'd have choked to death. Now she was both sedated and in restraints. With the way the patients were agitated tonight, it would be almost impossible to help them until daybreak. Jenny hated to admit it, but the best that she could do was try to keep them all safe until morning, try to soothe them, and assess them anew in the morning.

The lights were off in the empty room. Jenny glanced inside as they passed, just as a fresh barrage of lightning splintered the night beyond the glass. It lit up the room with flickering flashes, casting strange shadows.

"Did you see that?" she asked.

"Lightning, Dr. O'Neil?" Elissa asked, sounding almost amused, as in, *Of course we saw it, woman, it's been going on for hours.*

"It looked almost blue," Jenny said.

"I noticed that earlier," Marlon told her. She looked up at him, but he averted his gaze, as if for some reason he did not want her to see his eyes. She wondered if he was spooked by the lightning, too, and embarrassed by it. "It seems even bluer now. I figured it was something to do with the rain, the way it reflects the light."

"I guess," Jenny said.

As the thunder accompanying that blue lightning cracked the sky, she passed her ID in front of a sensor plate and the door into the secure section buzzed. Marlon yanked it open, letting Jenny and Elissa enter before him. The door clanked shut behind them and they started down the hall. Someone sobbed loudly, full of a sorrow that might only exist in their delusions, but was no less real for the fact. They passed several rooms whose doors were open, patients either drugged or restrained or both. Lightning sketched blue veins in the dark outside their windows. The lights in the corridor flickered, dimming slightly the way the lights in Jenny's house always did when she ran her hair dryer. Every time it happened, she held her breath. The hospital had already lost power once tonight and had to go to backup generators. The normal power had surged back on soon after, but she feared a total shutdown. It couldn't happen—the generators would prevent it—but as a doctor of the psyche, she knew that fear was never limited to the rational.

"Marlon, I want orderlies in this corridor every time a nurse is checking on a patient. On any patient who isn't restrained, even the ones who are sedated, I want an orderly in the room with the nurse."

"You've got it."

"Elissa," Jenny continued, looking at her clipboard. "Mr. Abrams tried to bite Dr. Nathanson earlier. He apologized. Said it was a new compulsion that he hadn't had before, didn't know where it came from. But most of his compulsions have been fairly benign if you don't count the damage he could do with scissors if we let him indulge his obsession with cutting other people's hair. The biting thing is new. I want him sedated for the night."

The nurse started to speak, but hesitated.

"Something to say?"

"Is that really necessary, Doctor?" Elissa asked. "He's kind of sweet, actually. And mostly harmless."

"It's the harmless that concerns me. Tonight's not the night for new compulsions. If you'd rather wait until he bites someone hard enough to draw blood or worse and we have to restrain him . . ."

"No," Elissa said quickly. "Of course not."

As they ran through the roster of other patients, blue light flickering all the way into the corridor from the open doors, they passed a police officer seated on a hard plastic chair. The patient inside that room, Wayne Pinsky, was dangerously bipolar and the suspect in a nine-month-old double homicide. Jenny wanted him out of the hospital as soon as possible. The court had remanded Pinsky here for observation. Tomorrow, Dr. Nathanson would be finishing his report on Pinsky with a final interview and examination. Soon after, they'd be rid of him.

Shouts came from the end of the corridor, and Jenny glanced at the clipboard in her hands, although she already knew who was making the ruckus. Sixteen-year-old Gregory Wheeler had been a repeat visitor to the unit over the years she had spent here. Greg had a history of paranoid schizophrenia and a cocktail of other mental issues that fed each other. Some of the drugs they'd tried were like putting out fire with gasoline. This year he had been steadily declining, succumbing more frequently to his recurring belief that there were very few humans left in the world, that other-dimensional aliens had infiltrated society and were now conspiring to steal his brain, which held some key to their own future which even he did not understand. The delusion was perfect in that he did not need to know what they wanted his brain for, only that they wanted it. Of course doctors and orderlies were all part of this secret invasion.

It had been difficult to get through to him over the past few days, but by testing several different combinations of drugs, they had seen some improvement and Jenny had hoped to send him home to his mother. But ever since the storm had begun, Greg Wheeler had spiraled down into the most terrifying depths of his delusions.

"The orderly that the Wheeler boy attacked . . ." she said.

"Oakes," Marlon supplied.

"Is he all right?"

"Minor concussion. He'll be out of work a couple of days."

"His nose isn't broken?" Elissa asked.

Marlon laughed. "It is," he said, touching his own nose. "But you do this job long enough, you're going to get your nose broke. It'll heal."

At the end of the corridor, two more orderlies appeared. They'd been the target of Greg Wheeler's torrent of verbal abuse, checking on his restraints. It had sickened Jenny to have to order Greg restrained. She had a soft spot for the gawky, floppy-haired teenager. But he was as much a danger to himself as he was to others. She only hoped that through a combination of counseling and drug therapy, they could get his perceptions back to normal. Right now he existed just as much in another dimension as these aliens he hallucinated.

A nurse accompanied the two orderlies who'd been checking on Greg. The trio patrolled the corridor warily, and Jenny thought they were smart to be wary. The patients and staff were all skittish now.

"All right," Jenny said. "Get to it."

Marlon and Elissa agreed and went farther along the corridor to meet their colleagues and pass along instructions. Jenny turned to the cop guarding the murderer Pinsky's door.

"Can we get you anything, Officer?"

The thin cop had a dark complexion, a prominent Roman nose, and a roguish smile. "If you can get me off Chief Kramer's shit list, doc, that'd be great. Otherwise, just a cup of coffee at some point, if you can swing it."

"Coffee we can swing," Jenny replied. "The chief's shit list is another story. What's wrong, Officer? You don't like our company?"

"I'm sure you're excellent company," the officer replied. "It's the setting that troubles me, y'know? The ambience."

Jenny smiled, her nerves settling down now that the Wheeler boy had stopped shouting. "I'll see what I can do about that coffee."

She started back toward the security doors. Passing by one of the open rooms, she looked in to see the blue lightning flashing outside. Thunder hammered the hospital an instant later.

"Lightning's too close for comfort," the charming officer said. "That one must have been right—"

Blue light flashed so brightly that Jenny threw up a hand to shield her eyes. The safety glass windows in the patient's room shattered and lightning struck the empty chair by the bed. Thunder rolled across the sky, shaking the entire building. Jenny cried out and fell to her knees and the cop stood, one hand on the wall and the other on his sidearm, absurd really, as if he thought they were under attack. More glass blew in somewhere on the wing.

The lightning didn't subside. It kept striking the building. Lights in the corridor popped and sizzled and blew. Elissa and one of the orderlies down the hall held on to one another. Marlon swore, but Jenny couldn't hear much of it over the thunder. A boom rocked the whole corridor, and it seemed like it came from Pinsky's room. Jenny forced herself to stand and looked in through the small window in Pinsky's door to see that part of the wall had been smashed in by lightning and the murderer's bed was on fire.

"Fucking hell!" she shouted. "Marlon! Get it open!"

As she ran for the fire extinguisher, tugging out the master key in her pocket that would open the panel, she realized that the thunder had begun to fade. The lightning had ceased. The electricity still sparked and the lights crackled on and off, but the moment had passed.

Jenny yanked the extinguisher out and ran back to Pinsky's room. Marlon had unlocked the door and hauled it open, and now he pulled the extinguisher from her grasp and led the way into the room, followed by the Italian cop, who had drawn his gun. With a few quick bursts of foam, the burning bedclothes were extinguished, as were the flames that had started to flicker up the dresser.

The cop lowered his gun. Pinsky posed no threat to them now. The killer lay frozen in a portrait of agony, his flesh charred, his eyes turned to gelatin in his skull.

"Holy God," the cop whispered.

"Not tonight, man," Marlon replied. "Not tonight."

Shouts came from the corridor. A buzz from down the hall indicated help was coming. Jenny left Marlon and the cop in Pinsky's room, but when she reached the corridor, the shouting turned to a scream.

The sixtyish OCD patient, Sid Abrams, sat astride Elissa on the floor, holding her down, biting her face. He tore the meat of her cheek, blood spraying, and as he chewed he cried copious tears, shaking his head and trying to apologize with a mouth full of her flesh.

An orderly tackled the old man off her, struggling with him on the ground. A nurse ran to help Elissa. Other staff streamed into the secure section, but even as they did, howls and cries rose from all of the occupied rooms. The blue lightning had done something, Jenny realized. It had more than upset them. The place was bedlam.

Her twenty-first-century psych unit had become a true madhouse.

Keomany and Octavian went through the front doors of the club side by side, bent low to stay beneath the roiling smoke still pouring out. The hot breath of the fire blasted against them as though trying to keep them away, but they forged on. Keomany knew that Octavian must have half a dozen ways to handle this fire, but with people trapped inside, they had to be careful. And the elements were her specialty.

The roar of the blaze filled her ears as they ran through the small foyer of the club, past a ticket booth and velvet ropes and the stool where the bouncer would have been sitting. The curtains that separated the foyer from the club were burning, flames licking up and across the ceiling. Octavian tore them down with his bare hands, unmindful of the hungry fire that tried to leap to his clothes. As his shirt caught fire he batted it out with a hand, and then they were in the main area of the club.

Tables were overturned. Chairs had been hurled aside. A section of the roof had fallen in and an upward glance revealed a ring of fire like the gullet of a volcano. One whole side of the club had been engulfed in flames, and Keomany assumed that this had been the location of the bar, where the blaze had begun. On stage, the band's equipment crackled and blackened and one of the raised drums tumbled to the ground as the whole kit gave way, melted by fire.

The girl outside had described a fight, and it was not over. At a glance, Keomany spotted seven or eight people down, some of them probably dead. Six were still standing, and she saw that they were interrupting a bloodbath. They lunged at one another, tearing with fingernails and teeth, punching and kicking and clawing. One woman drove a man down with an elbow to his throat and then began to kick him in the balls, over and over, until another man—his face savage and bestial—brought a chair down on her head and then fell upon her, sinking his teeth into her arm.

They've gone insane, she thought.

One of them might have been the vampire, but they were all so vicious she could not tell the difference.

"Like we talked about," Octavian said.

"Damn straight," Keomany agreed.

She planted her feet, let the heat of the fire buffet her, trying to burn her and suffocate her all at once. Monstrous, it roared, flames continuing to consume the club, working their way toward the corners they had not yet touched. The middle of the room had become a bonfire of tables and portions of the collapsed ceiling. Somewhere glass shattered, the heat blowing out windows.

Keomany closed her eyes, reaching one hand toward the hole in the roof and the other out toward the inferno where the bar had once stood. She had become far more adept at working with air and earth, with roots and plants, but she had dealt with fire before. Weather could be influenced, but never really controlled. Still, she had to try.

With a single exhaled breath, she thrust her spirit down into the earth, extending herself, searching for a place beyond the reach of the chaos storm that had begun to unravel Hawthorne. She felt the fire. Felt the rain. Tried to smother the one with the other. The wind howled inside the club, and that was not at all what she wanted. It only made the flames leap higher, ravage the walls faster, leap from table to table to fabric seat. But the rain came with it, this strange, warm rain whose source was a perverted nature. Still, rain was rain, and the fire did not like it. She could not bring more rain, but she could focus it, draw the clouds above more tightly together so that the moisture falling else-where in town would, for a few moments, fall almost entirely in this one place.

Impossibly, the fire raged higher, as though fighting back. But she had seen the blue core of the flames and knew that there was magic in them. She opened her eyes, and through the hole in the roof she saw blue lightning dancing inside the clouds that were colliding above the club, and she could picture it now . . . blue lightning strikes, blue fire eruptions. Had this been a mistake? Would it only bring more lightning?

"I can't control the fire!" she shouted, trying to be heard over the blaze.

Her voice was met with snarls and hyena laughter. Keomany turned in time to see a man running toward her, blood on his hands and smeared on his mouth. His eyes were wild and his teeth jagged and plentiful as he lunged for her. No time to dodge. He would be on her in a moment.

The beast-man cried out in pain as green electrical fire seized him, a sphere of magic that crackled like real flame. He struggled against it, but to no avail. The sphere contracted quickly and Keomany heard the air hissing out of it, and a moment later he tumbled to the floor, free of the sphere but unconscious. One of his legs looked broken. She had no sympathy.

"Peter!" she called.

Octavian had cast the spell that saved her. A man and woman hung ten feet from the ground in a similar sphere, all the oxygen being stolen from them. A shambling fat Asian man careened toward him from behind. With the noise of the fire and the entire sky's worth of rain pouring down upon them, Keomany could not be sure Octavian heard him. She reached down into the earth again. This time, so far away, she felt contact, just the lightest touch of the goddess. With a gesture, she brought the floorboards to life. Roots and branches sprang from long-dead wood, reaching up to twine around the gargantuan man. Flames raced along the floor and began to spiral along the roots, and she knew her mistake at once. Trapped in the prison her witchery had just made, the man would die.

"Something's controlling the fire!" she called to Octavian.

The mage shot out his left hand and an arch of golden light sliced across the club, knocking the other two beast-men from their feet. Then he spun around, staring at the blue core of the fire, and raised both hands.

"Vodilna roke odšla," he chanted. *"Pusti naravi z naravo. Je treba očistiti zunanjih vplivov!"*

The light that burst from his hands and his eyes turned from gold to amber to blinding red. The wind that flashed through the club had more power than the storm and it shook the building to its burning rafters, but when it had passed, Keomany stared at the ring of fire in the ceiling above.

The blue fire had gone, leaving only ordinary flames behind. The rain had already begun to subdue the blaze.

"This I can work with!" she said, grinning, twirling, and dancing, singing a song that she often hummed in the orchard.

The wind died but the rain came on. The fire began to gutter like a million dying candles, hissing as it subsided.

In seconds, the blaze had gone out.

"Well done," Octavian said.

With a wave of his hand, the crackling energy sphere vanished and the two lunatics within fell to the ground with a crash. The two he had cast aside with a concussion spell were beginning to stir.

"No sign of a vampire?" Keomany asked.

"None," Octavian replied. "These people have been cursed

somehow, turned savage. It may fade or it may not. Their best bet is us being able to stop the chaos here. We do that, and they should be all right. But they're not vampires."

"The one guy who nearly got me had some nasty teeth. Maybe that girl outside just thought she saw a vampire," Keomany said.

Octavian nodded. "Maybe."

But as firefighters and EMTs began to enter the burned wreckage of the club, Keomany walked farther inside, toward the motionless bodies scattered on the floor.

"Careful," a firefighter called to her. "This place is unsafe. The roof could come down on our heads. You folks should wait outside."

Octavian glanced at her and they shared a moment of quiet irony. They had just extinguished the blaze and put down the rabid freaks who'd been tearing each other apart in here, and he thought maybe they should wait outside?

Off to her left, just to the left of the stage, something moved. Keomany looked toward a platform that had been rolled off to one side, perhaps used for some performances but not others, and saw a figure rise. Clothes singed, coppery red hair wild and unkempt, the girl might have been nineteen or twenty. Though slender and of average height, she carried another girl in her arms as easily as she might have cradled an infant. Beautiful, her ocean-blue eyes bright, she walked toward Keomany and laid the other girl on the floor.

The injured girl coughed harshly, smoke inhalation having done its work. With her short-cropped black hair and the ring through her lip, she fit the description of Makayla, the friend who'd been left behind by the panicked girl outside.

"She'll be all right. Just see she gets oxygen. Too much smoke," the redhead said. She hesitated and started to walk away.

"Hold on," Keomany said, reaching for the redhead's arm. "That corner was on fire. How the hell did you—"

The copper-haired girl spun, silently baring fangs.

Keomany swore and stepped back. The vampire's eyes flashed a warning and she picked up her pace, hurrying out of the burned shell of the club. She could have turned to mist or rain, could have been a mouse or a fly, but she seemed determined to walk out on her own two feet. Keomany turned and saw Octavian talking to two EMTs.

"Peter!" she called. She wanted to shout, *Here's the vampire*, but since the vamp girl didn't seem to be hurting anyone, she didn't want to freak out the emergency workers. But the mage did not seem to hear her. "Hey, Octavian!"

Octavian spun around, eyes narrowed, alarmed by the edge in her voice. It had been a long night already, and they had known from the moment they'd entered Hawthorne that the chaos would only get worse.

Keomany gestured toward the copper-haired girl, but even as Octavian started across the scorched club to pursue her, the vampire halted in her tracks. She turned to stare at Keomany and then spotted Octavian approaching.

"You're Peter Octavian?" the vamp girl asked, her eyes filled with hope.

Confused, Keomany studied the two of them. Once upon a time, Octavian had been a vampire, and for a time he had led a group comprising both humans and vampires, trying to protect humanity from vampires who refused to give up the bloodthirsty ways of the past. He still worked with the UN, aiding their efforts to hunt rogue vampires.

"I don't know you," Octavian said, studying the girl warily.

"I'm Charlotte," the vampire replied.

"Are you registered?" Octavian asked.

Charlotte glanced away.

"You're a rogue," he said ominously. "Why aren't you running?"

She flinched as though the words pained her. "Maybe because I'm hoping that instead of killing me, you'll actually help me. Someone has to."

Octavian hesitated. Keomany inched closer to him, just in case the vampire girl tried anything—not that he would need her help for one vampire.

"Look," Charlotte said, her anger flaring again. "I didn't kill any of these people. I need your help. Come on. Seriously, don't you have bigger problems than one vampire girl who hasn't signed the Covenant?"

Octavian hesitated. Charlotte looked to Keomany.

"She has a point," Keomany said, keeping her voice quiet. Already the firefighters and EMTs were starting to pay close attention to this exchange, and she didn't want anyone to get hurt trying to interfere. Officer Connelly would be waiting for them outside, and the cops would be tempted to start blaming some of this nastiness on Charlotte once they found out she was a rogue.

"All right," Octavian said. "We'll talk, but not here."

"There's a café up around the corner that looked like it might still be open," Keomany said. She'd spotted it as they'd driven through the town center, a place called After Midnight Café.

"Fantastic," Charlotte said, flashing a pouty, sharp-edged smile. "I'd kill for a coffee."

Octavian narrowed his eyes.

"Oh, for fuck's sake," the vampire girl said, rolling her eyes in perfect teenager style as she turned and marched out of the club. "It's a friggin' figure of speech."

Keomany arched an eyebrow, amused. Octavian only looked troubled, but they followed the girl out into the warm blue rain and the burgeoning chaos of night in Hawthorne. Daybreak could not come soon enough.

8

Miles sat on a floral-patterned, high-backed chair in his mother's living room. The fabric smelled of flowery perfume and when he had sat down, it had exhaled the scent of dust and old age. It had been a quiet sort of house, even when Miles had been growing up, used to long silences or to stillness broken only by the voices of soap opera actors and news anchors. His mother liked to have the television on for company when she did her cleaning or folded laundry. *Had* liked to have the TV on. *Had* being the operative word.

His mother was past tense now. History. Past tense, past tension, passed on.

"Shit, Ma," he whispered to himself, scraping his palm across his eyes, swiping at a fresh trickle of tears.

He had been keenly aware of her mortality for years. Since the death of his father, when Miles had been only a boy, the idea that his mother would one day follow had haunted him. But in a way her presence had also comforted him when he had been lured into dark musings about his own eventual fate. His grandparents had been old and had passed away when he was small. But sad as they might have been, their deaths had seemed natural and ordinary. His father's, less so.

Now, though, with his mother gone . . . he was next in line. Miles knew he wasn't old, but it felt to him as though the Grim Reaper had touched his hand tonight, had slipped up beside him and breathed the same air. With no generation ahead of him now, he felt a new intimacy with death that he had always feared. It had come for his father so long ago, but now it had come for his mother as well, and too soon. She had still enjoyed cooking, still read her mystery novels, still painted flowers and ducks and the old grist mill from time to time. She had friends who loved her, including Tricia Bowker, who walked with her four mornings a week to keep their hearts pumping. Tricia would probably stop walking now, Miles thought.

With a shudder, he buried his face in his hands, bent over in the chair, trying to make sense of what he had lost today. He remembered coming in from sledding with his friends and his mom making him hot chocolate and indulging him when he wanted to stick his feet under the baseboard heater to get them warm. She had brought him shopping with her and he had sat patiently inside the circular clothing racks, hidden from other shoppers in a forest of dresses or blouses, waiting for her to finish. He remembered his birthday parties and how each one had seemed quirky and different; one year, they'd had a séance. His mother had loved parties and didn't mind if the other parents thought she was a little strange.

Miles had never told her about what happened the Christmas after the séance birthday party. He had been eleven . . . certainly old enough to tell the difference between dreams and the waking world. After a long Christmas day, his mother had gone to sleep and his Aunt Betty and her second husband, Uncle Artie—who had come in from Colorado for the holiday—were crashed out in the living room, nodding off in front of the television. Miles had gone off to the bathroom for a quick pee before bed, heavy with Christmas dinner and the exhaustion of postpresent ecstasy. Emerging from the bathroom, he had nearly run into Tim McConville in the hallway.

The trouble had been that Tim McConville—a boy with whom Miles had taken the school bus every day since the beginning of third grade—had dropped dead in September. A hole in his heart, a birth defect no one had been aware of until it killed him. Tim had been at Miles's eleventh birthday party, but he had not wanted to take part in the séance. He had left the room, deeply unsettled, though just why he could not say. Miles had located him in that upstairs hallway, just outside the bathroom door, crying.

The sight of the ghost sent him screaming down the stairs to his mother, who had led the way back up with her son shaking behind her. There had been no sign of Tim McConville, but Miles had never doubted what his eyes had seen, and his mother had never expressed any doubts either. She had believed him completely. God, how he had loved her for that.

He had seen the ghost of Tim McConville several times over the years, but he had never been as afraid as he had been that first time. When he was twenty-two and just home from college, he'd been up late watching an extra-innings Red Sox game and seen Tim standing behind the television, and he had tried to speak to the spirit of the dead boy. The ghost had not replied.

There had been several other ghosts as well, but no one he knew . . . just glimpses of translucent figures on the street or in the library, and once in a tiny Irish pub on East 19th Street in New York.

Ghosts. Miles tried to steady his breathing. His mother was dead. And what was that thing that had killed her? Was that a ghost?

The grief came at him in waves and he exhaled, letting the latest one pass. But along with the grief there had come shock and fear and confusion, and those came in waves as well. He sat up straight, swallowed hard, and, after a moment, somehow managed to control the fit of trembling that came over him.

Awful images flashed in his mind, things that filled him with dread. Just like the ghost of Tim McConville, he did not doubt the horror he had witnessed in his mother's bedroom. The first police officer on the scene and the EMTs who had followed had all looked at her and turned away. What could they say about the withered skin and her sunken eyes? She looked like some kind of papier-mâché creation, as though she had been laid out and dried in the sun for weeks. There had been suspicious looks, and he knew they wondered if she had been dead a long time, and he had only just called. Maybe they thought he was taking her social security checks or something.

But then Don Kramer had shown up and had mentioned seeing her just the day before, and none of them were going to argue with the chief of police, no matter how impossible it might be that this woman had been dead only an hour.

Miles felt bile burning up the back of his throat. *Ma. Oh, hell, Ma. What did it do to you?*

That was the question he did not want to ask, and he certainly had no desire for an answer. In his mind's eye he saw the horrible thing on top of her, hacking those smoke-scythes into her body and tearing out that nebulous light, that colorful radiance that looked almost like a butterfly . . . that bit of his mother's life, or that part of her soul, that it took with it when it fled the house.

Miles had known death all his life. He hadn't been prepared for his mother to die, but he had thought about it enough that he could have weathered it, could have managed the grief . . . if only he did not now have to ask himself a dreadful question. Was she at rest? Could she find peace beyond this life without whatever vital piece of her that thing had stripped away?

The stairs creaked under the weight of heavy footsteps. Miles turned to see Chief Kramer reach the foyer. The chief spotted him in the living room and came in to join him, perching on the arm of the sofa.

"Miles, I'm so sorry," Chief Kramer said.

"Thanks, Don. I appreciate you coming by yourself."

"Of course," Chief Kramer said.

He looked genuinely upset, and Miles believed he must be. The Kramers had lived two houses over for years. Don might have been three years older than Miles, but he had never teased the younger boy and always included him in the baseball games and touch football matches and street hockey games in the neighborhood. And young Don Kramer had visited the Varick house often, too. Toni Varick made the greatest cookies the world had ever known, and Don was always welcome. They hadn't been buddies, really—the age difference had been a major gulf in those early years—but Miles certainly considered Chief Kramer a friend.

"Is there anything you need?" Chief Kramer asked. "Right now, I mean?"

Miles shook his head. He tried to smile and knew he only managed a grimace. He threw up his hands, knowing his voice would crack with grief.

"I'll be all right," he said. "Thanks, though. I'm just going to sit here for a while, let it sink in, you know?"

Chief Kramer nodded. As they were talking, the EMTs had been carrying the stretcher down the stairs. Strapped to it was a black body bag. Miles tried not to think of the dried husk inside it. That thing wasn't his mother. His mother was gone.

As if to punctuate this thought, the EMTs put down the wheels on the stretcher, turning it into a gurney. The wheels rattled over the threshold as they rolled it out of the house, leaving only Miles and Chief Kramer, and just maybe the ghost of Tim McConville. Miles hadn't said a word to the chief about what he had seen, the demon or whatever the hell it was, in his mother's bedroom. Now he had begun to regret it. He hated the idea of Don Kramer thinking he had lost his mind, or been hallucinating or worse. But in a world where the public had been given ample evidence of the existence of demons—though many still didn't believe in them—would the chief have thought him crazy? And did it really matter? What could one middle-aged police chief, or an entire police force, do against demons?

"All right," Chief Kramer said. "Call me if you need anything, Miles. Truly. But I've got to head out. There was some kind of fracas down at the Troubadour and now the place is burning down."

"In this storm?"

"Looks like."

Miles shook his head. "What a fucked-up night."

Something rippled across Kramer's face—irritation, yes, but also a certain unease. But then he was retreating across the living room, headed for the exit. He had a job to do, and Miles didn't begrudge him that. After the phone call he'd had from Amber earlier and the unearthly thing that had killed his mother—the thing that looked exactly like the creatures Amber had described from her vision—he knew that it wasn't only *his* life that was unraveling tonight.

"I'll call to check up on you in the morning," Chief Kramer said, standing in the open door.

Miles lifted a hand in farewell but did not rise from the musty chair. "Tomorrow. Thanks, Don."

Then the door closed, and Miles was alone in the silence of his mother's house. For several minutes, he played the events of her death over again and again in his head. But then his thoughts began to slip back to the phone call he'd had from Amber right before he had gone up to his mother's room. He thought about her dreams. She had insisted they were visions, and if he had been hesitant to believe her before, he had no more reservations. Amber had described in perfect detail creatures just like the thing that had killed his mother. Hawthorne wasn't the kind of big city where most of the supernatural wars and skirmishes had been fought in the years since the world had learned the truth about magic and evil. But something evil had indeed begun to infest the town.

You should've said something to the chief, he chided himself. And he knew that he would. But Don Kramer might be the kind of guy who needed convincing, and a college girl's dreams might mean nothing to him if he refused to believe in the creature Miles had seen. No, he needed more than wild stories and visions to get the chief's attention.

Tonight he would sleep here, right in this chair, or on the sofa. He would give himself over to grief and exhaustion. But tomorrow . . . tomorrow he would start digging. He would talk to Amber, see if she'd had any other visions, and he would do some research. One word had resonated in those visions, and it had stuck in Amber's mind. Now it echoed in Miles's thoughts as well.

Navalica.

It had to mean something. If he could find out what, perhaps he would learn what had killed his mother.

And what he had to do to destroy it.

Amber woke abruptly, inhaling sharply as though she had stopped breathing for a minute. It took her a few seconds to orient herself to her surroundings. She still lay on the couch, her neck stiff from being propped awkwardly against the sofa arm. Stretching, she gave a soft moan and blinked, trying to focus her vision. The floor lamp in the corner still offered a wan golden light, but most of the illumination in the room came from the infomercials playing at low volume on the television. The clock above the cable box read 12:21 . . . not very late for a girl in college. On campus, there would be parties that were just getting started, or just getting good. But after the day she'd had, Amber was in no mood for a party.

She swung her legs off the sofa and sat up, rubbing her hands over her eyes. Her throat felt parched and, sleepily, she made a mental checklist of the steps between this moment and crawling into her bed. A glass of water. A visit to the bathroom. Removing the clip from her hair. Undressing. She had some eye makeup on, but she was too tired to clean it off tonight.

The house creaked with a gust of wind, and she heard the rain against the windows and on the roof and realized that the storm still raged outside. But as she listened, she thought maybe it had eased off just a little. That was something, at least. *And you didn't dream,* she thought, before immediately correcting herself. *You didn't have a vision.* What a relief to know that she could sleep without those hideous images invading her mind.

The murmur of the TV drew her attention. She grimaced at the sight of the bearded man on the infomercial. The guy had been dead for years, but they still had him hawking products. It was ghoulish. With a shudder, she dug around the cushions on the sofa for the remote control and clicked off the TV, leaving that dim floor lamp the only source of light in the room, save for the oddly bluish lightning that flickered outside from time to time.

A glance at the chair in the corner confirmed that Gran had gone to bed. She slept ninety percent of her life now, but Amber figured that she had earned a rest. Her chair was one of the electronic variety that raised itself until its owner was nearly vertical. Some days Gran didn't really need to use it, but most of the time she did so just for safety. Amber had suggested more than once that they install one of those lifts on the stairs, but Gran always clucked her tongue in irritation at such talk. She needed help getting up, but if she took her time and held the railing, she could navigate the stairs all right.

Until the day you can't, Amber always thought but would never say. She worried about that day, when her old Gran would come tumbling down. She had also mentioned many times that her parents might want to turn the back porch into a bedroom for Gran so she wouldn't need to go upstairs to bed, and even offered her own room on the second floor, so Gran wouldn't have to walk up to her room in the house's converted attic. Her parents were all for either option, but the stubborn old woman wouldn't hear of it. She didn't want to sleep on the porch or in someone else's bedroom. She wanted her own room. Amber thought it ridiculous, especially considering that Gran did nothing in that room except sleep, and never returned to it during the day. Once she came downstairs, she was down until bedtime, so she didn't have to do the stairs any more than absolutely necessary.

I hope I'm not that stubborn when I'm as old as she is, Amber thought now as she stretched again and then headed for the kitchen. She smiled. *Assuming I'm lucky enough to* get *that old in the first place.*

She filled a glass with ice water and carried it upstairs to her bedroom. Stripping to her underpants, she slipped on an oversized T-shirt that smelled fresh from today's laundry and then padded across the hall to the bathroom. After she'd relieved herself, she avoided looking at herself in the mirror as she washed her hands. If she saw the little bit of makeup she had on, she'd want to take it off, and she could feel the comfort of her bed calling to her.

As she stepped back into the hallway, a shudder went through her. The skin on her right arm prickled with gooseflesh and a damp heat that seemed to come from nowhere. She turned in that direction and her heart clenched in her chest.

In the gap of the partly opened door to her parents' bedroom stood a familiar, skeletal black figure, all stick limbs and night-dark tatters of fabric or smoke. The curved blades in its hands glinted in the blue light flickering from her parents' television set inside the room.

A Reaper. Amber couldn't breathe. This must be a vision. Of course it had to be. These things existed only when she closed her eyes.

But she knew it was not a vision. Cold fear burned in her, panic surging. She took two steps back, staring at the impossible and shaking her head. She bumped into the frame of the bathroom door and the Reaper whipped around to stare at her, pinpricks of ice blue leaking mist from the dark pits of its eyes.

"Out," she said, surprising herself with the firmness of her voice.

She shot out a hand, felt around for the switch outside the bathroom that would turn on the hall lights. Her palm brushed against the switch.

"Get out!" she screamed as she flipped it, bathing the hallway in yellow light.

The thing glared at her defiantly for a moment, and then a gust of wind struck the house with such force that Amber could feel the wall trembling against her back. The Reaper cocked its head as though listening to some distant call, then darted down the corridor and struck the window at the bottom of the attic stairs, passing right through the glass with a noise like a tremulous sigh.

"Oh my God," Amber said. Her hand shook as she raised it up to cover her mouth. *Not just my hand.* She realized her whole body was shaking.

The thing had looked exactly like the ones in her visions. The Reaper had been a wraith in the darkness, but when she had turned on the light she had seen it very clearly. It might be an insubstantial thing, almost like a ghost, but there was no denying that it was real.

"Mom," she said, realization striking her as she rushed toward their bedroom door. "Dad."

The door had been half open, and now she pushed it the rest of the way. It banged off the doorstop screwed into the baseboard, and Amber stood staring at her parents as they slept in the flickering light from the television. Or were they sleeping? Her heart fluttered inside the cage of her chest as she stared.

Her father stirred. He seemed to sense her standing there and rolled over.

"Amber?" he asked. "What was that noise? Something wrong?"

Not just something, she wanted to say. *Everything!* But how was she supposed to explain what she had seen in the hall? If she told him it came from her dreams, or visions, he would think it had been part of a dream. And could she really be so certain that it hadn't been some echo from a nightmare? She'd had a seizure this morning and been taken to the emergency room. Her brain had gone on the fritz for a while. How could she be sure this wasn't a by-product of that?

It wasn't. It was real.

Part of her felt so certain, so insistent. But if she had doubts, and she had seen the thing, what would her parents say? What else *could* they say, but that monsters—under the bed or in the hallway—weren't real?

"Sorry. I banged the door," she said, trying to hide the whimper of relief that came out with the words, now that she'd seen her parents were all right. "I didn't mean to wake you."

"What's wrong? Gran okay?"

Amber stared at the two figures in the bed. Her mother—always a notoriously deep sleeper—groaned and turned in the bed, putting her back to them, shutting out the disturbance.

"Yeah. She's in bed," Amber said. "I just had a bad dream, I guess. The storm's got me freaked out."

At last, her father turned his tired eyes upon her. His smile made him seem younger than his fifty one years. The light from the TV made the generous patches of gray stand out against the darker bristle of his hair, but still he looked more tired than old.

"Just a dream, honey," he said. "And just a storm. Both'll pass."

"Thanks, Dad. Sorry. Go back to sleep."

"Not sleeping that well, actually," Frank Morrissey replied.

Amber looked at her father, a little alarm bell going off in her head. "You having bad dreams, too?"

"Nah. Just stiff," he said, then illustrated the point by groaning as he stretched. She could hear his joints popping from across the room. He scratched at his right arm. "And itchy as hell. Hope I don't have the shingles again."

Amber nodded. "You'll be all right. All you need is a good night's rest, without your daughter waking you up 'cause she's afraid of a thunderstorm."

"I'll tell you a secret," her father said. "Nights like this, I'm a little afraid, too."

She smiled. "Night, Dad."

"Good night, sweetheart."

Amber turned to leave the room. As she went out into the hall, she heard her father moving around, trying to get comfortable again. He moaned softly, obviously in more discomfort than he had let on. Frank Morrissey often joked with his wife and daughter that once he'd hit fifty years old, the warranty had run out and he had started to fall apart. Her father, it seemed, was getting rusty. Amber wished he would exercise more. She vowed to herself that she would not surrender so willingly to the aging process.

With a nervous glance around the hall, she went to her room and climbed under the covers, but she had no intention of sleeping. She had left her bedroom door open and now she clicked on her reading lamp and picked up the Jodi Picoult book she'd been reading. Amber didn't want any more visions, no more bad dreams. And just in case they were more than dreams, she wanted to make sure her family was safe. If the Reaper returned, she would be awake and on guard, and she could at least shout a warning.

When the sun rose, she would sleep. She would miss most of her Thursday classes, but that seemed a small price to pay to make certain that the darkness in her visions did not infiltrate her real world, her real life.

Amber glanced out into the hall, then at the rain pattering her darkened window.

It wasn't my imagination, she thought. *I only wish it were.* But she didn't want to wake her parents again. Tonight, she would read. And tomorrow, when she woke, she would tell them about the things she had seen, both in her mind and in their house, and about the things she feared.

In daylight, she would tell them. It would feel safer.

Frowning, she glanced out the window again, thinking of the storm, wondering if there would even be daylight tomorrow.

Please, let me have some sunshine, she thought, sending the prayer up to a God she had never spent much time thinking about until tonight.

Forcing herself to look at the pages of her book, she tried to read. *Please.*

Dr. Jenny O'Neil stood at the nurses' station just outside the secure area of Hawthorne Union Hospital's psych unit and tried to persuade herself that there was a rational explanation for what had happened tonight. She held an ice pack to the side of her face, waiting for the OD of ibuprofen she'd taken to kick in, and stared at the door to the secure area, which stood propped open. She had never seen it propped open before, and it seemed strange and counterintuitive. The whole ward had gone apeshit. Half a dozen patients and one of the orderlies had experienced simultaneous episodes of psychotic aggression. Logic suggested that maybe leaving the door wide open wasn't the smartest thing in the world. The view down the corridor should have comforted her. There were eight or nine cops, half a dozen security guards, and at least that many orderlies, not to mention several doctors and a platoon of nurses. It looked like half the hospital had been detached from their normal posts to come and help clean up the mess.

"You sure you don't want something stronger than ibuprofen?"

Jenny glanced over to find a nurse named Lauren watching her. The woman had been on the job for a quarter century and had confided to Jenny that she had thought she'd seen it all, until tonight. Lauren looked spooked, and Jenny didn't blame her at all.

"You think I should prescribe myself some Vicodin?" Jenny said. "I think that'd be counterproductive."

Lauren made a valiant attempt at a smile. "Oh, I don't know. I think we could all use a little Vicodin right about now."

Jenny sighed and took the ice pack off her face. One of the patients had thrown her into a wall, but she was fortunate that had been her only injury. Elissa was up in surgery right now having her cheek repaired. It would take several rounds of plastic surgery to get her face looking even close to normal again. The image of that crazy bastard tearing at her with his teeth was stuck in Jenny's mind, and she knew it would haunt her when she tried to go to sleep. Maybe Vicodin wasn't a bad idea after all.

"I'll tell you this much," Jenny said, "someone better cover my shift tomorrow night, because I need to blow the cobwebs of this place out of my brain and the only thing that's going to do that is a little time away."

Lauren nodded. "Somehow I doubt that's going to be a problem," she said, then nodded toward the secure area. "Looks like you're wanted."

The police lieutenant who was heading up the investigation strode toward the nurses' station accompanied by a nurse named Franco, the only male among the psych unit's usual coterie. Sexist as it might be, Franco was often called on when there were unruly patients, a by-product of his being larger and more powerful than most of the orderlies. Tiny as she was, Jenny had never gravitated toward men like Franco, but she'd seen other women on staff swoon over him. The police lieutenant, on the other hand, was exactly her type—gruff and cynical, but also lean and handsome.

"Dr. O'Neil," the lieutenant said. "How are you feeling?"

"I'll survive," she said, wishing she could remember his name and wondering if her poor memory suggested a concussion. She ought to have one of the other docs have a look at her. "I don't suppose you have any idea what happened here?"

"An act of God?" the lieutenant suggested.

She knew he meant the death of the murderer, Pinsky, who'd been flash-fried by lightning that had broken through the wall of the building.

"Maybe it was," she said. "But I'm not just talking about that. Freak lightning storms aren't unheard of. I'm talking about the people who went . . ."

"You don't want to say *crazy*," the lieutenant observed.

"Let's say *rabid*."

The lieutenant looked troubled. "*Rabid* sounds right. As for what happened, I have no more idea than you do. I wish you could tell me that all of the patients who became violent were on the same medication. We'd at least have a starting point." ·

"I already told you, Lieutenant—"

"I know, I know," he said, holding up a hand. "I said, 'I wish.'"

Franco gave her a meaningful look. "I overheard one of the officers saying there was a similar incident at a club downtown."

"Really?" Jenny asked, surprised. "Tonight?"

The lieutenant seemed irritated at Franco—or maybe at whichever officer had let it slip—but he nodded. "It could be. There was a fire at the club and a lot of people were injured, but reports on the scene say there was an outbreak of violence before the fire. It might be nothing but too much alcohol, but . . ."

"But what?"

Lauren came out from the nurses' station and pulled Franco aside, giving him quiet instructions that sent him off toward the room of Sierra Langan, the fifteen-year-old girl who enjoyed cutting herself far too much.

The lieutenant seemed to be rethinking having told Jenny anything to begin with, but he forged ahead.

"Apparently they kept fighting, even though the building was on fire."

Jenny understood, then, why he had told her.

"Sorry, Lieutenant," she said.

"For what?"

"I take care of crazy people. I mean, the way you see it. But most psychiatric patients are not that complicated when you get to the bottom of it. Some can be helped and some can't. But each case is different. When it comes to something like this . . . mass psychosis or group irrationality—like the total abandonment of self-preservation required to stay in a burning building and keep fighting—doesn't fall within the usual parameters of my work."

His disappointment was obvious. It troubled Jenny that they were both looking to each other for answers and coming up with nothing. The only thing she could point to as potentially affecting the patients had been the weather. Bad storms were often disturbing to psychiatric patients, and for whatever reasons, she had always felt that the level of their agitation corresponded directly to how many of them were in the psych unit at any given time.

But weather couldn't account for this. Not even freaky blue lightning striking the building and blowing in a wall. Yes, it might make the schizophrenics even wilder than usual, but to send half a dozen patients into seemingly homicidal, bestial rage, and doing the same to a member of the hospital staff . . . ridiculous. If it wasn't the storm or the wrong medication, she couldn't begin to imagine what could cause something like this. Jenny wished she could leave the investigation to the police, but it wasn't just their problem. She and her colleagues would be studying the night from every angle, just as the cops would. But Jenny had a feeling they weren't going to find any easy answers.

The most important thing was that the crisis had passed. The patients who had erupted in violent rages had been restrained and sedated, though not without injuries to themselves and to members of the staff. Alarms had sounded. People had bled. Bones were broken. Pinsky was dead, but no one was going to cry for a homicidal maniac with so much blood on his hands. They were very lucky no one else had been killed while the orderlies and the rest of the staff were getting the whole thing under control.

"If you think of anything . . ." the lieutenant said, all furrowed-brow business.

Jenny smiled, wishing that the left side of her face weren't swollen and bruised. "You'll be the first person I call."

If the lieutenant had even the tiniest clue there might be some flirtation in her tone, he didn't show it. Her timing was not ideal. The truth was, she couldn't even really put her heart into flirting with the guy. The night's events had gotten under her skin too much. But she did want to know his name, for future reference.

She was about to ask for his card when she saw Marlon coming out of the secure area. He spotted her and hurried over, a worried crease to his brow.

"Dr. O'Neil."

"What's up, Marlon?" she said. "I don't like that look."

"You've got to come and see Gregory Wheeler."

Jenny frowned. "What is it? Don't tell me he's gone rabid all of a sudden?"

Marlon glanced from Jenny to the lieutenant and back again. "It's probably better if you come talk to him."

"*Talk* to him?"

"Can someone enlighten me?" the lieutenant asked. "My officers are still gathering information, but I don't think there was a Wheeler on the list of patients who had outbursts."

Jenny started walking. Marlon and the lieutenant caught up and the three of them hurried into the secure area, that propped-open door still troubling her. She paused a moment to release it from the magnetic catch and let it swing closed, hydraulics hissing.

"Greg Wheeler is a paranoid schizophrenic. Badly delusional," she told the lieutenant. "He's in the last room on the hall."

"Where the window shattered," the lieutenant said. "He's a kid."

Jenny almost corrected him, not about Greg being a kid—his parents were on the way down—but about the window. It hadn't been Greg's room where the wall had been so badly damaged, it had been Pinsky's. But then she remembered that the window *had* shattered in Greg's room. The frame was charred and the metal grate that covered the glass had been blackened. Lightning had hit the building in more than one place, but at least in Greg's case, it hadn't done more than break a little glass. If the wall had blown in, the boy might have been killed.

They passed police officers and security guards, nurses and order-lies. Many patients had been put in restraints in addition to being sedated. Some had been moved to other wards. Workmen were already in the damaged room boarding up the hole in the wall until more permanent repairs could begin. Pinsky's charred remains had already been taken to the morgue. Several nurses tried to talk to her, but Jenny asked them to hold their questions for a few minutes. Police radios buzzed with static, and she thought she heard frantic voices.

"Seems like the police department is having a rough night," she said.

"Chief Kramer has his hands full," the lieutenant confirmed. "I've never seen a night like this. Crank calls. Heart attacks. People hallucinating all kinds of things."

"How can you be so sure they're hallucinating?" Marlon asked.

The lieutenant glanced at him. "If you heard the stuff they're reporting, you'd know." He glanced back at Jenny. "So, yes, we're stretched pretty thin. Now that things are reined in here, I'm going to cut most of my guys loose. I'll leave an officer here until morning, just in case anything else happens—"

"God forbid," Marlon said.

"—and you can call me if you have any questions."

The lieutenant produced a card and handed it to her. Pleased, she pocketed it, then turned all of her focus on the mystery of why Marlon had dragged her down here in the first place.

They arrived at Greg Wheeler's room. A nurse stepped aside to let them through the door. Greg had been restrained earlier, so Jenny was surprised to find him sitting in a chair. His hair was combed and his clothes—a top and pants not unlike the scrubs the staff wore—seemed neatly arranged on him. When she walked into the room, he turned to look at her and a gladness filled Jenny, because she could see just from the look in his eyes that he *knew* her.

Greg smiled the disarming smile that she had come to recognize over the years. He only smiled like that when his paranoia had retreated, when he could like her and trust her. With that look on his face, he seemed like a completely different kid, sweet and intelligent and a little sad.

"Wow. Looks like there's at least one person around here who's having a good night," Jenny said.

Greg nodded, smile broadening. When he spoke, he was animated and a little goofy, and he offered her a self-deprecating grin and a shrug, rolling his eyes. He spoke to her as he would a friend—and why not, they had known each other more than long enough to be friends.

Except he wasn't speaking English.

Jenny stared at him. It wasn't gibberish, either. The words had a cadence and rhythm and a repetition of certain sounds and even phrases that made her feel certain it was an actual language, but it wasn't any language she had ever heard before.

"What the hell is this?" the lieutenant asked. "Where's this kid from?"

Jenny glanced at Marlon.

"Greg's from Salem," the orderly replied. "Right down the street."

"What's he speaking?" the cop asked.

Jenny thought that was a damn good question.

9

Octavian wasn't sure if the After Midnight Café had been designed to have a retro, fifties diner feel to it, or if it had just been that long since anyone had updated the décor. He and Keomany sat across the table from the vampire girl, Charlotte, in a red vinyl booth. In life, the vampire had been beautiful, with copper-red hair that hung in unkempt curls past her shoulders, and blue eyes that sometimes seemed to reflect back the colors around her. She had asked for his help, and Octavian would not turn her away, not even in the midst of this crisis. But she had him on guard. He read her fear and anxiety as genuine, but there was more to her than just that.

One look at her, and he knew she was hungry. Charlotte had an addict's smile, twitchy and unsure, nervous energy making her fidget in her seat. Yet he could see the struggle going on within her as she tried to hide that hunger from him.

"When was the last time you ate?" Octavian asked.

Charlotte glanced at the menu in front of her, eyebrows knitting in frustration.

"I'm not talking about anything on that menu," Octavian added, his voice lowered.

Beside him, Keomany sat up a bit straighter. He knew she had met vampires before, but despite that—and in spite of her intimacy with magic on an elemental level—she had no experience that would allow her to form an opinion about Charlotte. That would have to be Octavian's job.

"Are you saying—" Keomany began.

"Too long," Charlotte interrupted, glancing nervously at Octavian and then, almost demurely, down at her fingers. She alternated between drumming them on the table and scraping her nails against the plastic edging around the menu.

Octavian narrowed his eyes, growing very still. "You said you understood who I am."

Charlotte gave a hollow laugh. "Who doesn't? I mean, who of *us*?"

"I'm not one of you anymore," Octavian replied.

She shrugged. "As if it's that easy. I've heard about you. Read about you. Add in the time you spent in . . . well, in Hell . . . and you were a vampire longer than anyone. Long enough to evolve into whatever the hell you are now."

Irritated, Octavian bared his teeth, just the way he had sometimes done in the days when they were sharper.

"This conversation isn't about me, except to establish that you understand who you're dealing with. I've never heard of you, never met you, never seen you before. You've admitted that you never signed the Covenant, and that makes you rogue. I could kill you right now and be well within my rights. International law is on my side. It practically demands that I end you."

"Fine," Charlotte said, leaning forward on her bench, red vinyl crumpling as she moved. She tugged down the front of her tank top, revealing an expanse of white cleavage and lacy black bra. "Go for it. *End* me. Or, y'know, let me answer the questions you brought me here to answer."

Octavian bristled, but Keomany put a hand on his leg, under the table. He looked at her, saw the concern in her gaze, and he exhaled. What had gotten into him? Chaos? That made a certain amount of sense. The chaos that was quickly spreading through Hawthorne and saturating the community might well affect the people within its sphere of influence, even those connected to the supernatural. Perhaps, he thought, it would affect those individuals most of all.

The waitress arrived, cutting off whatever any of them might have said next. They ordered coffee all around, and Keomany asked for a slice of cheesecake. Somehow, that seemed to calm them all. There was something absurd about eating dessert in the middle of such chaos and hostility. Perhaps Keomany knew it, because she smiled and asked for three forks.

Octavian frowned as he noticed she was cradling one hand in her lap, and he realized she was still feeling the effects of her contact with the wraith earlier tonight. The trouble at the Troubadour, and now encountering Charlotte, had distracted him enough that he had nearly forgotten. Keomany had not complained, but watching her now, he knew that he would need to follow through on his earlier insistence that she rest tonight. He would cast a spell that would hopefully draw out whatever taint might be in her, or simply help her heal if it was only a matter of numbness and aching after the wraith had touched her. By morning, she ought to be fine. He needed her to be fine.

When the waitress departed, Charlotte opened her hands as though in supplication.

"Look, can we start again?" the vampire girl asked, her red hair falling across her face. Another day it might have made her sexy, but Octavian thought that tonight, the effect was altogether different. She seemed vulnerable, and very alone.

"Why don't we start with what you're doing here?" Keomany asked. "This whole town is falling apart. Peter and I are here to help, but the last thing we expected was an unregistered vampire."

Charlotte sank back into her seat. For a moment she looked like a truculent teenager, but then she softened, making herself breathe when she didn't need to—a cleansing breath, Octavian thought.

"None of this is my doing," she said. "I mean, if that's what you were thinking, you can unthink it. I've got nothing to do with this, except that I was in that club listening to the band when these people started trying to kill each other. It was that sudden, y'know? One second everyone's just listening to the music, maybe chattering about the thunder because they could hear it over the band, and then—like someone fired a starter pistol—they're going at each other, kicking and punching, grabbing anything they can use as a weapon, just tearing into each other. Fucking rabid animals."

Octavian smiled, reaching up to scrape his palm thoughtfully across the stubble on his chin.

"Okay," he said. "But that brings me back to my first question. It's been a while since you ate. You're as twitchy as a junkie looking to score. Were you at that club hunting?"

Charlotte tried to smile again but succeeded only in baring her fangs. "I don't hunt humans."

Octavian could practically hear the unspoken ending to that sentence: *anymore*.

"Look, just because I'm what you call a rogue, that doesn't make me a monster."

"Then why aren't you registered?" Keomany asked. "And how is it that you need our help?"

Charlotte nodded. She scratched at her arms and fidgeted a bit. "There you go," she said. "That's where we need to be in this conversation."

The waitress arrived, delivering their coffees and Keomany's cheesecake. As requested, she laid three forks on the table, but when she walked away, no one touched the cheesecake.

"Go on," Octavian urged.

Charlotte hesitated, holding her coffee cup in both hands as though to warm her. The rain pounded the plate glass windows of the café. The lights flickered from the storm.

"You swear you won't kill me?" the vamp girl asked.

Octavian stirred sugar into his coffee and raised it to his lips.

"No," he said, taking a sip, letting the heat of the drink sink into him. "But I promise I'll hear you out."

For the first time, Charlotte looked truly afraid of him, and a dreadful sorrow filled her, as though she had been hollow before and now that sadness was all that she could contain.

"I promise you'll get a running start," Keomany told her. "But that will have to be good enough."

Octavian glanced at her sharply, but Keomany ignored him. She stared at the vampire, rubbing her numb hand as if it had fallen asleep.

Charlotte glanced around, scratched her arms again, and ran her tongue over her fangs before nodding. "All right, fine. Whatever. It's not like I have a lot of other people lining up to help me."

She took a sip of her coffee, unsweetened, and grimaced at its bitter strength, but she did not add sugar or cream.

"You once knew a vampire named Cortez," Charlotte said, steadier now that she had the coffee cup to hold on to. She glanced at him and then looked away. "Seventeenth century, I think it was. Somewhere in Italy."

"I knew him," Octavian allowed.

"Wait, Cortez? As in the conqueror?" Keomany asked.

Octavian gave her a sidelong glance. "So he claimed. I was never convinced." He ran his thumb across the smooth ceramic rim of his mug. "What about him?"

Charlotte glanced out the window, watching rivulets of rain run down the glass. "I had just turned nineteen. My friends took me to this big party at this guy's house. I had spent my whole life as a good girl, y'know? No sex, no booze, no drugs. They had a fire pit in the back and everyone was hanging out, drinking. This one guy, Nick, took out his guitar and started playing, and the whole thing was just . . . it was bliss."

Her eyes began to fill, not with tears but with blood. She wiped it away, idly licking it from the back of her hand, barely even noticing what she'd done.

"This is stupid," she said abruptly, shaking her head. "I'm not going to bore you with my human life."

Despite his suspicions, Octavian pitied her, for he sensed where the story was headed . . . somewhere that shouldn't have been possible.

Keomany had not touched her coffee. Now she put her hands over it, perhaps hoping its warmth would take away the numbness, and shivered.

"There were drugs. Cocaine. Ecstasy. I wanted to leave but my friends—such as they were—wanted to stay. I got pissed off and left without them. This was in San Diego, okay? Pacific Beach. I guess I could've called a taxi, but I decided to walk home, burn off some of my anger. It's a party town, but that area's usually pretty safe. Usually.

"I was so mad, I barely heard the van pull up beside me. Two men—I thought they were men—dragged me into the back. Duct tape, a black hood . . . it's fucking redundant, right? You've watched that scene a thousand times in movies or on TV. It's trite."

Charlotte faltered, licking her lips and once again dabbing at the bloody tears in her eyes.

"Unless it's happening to you," Keomany whispered.

Charlotte glanced at her sharply, almost angrily. Octavian could feel the pain emanating from her.

"Yeah," the vampire girl said. "Damn fuckin' straight. It's not trite when it's happening to you. When you're screaming and then you can't scream anymore. When they're beating you. When they do whatever the hell they want to you. When they *play* with you."

She smiled, and with her long fangs and the blood smeared around her eyes, she had become something terrifying.

"I survived," she said, uttering a horrid laugh. "And what was my prize for surviving all of the things they did to me? They said I was tough. They said Cortez wanted survivors. Fighters. And they brought me to him, and he took care of me, nursed me back to health . . . and then he killed me, and made me *this*."

She looked down at herself in disgust.

But Octavian had forgotten his sympathy for her. He set his coffee down.

"Charlotte," he said. "Look at me."

The vampire girl did so. The waitress chose that moment to approach. Likely, she meant to ask them if there was anything else they needed, but when she got a look at Charlotte's face, she made a tiny yelping noise and then muttered something about God as she hurried away.

Octavian ignored her, focused entirely on Charlotte.

"What year did you die?" he asked her. "What year were you turned?"

The girl laughed hollowly. "What do you mean, 'what year?' *This* year. I turned nineteen in February."

"But Cortez died in London, during the Blitz."

Charlotte frowned. "World War Two?"

"Yes," Keomany said. "World War Two."

Octavian could feel Keomany staring at him, but he kept his focus on the vampire girl. "Cortez has been dead all this time. Most of his coven died in a single night's bombing. Whoever turned you, it wasn't Cortez."

The girl looked confused. "Well, whoever he is, he certainly hates you."

"So, there's some rogue out there creating new vampires—" Keomany began.

"A lot of new vampires," Charlotte said. "There were dozens just in the one building in L.A. where he kept me. And the guys in the van? They aren't the only ones. They hunt, have their fun, and pass on the best 'candidates' to Cortez."

"I don't understand," Keomany said, turning to Octavian. "How is it possible that an operation of that size can exist without Task Force Victor finding out about them?"

Octavian pushed his coffee mug away. He'd lost interest. Charlotte's story weighed heavily on him. Task Force Victor was a joint United Nations operation. Allison Vigeant—one of Octavian's closest allies, one of his shadows—had once hunted vampires for them. If TFV knew about this "Cortez," the group would have been wiped out, which meant they did not know. But someone had to. That many people disappearing, that many new vampires being created. Someone had to know.

"Is this Cortez connected to what's happening here in Hawthorne?" Octavian asked.

"What?" Charlotte said, frowning. "No. I took off months ago. Cortez wanted us all to be killers, to be what he called 'real vampires.' We were forced to . . . to feed." She shuddered. "I'm not a killer. I get hungry, yeah. But I'm young and pretty enough that if I want blood, I never have to force a guy to give me some, y'know?"

Octavian nodded. He could imagine that, especially in a world that knew vampires were real, it would be a simple enough matter for a girl as lovely as Charlotte to persuade a young man to part with some of his blood.

"All of us were supposed to hunt, eventually. They sent me out with two others who had been recently turned. But we'd talked in advance and agreed we weren't going to kill to feed ourselves, and we sure as hell weren't going to kill for Cortez. We had a babysitter, of course— one of Cortez's faithful, who was there in case something went wrong, or one of us decided to run. He wasn't ready for all three of us trying to run. It turned ugly fast. Ugly and bloody."

Charlotte shrugged. "But here I am. I don't know if Cortez is look- ing for me. I'm gonna guess no. His operation's too ambitious for him to chase down one girl from Pacific Beach. Anyway, I made my way east—wanting to put as much distance between myself and him as possible—and ended up in New York."

"You're not in New York," Octavian reminded her.

"I was. And that's the weird thing," Charlotte said. "I've been living in New York. I work in a theatre on Forty-fourth Street. This morning I was going to an acting class, and halfway there I felt this *compulsion*. Maybe that's the wrong word. It didn't feel like something was driv- ing me, but luring me. The savage part of me . . . the demon taint, right?" She nodded at Octavian. "It reacted. I felt like a sailor in some old myth, like the sirens were singing and I had no choice but to come to them."

"And when you got here?" Keomany asked, sipping at her coffee and making a face, as though the cream in it had spoiled.

Charlotte threw up her hands. "Nothing. I felt it under my skin. Felt it rattling around my skull. But once I got into town, I had no direc- tion. I'm hugely on edge, ready for a fight. Hell, I want one. I feel like I just want to *hurt* someone."

She smiled, but it turned into something resembling a snarl. All through their time in the café, she had been fighting the hunger that gnawed at her, and Octavian thought she had been struggling to rein in the irritation the chaos around them was causing . . . the aggression growing in all of them. And now she'd put it into words.

"I wouldn't, though," Charlotte said. "Not without a reason."

Attempting a smile again, she picked up a fork and dug into the cheesecake, popping a bite into her mouth.

"Maybe not," Octavian said. "But you'll understand if we want to keep an eye on you."

"Absolutely," Charlotte replied over a mouthful of cheesecake. "Hell, I want you to. The feeling isn't gone. It's still buzzing in my head, so I can't exactly leave here. I tried to, before I went to the club, but it's like I can't make myself. The dark part of me wants to be here. But if I'm going to be here, then I want to help you. And when it's all done, show me where to sign, and I'm totally on board with the Covenant. I never wanted to be a rogue."

"What about this Cortez?" Keomany asked.

Octavian had been wondering the same thing. "It doesn't sound like his operation is connected to what's happening here. So we'll deal with Hawthorne first, then we'll worry about this impostor pretending to be Hernando Cortez."

"Assuming we survive," Keomany said drily.

Charlotte stared at her, upset by the words, and then she laughed. "Aren't you a ray of fucking sunshine? I thought you Wicca-chick earth mommies were supposed to be all sweetness and light."

Octavian couldn't help smiling. The girl might be a vampire, and she might be bristling with unspent violence, but he liked her.

"Absolutely," Keomany said. "Sweetness and light. Until dark magic starts messing with our goddess. Then we're all business."

"Good to know," Charlotte replied.

Octavian saw the corners of Keomany's mouth twitch as she fought a smile. Her instincts probably told her not to, but it was obvious that she, too, had been charmed by the vampire girl.

"All right," Keomany said, turning to Octavian. "Assuming Charlotte here isn't going to rip my throat out in the next sixty seconds, what's the plan?"

Her voice had a tired rasp and Octavian could see she was exhausted. A glance at the clock confirmed that midnight had come and gone, the hands ticking toward 1 a.m. Though Octavian was flesh and blood—technically human, and mortal—he had acquired such magic that he could go without sleep or sustenance for long periods, if circumstances required it. Keomany might be a powerful earthwitch with a direct line to Gaea, but she had never mastered the kinds of magic that Octavian had spent a thousand years in Hell perfecting.

"You're not going to like it," he warned her.

"Try me," Keomany said.

Octavian glanced at Charlotte, then back to Keomany. "If you can't pinpoint the source of all of this, then more traditional methods are called for. That means poking and prodding, asking the wrong people the right questions, sticking my nose in where it doesn't belong. With all the years I spent playing private detective, I have a little more experience in that area than you do."

"Granted," Keomany said.

"You're going to head over to the hotel. You can check us in—"

"Bullshit—"

"—I'm going to have a look at your hand, try to dispel whatever's troubling you, and then you're going to head over there and get some rest," Octavian continued, ignoring her interruption. "It's the only rational thing to do, Kem. You might not be bleeding, but you're injured. If I find any decent leads, anything to direct us to the source, I'll come and wake you. But if this thing is still raging tomorrow—and we both know it will be, unless I get lucky tonight—I'm going to need you sharp and focused in the morning."

He saw that she was reluctant, but she couldn't argue his logic, especially given how hard she was rubbing her numb hand.

"What about Little Orphan Charlie?" Keomany asked, nodding toward the vampire girl.

"Shit, really?" Charlotte said, smirking. "I'm right here. I can hear you."

"I'll take her with me," Octavian replied. "It'll keep her out of trouble. And it never hurts to have a shadow on your side."

Charlotte ate another forkful of cheesecake. "Is that what I am? I'm a shadow now?"

Keomany slid the plate of cheesecake back in front of her and picked up a fork. "They're the same thing, honey. But the ones who *want* to be called vampires . . . they're still the monsters the old stories made them out to be. If you want to be something else, that's going to be up to you."

The Sea Foam Hotel looked closed, not for the night, but forever. Aside from a single security light that shone into the parking lot, the place was dark. Some of the guests must have had lights on in their rooms, up reading or watching television, but Keomany assumed that they had drawn the shades against the eventual sunrise, because as she approached the entrance, she thought the place looked completely abandoned. Still, when she tugged the door, it swung open, and now that she was out of the rain—standing under the hotel's dripping awning—she saw that dim lights burned within the lobby.

For a moment she hesitated, afraid to go inside on her own. It wasn't the hotel that frightened her so much as the prospect of being alone on a night, and in a town, that bristled with dark chaos magic. Anything might happen. The ground might split open and swallow the Sea Foam Hotel and its outdated stucco façade in the blink of an eye, and she didn't want to die alone.

Keomany took a deep breath. *You've been alone against dark magic before,* she reminded herself. *You can hold your own.* Sometimes she forgot just how powerful an earthwitch she was. That didn't mean she had nothing to fear, only that she had the magic to fight back.

She turned and gave Octavian a wave. He nodded and put the car into gear, pulling out of the parking lot. In the passenger seat, Charlotte raised one hand in a small salute, and Keomany wondered if they were making a terrible mistake. The girl had charm and she had told her story convincingly, but they really knew nothing about her. Still, it seemed absurd to worry. If Charlotte betrayed him, Octavian would incinerate her in a heartbeat. Most people had no idea just how deadly powerful a mage he was, and would be terrified if they ever witnessed that power in action. Charlotte posed no threat to Octavian, and perhaps the vampire would turn out to be helpful.

It felt strange, though, watching them drive away, off to patrol the darkened city like some kind of magical vigilantes. She ought to have been with them.

She flexed her fingers. Already the unnerving cold and the ache that she'd felt from the moment the wraith had slashed her with that strange black knife—the blade passing right through her arm—had begun to abate. Her skin prickled as though her hand had fallen asleep and the blood had just started flowing again. But Octavian had insisted that if she wanted to be sure his spell would do its work, she needed at least a few hours of sleep. Reluctantly, she had agreed.

Weary and troubled, she hitched up the strap of her travel bag and entered the hotel, striding across the lobby. She thought she might have to make a ruckus to get service, considering the lateness of the hour, but before she had even reached the desk a twentyish guy with patchy skin and leftover baby fat emerged from a door behind it.

"Help you?" the clerk grunted.

Keomany was too tired to even get irritated by his attitude. "I called ahead. Adjoining rooms. The name is Shaw."

The guy typed something into a computer, scanning the screen with a sigh. "Yeah, here you are. Kee-o-menny. What kind of name is that?"

She let out a breath. "Can I just get my key? I need sleep."

"Huh? Yeah, sure." He banged at the keyboard a bit—*tak, tak, tak*—and then pulled out a plastic key card, slipping it into a machine to be coded. "You'll be in 325. Mr. Octavian will be in 327 when he arrives."

"Give me his key as well, please. You can put both rooms on my card for now."

The guy had been a bit brusque and his social skills left something to be desired, but he wasn't a complete moron. He could see that he had annoyed her, and he gave her Octavian's key without further inquiry.

"Here you go," he said, sliding both room keys across the counter to her. "Just FYI, the Internet's down for some reason."

Like her cell phone. *And probably everyone else's,* she thought. Keomany shivered, then forced herself to smile. "Must be the storm."

"I guess," the clerk said, not sounding convinced.

She rode the elevator in silence. Walking down the third-floor hall-way, she heard a baby crying loudly from one room and a woman pleading with the infant to be quiet. From another room came the sounds of a couple fighting. At the door to her own room, as she slipped the key card into the lock, she overheard hysterical laughter coming from Room 323, next door. Despite the lack of lights visible inside those rooms from the outside, many of the guests were up late tonight. The chaos magic surging through the storm had begun to seep into everyone.

In her room, she experimented with her cell phone, but it remained frustratingly uncooperative. Even out on the balcony, she could not get a flicker of a signal. Locking herself in, she washed up in the bath-room, brushed her teeth, and then threw herself into bed, burying her head under a pillow to keep out the sounds of fragile people beginning to shatter. She wanted to help them, and that meant locating the source of the chaos. Tired as she was, and despite the remaining numbness in her hand and Octavian's insistence, lying in some hotel room while the town fell apart seemed wrong.

On the other hand, as ugly as some of the things happening in Hawthorne were, the town was not quite unraveling. Not yet. She would do more good after a few hours' sleep, with the daylight driv-ing away some of the shadows. It might be easier to pinpoint the source then, as well.

You're here, she told herself. *The useful thing to do is get some sleep.*

Eyes closed, curled in a fetal position, she forced herself to relax. Her breathing evened out and she felt the heaviness of her weariness begin to drag her down. As she did most nights, she reached out like a child for a favorite stuffed bear, but instead of using her hands, Keomany reached out with her spirit. She wanted to touch her god-dess, to feel the comforting presence of Gaea, to tap into the current of energy that ran through all of nature. As it had earlier in the day, that current proved difficult to find, but eventually she sensed it—and Gaea—just out of reach. Something tickled at the back of her mind. She could feel the goddess, and she had the sense that Gaea might be focused on her, trying to tell her something, to give her some message that she was not in any position to receive. She thought of her cell phone, and the hotel's wireless Internet, and she understood how completely cut off they were from the outside world.

You could leave, she thought. *Get out of Hawthorne right now, before it becomes so dangerous that escape is impossible.* Before the magic insinuating itself throughout the town became powerful enough to trap her here.

It was an idle thought, but still she felt guilty. She would never abandon these people to the twisted magic that had begun to envelop their homes and lives.

Drifting toward sleep again, Keomany reached out and touched the ocean. It had a taint of the chaos that had touched Hawthorne, but could not be fully infected by it. The ocean was too powerful, an engine of natural forces at work. But that taint she had sensed earlier— though faded—remained. And now as she felt heavier, surrendering to sleep, she realized that she sensed that same taint elsewhere in Hawthorne, not just a generalized malaise, but the specific dark taint that lingered just offshore. But this smear of chaos on the natural order of things was not at sea . . . it was on land, just a few miles away. For a frustrating quarter hour, she fought the pull of sleep as she tried to pinpoint the location of that taint. But she could not get a fix on its position, only the general direction in which she might find it if she set out in pursuit.

I'll tell Octavian, she thought. But without cell phone service, she had no choice other than to wait for Octavian to return. Next door, the laughter had ceased, and down the hall, the baby had stopped screaming, though whether that boded well or ill, she refused to speculate.

Sometime in the small hours of the morning, without Octavian ever having turned up to retrieve his room key, Keomany at last surrendered to sleep.

Chief Kramer stood on top of his patrol car in the rain, gun warm in his hand, uniform plastered to his body. The wind gusted nearly hard enough to topple him off the car, and as he fought to keep his balance, three more dogs came bounding and snarling from out of the storm. One came from beneath the car, the others from a cobblestoned alley beside the Enchantment Bakery.

Kramer shot a German shepherd in the head, blowing it back into a puddle, dark matter spilling out of its shattered skull. The other two continued to growl, splitting off from each other, one headed for the front of the patrol car and one to the rear. Kramer forced himself to stand up straighter, trying to keep his balance in spite of the vicious dog bite on the calf of his left leg. Blood streamed down into his shoe, soaking through his cotton sock.

"Fuck this," a voice crackled on the chief's radio.

Kramer didn't have time to snatch up the radio to reply.

"Don't do it, Jim!" he shouted, as the black Labrador leaped up onto the trunk of his car.

The chief put two bullets into the black Lab and the dog's bloody carcass flipped backward off the trunk and hit the rain-slick pavement. The third dog snarled behind him and he spun, finger on the trigger, only to see the mutt scrabbling at the fender with its teeth bared, unable to make the jump onto the hood of the patrol car.

Officer Connelly had never been the best cop when it came to taking orders. Maybe that came from knowing one another so long, or maybe Jim just didn't think anyone should be able to tell him what to do, even the chief of police. He popped open the door to his own patrol car—Connelly and his partner, Tony Moschitto, had arrived on the scene only seconds after Chief Kramer—and climbed out into the rain, weapon drawn.

"Get back in the fucking car!" Kramer called.

From inside Connelly's patrol car, Moschitto shouted at him as well. Connelly had no intention of listening. If anything, Moschitto had only made him more determined. He held his gun out in front of him in both hands, imitating countless television cops, and aimed it at the mutt.

"That's an order, Jim! Get in the car!"

"It's just a damn dog, Chief," Connelly snapped.

The mutt turned on Connelly, growling as it rushed at him. Chief

Kramer and Connelly both fired at it, and at least one of them hit it, because the dog whimpered and sprawled to the ground, twitching and bleeding. Counting the shepherd and the Lab, there were half a dozen dead dogs scattered around the two police cars, all of them shot in the mere minutes since Kramer had first pulled up to the curb and gotten out of his vehicle, responding to a 911 call the dispatcher had patched through to him.

Connelly started to holster his weapon, obviously pleased with him-self.

"It's just a damn dog, yeah," Chief Kramer agreed. "But the call that came through said there were dozens of wild dogs running in a pack, Jim. Dozens. Do the fucking math and get back in the—"

A howl silenced him. The rain pelted the cars loudly and the wind moaned around them, but another sound rose above the noise of the storm. Whining, growling, and snarling, they burst from darkened doorways and beneath sidewalk benches, lunged through the broken glass of the apartment building from which the 911 call had originated, and surged toward the two police cars. In the dark and the storm, Chief Kramer could not count them all, but he thought there might be as many as twenty.

Connelly wasn't the only one who should get back in his car.

"Chief!" Connelly called.

Kramer jumped onto the hood but his wounded leg gave way beneath him. He collapsed onto the rain-slicked metal and rolled off onto the ground, pain shooting through his leg. His elbow smashed down onto the pavement and his gun spun free, sliding several feet through the driving rain.

He heard the dogs howling, yipping in savage victory, and knew he would feel their teeth any moment. Connelly yelled for him, came run-ning, and popped off a couple of shots. And where the hell was Moschitto? Still in the goddamn car, which was fine when his chief wasn't about to get torn apart by a pack of wild dogs, the son of a bitch.

Kramer scrambled for his gun, pain searing his leg and his elbow— had he cracked bone?—and as he reached for it, he looked up into the sickly yellow eyes of a Doberman. It snarled, lips drawing back to reveal teeth stained with blood, strings of raw flesh caught in its jaws. It had already killed tonight, this dog.

He lunged for the gun. The Doberman shot forward, jaws opening.

Connelly shot it twice, then started firing at the others, but there were too many of them. Far too many. They slammed into Connelly, jaws flashing, claws raking his flesh, dragging him down to the ground as they drove their snouts into the soft places, his throat and his stomach, and began to rip him open. Kramer retrieved his gun and tried to help, but after just a few shots the weapon clicked on an empty chamber.

They were both going to die.

Headlights washed over the dogs, backlighting them, revealing how many there truly were, and he wondered if what he was seeing was every dog in Hawthorne. Then tires skidded to a halt, spraying an arc of rainwater. Some of the dogs turned toward the new arrival, others merely hesitated, but that hesitation was enough.

The car's front doors opened and two people stepped out. The dogs were on them instantly. Snarling, jaws snapping, they attacked the pretty redhead on the passenger side, biting and clawing. Chief Kramer shouted, frantic, thinking she would go down in a mass of undulating fur and tearing flesh like Connelly. Instead, she began to kill them, picking up a collie and snapping its neck, grabbing a bulldog and smashing it against the pavement. Blood—hers and the dogs'—mixed with the rain.

The driver of the car did not fight the dogs. He destroyed them. Tall and grim as a reaper, already soaked with rain, he put out his hands and brilliant golden light erupted from his palms. Like Zeus's lightning bolts, he hurled that crackling fire at the dogs nearest to him and they were incinerated where they stood, flaking away to cinder and ash in seconds. Others ran at him, but now he made his hands into fists and the golden light vanished, replaced by a strange pink glow that made Kramer think of something being born.

The man dropped to a crouch and slapped his palms onto the pavement. That pink glow spread out in all directions and a shock wave traveled beneath the street, jarring Kramer and shaking the cars, cracking glass and setting off alarms. The dogs were all thrown to the ground by the tremor, but the man—the magician—kept walking.

As the dogs tried to rise, the magician contorted his fingers, muttered something that sounded more like a growl of his own, and then opened his arms wide, still striding among them.

"Sleep," he said.

And the dogs obeyed. They crumpled to the ground, deep in slumber, innocent as newborn pups. Two of them had somehow been out of range of his influence, and they darted into the alley, fleeing from the magician. He put out one hand, fingers hooked into a claw, and blue lightning arced from his empty grasp and froze the animals where they stood. In the rain, Kramer could not tell if they had become stone or ice, or somehow been frozen as flesh and blood, and he did not want to know.

The magician stood over him, reached down a hand to help him up.

"From the insignia on your vehicle, I take it you're the chief of police."

"Don Kramer," the chief said, taking the offered hand and rising to his feet, limping badly on his wounded leg.

The redheaded girl came over to join them, her clothes torn and soaked through with blood and rain, but otherwise somehow unharmed. She smiled brightly, as though greeting an old friend. The girl had perfect lips. A beautiful smile. Her fangs gleamed in the headlight glare from the car she'd arrived in.

"Hi," the vampire said. "I'm Charlotte."

"Peter Octavian," the magician said, nodding in greeting.

"I know who you are," Chief Kramer told him. He glanced around at the sleeping dogs. "Who the hell else *could* you be?"

"I wish I hadn't had to kill some of them," Octavian said, looking at the place where he'd gotten out of his car with real regret.

Tony Moschitto chose that moment to finally get out of his patrol car. Gun out, he walked carefully among the sleeping dogs, then stared in fear and wonder at Octavian and Charlotte.

"I've come to offer what help I can, Chief," Octavian said. "You've got chaos magic building up in Hawthorne, and if we can't figure out where it's coming from, it's only going to get worse."

Kramer had seen video footage of some of the places Octavian had shown up to help. He had often wondered if the magician and his associates kept things from getting worse, or if their presence made them worse. He supposed he was going to find out. After what he had seen tonight—black wraiths wielding curved daggers, people driven to try to kill each other, massive animal attacks—he had known something unnatural was unfolding in Hawthorne . . . something he didn't have the knowledge or experience to combat. Octavian did, which meant that he would have to roll the dice.

"I hope to God you know what you're doing, Mr. Octavian," Chief Kramer said, glancing again at the dogs. "Have you made any headway figuring this all out? How long until things get back to normal?"

"We're working on it, Chief," Octavian told him, pushing back his rain-soaked hair. "But I can almost guarantee that it's going to get a lot worse by the time we figure out how to stop it. If we haven't sorted it out by noon tomorrow, I'd recommend you evacuate the town."

Kramer cringed. "The mayor will never go for it."

Charlotte laughed. "Maybe not tonight. But ask him again over lunch. If this stuff keeps getting worse, he won't have much choice."

"It'll have to get better once the sun is up, won't it?" Kramer asked. "Isn't that the way this stuff—evil, dark magic, all of that—usually works?"

"Sometimes it does, and sometimes it doesn't," Octavian said, his eyes cold. "But look at the sky, Chief. The night's only going to last a couple more hours, but that doesn't mean the sun is going to come out today. Whatever happens next, I suspect we'll be doing all of our fighting in the dark."

———————— ✳ ————————

10

Amber stands in the hot rain and stares up into the eye of the storm. The clouds swirl into a dark, undulating whirlpool in the sky, as though a hole has been punched through the atmosphere and the storm is pouring into space, bleeding chaos out into the universe. Her face upturned, she revels in the hot rain, in the baptism of anarchy that blesses her anew with every drop.

Voices are raised around her, some in pain and some in terror, some in anguish and some in worship. With a silent laugh, she glances at the clock tower jutting up from the town hall and sees the goddess there, her arms raised to the storm, which even now washes away the blood of her victims. Wraiths dart through the air above her, riding the wind currents, and they open their mouths and vomit blood and gore down upon their goddess like diabolical crows feeding their babies. The goddess opens her mouth and accepts the offering, swallowing what she can and allowing the rest to splash her face and sluice down over her breasts and arms and belly.

Amber shudders at the sight. She blinks, trying to remember who she is, and why she is here. Shaking, she glances to either side and finds that she is flanked by skeletal wraiths clothed in tatters of black smoke, their carapace faces blank and cruel, all grasping those deadly, curved blades. Terror blooms instantly within her, and yet the wraiths seem not to notice her at all.

The goddess screams, her voice a cacophony, a thousand maniacs shrieking in disharmony. Other wraiths dart down from the storm, dragging fluttering creatures of iridescent light on the blades of their scythes. They feed the goddess, who is greedier with these gifts, gobbling them down without wasting so much as a strand of that light. The blood she had thirsted for was as nothing compared to her desire for these shifting, glowing treasures.

It is an abomination. Amber can barely stand the sight of this hideous devouring. Despite the fear that infuses her very essence, she must do something. Yet as she tries to move, to slip away from the wraiths clustered around her, she realizes that she holds something clutched in her hands and that she cannot seem to unclench her fingers. Her limbs are stiff and aching, and she looks down to find the source of her discomfort.

She is nude. Her skin is a black so dark it is blue, a terrible indigo that has hardened and cracked at the joints, a carapace beginning to form around her muscle and bone. In her hands, she grips the handles of twin ebony scythes.

Amber throws her head back and screams into the storm, hot rain spattering her skin . . . yet it is not her skin anymore.

When her voice is raw and her scream dies, she is startled by the silence around her. Save for the wind and the rain, she hears nothing, but she can feel their attention on her. Staggered by the weight of the dread that bears down upon her, she gazes around in expectation that the wraiths are about to descend upon her with their blades flashing. Instead, she sees the goddess up on her ledge on top of the clock tower . . . and watches the hideous queen of chaos fall to her knees and reach downward with the yearning of a spurned lover.

The wraiths shuffle aside, opening up a path among them. On the wind-and-rain-swept pavement their parting has revealed dead dogs and cats and the skeletons of birds. There are human bodies, though only a very few, ruined and trampled. From beyond the cluster of adoring wraiths comes a solitary human figure, a burly man with his eyes downcast. He walks as though his limbs are controlled by some invisible puppeteer, feet lifting and falling, knees bending . . . and he never looks up.

In his arms he carries some sort of offering, and Amber understands immediately that this is the thing for which the goddess has yearned. As the man staggers closer, Amber shifts, feeling her stiff limbs grow light as mist, becoming intangible for a moment before coalescing once again.

In his arms he carries a small iron box, strangely shaped, its locks broken.

No rain falls upon the man or the box, as though the storm hesitates to touch him.

The man raises his eyes at last to gaze upon the goddess, and Amber gets a look at his face, realizing that she knows him.

Norm Dunne, her friend Tommy's father.

He falls to his knees and places the iron chest on the cracked pavement. The moment he is no longer touching it, the rain punishes him for letting go, the storm beating down upon him. Norm lowers his face until he can rest his forehead on the street, and his body shakes until Amber understands that he is sobbing.

The wraiths begin to surround him, slowly encroaching upon him, their blades gleaming wetly in the rain.

Amber wants to scream again, but she has lost control of her own limbs. Instead, she finds herself drifting toward him along with the others. Her hands lift of their own accord, her black scythes thrusting ahead of her. She tries to hold them back, but they pull at her like hungry dogs struggling to be unleashed, and she knows they will not be satisfied—that she will not be sated—until they are stained with Norman Dunne's blood.

The buzzing of her alarm clock invaded Amber's slumber, insinuating itself into the fog of her sleeping mind and growing in irritation until, at last, her eyes opened into narrow slits. With a frown, she let her brain sift through the sounds around her. Yes, the alarm clock buzzed, which was strange since she had it set to *RADIO*. Instead, it emitted a crackling static drone. The rain still beat down upon the roof and pelted the windows, but now it sounded more like sleet. The storm made the timbers of the house groan, as if its foundations were barely able to stay buried in the ground.

She took a deep breath and glanced at the window, wondering for a moment why everything seemed so off. So wrong. Then she had it—beyond her gauzy white drapes, through the glass, the darkness remained. Her alarm clock showed that 7:30 a.m. had come and gone, but the sky had lightened only a few shades, from night-black to the deepest storm-gray.

The idea of dragging her ass out of bed and going to class made her want to bury her head under the pillows. She had begun to do that very thing when her mind at last reached a state of wakefulness full enough that the details of the previous day returned to her, and she froze. Fragments of her dreams and visions flashed across her mind. She remembered the thing she had seen in her house last night, and her certainty that she would never be able to fall asleep after such a fright. Obviously she had managed it, but doubted she'd had more than four hours' sleep, all told.

Get up, she told herself. *Do something.*

The idea almost made her laugh. She was a college kid. What the hell could one twenty-one-year-old girl do against the kind of evil she knew was brewing in Hawthorne? If the things from her visions were now stalking the real world, all she wanted to do was run and hide, or maybe scream.

But it was here. In my house. And her family lived in that house. They were all in danger, and so were most of her friends. Something had to be done. If she let fear get in her way, she might as well surrender their lives, and her own life as well, to the ancient evil poisoning Hawthorne.

She slapped a hand down on the alarm clock, silencing the buzz, and threw back her sheets. Her mother had left a basket of clean and folded laundry next to the bed, and she dug through it and yanked out a pair of blue jeans and a dark red top. Stripping out of her T-shirt and panties, she put on clean underwear and then the clothes she'd selected. She slipped her feet into scuffed black lace-up shoes—in this storm, flip-flops just weren't going to do the job.

At her bureau, she grabbed an elastic and tied her hair back into a ponytail. A quick glance in the mirror revealed dark circles beneath her eyes, evidence of a night of limited and fitful sleep.

In the midst of the sound of the rain on the window came another sound, a scritch-scratch noise that might have been a branch scraping the glass, bent by the wind, if there had been a tree that close to the house. Amber studied the reflection of her bedroom window in the mirror, seeing only darkness and rivulets of rain sliding down the glass. She realized she had stopped breathing and forced herself to exhale, then inhale. She couldn't let her fear get the better of her before she even left the house.

In the mirror, she saw something move.

Amber spun and saw the face outside the window, the flat, black, expressionless countenance of a wraith.

Her hand reached out and snatched her hairbrush from the bureau. Instead of fear, rage surged up inside of her and she hurled the brush at the window, screaming at the creature to go away. The brush thunked into the window frame and fell to the carpet, even as the wraith slithered away.

Amber ran to the window and looked out to see it clinging to the outside of the house, the tatters of its clothing half-mist and half-fabric. Where it had hidden its blades she could not tell, but it clung to the siding like a salamander. As she studied it, the wraith glided upward, crawling toward the third floor, where her Gran would be sleeping.

"No," she said. "No way."

Her fear returned, but this was not fear for herself. It was fear for the old woman whose words she found so difficult to understand, but whose love for her family had always been in evidence.

Amber bolted from the room, frantic, her heart thudding in her chest as she mounted the steps to her great-grandmother's attic apartment. *Not Gran,* she thought. *You can't have her.*

She thought of all the times Gran had cooked for her, and taken care of her when she was little, and sat in her chair knitting while Amber watched whatever foolish TV show had been her favorite that month. Gran liked soap operas and the Three Stooges, and would laugh at both, which had always made Amber laugh, too. Fear carved into her heart and squeezed the air from her lungs, and she took the stairs two at a time until she burst onto the landing at the top of the stairs and saw that Gran's bedroom door was slightly ajar.

She nudged it open and hurried in as quietly as she could manage.

Gran snored. Sometimes it annoyed the hell out of Amber, but this morning it was the most beautiful sound she had ever heard. The old woman lay on her bed, deep in slumber, snoring deeply. The gray light of the storm-shrouded day filtered through the curtains, but there was no trace of the wraith. Still, it wasn't until Amber hurried to the window—careful not to tread too heavily for fear of waking Gran—that she managed to exhale. The wraith had been on this side of the house. She saw no sign of the thing now, but was it still out there?

Only one way to know.

She hustled down two flights of stairs, flung open the front door, and ran out into the rain. Turning, she began to scan the outside of the house, but even as she did so, she felt the rain on her face and arms and shuddered in revulsion, as though what poured down out of the storm was the blood of innocents. As in her visions, the rain felt hot. It soaked through her shirt and slid down her skin, and she wanted to run from it.

But first she had to make sure her family was safe, so she made a quick circuit of the house, moving back far enough that she could see all of the windows and even the roof. She saw no sign of the wraith, but now it felt as though there were eyes upon her and she spun around and looked at the roofs of nearby houses and the branches of trees and the power lines that were strung along the street. Nothing.

But in the distance, above the twin spires of the church's bell tower and city hall's clock tower, the sky swirled inward and upward, as though the storm were draining into some upper level of the atmosphere. Amber froze, terrified of what she might find if she were to go downtown and approach the clock tower.

No, she told herself. *I won't be going there. Not for anything.*

There could be no hiding from this now. The whole world knew that real evil existed, and that dark magic could destroy lives and poison whole peoples. But a small town like Hawthorne was used to its own tiny evils, its small bits of dark intention that sprang from human nature. Real evil, the sort that might tear down all of their hopes and dreams and steal their souls, destroy their lives, didn't happen here. This was Hawthorne, Massachusetts. It just didn't.

Yet now it had. And Amber knew things about it that she wasn't sure anyone else knew. Her visions had to mean something, and that meant she had to act. But would people like the mayor and the police chief have admitted to themselves by now that what they faced was dark magic? Real evil? She wasn't sure. She should call the police, or go to the station, but she realized that the first people with whom she needed to share her fears were her parents.

Skin stinging from the hot rain, she went back into the house and ran up to her room, pulled on a dry shirt, and spent a moment searching her closet for a raincoat, without luck.

Quiet as she had tried to be because of the early hour, she felt sure she had made enough noise to rouse her parents, but when she went to their room she found they had not stirred. Frowning, she approached their bed. Sometime during the night they had moved together, her father spooning her mother from behind, one arm thrown over her, his face nuzzled against the back of her neck. She had a moment to think of this image as sweetly romantic.

And then she narrowed her eyes and studied the arm that her father had around her mother. She had attributed its dark hue to the gloom of the stormy morning filtering through the curtains, but as she moved closer, she saw something that startled her so badly she froze on the spot. The arm had no hair on it. It had become thinner overnight. At the elbow was a visible joint, the skin clinging so tightly to the bone that it seemed more like a shell.

Like the carapace of an insect or a crustacean.

"Daddy?" Amber whispered, feeling like a little girl again . . . a little girl trapped in a nightmare from which her parents could not save her.

She inched closer. Her father's forearm had turned so dark it was nearly black. And that bruise-black flesh had spread. She saw her mother's bare foot sticking out from beneath the covers, and it had also changed. Amber's breath came in tiny, ragged sips and she began to shake her head in denial. Yet she could not accept it, even then.

Not until she saw their faces in profile, and realized that all signs of age had gone away. Their skin had begun to smooth and harden and darken.

And they no longer had mouths.

Amber screamed and staggered away from the bed, turned and fled from the room and the house, thinking of the police. Chief Kramer. He and his cops—some of them people she had known her whole life—wouldn't be able to do a fucking thing, but the chief would know what to do. Who to call. Dark magic had poisoned Hawthorne—*it's poisoned me!*—and it had to be stopped before her parents had been transformed completely. That had to be what was happening to them, she knew. There could be no mistaking it—the thinning of the limbs, the coloring, the carapace—they were turning into wraiths, just like the one she had seen slithering on the outside of the house, and the one in the corridor the night before.

And then it struck her, hardest of all—that in her dream this morning, *she* had been one of those things. Amber thrust her hands out and stared at them, pushed up the sleeves of her jacket and felt her skin. She reached up to feel the contours of her face.

I'm still me, she thought. But for how long?

With a glance upstairs, she wondered how she could help Gran. Her parents were sleeping—her scream hadn't woken them, so maybe they would keep sleeping until they had been completely changed—but how was she supposed to get Gran out of the house?

Then it struck her that Gran hadn't woken either. She'd screamed so loud that there was no way the old woman hadn't heard her, no way that it wouldn't have roused her from her bed if she had been capable of getting up. Amber hadn't gotten a good look at her skin beneath that bedspread, but a dreadful certainty filled her now, and she knew what she would find.

"Oh, no," she whispered to herself, feeling more alone than ever.

She whipped out her cell phone and tried it, but couldn't get a signal. Running to the kitchen, she picked up the house phone to find it dead, not so much as a busy signal. Just blunt nothingness.

There was nothing else she could do, except run. She tapped her pocket to make sure she had her keys. Her car was still parked back on campus. Ben was supposed to drive her back to pick it up, but she had a key to her father's Jetta, and he sure as hell wouldn't be using it today. She raced out into the hot, oily rain for a second time.

She slammed the door behind her, twisted it to make sure it had locked, and then turned to sprint to her father's car, colliding with someone who grabbed at her as they fell in a tangle of arms and legs, hot breath on her neck. Amber screamed, thinking a wraith had come for her, but then she felt ordinary human skin and the touch of gentle hands, and she focused on the face above her.

"Amber," Miles Varick said. "It's all right. It's me."

His eyes were red from exhaustion or tears or both, but he was not a wraith. Not a monster. Just a man.

"Professor Varick," she breathed. "Oh, thank God."

"You're okay," he said, and it sounded like a promise. "But we need to talk."

Keomany woke to feel a gentle hand brushing her hair away from her face, and a soft voice telling her it was time to get up. A purr of contentment rumbled in her chest and she nestled deeper under the covers for a moment, her subconscious chasing the strands of a dream that had been deliciously carnal. Then she heard another voice—a girl's voice—and her brow furrowed.

"Kem, rise and shine," the male voice said again, a pleasingly sexy rasp.

Coming further awake, she stiffened with recognition and opened her eyes. Peter Octavian sat on the edge of her bed, smiling the lop-sided grin that always made something inside her give a little growl. Keomany didn't have romantic feelings about Octavian—he was with Nikki, so there was no point—but he spent so much time under the weight of grim thoughts that when that grin appeared, it radiated warmth and charm and a swagger that was unmistakably sexual.

"I hate to wake you," Octavian said, his gray eyes dark, the silver flecks swirling as though caught in a storm, "but we have a lot to catch up on, and a meeting with the chief of police in half an hour."

"What time is it?" she asked.

"Just after seven."

Keomany stretched, belatedly realizing she was barely covered. During the night she had kicked off the bedspread and the sheet now veiled only one leg, leaving the rest of her clad only in skimpy pink panties and a T-shirt that her nighttime squirming had twisted up around her.

"Oh, shit," she said, laughing uneasily. "Sorry."

As she yanked up the sheet to cover herself, she looked past Octavian toward the sliding glass door that led to the hotel room's tiny balcony. Charlotte stood there, her clothes tattered and torn, the ruin of her top leaving very little to the imagination. Her bright red hair was dark against the dour gray morning beyond. The vampire girl watched her with a sliver of a smile, as though she suspected Keomany's exposure had been no accident. Keomany wanted to protest the presumption, but knew that she would only draw Octavian's attention to her discomfort, and did not want to do that.

Get a grip, woman, she thought. *It's Peter. He's your friend. And so is Nikki.*

That was true enough, but between the dream she'd just woken from, the overall absence of any physical intimacy in her life, and Octavian sitting there on the edge of her bed, she had to work to remind herself. Maybe it would have been easier for her to dispel the frisson of erotic tension with which she had woken if she had not caught Octavian, in that moment before she covered herself, casting an appreciative glance along her body.

"I need a shower," she said.

Charlotte laughed, exposing her fangs. "I'll say you do."

Octavian shot her a hard look. "What's that supposed to mean?"

Charlotte blinked, stung. "Nothing."

Keomany arched an eyebrow, wondering if he was being coy or if he really didn't understand the crack, couldn't sense the strange dynamic he had created by rousing her from sleep. Men always missed that sort of thing, but Octavian had been born in the fifteenth century—surely he must have learned something about women in all that time. If not, all the better for Keomany. The last thing she wanted was for him to get the wrong idea and mistake her being flustered for some profound attraction.

"I'm just teasing her," Charlotte added.

"Well, don't," Octavian said, standing and moving away from the bed. "If you're with us in this thing, then you're with us. Time is short, and there's nothing funny about the night we just had, or the situation this town is in."

He turned to Keomany. "How's your hand?"

Her brow furrowed. She'd forgotten all about it. Flexing her fingers, she smiled.

"Right as rain," she said.

Octavian nodded. "Excellent."

Keomany rose from bed, wrapping the sheet around her waist. Again she studied Charlotte's clothes and felt a twinge of jealousy as she wondered about the night Octavian and the vampire girl had spent together.

"Maybe you should tell me about last night," she said. "How is it you ended up half naked?"

Charlotte nodded, but without a trace of a smile. She seemed to have taken Octavian's instruction seriously. She crossed her arms and leaned against the wall next to the rain-pattered window.

"More of those spooky black smoke dudes," Charlotte said. "Plus all the dogs in town went rabid. Then half a dozen kids set their houses on fire, pretty much at the same instant, with their families inside. Kept us busy. The rain of toads didn't help."

Keomany gave her a withering look. "Rain of toads? Really?"

Octavian stood at the foot of the bed. "She's not joking. I wish she were. They rotted down to almost nothing and were washed away by the rain, but the damage was significant. I'm just glad it happened at night."

"Holy shit," Keomany whispered.

"Yeah," Charlotte said. "Long night. And don't get me started on the wasps."

"Wasps?"

"Roving swarms," Octavian confirmed. "Although now that it's morning, I haven't seen any. There's no sun to speak of out there, but it's still there, behind the clouds. Hopefully the chaos will wane during the day."

It's still there, behind the clouds. The words made her think of Gaea, and the way she could feel the goddess in the distance, the purity of nature just out of her reach.

Troubled, Keomany cinched the bedsheet more tightly around her waist, gathering it up so she wouldn't trip over it as she moved toward the bathroom.

"Look, let me take a quick shower. I'll throw my hair in a ponytail and put some clothes on and we'll go talk to the police. On the way you can explain how it is we've got a meeting with the chief, and what you've got planned."

"Fair enough," Octavian said.

"Actually," Charlotte began, "I was sort of hoping you might have something I could wear."

Keomany studied her ruined clothes.

"I'm sure I've got something," she said.

The gratitude in Charlotte's eyes was startling. Keomany went to her travel bag and rooted around, pulling out a fitted white T-shirt and a pair of dark brown jeans. She herself could wear the ones she'd had on the night before, which she had hung over a chair to dry. She tossed Charlotte the clothes and the vampire mumbled her thanks.

The girl had not been a vampire very long and retained most of what Keomany imagined must have been her human personality. She tried to be tough and sexy, all sharp edges and attitude, but within her was a girl who could feel awkward and lonely, and at last Keomany understood why Octavian had kept her with him all night. It wasn't only that he wanted to keep track of her, to protect Hawthorne from a rogue vampire. He wanted to protect Charlotte, too, from the world, and from the savage hunger that she had confessed was gnawing at her.

That, too, seemed to have abated somewhat with the day.

"You've had blood," Keomany said, staring at her.

Charlotte glanced away, embarrassed. "The dogs went crazy, killing people. We had to put them down."

Keomany wished she hadn't asked.

"Peter, why don't you go back into your room?" she suggested. "We'll be ready in just a few minutes, and then we'll head to the police station."

Octavian glanced back and forth between them, as if it worried him to think of leaving Keomany and Charlotte alone together. After a moment, he relented, and went through the connecting door into his own hotel room, closing it behind him.

Keomany headed for the bathroom, but stopped just inside and looked back out at Charlotte, who had already stripped off the torn remnants of her shirt.

"Those should fit," Keomany said. "If you need a brush or any-thing—"

"I'm good," Charlotte said, cutting her off. She stood in her blood-stained bra and pants, a strange look on her face, liked she'd just discovered something deeply unpleasant. "Thanks for the loan, but we're not, like, girlfriends now or something."

"Okay," Keomany said. "Thanks for clearing that up."

She started to close the bathroom door.

"And don't worry," Charlotte added. "If you want to jump the magi-cian's bones, I won't get in the way. He's way too old for me."

As Charlotte pulled on the white T-shirt, Keomany froze, staring at her, wondering how much truth there was in the presumption. After a moment, she decided the answer was none at all.

"It isn't like that. He's a good man, and easy on the eyes. But he's involved with someone else. We're just friends," Keomany insisted.

Charlotte sneered her doubt. "Yeah. Keep telling yourself that."

"He's your friend now, too," Keomany said. "After the night you just had ... trial by fire, right? That forges something between people."

"I'm a vampire," Charlotte said, as she slipped out of her ruined pants and reached for the clean brown jeans, steadfastly refusing to meet Keomany's gaze. "That pretty much means I don't have any friends."

Keomany had liked Charlotte almost from the moment they'd met. This morning, she had found the girl's sharpness irritating, but she saw the pain beneath the attitude, saw the girl who had turned nineteen only this year, before a vampire had ended her old life and transformed her into something new.

"That's not true," Keomany told her.

Charlotte rolled her eyes.

"Seriously, Charlotte. That kind of thinking comes from Cortez. The guy who murdered the old you. It's what makes you a rogue. But you don't have to stay a rogue. The truth is, if you don't think it's possible for you to have friends, you're probably going to die again very soon. Forever, this time."

Charlotte seemed like she might think that wasn't a terrible idea, and for a moment, Keomany thought she would say so. But then the vampire girl zipped and buttoned her pants and went to retrieve the sodden shoes she had slipped off before changing, and the moment had passed.

Keomany closed the door, turned the water on in the shower, and as it began to steam up the bathroom, she tried not to think about how easily a vampire with trust issues could get them all killed.

Miles Varick sat behind the wheel of his car and let Amber's story sink in. In the passenger seat, the girl shuddered and fidgeted as though she wanted to run, not to get away from him but just to be running . . . to be doing something to escape the unnatural horror that was spreading through Hawthorne. But he knew she would not run—not with her parents and great-grandmother still in the house and somehow under the influence of the dark goddess from her visions.

There in the stillness of the car, windows veiled by the driving rain, which pounded on the roof and the hood with such force that the noise made him want to scream just to drown it out, they shared their terrors. Miles told his student about the black wraith-thing that had ripped the life from his mother, and Amber told her professor about seeing one of them inside her house, and another outside this morning. But what stunned Miles the most was her revelation about the transformation her parents seemed to be undergoing.

Sometime during this exchange of fears, they ceased being professor and student. Miles took a long breath and turned to study Amber. He had long since recognized the bond of friendship—a thing he had rarely felt for his students in the past. That was why he had been so concerned about her yesterday, and why she had called him last night. But now they were allies as well. Whatever happened next, they were in this together.

"So, what now, Professor?" Amber asked, emotion choking her voice. "We've got to do something. I can't just . . . I can't let this happen to my parents."

Miles thought about his mother, images of her murder flashing in his mind. He blinked hard, trying to force the memory away, but any time he closed his eyes the images only became more vivid and horrible.

"A lot of people must be suffering in Hawthorne, right now," he said. "And maybe beyond. The phones are out. On the way over here I saw a lot of people packing up and getting out of town. I hope they manage to leave, but I have a terrible feeling that whatever power is behind all of this, it won't want to let them go."

Amber stared at him. "We need to go to the police. Talk to Chief Kramer."

"I've been friends with Don Kramer most of my life," he replied. "But think about it, Amber. What do we have to tell him that he hasn't already heard from dozens of other people? I'm sure my mother isn't the only person these wraith-things have killed."

He hesitated a moment, a fresh wave of grief sweeping over him. Amber must have seen his pain, because she reached out and squeezed his hand. Something passed between them. Miles took comfort and strength from her, but they both seemed somehow calmer. He tightened his own grip on her hand and nodded, searching her eyes. The inside of his car seemed to grow smaller. In the stillness, surrounded by the roar of the rain on the roof and hood and trunk, they breathed each other's air. In their fear, a strange but intense intimacy was born.

"I can't do nothing, Professor," she said.

"Miles," he said. "This isn't a classroom, Amber. This is life and death. Call me Miles."

She nodded. "All right, Miles. If not the police, then what do we do? My parents are turning into monsters. And my Gran looks like she's in some kind of weird coma."

"You've been having these visions . . . both awake and asleep . . . since yesterday morning," he said. "It's possible that some of these bizarre phenomena manifested prior to the first one, but none that I know of. Whatever set off this chain of events, it may have begun that same moment."

"But why me?" Amber asked.

"The only way to answer that is to start deciphering your visions. But every moment that passes, these things are out there preying on people, so we need to be smart about it. From what you've told me, I don't think there's any doubt that the goddess in your visions is the source of this chaos."

"Navalica," Amber said, her gaze distant as she recalled her visions.

"We have to find out whatever we can about her."

"If the phones are down, I'm betting the Internet is, too," she said. "You're talking about what, going to the library, poring through textbooks and stuff? We don't have time for that. It could take all day. How many people are going to be dead by then? My parents are . . . I can't just leave them like that."

"What choice do we have?" Miles replied. "And what good are you going to be able to do them if you stay here? Without knowledge of how this is all happening, and what we're up against, we have no hope of stopping it. Stopping her, if this Navalica really is responsible."

"She is," Amber said grimly. But then he saw a hopeful spark in her eyes. "But maybe there's a more direct way to get answers. Remember I told you about the fisherman I dreamed about this morning? The one bringing that box as, like, an offering to Navalica?"

"Some kind of iron chest," Miles said. "But you said you didn't know what was in it. If you could describe it in detail, there might be clues—"

"I'm not talking about the box. I'm talking about the man," Amber said. "Norman Dunne. His son, Tommy, is a friend of mine."

Miles started the car, the engine growling to life. She was right. Research might be their only hope, but if there was a faster way to the answers they needed . . .

"Where does he live?" he asked.

"Head for the hospital," Amber replied, putting on her seat belt. "His father had a heart attack yesterday. I saw Tommy when I was leaving, after I'd had my seizure. I'm betting his dad is still there."

Miles gripped the wheel, eyes narrowing as something clicked into place, like the tumblers of a lock lining up.

"When, yesterday?"

"What?"

He turned to stare at her. "When did your friend's father have his heart attack? Yesterday morning, you said, but do you know when, exactly?"

"Why would I know that?"

Miles put the car in gear and pulled away from the curb in front of Amber's house. "If you saw him at the hospital right after your seizure, maybe Norman Dunne had his heart attack at the same time. According to your vision, he's connected to Navalica. Maybe he had a seizure, too. Or something else."

"Like what?"

"Let's find out."

11

Tommy Dunne was sick of the damn rain. On weekends and during bad storms he often slept until ten or eleven in the morning. During high school there had been Saturdays when he had stayed in bed until long after lunchtime had come and gone. But working with his father had gotten him into the habit of rising before dawn, which helped this morning. He had slept poorly and woken to find the weather had not improved. If anything, it had worsened.

Last night, his father had collapsed in his hospital room. What he had been doing out of bed in the first place, Tommy had no idea, but he spent the night worrying. Instead of recovering from his heart attack, the old man seemed to be getting worse. According to the doctor he'd talked to just before going home last night, his father's heart functions showed continued strain, but they were having trouble determining the cause. The doc had suggested it might be nothing but stress, but stress sure as hell hadn't caused the initial heart attack, so that didn't seem to make a hell of a lot of sense.

Before his collapse, Norm Dunne had told his son to get back out into the water. Tommy expected nothing less. They were working fishermen, which meant if they weren't out on the water, catching something they could sell, there wouldn't be money to keep food on the table or a roof over their heads. Worse yet, the insurance Norm paid too much for every month was going to cover only a portion of his hospital stay and treatment. Tommy knew his father would be worrying about that more than anything, even his own health. But he couldn't have taken the boat out yesterday afternoon—not with the way the tide had receded so far from shore. And though the tide had come back in during the night, the seas were so rough that he knew he would never be able to take her out by himself.

In his heart, Tommy was happy to have the excuse. He didn't give a shit about fish, or about the bills, or even the insurance. All he cared about was his dad. They had not always seen eye to eye, but without a mother in his life, his old man was all he had. He had never thought about it before, but thinking about his father having a heart attack—maybe dying—had made him understand that Norm Dunne wasn't just his father, but his best friend. For a kid who'd rolled his eyes a thousand times at things his father had said, it had been a startling epiphany. But his father had been the one constant in his life. They were together through everything. The idea of losing him was almost too much to handle.

After a fitful night's sleep, Tommy had woken just after 5 a.m. He had rolled over and closed his eyes and waited, but sleep never returned, and so he had risen and made himself scrambled eggs and toast, showered and eaten breakfast, all the while watching the clock and waiting for visiting hours to begin at the hospital. But patience had never been his strong suit. He needed to see his father, to reassure himself that the fears that he had nursed overnight were unjustified.

The windshield wipers swept sheets of rain off the glass as he pulled into the visitors' parking lot. The hospital seemed dark, but he thought it must only be the gloom of the stormy morning—surely if they had lost power, they would have evacuated the patients and someone would have notified him. The phone hadn't rung—not at home, and not his cell. Tommy parked and dug out his cell phone. Flipping it open, he saw that he had no signal at all, and the anxiety that had plagued him all night began to gnaw at his insides.

He climbed out of the car and slammed the door, pocketing his keys and phone. As he ran for the shelter of the building, the rain felt hot and oily on his skin. It gave him the creeps.

Sirens wailed, cutting through the roar and gust of the storm. Tommy glanced back and saw an ambulance headed for the emergency room doors, where two others sat silently, their lights flash-ing. For the first time he noticed the people hurrying back and forth from the open doors—doctors and EMTs moving patients on gur-neys—and he wondered if that kind of ER traffic was normal. Even as the thought crossed his mind, he heard another siren rising in the distance.

Then he had to get out of the hot rain. The doors slid open and he went into the lobby, where he stopped to blink in surprise at the number of people there. The benches and seats were all taken, and maybe two dozen people stood around the information desk. Others were passing through, whole families headed for the elevators. A few uniformed police officers were positioned in the lobby, and Tommy saw Lisa Landry—a reporter for the *Hawthorne Letter* interviewing a fortyish black woman with a bruised face and a bloodstained blouse. A guy with a fancy camera, complete with a huge flash contraption, was taking photos of the two women, and Tommy figured he must also work for the paper.

Some strange shit had gone down in Hawthorne yesterday, but from the looks of the hospital lobby, the night had been much worse. And if the lobby looked like this, he couldn't help but wonder how crammed the waiting rooms must be, never mind the ER.

This is nuts, he thought, cutting through the throng and making his way to the elevator. There were so many people waiting that he couldn't get on the first one and had to jam in with a large group to claim a spot on the second. Only when he had reached the fourth floor, where his father's room was, and bypassed the waiting area, did he manage to escape the foot traffic.

Tommy had always thought of hospitals as torture chambers. He'd had food poisoning once and been brought to the emergency room, where they had put him on one of those awful beds in which it was impossible to get comfortable. They'd given him drugs to stop him from puking and a saline IV to rehydrate him, but after the first hour he felt certain he would rather have been dry-heaving blood and stom-ach acid if it meant not having to spend another minute in that bed.

Torture.

As he strode down the corridor he found himself paying more attention than usual to the people around him. Visiting hours wouldn't start for twenty minutes or so, but no one bothered to try to stop him. The nurses all looked troubled and some of them were obviously exhausted, their eyes punctuated with dark circles and their faces slack. There were orderlies whose expressions were closed off and grim, one of them with a nasty shiner. Something about them troubled Tommy, and it took him a few seconds to realize what it was—they were too damn quiet. They were all going about their duties like the walking wounded, like they had seen things they wished they hadn't and were haunted by them.

Somewhere nearby, a cell phone began to trill. Machines beeped. He glanced into rooms as he passed and saw that where there had been empty beds the previous evening, there were no longer any vacancies. Did his father have a new roommate? Probably.

His shoe slipped on something and he flung out his arms, just managing to keep his balance. When he turned to see what he had slipped in, his nose wrinkled in disgust. *Looks like piss. Smells like piss, too.* And that last item was weird, considering how often people moved through these corridors with mops and disinfectants, making the whole place smell like medicine and death.

With all of these troubling thoughts swirling in his head, he reached the door to his father's room and froze, trying to make sense of the tableau before him. His father shouldn't be out of bed. The doctors were trying to figure out why his heart kept racing and seizing. Unless he'd undergone a drastic change in his condition, he should be laid up, attached to machines . . .

Tommy stared, his brain allowing him to see it all now.

His father was still attached to the machines. Some of the monitors had pulled off his skin. The machines had been silenced, but their readouts were flashing alarming colors. Norm Dunne stood with his back to the door, dressed in pajamas that Tommy had brought from home. In his hands, he held a metal IV stand, and as Tommy looked on, his father raised it over his head like a hatchet and brought it down.

Norm Dunne had gotten a roommate overnight after all. And now he was trying to kill the man.

"Jesus, Dad, no!" Tommy shouted.

But the IV stand came down again, this time with a sickening crunch, and when Norm swung it upward, droplets of blood flew from the metal. The old Hispanic guy in the bed groaned and began to pant like a dog, maybe the only noise he could make—full of pain and terror and desperate sorrow—and Norm paused and cocked his head as if listening to a melody that pleased him.

Tommy stood paralyzed, unable to move or speak beyond his initial shout. In utter horror and confusion, he shook his head, trying to deny what he was seeing. He heard footsteps coming from the corridor behind him, someone at last responding to the silenced alarm on the machine that monitored his father's heart.

His father tensed to swing the IV stand again.

"Dad, stop!" Tommy snapped, bolting at his father, his voice and body unfrozen. Images of their shared past filled his mind—his dad wiping away a tear when he brought Tommy to his first day of school . . . throwing a football in the backyard in the twilight of a long summer day, still smelling of fish guts . . . chauffeuring Tommy and Annie Slason on their first date in the sixth grade, wearing the black chauffeur hat and everything . . . teaching Tommy how to work the nets, and putting salve on the abrasions on his hands after that first day . . .

His father turned on him, snarling, holding the IV stand like a baseball bat. His eyes had turned black as tar, and at their centers were pinpoints of bright light like distant stars. Norm Dunne stared at his son as if he had nursed a hatred for him all of his life.

"For the goddess," his father said, black fluid dribbling from his lips, turning his voice into a wet growl.

Then his father lunged, cocking the IV stand.

Tommy got the hell out. He hurled himself backward, turning to flee the room. He hurtled into the corridor, slamming into a young nurse, who staggered back and crashed into the opposite wall. Off balance, Tommy careened across the hall and lost his footing, went sprawling into an empty gurney, then pushed off and bolted.

But he had lost precious seconds.

"Mr. Dunne, what are you—" the nurse began.

And then she screamed, and the IV stand swept down toward her. Every ounce of sense Tommy had ever had told him to run, but he couldn't let his father do to the nurse what he'd done to the old man. He reversed direction, threw out an arm, and stopped the IV stand as it came down. Twisting it around, he held on with both hands, using it as a bar to shove his father back. As a teenager, he had wondered how much stronger he would have to grow, and how much older his father would have to get, before he would be able to take his old man.

Tommy hadn't gotten there yet.

Norm yanked the IV stand toward him with one hand, and with the other he smashed a fist into Tommy's face, breaking his nose and splitting his lip. Norm tore the IV stand from his grasp and hit him again, this time with such force that the blow drove Tommy to his knees.

"Dad, please," Tommy said, looking up at his father's black, pinpoint eyes. "Stop."

Norm grabbed a fistful of his son's hair, hoisted Tommy off the floor, and hit him again. And again. Blood flowed from Tommy's nose and mouth. He could taste the copper tang of it on his tongue. Blackness swam in at the edges of his vision. When his father picked him up by his shirt and belt, Tommy could not fight back.

His father hurled him into the wall. Something cracked inside Tommy Dunne, and he slammed down on top of the gurney in the hall, then tumbled off it and hit the linoleum. His eyes flickered open and closed and he saw a pool of his own blood forming around him. He heard shouting and retreating feet, and he thought his father must be running.

He killed me, Tommy thought. *My dad killed me.*

And then he slid into oblivion.

Keomany watched as Octavian scanned the jammed visitor parking lot at Hawthorne Union Hospital for a second or two, then turned up the drive reserved for ambulances and other emergency vehicles. He drove onto the grass alongside that lane and killed the engine.

"You're just going to park on the hospital lawn?" Keomany asked as he popped open his door and began to climb out into the rain.

Octavian glanced back inside at her. "Daybreak hasn't given us much of a reprieve. No more wasting time." He gave her a mischievous grin. "Besides, I think most of the town's a little too busy to worry about towing my car."

He swung the door shut.

In the backseat, Charlotte snickered. "I know I was, like, *made* to hate him. But I totally want him," she said, in a just-us-girls conspiratorial tone that made Keomany wince. "The swagger just gets me, y'know?"

Keomany opened her door, glancing into the backseat. "Again, he's in a relationship."

Charlotte smiled, fangs glinting in the gloom of the car. "He's been around practically since the Dark Ages. My guess is he's had a lot of relationships and outlived them all."

"Listen—" Keomany snapped.

"Please, don't lecture me," Charlotte said, rolling her eyes. "The guy's yummy. Let's not pretend being around him doesn't get you buzzing in all the right places. If you're not going to act on it, that's fine. All the more for me."

The vampire girl opened her door and plunged into the storm with inhuman swiftness, leaving the door hanging open. Keomany climbed out, shut both doors, and started after her. She didn't want to seem like she was chasing Charlotte, but the hot rain felt so slick and viscous on her skin that she ran just to be out of it.

Ahead of her, she saw Octavian stride through the sliding glass doors of the emergency room with Charlotte in pursuit, her red hair bright even in the gray rain. The whole town had been infected by chaos, but Keomany knew now that it was the way the infection spread and created blossoms of discord and madness that was the true threat. She had faith in Octavian, and in herself. They could stop this. Gaea lingered just out of her reach, yearning to cleanse the contagion from this place. All could be healed again. Unless their efforts were undermined by small blossoms of chaos that grew so close they could bloom unnoticed. The wild, savage streak in the vampire girl had been augmented and intensified by the dark energies threaded through the town, churning in the chaos storm. This wasn't the time for the kind of mischief she seemed to delight in stirring up, but like the blood thirst that gnawed at her, she could fight the urge only if she wished to, and even then, for only so long.

The doors shushed closed behind Charlotte, and Keomany ran even faster after her.

Octavian could feel the chaos around him now, its dark energy prickling his skin and making the small hairs stand up on the back of his neck. It touched him, coated his skin with a layer of filth just as unpleasant as the hot rain outside. The miasma of chaos was intangible and invisible, existing only on some etheric plane, but he felt it just the same, and it had been growing worse with every passing moment since the sun had come up. Keomany had predicted that they would have two or three days before the dark energies swirling in Hawthorne hit critical mass, reaching their full power and potentially destroying the entire town and all of its people. Instead, it had been not quite twenty-four hours since Keomany had first sensed the disturbance here, and Octavian could feel the power building. The air crackled with it. He still believed that the daylight—beyond the veil of the storm or not—would have a tempering influence on the evil festering here. But by nightfall, all hell would surely break loose.

The emergency room hummed with the voices of a throng of people, most of whom had sustained bloody injuries overnight. There were broken limbs and gashed faces and two men who looked like they had beaten each other half to death and then come to the hospital together. A middle-aged Asian woman vomited noisily into a paper bag while her daughter tried to comfort her and held her hair away from her face. The woman had blood and snot dripping from her nose and tried to catch her breath between bouts of retching. She wasn't the only one who looked sick, like some kind of poison had gotten inside her. Octavian realized that was precisely what had happened.

Closing his eyes, he tuned out the cacophony of voices around him—all those people waiting for help, knowing there were dozens inside already being treated—and reached down within himself. At the core of himself burned a magic that he nurtured every day. Of all of the sorcery he had learned in the thousand years he had spent in Hell, this was the greatest— to find within himself the magic that had lain dormant in humanity for thousands of years, and ignite it, and make it grow and become his own second nature. So much of what he could do now—not the spellcraft but the instinctive magic, the combat sorcery, came from that core. And something else.

Octavian smiled, because it felt good. Very, very good. Golden light shimmered at the tips of his fingers and sparked along his palms. An unseen wind danced around him and rustled his clothes and hair, and he could see the golden light misting in front of his eyes, spilling out of them.

"Be well," he whispered, and the words were the courier.

The magic flashed up and spread across the ceiling, falling like gold dust. It slid through the cracks beneath the doors into the treatment area and the open window of the receptionist's desk and he watched it go, exhaling.

The Asian woman stopped vomiting. She took several deep breaths, eyes wide, as though she expected another round of convulsive retching any second, but none came. Even her pallor seemed less sickly. Some people tried to brush the gold dust from their clothes and skin, but it vanished like snowflakes melting as they landed on warm pavement. Several had noticed him and now turned to stare, some with fear and others with wonder. Octavian hated to make a spectacle, but if he could not purge all of Hawthorne so easily, the least he could do was help cleanse the dark chaos poison from this handful of people.

The wounded were still wounded. They still bled. They were still in pain. But those who had been ill, he had made well.

"What did you just do?" a voice asked from behind him.

Octavian turned to see Keomany and Charlotte side by side, staring at him. He would have smiled and dismissed his actions with some offhanded remark, but off to their right, in a corner by the door, a uniformed police officer—darkly handsome, perhaps Italian or Greek—had drawn his gun and held it in both hands, aimed at Octavian's chest.

"Damn good question," the cop said. "I'd like an answer. What the hell was that?"

Keomany shuffled aside. Charlotte swore but managed not to reveal her fangs, and Octavian was grateful of that.

Octavian lifted his hands to show he meant no harm. "My name is Peter Octavian. Last night, my friends and I were working with Chief Kramer and some of your fellow officers to fight the magic that's attacking your town. The chief asked us to meet him here."

The cop looked doubtful, but his gun wavered. At least one member of the Hawthorne police force had been killed last night, and Octavian suspected that there might be more than one. Octavian saw the fear and grief in him and knew that he must have seen awful things overnight and might now be worried about the people he loved. Men in such circumstances could do foolish things.

Keomany took a step toward Octavian, raising her hands as well in a placating gesture. "Officer, I know it's been a long night and it doesn't seem like it's getting any better. But we're here to help."

"You're supposed to meet Chief Kramer here?" the cop asked slowly.

Octavian nodded. "We are. Check in. You'll find out that we're telling the truth."

The cop glanced over at the people who had been sick, many of whom were standing, looking around in bewilderment as though they were only waiting for the standoff to end so that they could go home. But it was clear they were better.

At length, the cop nodded and pulled out his phone, then seemed to remember it wasn't working and grabbed a hand radio from his belt instead. Bursts of static erupted from it intermittently, but he managed to have a short, muttered conversation, and when it ended he holstered his weapon.

"Come with me," he told Octavian and Keomany, with a curious appraising glance at Charlotte. "The chief's up in the psych unit."

"I imagine there was a lot of trouble there last night," Octavian said, as they all fell in behind the cop, whose name badge he now saw read *TAGLIATELLI*.

Officer Tagliatelli would have been a poor poker player. His expression turned grim, and Octavian knew that they had lost at least one officer to violence in the psych unit. But then Tagliatelli's eyes lit up with confusion and curiosity, and he knew it was not the violence that had brought Chief Kramer to that particular wing of the hospital this morning.

"Something interesting as well?" Octavian asked.

"You'll have to talk to the chief about that," Tagliatelli replied. "Sorry about drawing on you, though. We're just not used to . . . y'know, magic, around here. Good or bad. I think I've drawn my weapon once since I became a cop, but with all of the craziness right now, we're all pretty on edge. A patient went nuts a little while ago, beat some people up and took off. I mean, why not just check yourself out. It's like the whole town's an insane asylum. Makes the psych unit look like a bunch of accountants talking numbers."

"Understandable," Octavian said. "It's an ugly day."

"I'll take you up there," Tagliatelli said, leading the way through the waiting room and past the reception desk.

Octavian gestured to Charlotte and Keomany, and the three of them followed the cop into the heart of the ER. He could feel the fear and smell the sickness around him and he wished he could stop and do whatever he could for each person who was ill or wounded or crushed by fear, but the only way to help them all was to put an end to the chaos.

Tagliatelli gestured to a hospital security guard. The man nodded and went out to monitor the waiting room. Out of the corner of his eye, when he knew her attention was elsewhere, Octavian watched Charlotte. The vampire had been twitchy and skittish all morning, and he knew it wasn't just the agitation of the chaos in the air or a hunger for blood. Charlotte had been made into a vampire by Cortez, and he subscribed to an antiquated idea of vampirism. At their core, vampires were shapeshifters, able to change themselves on a molecular level.

For more than a thousand years they had been infected with beliefs ingrained in them by the church, purposely laced through their community to limit their power. They'd been made to believe that there were only certain forms they could take when they shapeshifted, and that the sun would burn them, the latter a form of psychosomatic suicide—as shapeshifters, if they believed they would turn to fire and ash, they had.

Octavian and his long-dead lover, Meaghan Gallagher, had helped to change all of that, to free vampires— shadows—from the limits the church's cunning had placed on them. But some had enjoyed being the creatures of nightmare the church had painted them as, who had loved being monsters. Predators. Cortez and his ilk shunned the sunlight, cleaving to the vampire myths of old.

And so Octavian watched Charlotte. She had been turned and taught by Cortez, but he wondered if she had spent much time in the sun since she had fled his coven. He had a feeling she had experimented very little with walking beneath the sun, perhaps afraid to experiment. Even with the storm blotting out all but the dimmest light that filtered through the clouds, she seemed troubled by it. Now that they were indoors she seemed to have settled a bit. He hoped she could get over any skittishness quickly. He needed to be able to rely on her.

They reached the elevator, where nurses and patients waited.

"I'm sorry, folks," Tagliatelli said. "We need to get up to the third floor immediately. Police business."

"They don't look like police," a craggy-faced old nurse said, staring at Octavian and his friends.

"Never said they were," Tagliatelli replied simply, ignoring the woman's glare.

The elevator doors opened and the four of them stepped on. None of the patients waiting looked to be in dire straits, so Octavian didn't object when Tagliatelli held up a hand to prevent anyone else from boarding. The doors shushed closed and the officer hit the button for the third floor.

As they ascended, Tagliatelli cast appreciative glances at Keomany and Charlotte.

"What are you two, his personal assistants?" the cop asked, trying to hide his lecherous implications behind an innocent look that didn't quite work.

Keomany shot him a withering glance. She pointed a finger at herself.

"Earthwitch," she said, then pointed at Charlotte. "Vampire."

The cop flinched and turned a fearful gaze on Charlotte, who grinned widely enough to reveal her fangs and waggled her fingers in a childlike wave.

"Jesus," Tagliatelli said, facing forward and staring straight ahead as the elevator eased to a halt.

When the doors opened he practically jumped off. Octavian waited for Keomany and Charlotte to step out before he followed. Tagliatelli rushed ahead of them, no longer bothering to try to make small talk. That was good. It was too grim a day for small talk.

As they approached a turn in the corridor, Octavian spotted the police chief waiting for them by the nurses' station outside a secure wing of the floor. Chief Kramer was in the middle of a conversation with a grave-looking doctor, a diminutive woman who seemed exhausted, but broke off the instant he saw them coming.

"Chief, this is—" Tagliatelli began.

Kramer ignored them, extending his hand. "Mr. Octavian, thanks for showing up."

Octavian nodded. "I told you last night, Chief, that's why we're here. I just wish we'd been more successful last night in figuring out the source of all of this."

"I appreciate that," Chief Kramer said, then turned to the vampire girl. "Good morning, Charlotte."

"Peachy," Charlotte replied.

The chief had not been very comfortable with Charlotte in their brief meeting last night, and he seemed even less so this morning. Sometimes Octavian forgot that most of the world had still never seen a vampire outside videos on television or the Internet. She made Chief Kramer nervous, but Octavian thought that was probably for the best. The chaos around them had made everyone unpredictable, and with her hunger, Charlotte would be even more so. Octavian had caught her looking at him from time to time with a certain salacious glint in her eyes. He would have to have been blind not to see the sexual mischief there, but he wondered how much of that was really her and how much was the influence of chaos.

She would bear watching.

"Chief Kramer, this is my friend Keomany Shaw," Octavian said. "Keomany, Don Kramer."

The chief shook Keomany's hand, sizing her up. Octavian had told him she was an earthwitch and could see the man trying to match his own personal image of what an elemental witch might look like to this lovely, slender creature. Keomany was half-English and half-Cambodian, and the combination of her parents' two heritages had given her a rare beauty.

"This is Dr. O'Neil," Chief Kramer said, indicating the pale, petite woman in her lab coat. "She's had a hell of a night."

They all exchanged greetings, and then Kramer turned to Octavian.

"I wanted you all here so we could compare notes, see if anyone's learned anything that will help us get to the bottom of this. The weird shit has tapered off a little since dawn, but it hasn't stopped, and there are new twists by the hour. In some parts of town, the plants and trees and grass have all died, but in a couple of neighborhoods it's all grown out of control, like jungles sprouting up from nowhere. More and more people are just flipping out, turning feral. My department hasn't been able to keep up with all the fights, and the ones they can stop, they're not arresting anyone. Just sending them home. Sinkholes are starting to open up . . ."

Chief Kramer paused, glancing from Octavian to Keomany and back.

"I guess what I'm saying, folks, is that I hope you've got some good news. Tell me you can figure out the cause of all this."

"I wish we could," Octavian said. "We know what it is, Chief. But Keomany's tried pinpointing the source with no luck. If we can't find the source, maybe we'll have better luck finding a trigger."

Kramer nodded. "I'm not used to all of this stuff, but I had the same thought. I talked to my officers, tried figuring out a timeline. Looks like the first thing anyone noticed was all the dairy products spoiling in some parts of town."

Octavian narrowed his eyes. The chief seemed irritated, a little on the defensive. Back in the days when Octavian had played detective, he'd seen it before, cops who bristled at the suggestion that anyone else might be able to do their jobs better than they could. Under the circumstances, Chief Kramer had mostly seemed happy for the help during the night. Octavian hoped the man was smart enough not to start getting territorial now.

"In some parts of town?" Octavian repeated.

"I take it back," the chief said. "As far as I can tell, it happened everywhere, just not all at once. It was like a wave."

"A wave," Keomany said.

Octavian exchanged a glance with her.

"Where did the wave start?" Charlotte asked.

Chief Kramer gave her a surprised look, but Octavian was glad she'd asked. It showed that the vampire was focused, despite the chaos within her and the daylight without, both distracting her. It was the very question he'd been about to ask.

"It seems like it started from the coast and rolled through town east to west," the chief said. He looked tired, dark smears under his eyes, but he perked up now. "The way the tide went out so far, like a tidal wave was coming in or something . . . do you think this started in the ocean?"

Octavian glanced at Keomany.

"It's where we went when we first came to town," Keomany told the chief. "I don't think it's the source of the magic causing this, but I definitely sensed something unnatural there."

"It's a start," Chief Kramer said. "But what do we do? Send divers down? We wouldn't know where to begin."

"Let's take this from another angle," Octavian said. "Other than Charlotte over here, has anything been reported that seems occult to you? I don't mean the effects of magic, all this chaos, but something more than that, anything your officers have run across, or anyone who seems to know more than they should—"

From the chief's reaction, Octavian saw that he'd hit on something. "What is it?"

"The reason we were up here to begin with," Chief Kramer said, gesturing at Dr. O'Neil, who still stood beside him. "One of my people was murdered in the psych unit last night. Dr. O'Neil's staff and patients took some hits as well. But one of her patients . . ."

The police chief glanced around, turned to Dr. O'Neil, and then smiled wanly.

"Maybe you'd all better hear this yourself. Could be it'll make sense to you."

12

The ghost was waiting in the elevator when Miles and Amber got on. Or, at least, that was how it seemed. Over the course of his life, prompted by his first brush with the supernatural as a child, Miles had studied various occult phenomena, but all of his research and his various encounters with roaming spirits had no handle on the behavior of ghosts. All of the supposedly true stories he had ever read had provided no consensus. For all he knew, the ghost might have been following him all morning, just out of sight, and only manifested as something he could see at the moment that the elevator doors swept open and he and Amber stepped on board.

Amber didn't seem to see the specter at all, but to Miles—whose breath and voice had caught in his throat—the ghost had an undeniable presence. Transparent, yes, but it had dimension and a certain weight, as though if he tried to touch the spirit it might feel like he was pushing his hand into water. He didn't dare test the theory.

"Professor?" Amber said as the doors slid shut, edging closer to him to make room for the four other people in the elevator with them. "Miles? What's wrong? Are you feeling all right?"

He couldn't reply. His palms began to itch and he felt a trickle of sweat run down the back of his neck. Suddenly his clothes seemed too tight. He glanced around, but no one seemed to see the ghost except for him, not even Amber.

Close your eyes, he thought. *It'll go away.*

But he wasn't sure if that was true, and if it was, he wasn't at all certain that he wanted the ghost to disappear. After all, he hadn't seen Tim McConville for more than a decade. The kid had been his friend in a time when such a thing had an intensity that he'd found mostly lacking in his adult relationships. The years had flowed by him, or he by them, and Miles had grown older. But, just like his earlier encounters with the ghost, Tim McConville remained an eternal boy, a dead Peter Pan.

"Miles," Amber ventured again, nudging him.

He tried to give her a relaxed smile, but he knew it must be hideous and pained.

"Something strange is happening," he said quietly, trying not to draw the attention of the other people on the elevator.

"Really?" Amber said. "You're just figuring that out?"

"Something else," he replied.

Now they were all staring at him, listening, waiting for him to explain. But he refused to meet anyone's gaze—not a stranger's, not Amber's, and not Tim McConville's, though the ghost regarded him with imploring eyes. Instead, Miles watched the numbers above the elevator doors, cursing the age of the rattling old machine.

At last it slowed and the doors slid open. He was the first one off and he stood in the corridor while the others flowed around him. When Amber touched his arm, he flinched.

"Hey," she said. "Don't freak out on me. I need you."

Miles took a deep breath. Fear and loss had made them conspirators now, created an intimacy between them to which he could not help but react. A rush of sudden arousal startled him. Where had that come from? Amber was attractive, but he had never reacted to her like this. The heat racing through him reminded him of the effects of certain drugs, and he wondered if that was it . . . if there was something in the air, getting into his blood.

He shook himself. "Sorry. I'm okay now."

He hated to lie to her.

The ghost of Tim McConville had not exited the elevator—its doors had shushed closed without the specter emerging—but now it stood just a few feet ahead of them in the corridor, an impatient expression on the transparent face of the dead little boy.

"You're sure?" Amber asked, still very close to him. Close enough to whisper. Close enough for a kiss.

Miles pushed the thoughts away. She was supremely desirable, no doubt. But he felt sure this rush of intimacy was a symptom of logic and order unraveling in Hawthorne, and in him.

"I'm sure," he said. "Come on. Let's talk to your friend Tommy."

They started down the corridor, looking at the numbers outside the patient rooms and the names scrawled on white boards beneath them. The ghost watched them pass. After he had seen the spirit of Tim McConville as a child, Miles had found comfort in the knowledge that there truly was an afterlife, that the soul continued on after death. But now he tried not to look at the ghost, tried not to think about what it meant that the spirit of his dead friend could still be lingering after all of these years. What did it mean for heaven? What did it mean for faith?

"Excuse me," Amber said, stepping in the path of a male nurse in blue scrubs. "We're looking for Tommy Dunne. Thomas, I mean. Thomas Dunne."

The nurse studied them as though they might attack him at any moment. Nervous, obviously wishing he were anywhere else, he glanced around as if hoping someone else would answer.

"Are you family?" he asked at last.

"I'm his uncle," Miles said quickly, afraid that if Amber told the truth they might not be allowed to see her friend. Somehow he'd become a liar this morning. It didn't sit well with him.

The nurse seemed like he might ask for proof, but then his pager went off and he glanced at it.

"He's in room 513," the nurse said. "But he's not really up for visitors. You might not want to see him like this."

A scream echoed along the corridor, and then someone started to shriek about spiders. The nurse shuddered and brushed past them, apologizing as he went. Miles stole a glance at the ghost of Tim McConville, who waited for them farther along the hall. He had the idea that the ghost knew exactly where Tommy Dunne was, but he did not want to tell that to Amber.

Were other people seeing ghosts today, or just him? Was it just another of a million impossible things playing out in Hawthorne today? He thought it might be.

They had waited in line downstairs to ask what room Norman Dunne was in, only to find out that Mr. Dunne was no longer a patient at the hospital. They had been about to walk away when another woman behind the desk had muttered to the receptionist, asking if Norman Dunne was "the nut who'd run off." It had taken Miles only half a minute of quiet charm to learn that Norm Dunne had attacked members of the hospital staff and his own son and had somehow—despite the number of police and security guards in the hospital—managed to escape capture. It had been the receptionist's friend who had informed them, in empathetic tones, that the lunatic's son was now a patient.

Now Miles and Amber strode toward room 513, where the ghost of Tim McConville stood watch. They passed hospital staff, all of whom looked grim and some shell-shocked. One nurse glanced at them and seemed about to call out, to question their presence, out of habit ingrained in her over the course of her career. But an alarm went off in one of the rooms and she ran, instinct taking over.

Amber passed right through the ghost. Miles averted his eyes and walked around it, following her into Tommy Dunne's room. The lights were low and the room was suffused with the gray of the storm, the only sound the pelting of that slick rain on the window.

"Oh, Tommy," Amber sighed, and rushed to the side of the bed.

Norm Dunne had done a hell of a job on his son. Tommy's face and head were bandaged, spots of blood soaking through, and an IV needle pumped something vital into his arm. The kid was either deeply sedated or in a coma. Miles saw the chart in its slot at the end of the bed and glanced around, thinking he would have a look and see if he could make any sense of medicalese.

Something shifted in the corner of the room. Flickered like a candle flame. He assumed it was Tim McConville but stole a glance in that direction. All the breath went out of him. His heart raced, growing so loud it was like thunder in his ears.

"My God," Miles whispered.

The ghost in the corner, insubstantial as twilight, was not Tim McConville.

It was his mother.

"Mom?"

Amber turned and looked at him, the horror of Tommy Dunne's condition still etched on her face. But then confusion took over and she glanced into the corner to see what had caught his attention.

"What are you looking at?" she asked.

His mother wasn't alone now. As though the air itself had *breathed* him into existence there, Tim McConville manifested beside his mother's ghost. His mother's expression was filled with such sorrow, such disappointment, that it tore at his heart. Was this her final reward, such sadness?

"Miles," Amber said. "What is it? What do you see?"

He turned to look at her, sick of lying. "I see ghosts."

She stared at him. "What?"

Embarrassed, he glanced away. "It's not new. I mean, it isn't caused by whatever's going on in town. Not entirely. I haven't seen one in years, until today."

Someone shouted in the corridor. Miles heard running feet and turned to see one nurse running to an orderly, the fear that had been simmering in all of them rising to the surface.

"You need to get down to the morgue, right now," she said. "They need help down there."

Amber slipped closer to the door, eavesdropping. Miles glanced back into the corner and saw that both of the ghosts had vanished, and he wanted to cry out, to plead for his mother to come back. He wanted to reach her heart, and his own.

"What the hell for?" the orderly asked, out in the hallway. "There's nothing down there but dead people."

It was the nurse's laugh that got Miles to focus, a lunatic bark of laughter. He edged over to Amber and peered out. He could see the nurse's expression in profile, and she wore the kind of smile that was only ever used to stifle a scream.

"That's what I said," the nurse replied, her voice quavering. That smile widened. "Apparently some of them aren't dead anymore."

The orderly swore, but when he searched her face, he could see she wasn't joking. Shaking his head, he hurried away, leaving the nurse to tremble and reach up to wipe away tears from her eyes. Someone called her name and she took a deep breath, then rushed in the other direction down the hall.

"Did you hear that?" Amber asked.

Miles nodded slowly.

"It's not possible," she said.

"Who knows what's possible now?" he asked.

Her expression darkened, and then she looked as though she might be sick. "Oh my God. Isn't your mother . . ."

Miles glanced at that corner again, wishing the ghost would appear. But if his mother walked the corridors of Hawthorne Union Hospital now, he feared it was not as a ghost.

Amber took his hand in hers, squeezing it until he met her gaze.

"Let's go," she said.

He didn't ask where she meant for them to go. If something had desecrated his mother's remains, he had to do something. But they had come here for a reason. They had to find a way to stop the horrifying changes being wrought on Hawthorne, the hideous abominations that seemed to mount by the moment.

Miles cast a glance at Tommy Dunne's unconscious form.

"We'll come back," Amber assured him. "Tommy's not talking right now. If he has answers, they'll have to wait."

Octavian stood just inside the hospital room where the serial killer, Wayne Pinsky, had died. Plywood sheeting had been hastily bolted to the wall to keep the rain and wind from pouring through. In several places scorch marks blackened the wall, visible at the edges of the plywood.

He turned to look at Dr. O'Neil. "You said the lightning was blue. I assume you're not being poetic."

The diminutive doctor frowned. "Do I look like I'm in a poetic mood?"

"We saw blue lightning last night," Charlotte reminded him.

Octavian remembered, but he thought it might have been a trick of the light, some kind of shading caused by the storm clouds. If the lightning that had smashed the window and part of the wall here—and according to Dr. O'Neil, arced into the hallway—had been the vivid blue she described, that was something different entirely. He had known the storm was magical, but he had assumed that it had at least a core of natural weather phenomena. Now he realized he had been mistaken.

"Keomany," he said, "what are we dealing with, here?"

She glanced around, and he understood she was uneasy about discussing her theories in front of an audience. In addition to Charlotte and Dr. O'Neil, their group included Chief Kramer, Officer Tony Moschitto, and the brick wall of a head orderly for the psych unit, whom Octavian thought Dr. O'Neil had introduced as Marlon.

"Go ahead," Octavian told her. "Anyone who doubts you, or any of this, is welcome to come up with their own answers."

"All right," Keomany said. "I had a feeling about this before, but it's more than a feeling now. The storm is part of the chaos that's influencing everything in the town. That part is obvious. But I don't think the storm is even coming from anything in our world."

"Our world?" Marlon muttered. "What does that even mean?"

"It means there are others," Chief Kramer said. "Go on, Miss Shaw."

Keomany kept her eyes on Octavian for a second and then looked at Dr. O'Neil and Chief Kramer. "What a lot of people think of as Hell is actually a potentially infinite number of parallel realities. Alternate dimensions. Some evidence suggests that there might even be . . . let's call them slices of Hell . . . that are in our reality, but on planets so far away they might as well be other dimensions. The point is, in a lot of these places, magic is like water. Or even air. It fills these worlds like our oceans fill the crevices of *our* world. This chaos storm . . . it's coming in from somewhere else."

"What, like some kind of industrial accident?" Dr. O'Neil asked.

"That's possible, but I don't think so," Octavian said. "The creatures we've seen, these wraiths . . . they're serving someone, or something. There's a force behind this. But as we told Chief Kramer, we believe there was a trigger. Something started it. If we can't identify the source, then we need to identify the trigger."

Dr. O'Neil gestured for them to follow her. "This way, then. I don't know if it's going to help you, but there's someone you should meet. At the very least, you'll find it interesting."

Octavian glanced at the chief, who nodded.

"This is what I wanted you to see," Chief Kramer said.

The group hurried down the corridor, their sense of urgency only increased by the crackle of the chief's radio and the buzz of his cell phone. He answered, snapped instructions to the lieutenant he had temporarily put in charge of the police force trying to keep order in Hawthorne, and kept walking. The patients in the secure area of the psych unit seemed strangely subdued, or at least that was the impression Octavian had thanks to the lack of any appreciable noise coming from their rooms. It troubled him, reminding him of the way birds seemed to go quiet just before a storm struck.

A security guard stood at the end of the corridor, but he was hospital staff. The Hawthorne police had their hands full. Octavian imagined that soon almost all of the police at the hospital would be gone, leaving the orderlies and on-site security to deal with any outbreaks of violence and the frustration of those trying to deal with the long waits and crowded ER.

The door to the last room on the left stood open, but all was dark inside. Octavian glimpsed another boarded-up window. Dr. O'Neil crossed to the room on the right.

"Gregory Wheeler," Dr. O'Neil began. "Sixteen years old. Paranoid schizophrenic. His room was also hit by that blue lightning, but it didn't do him any harm."

She paused, then gestured to Marlon, who tugged at the key ring on his belt and went to unlock the door.

"Of course, that depends on how you define *harm*," Dr. O'Neil added.

"How do *you* define *harm*?" Charlotte asked, but her voice was absent its usual sarcasm. She really seemed to want an answer.

Dr. O'Neil gave her a strange look, but did not reply.

Marlon opened the door. The lights were low inside. The teenage patient sat in a cushioned chair that looked as though it did not belong in the room at all, and Octavian felt sure it had come from someone's office. It was not at all the sort of thing one put in the room of a psychiatric patient who might be in danger of hurting himself or someone else. But Greg Wheeler didn't look dangerous at all. In fact, he looked alert and calm, even curious, and as Dr. O'Neil led the way into the room, the kid looked past her and blinked in surprise when he saw Octavian, as though he'd recognized him. It wasn't a surprise, really. If Octavian wasn't precisely famous, he had certainly earned his share of notoriety over the past few years.

The chief came in with them, but Marlon and Officer Moschitto stayed in the hall.

"Greg," Dr. O'Neil said. "Chief Kramer and I wanted you to meet some people. This is Mr. Octavian, and with him are Miss Shaw and . . ." She trailed off and looked at Charlotte. "I don't think I caught your last name."

"Just Charlotte is fine," the vampire girl said, a glint of pain in her eyes. "I gave up my family name."

Octavian nodded to the patient. "Greg. It's nice to meet you. It seems you were very lucky last night, with the lightning."

Greg gave a small smile, as if to tell Octavian he had no idea what he was talking about, and shrugged.

Then he spoke, and Octavian blinked in astonishment.

"Friggin' gibberish," Charlotte said.

"I don't think so," Dr. O'Neil said. "It's a language. I've listened to him and there's structure to it, plus it's clear he's saying things that make sense to him. Watch his face and his hands. He's speaking. We just don't understand him."

"I do," Octavian said.

"So what language is it?" Keomany asked.

Octavian walked over and sat down on the bed, putting himself eye to eye with the boy. Greg Wheeler seemed entirely ordinary. Other than this strange shift in language, nothing about him suggested the influence of chaos or evil. He wondered if that was possible, if the teenager's schizophrenia—a kind of chaos in itself—could have altered the effect that the chaos storm's lightning would otherwise have had upon him.

"Peter?" Keomany asked.

Octavian glanced at her, arching an eyebrow. They were all watching him, waiting for an explanation.

"It's an Old Aramaic dialect that originated in ancient Chaldea. No one's spoken this language in well over two thousand years."

They were all staring. Octavian raised his eyebrows and smiled, acknowledging their astonishment. He shared it.

"How the hell does this kid know . . . what is it?" Chief Kramer asked.

"Ancient Chaldean," Octavian said.

"That. Yeah. How does he know it?"

"Not just him," Dr. O'Neil said. "How do *you* know it?"

Octavian glanced at Keomany and Charlotte and saw that they were both wondering the same thing. But he didn't feel like talking about his thousand years in Hell, and now wasn't the time. Instead, he turned to Greg and spoke to him in that dead language. The kid ought to have been scared, but he didn't seem frightened at all by this turn of events. They spoke for a couple of minutes while the others only stood and listened quietly, and when Octavian turned to look at them, he thought that Dr. O'Neil and the police chief looked unsettled, and maybe a little afraid of him.

"What did he say?" Keomany asked. "Does he know what's causing all of this?"

"He has no idea," Octavian said. "He's happy. His head is clearer than he can ever remember it being."

"There's some dark irony for you," Charlotte muttered.

"He can't tell us anything?" Chief Kramer asked.

"Not with words," Octavian said. "He still understands English but when he tries to speak it, Chaldean comes out. But he has no more sense of what's going on than we do."

"Shit," Chief Kramer snapped. "I thought for sure we had something."

"Wait, you said he couldn't tell us anything with words," Keomany said. "Which means there *is* something we can learn from him."

Octavian looked at Greg thoughtfully. "Maybe. With all the weirdness erupting all over the place, this could be just another example of that. But maybe it's not. Here's something true. At the end of the seventh century b.c., tribes of settlers began to arrive in Babylon. In a short time, they had completely taken over. These were the Chaldeans, and what was once Babylon became Chaldea. But no one—and think about this, with all of the historians and archaeologists who've made it their business to piece together the history of humankind—no one knows where the Chaldeans came from. They just began to appear in Babylon, and they spread, and they conquered."

"No one knows?" Chief Kramer asked.

"No one," Octavian echoed.

"Not even in Hell?" Keomany said.

Dr. O'Neil stared at her, then swung her gaze around to study Octavian.

Octavian did not smile. "Not the one I was in."

"You think they were from somewhere else," Charlotte said. "One of these other Hells that Keomany was talking about."

"I think it's possible," Octavian said.

"This is insane," Dr. O'Neil whispered, as if to herself.

"This is real," Keomany told her. "Trust me. I wish it weren't."

"The point," Octavian said, drawing their attention back to him, "is that the fact that he's speaking Chaldean specifically, and that—unless there's something I'm missing—we're not seeing a whole wave of people speaking various ancient languages, makes me think it *is* connected. Whatever this power is, whatever's brought this chaos to Hawthorne, may have originated with them."

Chief Kramer threw up his hands. "How do you get from ancient Chaldea to modern-day New England?"

Octavian had no answer, and he knew Greg Wheeler didn't have one, either. He thanked the boy, who asked him a favor.

"Dr. O'Neil, Greg says he would love you forever if you could get him some chocolate chip cookies."

The doctor, still in shock from the conversation she'd found herself in, smiled uncertainly and nodded. She went to Greg and put a hand on his shoulder.

"I'll make sure they bring you some milk, too," she said.

The boy thanked her in a language no one alive would understand. Octavian took a few steps toward the door, closing the distance between himself and his friends. Charlotte's eyes glinted with fascination and he felt her watching him hungrily, but he couldn't be sure exactly what it was she hungered for. Whatever it was, he knew he couldn't give it to her. Keomany appraised him as well, and he was surprised to see a similar look in her eyes.

"You're full of surprises," she said, reaching out to touch his arm.

He told himself that chaos was unraveling them all, playing havoc with reason, undermining logic. How else to explain the primal response he felt rising in him at her touch?

"So, what next?" the chief asked. "We're not any closer to an answer."

"We might be," Octavian replied, tearing his focus away from Keomany. "If I start with the assumption that this chaos magic is related to Chaldean sorcery, I might be able to come up with a way to tap into the flow, and trace it."

"Well, get on it," the chief said.

Octavian turned to Keomany and Charlotte, but before he could speak, the chief's radio crackled. Amid the static were screams and gunshots. Officer Moschitto poked his head into the room, face blanched white, his eyes wide. He clutched his radio like a life preserver.

"What the hell is this, now?" the chief snapped, grabbing at his radio.

Moschitto had the answer. "It's the morgue, Chief."

"What are they shooting at?" Kramer demanded.

Moschitto grew even paler, having to speak the words.

"The cadavers. They're shooting at the cadavers."

*

Miles flew down the stairs, taking them two at a time and jumping to each landing, careening off the walls. Amber came down behind him. Several times she called his name, and in the back of his mind he knew he should wait for her. A small voice inside him tried to insist that he send her back up, that she didn't need to see this or be a part of it, that he should keep her out of harm's way. But the voice was a tiny thing and could never have been loud enough to break through the roar that filled his head, the frenzy of panic and grief that sent him hurtling down the stairs.

He wanted the old world, the one he'd grown up in. He wanted the world where vampires and demons and magic were imaginary things, where he could pretend the ghosts he'd seen as a boy had been a singular, haunting experience, comforting evidence of the existence of an afterlife and perhaps of God and Heaven and other now quaint reassurances. He wanted an ordinary world, where his grief for the loss of his mother could never have been interrupted by the possibility that . . . the possibility that . . .

Rage filled him. Miles hated magic. It was obscene, what it could do.

They bypassed the lobby level. If they had tried to take an elevator, they would still be waiting up on the fifth floor. At every landing he expected to crash into a security guard, but they were obviously too busy to worry about people on the stairs. The cameras would show the two of them racing down the steps, but whoever was monitoring them probably had better things to do, just like the guards in the ER, and the ones who must already be in the basement.

Miles leaped to the landing where a metal door had been painted with an enormous *B* for *basement*. His right knee buckled and he slammed into the door, grunting in pain.

Amber caught up, hustling down the last few steps, reaching for him.

"Are you all right?" she asked.

"Just twisted it," he said. He had forgotten that he wasn't a kid anymore, that at forty-two his knees were no longer up to this kind of punishment. But the shock of pain had woken him from the lunatic rush that had swept over him.

Miles brushed his hand against hers, shaking with manic grief. "You should go back. It won't be safe."

Amber flinched, then shook her head. "Just shut up and go. Maybe you don't need me with you, but I can't face what's waiting for me at home by myself. I need a friend, and you're it. So let's go."

If he'd been capable of it, he might have smiled.

He yanked the door open and took her hand, and they rushed into the basement corridor together. No sign indicated the direction of the morgue, but gunshots rang out to the right, and he knew which way they had to go. They ran along the corridor, passing several testing labs where people crouched behind tables and machines, afraid of bullets, and other things as well.

Miles let go of her hand as they reached a turn in the corridor, but he didn't slow down. He turned the corner and only then did he stop short. Amber staggered to a halt behind him. Two police officers and three security guards—all but one of them men—stood in the corridor, backs to Miles and Amber. The cops had their weapons drawn. In front of them, outside the side-by-side entrances to the morgue and the autopsy room, dead people limped and staggered around almost aimlessly. A skinny middle-aged white man had been flayed open, maybe in the middle of an autopsy when he woke up, and his torso hung open as though his chest and abdomen had been unzipped, organs trailing behind him on the floor and hanging in loops. Two old ladies walked aimlessly, their eyes closed as if they were playing some kind of child's game.

There were bullet holes in most of the dead people. A fat, naked black woman had been shot half a dozen times. She had collapsed to the floor, but now she struggled to rise again, and one of the cops shot her in the face, eradicating her right eye and blowing shards of skull and drying brain matter onto the wall beside her.

Amber screamed.

The cops and security guards glanced back at them. One of the cops swung his weapon around, and Miles thought he might have shaken them out of fear and surprise, but he twisted back and aimed at the dead people again.

"You shouldn't be here!" one of the guards shouted, backing up a few steps to talk to them. He had gray hair and a paunchy belly and he looked terrified. In his hand, he held a Taser gun, but he hadn't fired it.

"What are you doing?" Amber demanded. "It's . . . it's wrong!"

"Are you high?" the guard asked. "They're fucking zombies!"

"This isn't a movie. You don't know what they'd do. They just look lost and sad. Those two old ladies don't even have their eyes open. You think they're going to eat you?"

"That's what they do!" one of the cops shouted at her. "Don't be stupid. The fat lady keeps coming for us. And these are just the ones who were on the tables. The morgue assistant who called it in said the ones in the drawers, they're banging to be let out!"

Miles turned and vomited on the linoleum. He wanted badly to cry. His eyes burned with the need to shed tears. But all he could muster was a nausea that retreated to a dull queasiness the moment he puked. For a second he leaned against the wall, trying to breathe, trying not to picture the dark inside of one of those morgue drawers. His mother wasn't out in the corridor, which meant she had woken from death inside a metal coffin, a drawer where she had been put into cold storage, covered with a sheet.

He wondered if she knew what had happened to her. The dead looked lost, Amber was right about that. But he had seen his mother's ghost upstairs, and he felt sure she must know. Even if her spirit had left her flesh behind, somewhere her consciousness knew that her remains had been desecrated.

"Just stop, you idiots," he said. "Stop shooting long enough to see if they try to attack you."

One of the cops shot the autopsy man in the chest, and Miles wondered what he thought he would hit. There were no organs in there, no further damage that could be done to make the corpse lie down, short of a grenade exploding.

"This is magic," Amber said. "It's got to be part of what's happening everywhere in town. It's not fucking *Dawn of the Dead*."

"How do you know?" the redheaded female guard snapped at her.

"There are vampires. You want us to treat the zombies nice until they eat our goddamn brains?"

Miles didn't want to argue anymore. The only one among the dead who seemed intent on reaching the living was the black woman, but she didn't look angry or evil or hungry. And as she looked up at them now, she had a faraway gaze as though her purpose lay somewhere quite distant. She tried to speak, but she had no voice.

Yet he thought he could make out the two words she tried to utter. He had no expertise in reading lips, but it seemed clear to him.

She said, *My baby*.

The woman wanted to reach her child. They might not all know who they were, or what had happened to them, but this one did.

Blind with grief, thinking of his mother in that drawer and the way her ghost had vanished upstairs, Miles could not stop himself. He ran through the blockade the guards and cops had set up. The female guard tried to grab him, but he shook her off and before the cops even knew what he was doing, he was between them and the dead woman who only wanted to reach her baby.

"You stupid bastard!" someone shouted at him. "What the hell are—"

The black woman, riddled with bullet holes, reached for Miles. A tremor of fear passed through him, but it was swept under by the current of his grief. He saw his sorrow reflected in her eyes, and he took her hand. She stepped toward him.

"Move aside, damn it! Move aside!" one of the cops was screaming.

One of them took a shot, but they didn't dare shoot Miles and they couldn't hit the dead woman without putting a bullet through him, too.

Amber screamed his name. He heard a scuffle and understood that she was trying to get to him, and the guards were holding her back. He saw the two old dead women bumping into each other, their eyes still closed. The autopsy man slipped in his own viscera and fell down. His heart broke for all of them, and for his mother, and for himself. And he prayed the cops were wrong.

The dead woman wrapped her arms around him, sagging into him as though she wept, although—like Miles—she had no tears. She held him as though gaining solace from his kindness, and then she stepped back, her gaze straying once more to some faraway place where she must have believed her baby awaited her.

Miles turned to the cops, who stared in astonishment, mouths open in expressions that might have been comical if there weren't so much anguish in the air around them all.

"They're harmless," Miles said, his voice catching. "They're just in pain. They're grieving for themselves."

The guard who'd been holding Amber released her, and she stepped up beside the cops.

"We've got to figure out a way to make them dead again," she said.

Miles nodded. She understood the obscenity here, what this twisted magic had done to them. This was an abomination.

He heard the shuffle of footsteps behind him and the whimper of someone in fear. Before he turned, he saw Amber's eyes go wide in surprise, and saw the cops raise their guns and take aim again.

Miles spun to see two people emerging from the open door to the morgue. One wore a white lab coat, maybe the morgue assistant who had called in this horror in the first place. The other held him from behind, a scalpel to his throat, a puncture wound in his neck already weeping blood.

The man who held the morgue assistant had been burned to death, his skin cracked and charred. Where his eyes ought to have been were ruined, blackened pits, but his grip on the terrified morgue assistant was strong.

The burned corpse smiled.

"Pinsky," one of the cops said.

"This one's not harmless," said the other. "He's a fuckin' serial killer."

Amber tore free of the security guard holding her back and brushed past the two cops, who shouted at her to get the hell out of the way. She grabbed Miles by the arm and pulled him aside, out of the line of fire, but she saw in his eyes that he had no fear of the policemen's bullets just then.

"Do it!" she shouted to the cops. "Shoot him!"

"No shot!" the younger cop snapped.

The two policemen shuffled forward, guns trained on the charred cadaver who had taken the morgue assistant hostage. Amber felt her stomach churn every time she glanced at that dead man and saw the scorched, empty pits of his eyes and the bones jutting through skin burned paper-thin.

"Even if they had a shot," Miles muttered to her, "it wouldn't stop the thing. They've all got bullet holes."

She knew it, but to hear him speak the words chilled her. Amber stared at the wide, terrified eyes of the morgue assistant as the burned man walked him backward toward the elevator at the end of the corridor. The scalpel had already drawn a thin red line on the hostage's throat, opening up a puckered wound that began to weep blood.

One of the cops took three quick steps forward, and the burned corpse twisted his hostage around to make sure the morgue assistant stayed between him and the police. The other cop took a shot, winged the dead man's shoulder, and both corpse and hostage froze. A sneer of fury contorted the burned man's face, cracking charred flesh, splits in his cheeks showing raw, bloody meat. The burned man was pissed, and he jabbed the knife an inch into the morgue assistant's throat.

The hostage screamed and began to beg and plead, tears rolling down his face. The burned, eyeless corpse smiled and backed toward the elevator, the morgue assistant helping him now, walking carefully backward, afraid to do anything but comply with the dead man's every whim.

Amber felt useless and helpless. She choked on a scream, unable to let it out. She shook her head and a terrible sorrow embraced her. In a time of impossible things, this moment would be branded on her soul forever, poisoning her sleep every night. She'd overheard the cops . . . in life, this man Pinsky had been a murderer, a serial killer. Now some anarchic magic, some convulsion in the chaotic sorcery plaguing Hawthorne, had given him a semblance of life. The other revived corpses wandered aimlessly or sought out some simple comfort, but Pinsky's mind held only one purpose—to survive, and kill again.

Pinsky jerked his hostage back, nodded his charred skull at the elevator, and Amber saw the light of understanding flicker in the morgue assistant's eyes. Trembling, his neck bleeding badly, the man reached out and pressed the elevator call button.

A quiet sob wracked Amber's body and she clung to Miles's arm, almost hiding behind him as the true abomination of this horror became clear to her.

"Oh, my God," she whispered. "He can still see."

As if he'd heard her, the dead man turned toward her, brow crinkling so that the skin split. Those empty, charred pits stared at her. Amber froze, wanting to scream and run but afraid that he would pursue her. Her rationality had all but fled. The police shuffled forward, not shouting at the killer the way they might have if he were alive. They seemed at a loss as to what to do. Shooting the corpse did nothing, but if they tried to rush him and take him by force, he would murder the morgue assistant.

One of the old women shambled toward Amber and Miles, and for a moment her view of Pinsky and his hostage was obscured.

She heard the ding of the elevator arriving. The doors slid open to the sound of voices, and Amber saw that the elevator had passengers. She saw police uniforms and a momentary relief washed over her before she remembered that bullets did nothing, that the police could *do* nothing.

Pinsky spun as the voices cut off. As the elevator's passengers saw him, the burned corpse twisted his hostage around and backed into the wall. The killer had nowhere else to go. Charred eye sockets narrowed.

"You've gotta be shitting me," Chief Kramer said, slapping his hand onto the elevator door to keep it from closing.

The chief and another cop who Amber didn't know sidestepped off the elevator, not wanting to turn their backs on Pinsky. There weren't alone. A red-haired girl about Amber's age practically leaped out, stalking toward the killer.

The morgue assistant howled as Pinsky stabbed him again.

"Please!" he said, tears streaming down, his voice, his whole body shaking. "Help me."

Two people were still on the elevator, a beautiful Asian woman and a tall, lanky, good-looking white guy in need of a shave. At first glance they looked ordinary enough, but a weird light flickered in that enclosed space, and Amber thought it seemed as though a breeze gusted around them.

"Who the hell is that?" Miles asked.

Even the dead people in the corridor ceased their shambling and seemed to awaken from their death fugue and turn to look at the two people in the elevator.

The scorched killer slid his back along the wall, holding the weeping, bleeding morgue assistant in front of him. Black flakes of burned skin smeared with grotesque fluids on the wall as he worked his way toward the elevator, obviously intent upon getting on board. Either Pinsky hadn't seen the people in the elevator, or he counted on the knife he held to his hostage's throat to prevent anyone from interfering.

The elevator door started to close.

The man inside whipped out a hand to stop it, and Amber saw a penumbra of purplish light crackling like fire around his fingers. He stepped off the elevator, reached his other hand toward the murderous corpse—this one sizzling in a sphere of golden light—and made a single gesture, a twitch of his wrist. The knife jerked from Pinsky's burned hand, snapping off charred fingers, and the blade clattered to the floor.

The fat woman fell to her knees and covered her face as if weeping. The two dead old women crashed into each other. Autopsy man flailed on the ground in a smear of his own entrails. They all felt something, reacting like animals to an oncoming storm.

Pinsky sneered, the skin of his left cheek splitting, revealing yellowed bone. He grabbed the morgue assistant by the throat, intent upon murder.

The tall man gestured again and the morgue assistant was ripped from Pinsky's grasp and flung toward Chief Kramer. He staggered as he collided with the chief, and both men fell down.

The redheaded girl hissed, her eyes glinting horridly, and Amber froze as the girl lunged at Pinsky, baring fangs. A vampire, Amber thought. *Ohmygodanactualvampire*. And then the vampire girl drove the burned corpse of the killer into the wall and began to tear at his insides, and Amber wanted to be sick.

As the Asian woman slipped out of the elevator behind him, the tall man fell to one knee in the corridor, raised his right hand—which sizzled and throbbed with that purple-black glow—and slapped his palm down onto the linoleum. Like the surf rippling across the sand, that color flowed down the hall, crawled the walls, spilled into the open door of the morgue, flared brightly, and then began to fade.

The dead collapsed like hanged men cut down from the gallows, bodies flopping to the linoleum. The vampire girl jumped back from Pinsky as the killer fell. His body hit the ground with a dry crack, his burned corpse splitting open like a rotten pumpkin. The stink wafted down the hall. Cops and guards, even Miles, all staggered back in disgust, covering noses and mouths. Chief Kramer swore loudly and looked like he might puke.

Amber's own stomach churned, but she managed to keep from being sick.

Her gaze locked onto the tall, lanky man, and the words came unbidden to her mind. *Magician,* she thought. *Sorcerer.*

"Miles," she said, turning to look for him and spotting him kneeling beside the corpse of the heavyset black woman.

She hurried to him and knelt beside him, troubled by the faraway look in his eyes.

"Hey," Amber said, tugging his sleeve.

"She just wanted her baby," Miles rasped.

Amber shook him. "Miles!"

At last he turned and his eyes seemed to focus on her. She pointed at the newcomer. The magician.

"We need to have a talk with *that* guy."

"Tell me again," Octavian said, as he strode down the fifth-floor hall with this new girl, Amber Morrissey, at his side. "What exactly did your friend Tommy say about his father's heart attack?"

"Not much," Amber said, hurrying to keep up with him. "I don't remember the exact words. Does it matter?"

"I don't know," Octavian admitted.

A nurse spoke up, demanding to know what was going on, but Chief Kramer led their grim parade, and he ushered the woman aside with a determined glance and a curt remark about police business. The rest of the hospital staff parted in front of them, and Octavian understood. The chaos in Hawthorne had not reached total anarchy, and perhaps it never would, but he suspected that all of these people must feel their world unraveling around them. Things were not right—not right at all. People were dying. Black wraiths assaulted victims in the privacy of their homes or in the shadowy corners of the town. The tide behaved wildly and toads rained from the sky. Dogs savaged their owners, birds smashed their bodies to pulp on pavement and glass, and bizarre lightning made mad children speak in dead languages. Corpses rose.

Octavian and his companions walked with purpose, and those who saw them moved aside with eyes full of hope that someone had a plan to put a stop to it all.

Keomany had been walking beside the chief, but now she dropped back so that she and Octavian flanked Amber.

"You said you saw his father in a vision," Keomany reminded the girl.

"Kind of a vision," Amber said anxiously. "More a dream. But it was like the others. It's more than a dream. Look, I know it sounds crazy—"

Octavian halted, reaching out to take Amber's hands in his. Chief Kramer kept walking toward the Dunne boy's hospital room, but the others all came to a stop as well. Charlotte had been walking with Officer Moschitto and Amber's college professor—Miles Varick. Was there something more between Amber and Varick? Maybe, but it wasn't Octavian's concern.

"Stop apologizing for the things you don't understand," Octavian told her. He squeezed her hands, allowing a trickle of magic to flow along his arms and into her, soothing her, giving her focus.

Amber had been frantic since the moment she had rushed at him down in the hall outside the morgue, telling him about her visions, and the wraith who'd murdered Miles's mother, and the hot rain and an old iron chest.

"Breathe," he told her.

A nurse hurried by them, huffing in irritation at the traffic jam in the corridor.

"I'm okay," Amber said, glancing at Keomany and then at Charlotte, Miles, and Moschitto. She looked back at Octavian. "Please, let's just go talk to Tommy."

"We will," Octavian promised. "In just a second. But first, focus. You saw your friend Tommy's father in a vision, bringing an old chest as an offering to this goddess."

"Does she have a name?" Keomany asked. "The goddess."

Amber glanced at Miles, then nodded. "Navalica."

"Does it ring a bell, Mr. Octavian?" Miles asked. "I've studied a lot of occult history, and I've never run across it."

Octavian felt a flicker of recognition, but then it was gone. "I don't think so, Professor," he said, glancing at Keomany. "But I'm willing to bet we can trace her back to ancient Chaldea."

"Why Chaldea?" Miles asked.

"A story for later," Octavian said. "In the end, it probably doesn't matter. We know the most important part—an ancient goddess of chaos has come to this town, pissed off, and decided to make life ugly for everyone."

"What does she want?" Amber asked.

Charlotte snickered. "I'm going to guess chaos."

Octavian noticed that Amber flinched and moved away from the vampire girl.

"She may have some other goal," he said. "But for now, let's focus on finding her, and figuring out how to stop her. If you're right, and Norman Dunne's heart attack coincided with your seizure yesterday morning, when he was out fishing with his son . . ."

"Maybe they caught something," Amber said in a quiet voice.

"Exactly."

"Let's go find out," Keomany said, and started to hurry after Chief Kramer.

They all followed. Octavian saw no sign of the chief, and realized he had already reached Tommy Dunne's hospital room and gone inside. Amber picked up her pace until she seemed about to break into a run.

But then they reached Tommy's room, and Amber led them in.

Chief Kramer stood at the foot of the hospital bed and as they entered, he glanced at Octavian.

"The boy's awake," said the chief.

Octavian looked from Chief Kramer to the beaten and bandaged face of Tommy Dunne. "And the iron chest?"

Tommy had been staring at Amber, pleased to see his friend, grimacing with pain as he tried to sit up. At the mention of the chest, he looked at Octavian and the others.

"We did find something just like that," Tommy said. "An old metal box with worn leather straps. My . . . my dad was opening it when he had his heart attack."

Thoughts of his father—the man who had always loved him but had now tried to beat him to death—gave the young man pause. Octavian saw the pain and confusion in his eyes.

"Tommy, I need you to describe this chest," he said.

"There's not much to describe," Tommy replied, reaching a hand up to probe gingerly at the bandages on his head. He winced. "I'd guess it's maybe a foot and a half long, probably nine or ten inches high and deep. The leather straps were worn away, like eaten away, y'know? Old and just rotted or whatever. There were two locks, heavy latches, and the top—the lid, right?—was kind of a weird shape. Not round or square, but kind of edged. If I'd paid attention in geometry, I could give you a better idea."

"Go on," Chief Kramer prodded.

Tommy took a deep breath and continued. "Well, I guess the weird thing is that it looked like it had been made a long time ago, like it should be in a museum, but the metal—I'm thinking iron—it should've been affected by being in the ocean, right? I've seen stuff brought up from wrecks by salvage guys and it's all pitted and worn by the salt. But other than the leather straps, this thing looked brand new."

"Were there any marks on it, anything carved into the metal? Words or symbols?" Keomany asked.

"Nothing," Tommy said, but then he hesitated.

"You just remembered something," Octavian said, glancing at Amber as he moved closer to the hospital bed. "What is it?"

"On the locks," Tommy replied, face set in concentration. "I barely noticed at the time. My dad was already trying to break them open. But on the metal of the latches, there were marks that looked like flames, a weird circle of individual flames like the burning wicks of candles, and then something in the middle that looked almost like a bird."

Octavian flexed his fingers, a flicker of magic rippling through him. "They, the Seven," he said, "proceeding from the west, rising from sea, descending from mountain."

A hungry intelligence lit up Miles Varick's eyes. "What is that from? Assyria? It sounds familiar."

"That design, the ring of flames around a bird, you've seen it before?" Charlotte asked, sidling up beside him almost like an animal investigating his scent. The thought made him study her more closely, wondering just how feral all of this chaos would eventually make her.

"You're close, Professor Varick," Octavian said. He glanced at Chief Kramer and Keomany. "Earlier this morning, we met a young psychiatric patient here in the hospital whose room was struck by arcane lightning, and who now can speak only in ancient Chaldean."

"Chaldean," Miles echoed. He turned to stare at Tommy Dunne. "The circle of flames . . . do you remember how many there were? Could there have been seven?"

Tommy gave a small shrug, wincing with pain as he did it. "I guess so."

"The Maskim?" Miles asked, turning to Octavian.

Keomany rapped her knuckles on the wall. "Come on, Peter. Don't keep us in suspense. This town is falling apart. People could be dying out there."

"People *are* dying out there," Chief Kramer said.

Octavian nodded. "You're right. And Professor Varick's on the right track. The ancient Chaldeans had a complex theology, including a hierarchy of gods and demons. There were ranks of demons, like the orders of angels in Hebrew beliefs. The most powerful and most evil of Chaldean demons were the Maskim, also called the Seven, and sometimes the Seven Flames."

"And you think these demons are, what, being reborn on Earth here in Hawthorne?" Chief Kramer asked. "I mean, here, of *all* places?"

"Impossible," Miles said.

Octavian shot him a dark look. Amber reached out and took her professor's hand, and Octavian thought there was more there than the concern of a favored student.

"From what little I can remember reading about the Maskim, if they were here, we wouldn't be," Miles said. "Hawthorne would be a smoking pit."

"Agreed," Octavian said. "I don't think we're dealing with the Maskim."

"Then what—" Officer Moschitto began.

"The symbols Tommy saw engraved on the latches of that chest," Octavian said. "I've never seen anything like them. But if these are the pieces of this puzzle—Greg Wheeler speaking Chaldean, that symbol, and everything that's happened thus far, all the chaos—I think we have to assume those seven flames are *the* Seven Flames, the Maskim. Which raises the question, what the hell is the bird in the center of that circle of flames?"

Charlotte went to the window and peered anxiously out through the dark and the rain. Octavian thought she looked like she'd heard the call of the wild and wanted to run. To howl. He could feel it inside him, as well, an energy that had nothing to do with the magic at his core, and everything to do with his basest, most carnal instincts. He wanted to fight. He wanted to fuck. He glanced around and saw that they were all edgy. They had been feeling it all morning, and the effect—wherever it came from—was getting worse. He glanced at Keomany and she flushed, as if with guilt, and glanced away.

"An eighth demon?" Amber asked, sliding closer to Miles, the two of them almost rubbing up against each other.

Octavian looked at Miles. "There's an older myth. It isn't strictly Chaldean, but from all of the magic theologies of the region— Babylon, Acadia, and a lot of others. The Chaldeans had mages, of course. The Magi, the three 'wise men' who brought gifts to the newborn Jesus Christ, were descendants of Chaldean mages. The Chaldeans had vampires, too—"

"Wait," Keomany said, "I thought Christ himself was the first vampire."

Octavian took a deep breath. He had learned so much in Hell . . . so much that the rest of the world had forgotten.

"Okay, quickly," he said, "you've all read the story by now of how the Christ faced demons in the desert, and how they savaged his flesh. Had he been anyone else, he would have become evil, a twisted mockery of life wearing his own face. But the divine power in him prevented the taint from spreading in him . . . up until he died, and

Divinity—what Christians call the Holy Spirit—left him. When God had no more use for the shell once inhabited by the Christ, it became something else. Something new. Shadows, like Charlotte . . . what we think of today as vampires . . . are a combination of demonic contagion, human flesh, and the divine influence passed down from that conflict in the desert.

"But those creatures . . . the things Jesus fought in the desert . . . they were the original vampires. Pure evil, with no trace of human emotion or divine light to temper that darkness. They haven't been seen in this world for two thousand years, not since the Christ himself eradicated them."

"What does any of this have to do with the Seven?" Keomany asked, her voice filled with an urgency he understood quite well. They needed to get out of this room, out of this hospital, and find something to fight, before they lost control of themselves.

"Short version—"

"Too fucking late for that," Charlotte snapped.

Octavian ignored her. "This ancient vampire species, the Innin, were never born. They were created in a storm of chaos that tore holes in the walls separating the human world from the demon realms, as if a chemical reaction of dark magic and our reality spawned them."

"Holy shit," Officer Moschitto muttered.

They were all staring at him, but Octavian ignored them, forging ahead.

"Do you think these wraiths are—what did you call them—Innin?" Amber asked, pushing her hair behind her ears.

"I don't. Maybe they're related, but I think they're something else entirely. That's the point. This maelstrom of magic . . . other cultures that existed at the same time as the ancient Chaldeans claimed that it's where the Maskim came from, too. Like the maelstrom, that chaos was some kind of womb that gave birth to monsters."

"But where did the storm come from?" Miles asked.

Octavian looked over at the rain-slick window. Charlotte stood looking back, and he saw that she had bitten into her lip and now licked the blood from her mouth.

"According to one of the clay tablets found by de Sarzac during the excavation of the Sumerian city of Lagash, the storm had a mother."

The people in the room had fallen silent, staring at him. The rain pelted the window and the wind shook the building. Hospital noises continued in the corridor, but in that room, no one breathed, until at last Amber spoke.

"Navalica," she said.

Octavian studied her frightened eyes and saw the moment when grim determination made her stand a bit straighter. She wanted to live. She wanted to fight. He admired her for that.

"Time had eroded some of the tablet. No name could be found for the mother of the maelstrom. But I suspect it may be her, yes. The pieces connect."

"But why here?" Chief Kramer demanded.

"Why anywhere?" Miles whispered.

"We'll find an answer," Keomany said. "While we're all trying to stay alive, we'll find an answer."

"The important thing," Octavian added, "is that all of this is going to get much worse if we don't stop it."

He looked at the young man in the hospital bed. "I believe if we can get that iron chest, we'll understand much more about why here, and why now. If Amber's visions hold true, your father means to get it and bring it to Navalica. We need to get the chest before he can do that."

Tommy brightened, looking for the first time like something more than an injured child, and more like a man. He glanced from Chief Kramer to Amber and then pushed himself up into a sitting position.

"He doesn't know where it is," Tommy said. "The last my dad knew, it was on the boat. We left it there when the ambulance came to take him to the hospital. But I went back yesterday after I left the hospital. I . . . I thought it might be valuable and I wanted to make sure no one took it."

"He's under the influence of the goddess," Keomany said. "It's possible he can sense the chest. That he'll find it anyway."

Chief Kramer stood straighter, grasping at something he understood, a purpose he could claim.

"Maybe, but this gives us a chance of getting to it before he does. Where is it, Tommy?"

"I brought it over to Mr. Hodgson's house," Tommy said.

"Bill Hodgson, the lobsterman?" Chief Kramer asked.

Tommy nodded. "He's always telling stories about diving on old wrecks and things he brought up from the bottom. I thought he could figure out where it came from and what it might be worth."

Chief Kramer looked at Octavian. "I'll get my car and meet you out front."

Octavian nodded. "Let's go. We've wasted too much time already."

But as they all began to move toward the door, Amber shouted and blocked the way.

"No," she said, eyes wide, shaking her head. "No way. My family is . . . they're infected or something. The only reason I left them was to find help. I know you had to figure this all out, and I get that you have to find this treasure chest, or whatever the hell it is, but I can't go anywhere but home. I *left* them, don't you understand? I need *help*."

Octavian glanced at Keomany and Charlotte.

"We'll help," Keomany promised.

But Octavian's attention had caught on a single word.

"What do you mean, 'infected'?" he asked.

"They're changing," Amber said, taking Miles's hand. "They're changing into those things."

An icy shudder went through Octavian. "Wraiths, you mean? Like the one that killed Professor Varick's mother?"

Amber nodded. "My great-grandmother looked like she was changing, too. I tried to wake her, but I couldn't, and then I ran out of the house, and saw Miles, and we thought if we talked to Tommy and figured out how it all started, we could stop it. I could save them."

Octavian didn't like the sound of that at all.

"Chief Kramer," he said, "Keomany, Charlotte, and Professor Varick will go with you. I'll stay with Amber. Whether you get to the chest before Norman Dunne or not, catch up with me at Amber's house."

Amber's expression softened. "Thank you."

Octavian said nothing. He had seen these wraiths in action, and it had never occurred to him that they might have begun as humans. Nor had Chief Kramer mentioned anything about people vanishing, or any other instance of such a transformation.

Charlotte stood next to him. "You don't want me with you?"

Keomany shot her a sharp glance that could only have been jealousy. The chaos that had been unbridling the urges of so many had created a dangerous dynamic among the three of them, almost without Octavian's realizing it. Much better for them to be parted for now. He thought of Nikki and wondered if she had begun to worry yet that she hadn't heard from him. The lust that rose in him, the animal passion of it, looked at Keomany and Charlotte—a witch and a vampire—and wanted the magic in them, something he could never get from Nikki. He wondered if it was only the chaos, or if the desire had been in him all along.

"You stay with Keomany," he told Charlotte, aware of the others all watching him. "If you run into trouble, the two of you are better off together."

Chief Kramer had his radio out as he went into the corridor, Officer Moschitto at his side. Amber thanked Tommy Dunne, and then she and Miles followed the policemen. Charlotte went next.

Keomany said nothing, only walked over to Octavian, took his hands, and pressed her body against him. A fire of lust ignited inside him. He could feel every curve of her, and it felt to him as though she burned with a heat that prickled his skin, even through his clothes. She stood on her toes and pressed her lips to his throat in a kiss that weakened him for a moment.

Then he pushed her back, held her away from him.

"No," he said.

She turned her face from him in shame. "I know. It's making me crazy."

"It's going to make us all crazy before too long."

And then Keomany was gone, she and Charlotte hurrying down the corridor with Moschitto, Professor Varick, and the chief. Octavian turned and thanked Tommy, who stared at him in fascination, and then walked out into the corridor, where Amber awaited him.

"My family," Amber said as the two of them rushed down the hall. "Do you think you can help them?"

"I'll do whatever I can," he said.

Octavian wanted to reassure the girl, to promise her that her parents would be all right, but he didn't have the heart to lie.

14

The storm had grown worse. As Octavian sped through Hawthorne, the rain drummed on the roof of the car and punished the windshield with such force he thought the glass would crack. He bent over the steering wheel in search of a clear view, but the hot rain had turned even more oily, and the wipers did little more than smear it into long streaks. As he rounded a corner, the tires skidded on slick pavement, forcing him to slow down.

A wraith flitted across the street, black smoke and skeletal piping outlined in the headlights, before vanishing into the rain. Octavian tapped the brakes, slowing further.

"Don't stop," Amber said from the passenger seat. "Please."

Reluctantly, he drove on. She was right, though. The only way to help the people of Hawthorne was to find Navalica and destroy her, to end this storm and send the wraiths back to wherever they had come from.

"There are more of them, I think," Amber said, peering out her window.

They had seen at least a dozen in the scant miles they'd traveled from the hospital, clinging to houses and perched on roofs, slipping through windows and doors. The chaos magic that prickled Octavian's skin and suffused his heart with a simmering violence and lust had gripped many people in Hawthorne. The evidence was all around them. Though most of the residents remained indoors, they had seen a mob chasing a man down a narrow side street, three separate bloody brawls, and various couples fucking savagely on street corners and up against buildings. In the storm of anarchic magic, illuminated only by flashes of crisp blue lightning, it had become impossible to tell the difference between sex and rape.

A wraith flashed by the window, flying ahead of the car into the churning storm, dragging an amorphous butterfly of color-shifting light beneath it on the hooks of its curved blades. What were they taking from people, Octavian wondered. Souls? Vitality? Morality?

"There may be more," Octavian said. "Or they're just not as worried about being seen now. The storm's getting stronger. It's building to something. Whatever purpose they serve, they're not trying to hide it anymore."

Octavian thought another moment, troubled. The girl beside him was beautiful, her body young and ripe, and he could sense that the chaos had worked its dark, twisted magic on her hungers just as it had on his own. But she was young, still in college, and he was in love with someone else. There was nothing between them. They didn't even know each other.

He noticed her squirming in her seat and saw her frustration. The things the chaos did to her were making her angry. Like Octavian, she refused to give in to those baser instincts. But the wraiths had no such hesitation.

"It could be that they're just excited," he said quietly, his voice barely audible over the pounding rain. "They're in a frenzy."

Amber settled back in her seat, gaze lowered, as though she no longer wanted to see what the storm had brought to her hometown.

"So, what, they're like sharks when there's blood in the water?" she asked.

Octavian didn't think she meant for him to answer, so he kept quiet. He glanced in the rearview mirror and saw the blue lights of Officer Moschitto's patrol car flashing. Chief Kramer had decided that they should have a policeman with them to add an official element to whatever actions Octavian might have to take. The chief did not understand that *official* meant nothing now. The police might help some of the people in town make it through the next few hours, but when it came

to surviving to see another sunrise, the chief and his officers were not
a factor.

"Turn left on Herman Street, right up here," Amber said.

Octavian signaled for the turn, that tiny gesture a small victory for
order.

But then he saw the car ahead. An old Honda had gone over the
curb, scraped its passenger side along a telephone pole, and then
crashed into a stone retaining wall in front of an old Victorian set back
from the road.

"Mr. Octavian," Amber started.

"I see them."

There were people in the car, and they were screaming. He counted
three, but he couldn't be sure because the wraiths had come. They
darted around the car, long thin arms flashing in through shattered
windows, curved blades hacking and tearing. The rain and the wraiths'
tattered clothing whipping in the wind blotted out much of their view,
but the screaming continued. Arms flailed but passed through the creatures. They could reach into their victims' flesh, into their very souls,
and no one could touch them.

"That's Mrs. Robideau's car!" Amber said, sounding much younger
than her twenty-one years. "They live right down the street from me."

Octavian aimed his car at the Honda, turned on the bright lights,
and laid on the horn. He hit the brakes, and the tires skidded on the
oily pavement. The wraiths were in a frenzy around the crashed
Honda—sharks in the water, like Amber had said—but now they all
looked up. The bright lights seemed to strip some of the mist away
from them, leaving them nothing more than slim black bones, but the
effect lasted only a moment.

They darted away from the Honda. Octavian slammed the car into
park and popped open the door, his skin prickling with magic summoned up by instinct. A rich silver light leaped in arcs of energy
between his fingers as he stepped out into the rain, but already they
were fleeing. He counted five wraiths, and three of them had those
amorphous colorful lights speared on their blades, dragging beneath
them.

Octavian didn't know exactly what they were stealing from people, but he had seen souls manifested in the world before, and they looked nothing like this. He suspected it was something that fed chaos, that the wraiths fed on human passion or imagination.

Officer Moschitto pulled up, tires skidding so badly on the slippery rain that his patrol car bumped the curb and the big blue mailbox on the sidewalk.

"You know where Amber lives?" Octavian asked as the cop jumped out of his car.

"Just around the corner," Moschitto replied.

"Do what you can for these people and catch up to us there," Octavian said, and he slid back behind the wheel of his car.

"They all took off in the same direction," he said. "Maybe it's a coincidence, but we're going the same way. The wraiths were headed toward your house."

Octavian put the car in gear and hit the gas, the tires spinning as he made the turn onto Herman Street. Amber's house was number 136, and he bent to stare through the smeared windshield, searching for any sign of the wraiths, hoping he was wrong about their destination.

It took him several seconds to realize Amber hadn't replied. Frowning, he glanced at her and saw that she was staring down at her hands, which were turned palm upward.

"Amber?" he ventured.

Over the drumming of the rain on the car, he hadn't heard the sound at first, but now he could make out the low hitching of her breath, and he saw the tears on her cheeks.

"Look at me," she said.

Octavian skidded to a halt again, only blocks from her house. Blood running cold, he turned on the interior light. He clenched his jaw to keep from cursing out loud, because he didn't want to scare the girl. He was the sorcerer, the one who had lived a life that to her must have seemed almost eternal. If he didn't know how to help her, she would think her death was imminent. Octavian thought it might be.

The skin of her forearms had taken on a darker tint and begun to harden. It had an almost chitinous texture, like the shell of an insect. Her fingers had grown longer and narrowed; soon they would be claws.

"When did this start?" he asked.

Her head shook and she gave a tiny shrug. "I was itchy. I scratched . . . I thought it was just itchy," she said, an edge of hysteria in her voice. Then she looked up at him. "What will it feel like, do you think? Being one of them?"

Octavian reached out and touched her arm. She flinched, then stared at the silver light sparking from his hand.

"What are you doing?" she asked.

"Does it hurt?"

"A little."

"Give me your hands," he said.

She turned to him, there in the illumination of the dome light with the rain pounding above them and the darkness of the storm cradling the car, rocking it with gusts of wind. They linked hands, and Octavian closed his eyes.

"What are you doing?"

"Hush," he said.

Octavian felt the magic within him reacting to the dark magic infecting her, transforming her. He let his mind slip back to his centuries in Hell, to demons and twisted souls he had encountered there, to things that had tried to taint him and enslave him. The filth of those things, their poison, felt something like this.

He took a deep breath and exhaled, forcing away the violence and lewd thoughts the chaos storm had raised within him. A second breath, and this time when he exhaled, he let the magic flow from him, the energy of it crackling along his arms and through his hands, then spreading up Amber's arms and engulfing her in silver light. She let slip a tiny noise, a gasp of surprise or pleasure or both.

Octavian spoke.

"Káto apó to dérma kai sto esoterikó ton ostón, píso apó ti génnisi kai tin koiliá tis mitéras tou, katharízei tin kardiá kai sárka ólon ton dilitiriáseon, káthe kakó, kai i kilída tis skoteinís mageías."

Amber's eyes fluttered as if she were waking from a dream. He released her hands and she reached up to wipe her tears.

"It stopped itching," she said, but when she held up her hands, they remained altered, the flesh of her arms like hard carapace, her fingers like claws. "But . . ."

"I did a purification spell," Octavian said. "It might cleanse you completely, or it might only slow whatever is being done to you. If I can figure out the nature of this transformation, that will help."

She stared at her hands, horror etched on her face. Octavian could feel her fear and uncertainty, but he needed her attention.

"Amber," he said firmly. "Your family."

She nodded. "Drive."

The tires spun as Octavian hit the gas. They spoke not a word as the car sped through the storm, engine growling, houses flashing by in the unnatural dark. He had felt the dark power working inside Amber and wondered how many hours had passed since it had first begun its work on her parents and great-grandmother.

"Right here," she said. "On the left."

He turned into the driveway of the well-kept, bone-and-rose-hued Victorian and killed the engine. It loomed above them, almost brooding, and Octavian felt a presence filling the house as though the walls were its womb and it cried out to be born.

"There!" Amber said, pointing at a wraith darting in through a second-story window. But there were others, some on the roof and some flitting around the turret at the top like wasps around a nest.

"Stay in the car," he told her, stepping out and pocketing his keys.

Amber got out. "I don't think so."

She rushed for the door, slipping on the driveway a little before regaining her footing. Octavian chased her, passed her, reached the front door first and didn't let her bother using the keys she fumbled from her pocket. With a wave of his hand, the door swung inward.

A wraith lunged out at them. Amber screamed as Octavian thrust both hands forward, hurling concussive magic at the thing. The spell passed right through it and struck a table in the foyer, shattering a vase and smashing framed family photos, and then the wraith was upon

Octavian, black blades flashing, ripping into him without cutting his skin. They slashed at his consciousness, at his mind, and he shouted in pain and confusion.

He staggered back. Amber screamed again and it hesitated.

Octavian snarled, reached out, and thrust his own hand into the black, smoky ribbons that were its garments. He muttered words learned in the torment of Sheol and the smoke solidified. His fist closed around the narrow pipe of its neck and he summoned a deeper magic, old as angels, and the wraith stiffened, then froze solid, its essence turned to anthracite coal.

With a kick, he shattered it.

"What did you—"

"Go!" Octavian snapped. "Where's your parents' room?"

Rain-slicked hair veiling her face, Amber bolted, leading him through the foyer and up the first flight of stairs. His skin prickled, a dim golden light dancing from his fingers as he pursued her, glancing around for any other wraiths.

Amber stopped in the open doorway to her parents' room, then backpedaled until she hit the corridor wall. Octavian hurried past her and entered the room.

The Morrisseys lay in their bed, eyes closed, limbs contorted as though they had been sleeping poorly. The bedclothes had been tossed or kicked aside. Amber's mother wore a nightshirt bearing the image of Tweety Bird. It had rucked up to just beneath her breasts, exposing her plain white underwear. Mr. Morrissey wore pale blue boxer shorts.

There were barely recognizable as human. Their facial features had almost completely vanished, the flesh hardening and smoothing out, turning into the same black plating that the other wraiths had for faces. No hair remained. They still had human weight and heft, but their bodies had withered horribly, thinning so much that soon they would be nothing but skeletal piping, like the creatures flitting around outside their house.

"No," Amber said. "Please, you've got to help them."

Seconds ticked by as Octavian stared at them, racking his brain for some spell that might reverse what was being done to the Morrisseys.

In the vast store of occult knowledge he had acquired in Hell, there must be something, but he did not have time to think on it, and the Morrisseys didn't have time to wait for him.

Cursing under his breath, he raised his hands and sketched at the air. His muttering turned into a spell, and the color began to drain from everything in the room. The furniture, and Amber's parents, started to fade until they were almost ghostly themselves, their pallor turning a strange sepia. Octavian backed into the hallway.

"What are you doing?" Amber demanded.

"Buying time. I've frozen them in a single moment. If stopping Navalica doesn't heal them, and you, they'll stay like this until I can figure something out."

Amber tried to reach into the room, her fingers bumping against an invisible barrier in the open doorway.

"Where is your great-grandmother's room?" Octavian asked, looking around.

That woke her up. "Top floor."

Octavian ran. Down the hall, he saw something flitting from room to room, but he did not slow as he mounted the next flight of steps two at a time.

"Do you think they were all people once?" Amber asked, huffing with effort.

"Looks that way," Octavian said.

Then there was no more time for questions. They reached the third-floor landing and rushed toward her great-grandmother's room. The door stood halfway open. A low whisper of motion, like silk on silk, issued from the bedroom. Octavian nearly barged in, but paused, listening to that sound. Amber made a small, urgent noise behind him as he reached out and gave the door a light push.

It swung inward.

The wraiths slid against one another, brushing together like animals huddled for warmth. There must have been nine or ten of them around the old woman's bed, and several of them clutched undulating masses of light and color, as though stripping it from the old woman's flesh. Others had their smoky hands plunged deep inside her.

"Oh, no. Gran," Amber whispered.

The wraiths all looked up, almost as if she'd screamed.

Octavian charged into the room. His left hand snapped up and he cast the spell that brought their intangible essence in synch with this dimension. The one at the front door had hurt him because he hadn't anticipated its true nature, and he wouldn't allow that to happen again.

He thrust out his right hand, summoning all of his strength, tapping the core of magic in him that burst out in a wave of concussive force. Wraiths blew back into the walls and crashed through windows. One hit the ceiling. A crucifix fell from the wall and snapped in half when it hit the floor. Knickknacks tipped over on a shelf. A lamp shattered.

"Kill them," Amber said, hatred in her voice, the chaos in the air giving her a savage edge.

Octavian grabbed the nearest wraith, working the hex that would transform its smoke into anthracite, just as he had done to the one downstairs.

But then he heard Amber cry out.

"Gran?" the girl said.

Octavian turned and stared. The old woman had begun to change, but there was no carapace, no black smoke, no skeletal bone structure. As he and Amber watched, her youth and vigor were restored, but her body altered, shifting, growing. Her skin darkened not to black but to a pale blue and her chest pulsed and blossomed as new breasts pushed out from her flesh.

Her hair ignited in cold, blue-black flames, and then that indigo fire was her hair.

"Oh, shit," Octavian whispered.

Amber staggered backward, crashing into the wall. The wraiths began to shake and fall to their knees. The figure on the bed sat up, eyes opening wide, gleaming golden yellow.

The goddess Navalica looked at Octavian and began to scream.

Miles felt like he now lived and breathed in a nightmare that would never end. He could feel his heart beating in his chest, knew that this wasn't a dream, but neither did it feel entirely like reality. Whatever happened to Hawthorne now, his life had reached its apocalypse, and everything now was only him wandering in the ashes of the world he'd once known.

He sat with Keomany Shaw in the back of Chief Kramer's car. The vampire girl, Charlotte, was in the passenger seat in front of him. Miles himself had offered to let the girl ride shotgun, but not out of any sense of chivalry. The tension between Keomany and Charlotte was palpable and he thought it best to separate them. He was also not thrilled about the idea of being trapped in the back of a police car with an irritable vampire. Don Kramer had a gun, at least.

"Are you all right, Miles?" the chief asked. "You're awfully quiet back there."

Miles glanced at Keomany, who studied him curiously.

"I suppose I'm feeling a bit guilty for letting Amber go off without me. We've been looking after each other through this."

Charlotte snickered, turning a lascivious gaze upon him. "Oh, is that what you call it?"

Miles frowned. "She's half my age."

"Yeah," Charlotte said, "the good half."

Behind the wheel, Chief Kramer smiled but said nothing. Miles wanted to protest further, but he didn't want to make a fool of himself. The chaos storm had done something to all of them, made them more aggressive in a variety of ways, and stirred lust for sex and violence in them. He could see it in the others and feel it in himself. From the first day of the semester he had liked and admired Amber, and now he felt as if this filthy magic had perverted his fondness for her. Perhaps it was better that they were apart for now.

The chief had turned on the blue lights and as he drove through the rain, Miles could see the pale, ghostly color flashing off parked cars and the dead, unblinking eyes of darkened house windows. Chief Kramer had pulled a pair of officers away from the hospital and the two uniforms followed in another car, just behind them, but both patrol cars proceeded without sirens. No one was on the street, so there hardly seemed any point. But Miles thought there was more to it than that—sirens were an announcement that the police were on their way, like the cavalry, and all would be well. One glance at Don Kramer's eyes in the rearview mirror, and it was clear to Miles that the chief didn't have the confidence to use the siren tonight.

"How far to . . . what was his name?" Keomany asked.

"Bill Hodgson," Chief Kramer said. "He lives on Sweeney's Point, on the north end of town. Sandpiper Hill overlooks the water. A lot of ship owners built homes there when Hawthorne still thrived as a port. When they moved on, it was all captains up there. Now it's dentists and advertising executives who get to work at home."

Charlotte pushed her damp hair away from her face, the red darker now that it was wet. "I thought you guys said he was a fisherman?"

"Lobsterman," the chief corrected. "He is. Hodgson's grandfather built the house way back when. In those days, the family had a lot of boats in the water. Now it's just the one, with Bill as skipper, but when he was in his twenties, he used some family money to open up the Surfside Restaurant, and he still owns it. Does just fine for himself, Bill Hodgson."

"Sounds like a nice life," Keomany said.

"Doesn't it?" Chief Kramer agreed.

"The Dunne boy said he was some kind of expert on sunken ships," Miles said.

The chief glanced at him in the rearview mirror. "You don't know him?"

Miles almost managed to smile. "You know me, Don."

"You're something else, Miles," Chief Kramer said. He glanced at Charlotte. "He grew up in this town, but he hardly knows anyone."

Miles felt Keomany studying him.

"But you stayed here," she said, and he understood what she was saying. What she was asking. If he had such little interest in his hometown that most people were strangers to him, why had he taken a position teaching at the university in town instead of trying to find a job elsewhere?

"I went to college in New York," he said. "But I hated leaving my mother alone."

Charlotte laughed. "Mama's boy. No wonder you're single."

Miles had to stifle the urge to strangle her with the strap of her seat belt. She would likely have killed him seconds later, but the vampire girl's sneering had begun to get to him. He wondered if she was always like this, or if it was just chaos talking.

"I wasn't always single," he said, and then wondered why he'd said it. He didn't have to justify anything to these people.

"Charlotte," Keomany said, her voice low and dangerous. "You want to keep your catty fucking comments to yourself?"

"I really don't," the vampire replied, grinning.

"You're lucky Peter didn't kill you."

Charlotte's eyes flashed excitedly. "He doesn't want to kill me. He wants to *do* me."

Miles watched Chief Kramer's nervous eyes in the rearview mirror. He might be the chief of police, but what was he supposed to do if these two gave in to the chaotic influence and went at each other? A vampire and a . . . what had the chief said Keomany was? Not just a witch, but an earthwitch. Some kind of elemental sorceress.

"More things in Heaven and Earth, Horatio . . ." he muttered.

"What?" Charlotte snapped, glaring at him, spoiling for a fight.

"*Girl,*" Chief Kramer said, his tone so stern that they all turned toward him. He kept his hands firmly on the wheel, looking out through the oily, rain-slicked windshield.

"Who're you calling *girl*?" Charlotte demanded.

Chief Kramer ignored the question. "You need to decide whose side you're on."

Charlotte glanced back at Keomany. She grimaced, her fangs glinting in the blue light that flashed into the vehicle from the police car behind them. Her eyes danced with violence. She looked like she might crawl out of her skin, like a junkie badly in need of a fix. But then she smiled.

"I'm on your side, Sheriff."

"Chief," Kramer corrected.

"Whatever."

"Good," the chief replied. "Because we're here. And Norm Dunne beat us to it."

As Chief Kramer hit the brakes, Miles grabbed hold of the seat in front of him. The car skidded to a halt, and then everything happened quickly. The chief left the car running as he jumped out, hand going to his gun. Charlotte moved so quickly that she was out of the vehicle almost before he was, leaving Miles blinking stupidly in the backseat.

"Charlotte, the door!" Keomany yelled, and only then did she remember that the backseat had no door handles.

Miles bent to look through the door Chief Kramer had left open. Keomany might be in a hurry to get out, but he wasn't sure that he shared her urgency. This was police business now. He wanted to help, but he'd been brought along to secure and examine the chest that the Dunnes had brought up from the water, not for a confrontation involving cops and their weapons. Even the aggression wrought within him by the chaos storm didn't override his dislike of guns.

"Forget it," Keomany said angrily.

She put a hand on the window and it grew suddenly cold in the back of the car. Miles shivered as icy air gripped him, and he realized he could see his breath. The window frosted over and Keomany shifted in the seat, leaned back, and punched her boot right through it. As she reached through the shattered window and opened the door from the outside, Miles hesitated. How much of what happened from now on would be dictated by the chaos worming its way inside them?

"Come on," she said.

Heart pounding with anticipation of the possibility of violence, he slid across the seat and climbed out after her. Only as his shoe crunched it underfoot did he realize that she had not just frozen the glass, but turned it to ice. Already it was melting.

"Put it down and back away, Mr. Dunne!" one of the cops shouted, moving past Miles and Keomany, his gun leveled.

Miles took in the scene in an instant. Lights burned in some of the houses on Sandpiper Hill Road, but in the rain and mist they were only blurred beacons. The two police cars were parked at hard angles in front of a hip-roofed Georgian surrounded by trees and prickly bushes. The screen door hung partially off its frame, the main door wide open.

Beyond the house, a rocky ledge overlooked the ocean. Metal railing indicated the stairs that led down to the water or a beach below. Out over the Atlantic, the storm churned and roiled, but within the clouds was a dim light that reminded him that outside the Hell that had swept over them, it was daylight. Hell, it was morning. He had forgotten.

"Norm, I'm not messing around here!" Chief Kramer barked, snapping Miles back to the nightmare that had ensnared them all. "Put the damn box down."

Miles blinked. He felt detached from reality.

Chief Kramer and his two officers surrounded a middle-aged man with graying hair and a long scar on the left side of his face. Norman Dunne might be in his forties, but his chest was broad and his arms were powerful. His hair and his clothes were soaked through by the storm, but the blood splashes on his shirt would never come out, and Miles understood that old Bill Hodgson—lobsterman and restaurateur—must be dead.

Norm Dunne held the iron chest in front of him.

"For the goddess," the fisherman said, as though he expected the police officers to understand, to lower their weapons and let him pass. As though murder were entirely reasonable.

The three cops surrounded him. Charlotte joined the circle, crouched and ready to pounce. *God,* Miles thought, *she looks hungry.* Chief Kramer barked at the vampire girl to back off, but Charlotte didn't move. Keomany kept her distance, but when Miles glanced at her, he saw that the wind seemed to swirl around her, as though she had her own private twister.

Dunne started to walk toward a gap between Chief Kramer and one of the other cops, but the chief got in his way, aiming at his chest.

"Not another step, Norm!" the chief barked.

Dunne cocked his head, almost birdlike. Inhuman. Miles noticed for the first time that his eyes were black.

"Bill?" Chief Kramer called toward the house. "You in there? You all right?"

Only the wind replied. They all knew that Bill Hodgson was anything but all right.

"Damn it, Norm, put the box on the goddamn ground right now!" the chief shouted, his voice cracking.

His nerves were frayed. The muscles in his neck stood out, and for the first time, Miles understood that Don Kramer wanted very badly to shoot Norman Dunne. To shoot someone.

Chaos.

Dunne's upper lip curled in disgust. Miles thought that in his chaos-twisted mind, the man must have only just realized they meant to stop him, that they did not worship his goddess. He started forward again.

A gunshot cracked the air, echoes bouncing off the storm and Bill Hodgson's house. Miles flinched and took a step back, looking at Don Kramer, but the chief hadn't fired his weapon. One of his men, a young guy with a crew cut and some kind of Chinese symbol tattooed on the back of his hand, had pulled the trigger, and he looked like he very much wanted to do it again.

And he might have to.

Norm Dunne glanced down at the hole in his shirt—in his chest—as fresh blood soaked into the fabric. This time it was his own blood, but the bullet had barely made him flinch. It seemed to mystify him, and he stared at the hole as the fluid leaking from his body and staining his shirt turned from red to darkest black.

Gripping the chest more tightly to him, Norm Dunne looked up and grinned.

"Shoot him again, for Christ's sake!" someone shouted.

It took Miles a couple of seconds to realize it had been him.

15

The police opened fire. Miles flinched with every shot as bullets punched through Norm Dunne's chest and arms. Chief Kramer shot the fisherman in the left knee, and the man's leg buckled. He went down on one knee, clutching the iron chest against him as if it were a child he would give his life to save. One of the other cops took aim and squeezed off a round that hit Dunne in the temple, and the impact rocked the fisherman over onto his side, where he curled into a fetal position, protecting the chest.

Miles looked at Keomany, but the earthwitch still stood in a strange vortex of wind she seemed to have summoned. It kept the hot, sticky rain off her, and he wondered if that was the point. Through the rain and the veil created by that wind, he could not read her face.

Charlotte stalked back and forth at the edges of the action like a predator awaiting the outcome, looking for an opening in which to attack.

Two shots hit Dunne in the back before Chief Kramer finally shouted for them to cease fire.

"Damn it, Norman, I want that fucking chest!" the chief shouted, approaching Dunne, keeping his gun trained on the man.

The fisherman hummed to himself, less a melody than a chant, and rocked a little, making Miles think of his cousin Angie's autistic son. But he made no move to surrender or give up the box, and Miles knew he would not. Black fluid like oil dripped from the entry and exit wounds in his back. Whatever control Navalica had over Dunne—he figured it must stem from the man's discovery of the chest—it was complete. The poor son of a bitch wasn't even human anymore. He should have been dead, and Miles thought Dunne would have been much better off if that were the case. Better to be dead than to live as some kind of black-magic puppet.

"Norm, don't make me!" Chief Kramer barked, bending over slightly, the tips of his shoes practically bumping into Dunne's back. He aimed his gun at the back of the fisherman's head.

Miles took a couple of steps forward. "Don, what are you doing?"

"What has to be done. Hawthorne's dying all around us, Miles. Being murdered. And if what's in that box can help me stop it, then I'll do whatever it takes to—"

"You can't execute the man!" Miles said. He looked to Keomany and Charlotte for backup, but received none.

Chief Kramer turned toward Miles, gun wavering, not as though he had changed his mind but as if he were trying to decide which of them to shoot.

"Are you nuts?" the chief asked. "This isn't Norm Dunne. Did you see his eyes? We just shot him a dozen times and all it's done is turn him into a petulant child. Reality's called a time-out, Professor. If you aren't willing to do what has to be done—"

Dunne shot out a hand and grabbed Chief Kramer's wrist and twisted even as the chief pulled the trigger. The bullet whined past Miles's temple. The two officers jockeyed for position, shouting to their boss, but Dunne dragged Chief Kramer to the pavement with him, pulling his gun hand into the same embrace in which he held the iron chest. The chief shouted, trying to extricate himself. He jerked and pulled the trigger, and an exit wound blew open in Dunne's back, even as the fisherman darted his jaws forward and bit deeply into Chief Kramer's neck.

With a backward jerk of his head, Dunne tore out the chief's throat with his teeth. Blood spurted from the gaping wound, spraying Dunne's face. The fisherman let go and curled around the iron chest again, snickering to himself as the chief's body jerked and flopped over, blood gouting from his throat.

Miles stared in shock, drowning in guilt. If he hadn't interrupted . . .

The remaining two cops started shooting again. Charlotte didn't wait for them to stop. The vampire girl leaped through the rain and landed in a crouch beside Dunne. The chief had wanted to handle this his own way, officially, but now his life was spilling out onto the road, and all bets were off.

The goddess's influence had given Dunne an inhuman strength, but vampires were superhuman. Charlotte jammed the heel of a boot down onto Dunne's neck, grabbed his right arm in both hands, and yanked up so hard that bones broke and tore through his skin as she peeled his grip off the iron chest. His black, chaos-tainted blood splashed her boots and she stood there on top of him, the rain plastering her clothes to her tight, perfect body, her red hair a wet veil hiding half of her face, mouth open in a sneer that revealed her fangs, which were much more prominent now, like needles jutting from her mouth.

God forgive him, he had never seen anything so arousing.

Charlotte pulled the iron chest from the grasp of Dunne's remaining hand, but as she started to turn away, the ruined man leaped to his feet and snagged her hair in his fist. The vampire girl glanced at him as if the attack meant nothing to her, but then a look of alarm crossed her face and she put the chest under one arm, prepared to fight him.

Keomany seemed to fly at them, carried on the vortex swirling around her, oily rain shedding from the wind she'd summoned. She halted ten feet from Dunne and seemed to dance in the wind, bringing one arm forward as if she were throwing a baseball. The wind uncoiled from her, snatched Dunne off the ground, and hurled him with terrible, bone-breaking force into the chief's police car, shattering the side windows.

Charlotte cried out in pain, surprise widening her eyes, and grabbed the side of her head where a chunk of her hair had been torn out. Strands of red hair were clutched in Dunne's fingers as he climbed to his feet.

Keomany pointed toward the ground. She groaned as though with terrible effort and Miles thought she might be crying, but the ground rumbled and then thick tree roots shot up through the pavement, wrapped around Dunne like the fingers of some ancient wood god, and dragged him to the ground, binding him there. He struggled but could not escape.

A squeal of tires made Miles whip around in time to see the two surviving cops taking off, their patrol car speeding away into the storm. Without Chief Kramer to keep them on the job, their fear had won out.

Keomany collapsed to her knees in the rain, the elemental magic she'd summoned gone as though only supreme concentration had kept it within her grasp. Charlotte carried the iron chest over and nearly dropped it in front of her, so keen was she to get it out of her hands. The moment she no longer had possession of it, she changed. One moment she was tantalizing flesh and blood and then she turned to mist, like steam over a city subway grating.

Charlotte rematerialized a few feet away.

Keomany stared at her. "Why didn't you shapeshift before, when he grabbed you?"

"I couldn't!" Charlotte said, a frantic edge to her voice. "Something about that fucking box. When I had it in my hands . . . I'm not touching it again."

Miles looked from one woman to the other, from earthwitch to vampire, and wondered why he hadn't run away with the cops. He didn't belong here. This might be his town, but it wasn't his world. He should be hiding in his basement right now, like most of the people in Hawthorne were probably doing.

And then Keomany looked at him. "All right, Professor," she said. "Your turn. Let's see what we can learn."

For a second he wasn't sure what she meant, but then she reached out and dragged the chest across the pavement toward her. A chill went through Miles. The vampire didn't want to touch the chest, and he had already seen what it had done to Norman Dunne, but Keomany wanted him to examine the contents?

"Come on, Professor Varick," Keomany said. "People are dying."

Miles thought of his mother. He thought of Amber, and her family, and his colleagues and friends who lived in Hawthorne. Last, he thought of Don Kramer, who had already died for this. He couldn't turn away, but he was no hero.

"You open it," he said to Keomany. "And I'll tell you whatever I can about what's inside."

Navalica shrieked, a banshee wail that made Amber clap her hands over her ears. The glass blew out of the windows of Gran's bedroom. The shriek jolted Octavian, who held his ears and staggered into a bureau. As the blue-skinned goddess stood and then began to float above her great-grandmother's bed, Amber screamed. The goddess, the demon, turned golden eyes toward her and its scream halted abruptly. Navalica smiled, and for a moment she saw Gran in that face.

"Quiet, girl," the goddess whispered, but her voice buzzed in Amber's ears like a nest of hornets. "I'll tell you when to scream."

Fear ran through Amber's veins like poison. The goddess knew her. She had Gran inside her, or something. Navalica stretched as though waking, and Amber realized that was precisely what had been happening. The goddess had been sleeping and now, somehow, from within Gran, she had awakened.

"What . . . what did you do with Gran?" she stammered.

Octavian moved into a fighting stance, a green light blossoming around his fists.

"End this now," he demanded.

The goddess sneered down at him, sickly yellow eyes brightening. "Kneel, little wizard."

"You've been gone too long, Navalica. No one in this world worships you anymore," Octavian said.

The blue fire of her hair burned higher, a halo of cerulean flame.

"Oh, they will," she said, her horrible, hornet-buzz voice stabbing Amber's ears. "And it will begin as it always has. With chaos."

She threw her arms wide. Octavian flashed his hands up, green light beginning to shimmer into shape as some kind of shield, but he was not quick enough. Like azure wings, chaos magic spread from Navalica's arms in a shock wave that cracked the walls and shattered windows throughout the house. Amber was blown backward into the door frame, smacking her head and dropping to the floor. Octavian slammed into the bureau again, then fell to his knees, where Navalica had wanted him from the start. The Reapers trembled and for a second their skeletal forms rippled as if they were only black smoke.

Octavian tried to rise, blood dripping from his mouth and nose. Navalica flew down from the bed, long black talons slashing his chest. Then she cocked back her arm and drove her talons into his chest, so long that they thrust out his back, tearing through bone and flesh and muscle just as easily as they had his shirt.

"Oh, my God . . . I can't . . ." Amber muttered, as she crawled into the hallway, climbed to her feet, and started down the stairs.

The image of Octavian—this famous sorcerer, or whatever—hanging from the goddess's bloody talons seared itself into her brain. His eyes had been wide with shock that Amber would never forget. If he could not help them, everyone in Hawthorne would be made to worship this creature or they would be killed. And what happened then? What about the rest of the world? If Octavian couldn't stop her, could anyone?

Rushing, heart hammering in terror, head ringing from when she'd hit it on the door frame, Amber gave in to utter panic. She lost her footing on the stairs and fell. Reaching out, she managed to get one hand on the railing, just enough to slow her down and turn her around, and then she tumbled the last half-dozen steps to the second-floor landing.

Blinking in surprise, she looked around in confusion. Nothing seemed broken. She felt all right. More than all right. She felt some-how stronger as she started to stand.

Another wave of blue light, of chaos magic, swept down the stairs and slammed into her, but this time she arched her back and let it caress her, shuddering with pleasure, flinching as she came.

Bent over, recovering, she looked around in confusion. *What the hell just—*

She caught sight of her hands. Her arms.

"Oh, no. Please . . ."

As she stood there, her skin was changing, darkening, withering.

She tried to scream again, tried to cry out, to speak, but her lips would not part to release her voice. She reached up and touched her face and found hardening skin, almost like soft shell, where her mouth had been.

No!

She wondered if she would still be herself when the change was complete, when she was one of Navalica's Reapers. She wondered if she would feel the horror, if she would still be able to cry . . . she prayed the answer would be no.

Another wave of chaos blasted through the house and again it staggered her, pleasured her. Then she heard a crash that shook the entire house. Splinter cracks raced up the walls. Feeling lighter than before, Amber turned to run into her bedroom, which was just beneath Gran's. But instead of running she *darted*, pushing off the ground and flitting across the hall and through the open bedroom doorway.

She stopped in front of the shattered window, the rain and wind blasting in from outside. The storm had grown so much worse. A web of blue lightning arced across the black sky. As she watched, it struck the Kanes' house, destroying the façade and setting it ablaze with a fire that the hot rain did nothing to extinguish.

Above, the goddess Navalica danced across the sky, blue as the lightning, clad only in gauzy veils that whipped around her body in the storm, her three sets of breasts bare. As she danced, she flew toward the center of town, as Amber had known she would. Her Reapers flew around her, capering excitedly in the air, and Amber thought of the wicked witch's winged monkeys.

And then she wondered why she was not following. Why was she not capering as well, nothing more than a slave to the goddess?

Stepping back from the window, she saw herself in the full-length mirror beside her bureau. The sight paralyzed her for several seconds, and then she stepped nearer to the mirror, studying her reflection. She glanced down at her arms and blinked in surprise when she saw that the withering effect had somehow reversed. Instead of black, her skin had turned a wine-color, a deep burgundy, her hair a gleaming shade of plum.

In her tank top and jeans, she looked bizarre and exotic, almost alien. Her eyes blinked back from within a black shell, but as she moved closer to the mirror she reached up to touch it and found it brittle. The skin at her jawline was dry and cracked and as she dug into it with her nail, she found an edge there, as if she wore a kind of mask.

Fascinated and disgusted but unable to stop herself, she began to work her fingernails into the flaking edges of her face, and then she felt something crack and give way. The carapace came away in her hands, breaking into pieces, and she let them fall to the floor.

"Oh, God, what am I?" she whispered.

She had a mouth again. Lips. Her face had been altered, had become a finer, smoother version of who she had been, a mask of wine-colored porcelain. But not a mask, that was wrong. The carapace, that had been a mask. She could speak. She could smile. This new face was still her.

But *how*?

And then she knew. *Octavian.* Whatever he had done to her, whatever magic he had woven inside her to try to reverse or at least slow Navalica's influence, had instead changed the very nature of her metamorphosis. Instead of becoming one of the Reapers, Amber had become this. But what was this?

She grabbed the bath towel she had used the day before from the hook on her closet door and wiped away the sticky residue of the carapace from her face.

"What the hell am I?" she said again, studying her face and her new body in the mirror.

"You ask me, you're beautiful," a voice rasped behind her.

She spun, the movement making her float a few feet backward. She alighted on the carpet, staring at the bloody figure in her bedroom doorway.

"Mr. Octavian?" she said, amazed. "I thought you were dead."

Octavian stood up straighter. Through the slashes in his shirt she could see the wounds Navalica had made, but they were smaller than she'd have thought, as if they'd already been healing.

"I survived seventy-seven years of torment in Tartarus at the hands of Temeluchus and his iron hooks, and you think I'm going to let this bitch kill me?" Octavian said, taking a deep breath as he stood, golden light spilling out of his wounds and enveloping him.

He closed his eyes a moment, then opened them, and for the first time she saw in his gaze how truly ancient he was.

"Not fucking likely."

Officer Moschitto had stopped to help the teenage girls who had crashed their car, frustrated by the delay, wanting to hurry after Octavian and Amber, to find out what had happened to the Morrissey family. It wasn't just his job; Mr. Morrissey had been his baseball coach when he was in elementary school, and he'd always liked the family. Instead, he'd had to see to these three girls. He thought they were seniors at the high school, but he wasn't sure. One of them was Janey Ebbetson, and he knew for sure she hadn't graduated yet.

If he'd had a working radio or cell phone he could have called an ambulance. But in the chaos, it was up to him to make sure they got to the hospital. The idea of bringing more patients to Hawthorne Union made him want to laugh—a weird hysteria had been bubbling inside him all morning—but he didn't want Janey and her friends to know what kind of hellish wait they had in store when they got there.

Janey looked all right. Officer Moschitto smiled to himself. The girl looked more than all right. That skirt ought to be illegal. He tried not to let her see the way his gaze kept straying to her ass as she bent to reach into the car, trying to help her friends. When she glanced back at him he looked away, but his eyes were drawn back again and again to the sway of her breasts against the rain-damp cotton of her shirt.

The other two girls were injured. The blond, Monica, had smashed her face against the dashboard and her nose looked broken, blood streaming out. The absolutely luscious black girl, Belinda, had smashed her knee on the steering column and her chest against the wheel.

"We've got to get them to the hospital!" Janey said, withdrawing from the car—she'd been in the backseat during the accident. She turned her pleading eyes on Officer Moschitto. "Dude, seriously. I think Belinda has internal injuries or whatever. This is . . . fuck, this is bad!"

Janey and Monica kept trying to use their phones, as if they couldn't get it through their heads that as long as the storm raged around them, they would not have a signal.

Officer Moschitto held the umbrella from his patrol car up to shield himself and Janey; the closeness to her, the damp slippery heat of the rain on his skin, beading up and rolling down her chest between her breasts, had his cock so hard that it hurt. It felt like it had been carved from stone. Really, more than anything, it felt like a weapon, and the urge to show it to her was so strong he could barely restrain himself.

Janey glanced down and licked her lips. It wasn't his imagination. He saw her do it, and then she shook her head like she was trying to stay focused. Officer Moschitto smiled and she returned the smile, and they laughed softly together.

"This is insane," she said, softly so her friends wouldn't hear her over the rain. "What's wrong with me? I think . . . I think someone may have slipped something in my drink at the party."

"You're not even old enough to drink," Officer Moschitto said, automatically.

Janey moved against him, under the umbrella. "What are you going to do, cuff me?"

He arched an eyebrow. "I might."

"Janey, what the fuck! Get us out of here!" Monica shouted from inside the car.

Officer Moschitto rolled his eyes. "Bitch."

Janey nodded. "I know."

"Belinda's breathing all weird. It sounds . . . it sounds wet. I think she's bleeding inside!" Monica cried. "Jesus, Janey! We need an ambulance!"

Officer Moschitto took a deep breath and then let it out. His hard-on didn't diminish, but he knew he had to get control of himself. He bit his lip hard, clearing his mind, and stepped back from Janey, who looked both disappointed and relieved.

"Look," he said, "we can't move Belinda. It's too much of a risk.

I'll stay here and take care of them as best I can. You take my car and drive to the hospital, get them to send EMTs out here immediately."

Janey looked past him, her face suddenly bathed in blue light.

Standing beneath his umbrella, half a mile from the Morrissey house, Officer Moschitto turned and saw chaos magic burst across the town like a slow-motion nuclear blast. The first wave set off car alarms and tore trees from the ground, blew out windows and knocked over fences. Blue light swept over everything. The hair on his arms and on the back of his neck stood up and his skin prickled as the chaos wave enveloped him and then rolled onward. He shook with something akin to laughter, but there was no joy in it, only madness.

From the broken-down car he heard screaming. He looked inside and saw that despite her injuries, Belinda was alive. Blood bubbled from her mouth, but she had a fistful of Monica's hair as she clawed the girl's face and eyes, hatred lighting her face with passion and fire. Monica punched her in the throat, over and over, but Belinda did not let go, dragging the other girl toward her for what looked to be a kiss, until Belinda bit into her lips and began to tear.

Janey watched, breathing hard, the rain sheeting off her. She grinned, slapping her hand on the roof of the car.

"Do it!" she urged, though it was impossible to tell whose side she had taken. Perhaps both, and neither. "Do it!"

The second shock wave of blue light slammed Officer Moschitto and Janey against the car. His arm struck her and, bathed in blue, she turned to glare at him with murder in her eyes. Screams came from houses near and far, a chorus that rose and spread like a hymn of pain and lunacy. Animals howled. The ground trembled and pavement cracked.

Moschitto punched Janey so hard that he felt her cheekbone crack. Her head bounced off the car and she went to her knees.

He threw his head back and opened his mouth, thrusting out his tongue like a child catching snowflakes. The oily rain tasted like blood to him, coppery and sweet. It was the best thing he had ever tasted and he let out a howl of pleasure.

Janey grabbed his crotch, fist bunching around the rain-soaked fabric of his uniform trousers and the painful hardness of his cock. He looked down and saw her hungry smile and grinned so wide it split the skin at the corners of his mouth. She unbuckled his belt and dragged his pants down, clawing savagely at the fabric. With a swift bob of her head she took him in her mouth, then down her throat, gagging loudly as she devoured him. He wondered if she would bite and found he didn't care. He fisted his hands in her hair and stared into her greedy eyes and knew they had both found paradise.

"More," he growled, tugging her up by her hair.

She whined as her mouth pulled off him, but then groaned more deeply as his hands reached under her tiny skirt and yanked aside her sodden panties. He threw her roughly onto the hood of the broken-down car and as he fucked her from behind, they both watched through the splintered glass of the windshield as Belinda and Monica murdered each other.

In a moment of sparkling clarity, Moschitto understood that this was happening all over town. He wondered if he should do something.

His hands wrapped around Janey's throat.

Then he remembered that he had a gun, and just the thought of it made him come.

Keomany figured that since Bill Hodgson was dead, he wouldn't mind them using his kitchen table. The iron chest that Norm Dunne had dragged up from the ocean bottom yesterday sat in the center of the painted wood. What had once been leather straps were now nothing more than a gritty residue, eaten away by what must have been centuries of saltwater erosion. But the chest itself had been perfectly preserved. She had studied the engravings on the locks that Tommy Dunne had described, anxious about opening the chest and suffering the same fate as his father. After several minutes she had realized magic was her only real option.

Charlotte remained outside in the storm, watching over the squirming creature that had once been Norman Dunne. But Keomany had needed Professor Varick with her.

"How do you do what you do?" Miles asked.

Keomany glanced at him quizzically. "Magic? You study. You practice. You meditate and you search within yourself for connections to the things outside yourself."

"But elemental magic," Miles said. "The kind of power you can tap into is unimaginable."

Keomany smiled. "Not for me, Professor Varick. It's just earthcraft. It's speaking to the goddess."

She saw the alarm in his eyes and shook her head. "Not Navalica. Gaea. The one who has given us our cradle and our grave."

Keomany rubbed her palms on the kitchen table, feeling through the paint, sensing the wood from which the table had been made, the trees from which the lumber had been cut.

"Besides," she said, "if you think I have power, you know nothing of real magic. What I can do is nothing compared to Octavian's sorcery. If magic is language, I speak only one, and he speaks every language ever conceived."

As she spoke, fingers of wood thrust up from the kitchen table and began to creep along the edges of the iron chest. They were not painted, but freshly grown oak branches complete with bark. Outside, with the storm all around and the only roots the thinnest sprigs deep under the pavement, it had taken every ounce of her concentration for her to manipulate the anarchic nature of this chaos-tainted place. Gaea's presence beyond the sphere of Navalica's influence was barely a whisper to her now, but that whisper remained inside Keomany's heart and allowed her to fight the poison of this place.

Or so she told herself.

Yet when she drew the wind around her, pushing against the storm and shielding herself against the hot rain, the power that suffused her did not feel pure. And when she had reached down into the ground and dragged those roots up through the pavement, making them grow and twist and grab hold of Norman Dunne, lashing him to the street, she knew that her earth magic had not tapped into Gaea's power, but into the unnatural stream of the chaos itself.

Fight the poison? She was fooling herself. The taint had wormed

its way inside her and now ate at her heart and her magical essence
like a cancer.

But this . . . the pure hard wood of Bill Hodgson's kitchen table,
untouched by the storm or the rain . . . it still held most of its natural
properties. Touching it, working it, helped to focus her and to allow
her to feel the distant presence of Gaea, yearning toward her just as she
was yearning toward the goddess. *Her* goddess. Nature herself.

"Amazing," Miles said.

The finger-branches wound about the iron chest to hold it in place
as others lifted the latches that Norm Dunne had shattered. When the
branches pushed the lid up, the chest opened with surprising ease,
almost as if it had wanted to yield its secrets to them.

Keomany thought of Norm Dunne's heart attack and madness, his
transformation from ordinary fisherman to chaos-puppet, and she did
not relish peering into the chest. But when seconds passed without
anything stirring inside that iron box, she glanced at Miles and they
both shrugged.

"I will if you will," he said.

Keomany felt a stirring inside her, born of chaos. She grinned. "I
bet you say that to all the girls."

Miles took a single, salacious glance at her breasts and then the two
of them bent forward to peer into the iron box. Keomany felt a strange
relief at the ordinariness of the contents, at least by the standards of
centuries-old secrets. There were three parchment scrolls, one quite a
bit older and yellower than the others, itself on a spindle of carved
mahogany. With the scrolls were five glass ampoules containing various liquids. One was clear, but the others varied in hue and viscosity.
Coppery grit floated in one. Another surely contained thick blood of
deepest red. Within the fourth, a yellowish tincture, floated a scarab
beetle. In the fifth and last, a milky, pearlescent substance that flowed
like mercury when she reached inside and tipped the ampoule back
and forth.

One by one, Keomany and Miles removed the contents of the chest.
There were small stone jars that, when uncorked, proved to have semi-
liquid dyes and inks inside them, as well as a pair of sharp, filed bones

that looked like crude knives and a pair of slender pieces of iron, sharply pointed on one end.

A crinkling of paper made Keomany look up. Miles had unfurled one of the scrolls—not the oldest, which he seemed hesitant to touch for fear of ruining it—and studied it with narrowed eyes.

"Can you read it?" she asked. "What does it say?"

Miles continued to study the scroll, his lips moving slightly as he tried to work out its message.

"It's in more than one language," he said. "The one I can sort of decipher is an archaic Latin dialect."

Keomany studied the materials arranged on the kitchen table.

"And?" she demanded, looking up at him. "What does it tell us?"

Miles exhaled. If he had looked terrified before, now he looked even more so, and nauseated as well.

"It tells us that we're screwed," he said, a hysterical edge in his voice. He turned the scroll around so that she could see the drawing of the nude blue goddess with her many breasts and her blood-dripping talons, standing on a pile of corpses amid a swirl of trees and mountains that all seemed to be swirling into a gaping hole below her.

"Chaos storm," Keomany whispered.

"I don't think Hawthorne's going to be in our world much longer," Miles replied. He bit his lip and exhaled, making a visible attempt to control his fear and sorrow. "She was a prisoner. All this time, Navalica was a prisoner. This chest must have been dumped hundreds of miles out to sea—"

"But how did it get here?" Keomany asked. "How did she get here?"

Miles shook his head. "You don't understand. She was already here. She's been here since this town was founded, and a prisoner elsewhere before that. They trapped her inside an illusion of humanity, of ordinary life, with a touch of dementia. And I think Amber's family has something to do with it."

"So, why now? How did she escape?"

Miles shrugged. "Maybe with other supernatural powers—gods and demons—slipping back into this world . . . she must have sensed them, somehow. Even unaware of it, she dragged the chest toward her, until poor Norm Dunne hauled it up from below and opened it.

"This," Miles said, gesturing toward the window, which rattled under the storm's assault. "All of this . . . it's just her waking up."

With a crash, the front door slammed open. Keomany jumped from her chair, knocking it to the floor, and gestured for Miles to return the objects to the chest. As he did, she rushed to the kitchen doorway, only to nearly collide with Charlotte.

"What are you doing?" Keomany asked. "Did Dunne get away?"

Charlotte glanced over her shoulder in fear. "Something happened. An explosion or something. All that blue lightning is spreading everywhere, and it's coming—"

The house shook, glass shattered, and sizzling blue light washed in through the door, streaming through the windows. The chaos wave blew Charlotte off her feet and she crashed into Keomany, who let out a scream as she and the vampire girl rolled across the kitchen floor in a tangle of limbs.

Keomany's heart raced. Emotions and desires roiled in her. Charlotte's breasts were pressed against her, perfect bow lips only inches away. The urge to touch her, to taste her, was almost as powerful as her desire to rend flesh and break bone, to revel in violence. She groaned, and it became a rhythm in her throat, a melody in her mind. She wanted to dance and scream.

The touch of her goddess saved her.

Blue light still shimmering outside the house, the glow spreading through the rooms, she looked within herself for the peace that Gaea had always brought her, and she found it there. Her tether to nature— the true nature of this world—was tenuous, but it remained, and it was enough for her to breathe.

Charlotte did not move for several seconds. She lay on top of Keomany without so much as the rise and fall of her chest to indicate that she lived, but then Keomany remembered that the vampire did not need to breathe.

"Hey, get up," she said.

Charlotte's eyes snapped open. Tiny pinpricks of red against black.

Slowly, her lips peeled back from her fangs and she hissed. Her head cocked back, and Keomany had a vision of the beautiful, horrible girl tearing out her throat.

With a gesture, the wind twisted around her, tore Charlotte from on top of her, and hurled the vampire girl across the room. Charlotte smashed into the cabinets above the kitchen counter. Doors fell open as she tumbled to the ground, the cabinet partially giving way, and piles of dishes and bowls slid out, shattering all over the floor.

She was up in an instant.

Between them, Miles Varick staggered to his feet. Blood trickled from a cut on his forehead that Keomany assumed he'd gotten when the blast of magic had knocked them off their feet. He wiped his palm over it, then stared at his bloody hand and started to laugh.

For an instant, all of the air seemed to be sucked from the room, and then a second wave struck, a blast of light that swept through the kitchen. This time they did not fall. Perhaps they were ready for it, Keomany thought, or perhaps they had already been infused with enough of the chaos in that magic that it passed through them more easily.

Charlotte leaped the distance between herself and Miles, grabbed the professor by the face, and slammed him down on top of the kitchen table.

"Stop laughing!" the vampire screamed, her lower jaw distending, fangs elongating into gleaming needle points. "It's not fucking funny!"

"Charlotte, no!" Keomany shouted.

She reached within and sought the voice of Gaea, the tether to her goddess. Wind gusted around her and she hurled it, conducting it at the two of them, grinding their hips together on top of the white table . . . and where was the iron chest? Damn it, where had it fallen in all of this?

But the vampire held on tightly, and only then did Keomany see the horrible truth—the savagery she herself had contributed to. Charlotte had slammed Miles down on top of those jutting wooden fingers she had summoned up from the table, the fresh oak branches that had held the damned box until only moments ago.

"Let him go!" Keomany cried.

With a snarl, her tongue snaking out, Charlotte turned toward her. Tears of bloody anguish ran down her cheeks.

"I can't!" the vampire cried, her voice a ragged scream of conflict between bloodlust and humanity. "I need it! Don't you get it? I'm just too goddamn hungry!"

Grinding herself against Miles—dying, bleeding Miles, with the branches jutting up through his chest, making bloodstained tents under his shirt—Charlotte lunged forward and sank those impossibly long needles into his throat. Her fangs changed, shrinking, and soon her lips were attached leechlike to his flesh, as she drank him.

Keomany screamed once more, reached out with the magic inside of her, and took control of the wooden table again. With a twist of her wrists, she jerked her arms back, and the oak fingers jutting from the table shot upward, becoming spikes, impaling Charlotte, who writhed atop them and shrieked in fury.

Too late.

Miles Varick twitched as his blood spilled out onto the table, dripping off the edges and through the seam where the table leaf would have gone. His head lolled to one side and he looked at Keomany, all traces of the salacious influence of chaos vanished from his eyes.

"Don't let me . . ." he said, throat bubbling with blood. "What happens if I . . . if I die here? Where do I go?"

Keomany stared at him, a new fear, unlike any she had ever felt, blossoming inside her.

"I'm sorry," she whispered. "I don't know."

16

Miles lay dying. Keomany could feel the chaos around them. It wasn't just in the hot rain, but in every intake of breath. The air held chaos magic, and Hawthorne itself had been tainted. It remained part of her world, but its fundamental nature had been altered, and she knew Navalica's influence must be spreading, no longer confined only to this one town. How far would her twisted magic reach? In time, would it envelop the world?

She shook her head. Such concerns were for later. The light had begun to dim in Miles Varick's eyes and the thought of letting his spirit leave his body in such an uncertain place, not knowing if his soul would be able to escape Navalica's dark magic, made her sick. If she let him die like this, in this place, she might be consigning him to a new kind of Hell. Keomany barely knew Miles, but he had seemed an honorable man, and she could not allow this to happen.

Charlotte moaned, but the sound turned into a low growl. Even in pain and twisted by hunger, the girl was beautiful, but it was a terrible beauty. She looked at Keomany with those black eyes, red irises expanding, and her upper lip curled back in hatred.

"Bitch," Charlotte snarled.

"You're not yourself," Keomany said quickly. "Just . . . just stay there."

Closing her eyes—the last thing she wanted to do with a hungry vampire in the room—Keomany exhaled and pushed her consciousness outward, searching for her goddess, for the tether that connected her to Gaea. For a second or two she panicked, but then she expanded her awareness farther, out into the chaos. She had to let it in, let herself feel it more than she would have wished, but she had no choice. Though her magic had allowed her to stifle the strongest and darkest of the urges that filled her, she needed chaos as a conduit so that she could reach the edges of Navalica's influence and touch the untainted world.

There. A smile spread across her face. She had found it, the distant, muffled whisper of the goddess. Gaea would not abandon her, and Keomany knew she must be equally dedicated.

"I'm talking to you, witch," Charlotte growled.

As Keomany opened her eyes, the vampire girl tried to tear herself off the sharp branches upon which she was impaled. Something inside her caught on a branch, maybe her rib cage, and she laughed.

The laughter chilled Keomany, but she took a deep breath and tried to focus, reaching out to Gaea. It had been hard enough to wield the elements before, but the wave of chaos magic that had swept through had made it much more difficult. Before she had been able to tap the pure essence of Gaea, but anything she did now would be tainted. She only prayed it would not be twisted too far beyond her intentions.

"Miles, can you hear me?" Keomany asked.

Charlotte laughed again. "Can *you* hear *me*?"

Then she changed. The weight of her flesh simply evaporated into mist, a small cloud that moved with its own dark purpose. The mist swirled and shifted and floated away from the kitchen table, and then began to take shape again.

But not a human shape.

With a fluidity Keomany had forgotten, Charlotte seemed almost to pour herself into a new form, that of an enormous wolf, its fur bristling. This time, her growl came from deeper in her chest, a place of even greater savagery, and the wolf that was Charlotte stalked toward Keomany with hideous intent. Somehow, despite her change, Miles's blood remained on the wolf's fangs.

Keomany reached toward Miles, keeping her breathing even, letting herself be suffused by magic even as she did her best to draw on what little purity lingered in the elements around her. If any of Gaea's influence remained, she needed to breathe it in, to wind it around her like a sheath. The wind that sprang from her hands and encircled her, whipping at her hair, gusted toward Miles.

The wolf leaped at her.

"No!" Keomany shouted, shifting to defend herself.

The wind caught Charlotte midleap, spun her around, and with a gesture Keomany slammed her against the wall. The kitchen clock fell to the floor and shattered, but the vampire was already rising, changing again. The wind gusted around her as wolf became bear, rising on its hind legs, opening its jaws in a furious roar. Keomany's magic could hold the shapeshifting leech at bay, but she could not kill Charlotte. She could not win.

You can't kill her anyway, she thought. *This is the bloodlust, it's Navalica's doing. She can't control herself.*

Keomany's heart pounded in her chest. Panic and chaos fed upon one another, and she glanced over to see Miles's head lolling over, his last breath rattling in his chest.

"Fine," Keomany muttered. "Two for one."

The magic felt as if it ripped its way out of her, and Keomany screamed as she tried to hold on to her rapport with Gaea. In that kitchen, she created her own storm. The wind lifted Charlotte and held her aloft, embracing her so fully that even when the vampire turned once more to mist, she could not escape.

Keomany took hold of Miles's hand. It felt cool, his heat bleeding out with his life, but reflexively his fingers closed on hers, and then opened again. His chest rose one final time, and his spirit left him with his final exhalation.

"Goddess, guide him," Keomany whispered aloud.

She let out another cry and with all of her heart, all of her will, she pulled on the tether that connected her to Gaea. For just a moment that bond strengthened, as though she had punched a real hole in Navalica's chaos storm. A great clatter arose as wood splintered, branches growing out of cabinets and chairs and floorboards, sprouting leaves. The wind smashed chairs against the walls and slung shards of dishware like razors around the room. One of them nicked her arm, but Keomany ignored it, enveloped by the surge of earth magic within her.

For a moment, she felt clean.

Something she could not see caressed her cheek, and it felt like gratitude. The ghost of Miles Varick or the goddess herself, she did not know. But as her pulse began to slow and the wind to diminish, she knew that his spirit had departed. Miles was dead, but she hoped that she had freed him from chaos and given him a path to peace.

Staggered by the effort, Keomany caught herself on the kitchen table. The toe of her shoe caught something hard and she cursed under her breath, glancing down to see the iron chest, its lid closed and somehow latched, as if it had its own protections. She chided herself— of course it did. That wasn't her sort of magic, but she knew enough of sorcery that she should've expected it.

"I hate you a little," Charlotte muttered as she became flesh and blood once again, mist sculpting itself into the perfect curves of her nineteen-year-old body. In the process, even her clothes had been repaired, broken down into their component molecules and then reintegrated.

Keomany braced herself, but when the vampire girl looked up, her eyes were no longer black, seeded with red.

"Only a little?" Keomany asked.

Charlotte nodded. She wiped the back of her hand across her mouth. "I'm still hungry."

"But under control?" Keomany asked.

"Yeah. Whatever you hit me with . . . I didn't even have a body and it felt like being electrocuted . . . cleared my head."

Keomany felt a stirring inside her, an urge toward violence and a sexual arousal at the sight of Charlotte, that reminded her she had only touched Gaea's essence, not been purified herself.

"But not completely."

"No," Charlotte agreed, smiling enough to show the tips of her fangs, her body still moving with the alert poise of a beast. "Not completely."

Keomany kicked the iron chest. "Then let's get this thing to Octavian."

Charlotte glanced at the corpse on the kitchen table, almost guiltily. "What about him?"

"I've done all I can for him. I set him on the right path, I think," Keomany replied as she bent down and hoisted the iron chest into her arms. "Let's see if we can keep the rest of us from following him."

Octavian pinned the scroll open on the coffee table in the Morrisseys' living room. He rolled the top up and let more of it unfurl from the bottom, reading as he went, but every movement caused a twinge of pain in his chest where Navalica had stabbed her talons through him.

"Are you going to be all right?" Keomany asked.

"In time," he replied.

"We're *out* of time," Charlotte said.

Octavian shot her a dark look. He didn't need the reminder.

"What does it say?" Amber asked.

When she spoke, Keomany and Charlotte both took the opportunity to study her more closely. Octavian had the impression that Amber's transformation from ordinary flesh and blood to wraith, or whatever she was now, had unsettled Keomany deeply. The earthwitch did not trust this new version of Amber. Charlotte, on the other hand, only seemed fascinated by the young woman's wine-dark flesh.

Amber didn't like it. She spun on Charlotte. "Stop staring at me!"

Charlotte held up her hands and took a step away. "Sorry. I just . . ."

"I know! I'm a freak. I get it, okay?" Amber snapped.

"Are you kidding?" Charlotte said. "Whatever the hell you are, it's totally hot. Makes me want to lick you."

"Oh, thanks. Like that doesn't freak me out even more!"

Charlotte laughed softly, mischief capering in her eyes. Octavian knew she had only been half joking. Despite all that was going on around them, and because of it, the house bristled with sexual tension. The chaos took the slightest urge and amplified it, so that they were all in an almost constant state of arousal. For him, simply being this close to Keomany in particular was torment.

Amber's grief at the news of Professor Varick's death seemed to have calmed her own chaotic agitation for the moment. She had gone quiet when Keomany told her, mourning in silence save for the occasional whimper. Octavian had decided that was best. Keomany had pulled him aside and informed him of the manner of Miles's death, of the effect the chaos wave had had on Charlotte, and he thought it would complicate things if Amber knew that Charlotte had killed her professor and drunk his blood. For now, it was better she not know. He needed all the help he could get, and he had the idea that in this new form, Amber might be very helpful indeed.

"Can we get on with this?" Keomany snapped.

He looked at her. For a moment she stared back with a steady ferocity, but then she glanced away. Neither of them wanted to acknowledge what they were both feeling.

"Charlotte," Octavian said, "can you check to make sure Dunne is still secure?"

The vampire girl glanced back and forth between him and Keomany, reading the tension there, flush with her own arousal and feeding off the sexual current in the room. If he needed any evidence that it had begun to wear on her, to drive her to the edge of her ability to keep herself under control, the fact that she did not comment on what she observed gave her away. Sarcasm and flirtation were her default settings, but she didn't even trust herself to go that far.

"Sure," she said, and strode to the window to peer outside.

Just when Octavian and Amber had been about to surrender their hope that their allies would return, Keomany and Charlotte had pulled up in a police patrol car. Norman Dunne was in the back, his wrists manacled and the chain of the cuffs looped through the D-ring on the floor. He wasn't going anywhere.

"He's still there," Charlotte said, her shoes crunching broken glass as she bent to peer out the window. "I told you he wasn't going anywhere."

Amber knelt on the rug beside Octavian's chair, looking up at him with pleading eyes, so strange in that exquisitely carved face. Her burgundy hair spilled around her shoulders.

"Why are you stalling?"

Octavian frowned. "I'm not stalling."

Keomany perched on the edge of the sofa, glancing from the scroll up to his face. "Yes, you are. I know you, Peter. Whatever you're trying to protect her from, just spit it out."

He inhaled deeply, trying to focus. The only way to do that was to concentrate on the scroll and not look at the women around him, especially Keomany and Charlotte, whose clothes were still damp and clinging from the rain.

"Navalica is what we figured," he said. "Chaldean goddess of chaos. Mother of the Seven. Though there is some hint in one of the other scrolls that her history goes back even further, that the Chaldeans were only the latest to worship her."

"The Seven," Keomany said anxiously. "Are they here, too? Are they coming?"

Octavian ran his fingers over the rough parchment of the scroll. "The most recent scroll only mentions them in the past tense. There's no history here of what happened to them, if they died or left this plane of existence, but there's also no indication that they remain tied to Navalica. We have to be prepared for anything, but unless we have some inkling otherwise, let's assume the Seven are off the board."

"Until they show up and tear us to shreds," Amber whispered.

"One ugly fate at a time, please," Octavian said.

She nodded, but her gaze was far away, lost in thoughts of death. He wasn't sure, but in the dim light of the living room, it looked as though her eyes had a newly purple tint.

"How did all of this happen?" Charlotte asked with a wave of her hand that took in all of Hawthorne. "I mean, how do you get from ancient Chaldea to some New England beach town?"

Octavian hesitated, glanced at Amber, and then rolled up the scroll and set it next to the iron chest.

"Amber's family," he said.

Her face might have taken on an almost alien cast, with its wine-red skin and ceramic perfection, but her metamorphosis into a wraith did not mean she was incapable of showing her emotions. Shock widened her eyes, and then he saw her features collapse into confusion and regret.

"I don't understand," Amber said.

Octavian glanced at Keomany before replying.

"Maybe you know this, and maybe you don't. If you trace the branches of your family tree backward, somewhere along there you have a family who were among the original settlers of this area."

Amber nodded. "Dmitri Poulos. He was a sailor."

"Greek," Octavian replied. "That makes sense. But the names don't really matter. They'd have changed with marriages a hundred times. Probably more. In the midseventeenth century, Dmitri Poulos arrives and makes his home here. Maybe he had a wife with him, but more likely, he found one among the other settlers, one of their daughters, I'd guess. Or in his travels, he met a girl in Boston or Providence or some other port, and brought her home."

"Adele Perrault. She was French-Canadian," Amber said, but now he could hear the fear in her voice, the desire for ignorance.

She was afraid of what he would say next, and Octavian wished he could tell her there was nothing to fear. But she was right to be frightened of this truth. It would hurt her. Scar her. Change her, even more than she had already been changed.

"But he would have had his mother with him, or grandmother, I suppose."

Amber shook her head. "I don't think so."

Octavian smiled sadly. He reached out and touched her hand, and when she flinched he was not certain if it was because of the sexual current that flowed through them all, or because she had seen herself in the mirror and despaired of ever being touched so tenderly again.

"Yes," he said. "The woman was with him."

Charlotte hurried to glance out the window again, checking on Norman Dunne. "Can you speed it up, for fuck's sake? If it's gonna hurt, just do it. Spare her the suspense."

Octavian knew what the vampire meant. Sometimes it was less painful to thrust the dagger in, rather than forcing his victim to endure its slow penetration.

"That woman wasn't Dmitri's mother," he said.

"You mean it was Navalica?" Keomany asked. "How can that be?"

The wind seemed to gust harder, sweeping the hot rain deeper into the house, where furniture and carpets were already ruined. The house shifted and creaked. But Octavian told himself it was only his imagination, that like the ocean, the goddess's magic ebbed and flowed. It would soon sweep them into a sea of chaos, if they could not stop her. But she was not here in the room with them. She did not know what magic was arrayed against her, and that was their one hope.

"When she had few left who would worship her, she went mad and turned on her people. That's the nature of chaos, of course. Entropy. The center cannot hold. She was too powerful for them to destroy, but they were able to weaken her. Her priests, the Chaldean mystics, knew magic that would contain her, and that is what they did. They removed her heart, the essence of her godhood and her power, and they sealed it inside an iron box with a recording of her history and the components they used for the ritual to bind her. But they could only bind her heart, not her flesh.

"To be certain that none of them would betray the others, that no one would try to free Navalica to curry favor with a mad goddess, they cast a complex web of spells, enchantments to make Navalica forget who she was, and to make the high priests forget as well."

Octavian looked at Amber. "But not only to forget. These enchantments made the high priests believe that Navalica was their responsibility. That they were family. Drained of her vitality, she looked like an old woman, and she has been in the care of the descendants of those priests—all of them under the same spell—for more than twenty-five hundred years."

Amber stared at him, her bloodred lips open in a tiny pout. Though her metamorphosis had given her the appearance of some kind of infernal succubus, in that moment he saw that she was still just a girl.

"Gran?" she said, her lips trembling. And she wept, silent tears sliding down that perfect wine-hued skin. "Gran was never . . . I mean, she was never *her*?"

"She didn't know what she was," Octavian said. "How could *you* have?"

"And the Reapers . . . the wraiths . . . There aren't any others, are there? No one else has been changed the way my parents have."

Octavian shook his head. "I don't think so. From what I've read, this is what happens. Living with her, constant exposure to the chaos inside her, causes the transformation. When it happens, the wraiths . . . what you call the Reapers . . . must have faded away, or left this plane. They went elsewhere, wherever that is, until Dunne opened the chest and Navalica started to wake. If I've got this right, it shouldn't have happened to your parents for decades yet, not until more generations were completely assured. But this plane is changing. The barriers that kept the supernatural out have deteriorated. Somehow, Navalica began to stir, and the ocean currents dragged the chest toward her, her magic working without her being conscious of it. And then Norm Dunne hauled it up from the bottom."

"So I would have been one, too, if you hadn't tried to help," Amber said.

"This is help?" Charlotte asked. "Turning you into this?"

Amber glared at her, and Octavian saw a true threat there. She wasn't a small-town college girl anymore. Vampire or not, Octavian thought Charlotte would do well not to test her.

"He did what he could," Amber said. "If not for Peter, I'd be her slave, along with the others. My parents would be out there right now, killing for her."

"This is insane," Keomany muttered.

Octavian squeezed Amber's hand, glancing up at Keomany. But beyond the earthwitch, he saw Charlotte watching him, and the urgency in the vampire's eyes startled him. He had taken too long. Sympathy for Amber, an attempt to be kind and gentle, had felt like the right thing to do, but he wondered what it might have cost them. Even now, the wraiths might be committing murder. And he had no idea what Navalica might be doing. Breaking down the barrier between worlds? Searching for her demonic spawn? He felt certain of only one thing: the infection of her chaos would be spreading.

He nodded at Charlotte. The girl might be a rogue vampire, but she had made it clear where she stood in this battle. Another rogue, one who believed the teachings of Hannibal or this new coven master, Cortez, would have surrendered immediately to the rush of chaos, to the insatiable hunger it created, and rejoiced in it. But Charlotte fought, and he was happy to have her on his side. Professor Varick's death had been regrettable, but she could not be blamed for that any more than the dogs driven mad by chaos could be held responsible for turning wild.

Octavian reached into the chest and began to remove its contents and set them out on the coffee table. The scrolls he placed on the floor in front of him—it would take him only moments to master the spells therein—and he arranged the stone jars of dye and the ampoules of liquid in even rows. The tiny bone knives and the pair of iron needles were last.

"You said her heart was in there?" Keomany reminded him. "But we didn't see any trace of organic tissue. Do you think Dunne took it out? Did something with it?"

Octavian's pulse quickened with her nearness. He breathed through his mouth so he would not inhale the scent of her. He thought of Nikki and wondered how she could possibly understand the world he had brought her into, and whether she could forgive him having rough, hungry sex with Keomany the way he forgave Charlotte for murdering Miles Varick.

A foolish question. Of course she could not. She would never understand the dark currents that ran behind the veil of the world or what had to be done to combat them, no matter how many times he pulled back that veil to show her.

"I think it must have been a real heart once upon a time," he said. "But she is a goddess. An entity like Navalica is not of flesh and blood the way we understand it. Her heart went into this box, but it was just as much her spiritual heart, her core, as it was a physical thing."

"And so, whatever we do," Charlotte said, "it has to start with ripping her heart out?"

Amber made a small noise. She looked up, wiping away tears, coming to terms with having her entire life redefined.

"I'm on board for that," she said. "All of this . . . this is my legacy. My family's entire history is wrapped up in keeping this bitch down. I'm not going to turn away from that now. Especially after what it's done to my parents, and to me."

"Good," Octavian said. "Because I have a plan."

"Finally," Charlotte muttered.

Octavian glanced at her. "Go and get Dunne. We all have a part to play in this. Even you."

They took the police car. Keomany drove, with Amber in the passenger seat and Octavian sitting in the caged backseat next to Norman Dunne, who held the iron chest in his lap. He had his eyes closed and rocked in the seat, murmuring to himself, a tiny smile at the edges of his mouth. The man's mind had been polluted by Navalica, and it pleased him to serve his goddess.

The wind and rain buffeted the car, but Keomany kept her hands tight on the wheel.

"It's hard to see," she said. "I wish I could clear us a path."

"You need to conserve your magic," Octavian reminded her.

She gave him a sharp look in the rearview. She didn't need reminding.

"Do you think Charlotte will be all right?" Amber asked. She turned to look through the grating of the cage, her skin a deep purplish-black in the darkness inside the car.

"There's very little that can kill a creature like her," Octavian replied.

Amber nodded thoughtfully, wondering, he presumed, what it would take to kill her, now that she was no longer human.

Octavian closed his eyes a moment, thinking, running it all over in his head. When he breathed in, he could taste her magic, and he could feel the rough caress of chaos on his skin. It prickled his flesh, made him keenly aware of his body and his carnal desires, in all forms. He forced his breathing to remain steady, but he could feel Keomany in front of him, so close, and he had seen the way she had been reacting to his presence, perhaps unconsciously, back at the Morrissey house.

The way she stood, as though magnetism drew them toward each other. The way she licked her lips with nervous anticipation. Octavian felt as though they prowled around one another in hungry circles.

When Navalica had been defeated and the chaos magic swept from Hawthorne and cleansed from their bodies and minds, he would have to decide if any of that attraction had been genuine. But not now. For now, he hated Navalica for making him jittery with sexual energy, for making him feel such bestial lust.

The plan, he thought. *The magic. Focus.*

In truth he did not need to go over the words in his head, to sketch at the air in rehearsal for the finger-contortions and hand gestures that would sculpt the magic he summoned into its proper shape, into the spells that would end this, if all went well.

If. Two letters. The most troubling word in the English language.

There were so many ways his plan could crumble into catastrophe, but he had not shared those concerns with the others. If it had been only Keomany, he might have been more up-front with her about the risks, but with Amber and Charlotte—he just needed them to perform the tasks he had assigned to them, and trust that he knew what he was doing. That he could win.

Keomany slowed, the tires skidding in the slick, sticky rain. She pulled to the curb and killed the engine.

"We'll have to walk from here," she said.

Amber was the first to get out, hot rain making her wine-dark skin gleam. It sluiced over her, sliding down her flesh as if she were made of glass. Her clothes clung to her, but they seemed strange now, hanging on her new form.

Keomany climbed out and opened the back door for Octavian. When he stepped out of the car, Dunne seemed to wake up from his peculiar, chanting trance. He scuttled along the seat with the iron chest on his lap, but Octavian slammed the door, trapping him inside, at least for the moment.

So close to Keomany, his hands shook with desire. He forced himself to look up the street.

The storm churned in circles above them, the wind whipping at them, rain falling in blood-warm sheets of gummy liquid. Reapers wove in and out of the clouds, circling like carrion birds. People staggered in the street, wandering into the town center, tilting their heads back to peer up at the city hall clock tower. Outlined against the glowing face of the clock, Navalica conducted the storm like a symphony, her arms outstretched, indigo hair burning with flames that no rain could extinguish.

The Reapers brought their bounty to her, undulating masses of shifting color, amorphous things that might not be souls, but which Octavian felt certain were some piece of the human spirit, some essential bit of ordinary chaos, perhaps the capacity to love or to imagine or to dream. They fed her, and she consumed those spirits, those elemental slices of humanity, with a voracious appetite.

Wraiths perched on the roof of the church.

"That's supposed to be me up there," Amber called, raising her voice to be heard over the storm. "In my vision, I was one of them."

"So what you saw has changed," Octavian said. "It was a warning, not a prophecy."

Amber glanced at him, expressionless, but then her eyes narrowed and he saw hatred and determination there. Her upper lip curled, revealing a bloodlust just as deeply ingrained as Charlotte's. But Amber did not want to drink it, only to spill it.

She opened the back door of the police car, reached in, and dragged Norm Dunne out. There was no need—he would have come eagerly— but Octavian understood the ferocity simmering inside of her, now boiling over at last.

"Walk," Amber said. "Go! Take it to her!"

Dunne did not acknowledge her, but he started walking, carrying the iron chest in his hands, raising it up as an offering, though they were still a block and a half from the clock tower. Her vision had been the key to this moment. Octavian knew that Norm Dunne was meant to be here, meant to bring Navalica that chest. And he saw no reason for her not to have it.

17

Keomany could barely focus on keeping one foot in front of the other. It felt as though her entire body were being torn apart, as if at any moment she would lose control. They walked the town square, where the church's bell tower and the city hall clock tower faced one another across the intersection. But with every yard, the air grew thicker with filthy, wild magic, and the rain turned so hot it almost scalded her. It stuck to her skin and created a film on her clothes, and she wanted to put her head back and howl.

Octavian matched her pace, just off to her left. Amber had gotten a couple of yards ahead. She'd been hesitant to let Norm Dunne just walk away, but Octavian had insisted. The three of them had hung back a little while Dunne lugged the iron chest along the block toward the intersection. Even now, through the rain, she could see him moving among the people gathered there. They parted for him, as if sensing that what he carried was important to their goddess. A low chant could be heard above the thunder and the rain. Blue lightning flashed every few seconds, illuminating the entire scene.

People had gathered in the intersection, many on their knees in worship to Navalica. But others had given in to their base urges, fucking and fighting with abandon. Sex and blood seemed almost indistinguishable in that gathering, and goddess help her, Keomany wanted to join them. She felt sympathy for Amber, for what the girl had endured, but she also wanted to hurt this strange wraith-creature, because she had seen the way Octavian had admired her new body.

Kill you, bitch.

Keomany faltered, staggering a few feet, and then halted. She forced herself to breathe. Back at Bill Hodgson's house she had been able to concentrate enough to sense the presence of Gaea beyond the fringes of Navalica's influence. She had touched the true nature of this world and it had restored her, allowed her to withstand the corrupting influence of the wave of chaos magic that had exploded from Navalica as she finally shattered the spells that had kept her ignorant of her true self, and woken.

But every step brought her closer to Navalica, and deeper into the heart of chaos. She tried to concentrate, to push her awareness out toward the edges of town in search of *her* goddess, but the pure car-nality forcing its way inside her, polluting her mind and soul, made it impossible for her to focus. Her skin prickled and her hands shook, so powerful was the lust within her. Aroused as she was, just walking—the friction of her stride—sent shivers of pleasure through her.

Get a hold of yourself, Keomany. This is it. The fight is here, and he needs you.

She took a trembling breath and covered her face with her hands, then slapped herself twice, forcing her eyes open.

Octavian stood in front of her. Startled, she jerked backward, but only for a second. Her breathing became ragged and her chest rose and fell too rapidly. Despite the rain her mouth had gone dry, and she wetted her lips with her tongue.

"Kem . . . you okay?" he asked.

His voice was shaking. *Goddess, no,* she thought. Bad enough that her own magic wasn't sufficient to fight the primal urge of chaos . . . What was she? Just an earthwitch! But if Peter Octavian, with all of his sorcery, could not keep himself from being corrupted, what hope did they have?

Octavian reached out to touch her arm, a fierce hunger in his eyes.

"We can do this," he said, and she could see him fighting it.

But then he touched her, and her knees buckled, and he had to catch her, and Keomany could not fight it any more. She grabbed a fistful of his hair and as he picked her up, she dragged him close and their lips met, and her whole body burned with desire for him. They kissed violently, mouths mashing together, tongues sparring, and she felt his hands on her, thrusting beneath her clothing, searching and probing, and she grabbed his face in both hands and guided him down, both of them buckling now and lowering each other to the slick pavement, that oily rain scalding them, rivulets running down the street toward the center of town.

Her mind retreated, surrendering to hunger. She scratched him, nails biting deep, and he bit her lip and made her bleed, and it made her shiver into orgasm. Her fingers worked his belt, then his zipper, and the rest of the world vanished. Octavian growled as he kissed her, tearing her blouse to get at her breasts, and as his rough tongue ran over her nipples and then he bit her there, she came again, this time with such ferocity that she nearly fell unconscious, tiny stars going supernova at the black fringes of her mind.

Nothing else mattered now. Keomany and Octavian had abandoned themselves to chaos.

Amber peered through the rain. Her senses had been enhanced by her metamorphosis, but still it was difficult to keep track of Norm Dunne as he moved through the crowd of worshippers. The wind gusted and she let it pass around her, rising off the pavement, intention alone enough to give her momentum. She hoped that in time, if this worked and they all survived, Octavian could help her discover what she had become and what it meant. It frightened her, but not as much as perhaps it ought to have. She felt powerful and beautiful and imbued with purpose, and those things were all very new to her.

Sounds behind her gave her pause. She frowned and turned, her mind already putting images to the sounds. Up ahead there were people who had given in to the chaos having sex in the rain. But the voices behind her had become familiar. She knew them. To hear them moaning and whispering in passion made no sense. But there they were, tearing at each other's clothes in the middle of the street. Keomany's breasts were bare, her jeans down around her knees. Octavian had his pants open and Keomany had torn his shirt to get at his flesh. Her fingers were twined in his hair, and his were cupping her ass, and—

"Are you fucking *kidding* me?" Amber shouted.

They seemed not to hear her. Amber shook her head, reached up to grab fistfuls of her own strange new hair. She felt the sexual abandon that came with the chaos magic, along with the savage aggression, but it had diminished after her transformation. Now she stared at Octavian and Keomany and then glanced at Navalica atop the clock tower, blue lightning dancing around her, illuminating her naked indigo flesh. The goddess's fire-hair had become a burning mane, a halo of infernal blue. More of the wraiths had begun to land on the ledges of the church's bell tower across from her, and some on the clock tower around her, all of them with heads bent, wordlessly chanting along with the humans below. Rows of people knelt in the town square, and now she could see Dunne again, far away, approaching the base of the clock tower.

This was happening right now. Right now!

With a furious snarl she darted toward Octavian and Keomany, floating by instinct, embracing the thing she had become. She alighted beside them, saw a flash of pale flesh as Keomany prepared to guide Octavian inside her, and Amber screamed.

"Enough!"

She picked Keomany up by one arm and the tangled clutch of denim between her legs and tossed her away. The earthwitch hit the pavement and rolled, and Amber didn't give a shit about scrapes or bruises. Half naked, exposed, Octavian looked up at her with a mad lust in his eyes. Amber leaped astride him, and he bucked against her as if he thought she meant to finish what Keomany had started. Instead, Amber grabbed him by the throat and pinned him to the street.

With the talons of her other hand, she slashed his chest, cutting deep enough to make him scream.

"This is magic!" she shouted into his face. "This is what you do! You have to be stronger than her!"

But even as she said it, she understood. Octavian might know a thousand different kinds of magic, might have extraordinary power by any human standard, but he had known that he was not strong enough to defeat Navalica face to face. Not with her in the flush of her newly awakened power. He had intended to use cunning to defeat her. That was why he'd made a plan.

Octavian looked down at his chest, saw his blood seeping from the gashes there, and glared at her with murder in his eyes.

"You little bitch," he growled, still poisoned by chaos. She'd hoped pain would wake him from its influence, but—

Something struck her, knocked her off Octavian, and she hit the street with metal and rubber clattering around her, disoriented. Blinking, she willed herself to rise, and felt herself fade right through the thing that had crashed into her and landed atop her.

Oh my God what am I now I'm like a ghost just passing through things . . .

Terror swept over her as she saw that what had struck her was a bicycle. Keomany stormed toward her through the rain, wind churning like a baby tornado all around her, and Amber understood that the witch had used the elements to hurl the bike at her. She should have been afraid, but she was not.

Her feet touched the pavement, solid again. Keomany had elemental magic in her hands, but she wasn't in her right mind. And Amber had become something supernatural, too. Her heart might still be human, but she had lost the fragility of human flesh. For now, she allowed that to be a good thing.

"Turn around, dumbass!" Amber said, pointing toward the clock tower. "It's happening right now! What we came here for!"

Keomany only sneered. But Octavian had begun to rise from the ground, one hand clutched over his torn-up flesh and the other hauling up his pants, trying to regain some of his dignity and self-control. She had gotten through after all, at least a little.

But not to Keomany. The earthwitch leaped at Amber, rage overcoming logic. Amber grabbed her, an unnatural strength filling her. She wrapped one arm around Keomany's neck and forcibly turned her to see the events unfolding in the town square.

Together, they watched as a pair of wraiths grabbed Norm Dunne and flew him upward. He ascended toward his goddess and she imagined him in ecstasy. He held the iron chest in front of him. The chanting rose to even greater volume and the rain tapered slightly, as if Navalica's focus on the chest had slowed it.

Dunne held the chest toward her, this thing that she needed so that she could never be harmed again, never be thwarted, never be caged.

Navalica took the iron box from him, and then gestured toward the wraiths, who backed up several steps and let Norman Dunne plummet to an abrupt death in the town square below.

Amber flinched in horror, remembering the man's amiable nature, his pride in his work, and his gruff love for his son. *I'm sorry, Tommy,* she thought.

As Navalica opened the chest . . .

The goddess would destroy the traitors' magic—their little binding spells and ritual oils. Navalica smiled, suffused with a power that she had only dreamed about in her long imprisonment, sometimes remembering while she slept what she really was, only to have the dream flit away upon waking. She hated them all for what they had made her.

Weak.

But the sigils for the ritual tattoos would be lost to history once the scrolls where they had written down the ritual were destroyed. The ingredients for the dyes, the measurements of the oils needed to brew the draught that had protected them from her . . . they would never be used again.

She would be worshipped. She would be fed. Forever.

Navalica laughed, full of such joy as she had never known. She opened the iron box, and her joy faltered. Her eyes narrowed. What was this? Where were the elements of the ritual? Where were the scrolls? Inside the chest was only darkness.

No. The air inside that box moved. Navalica turned it so that it would catch the light of her burning hair, and she saw the mist swirling inside. She did not understand.

And then the mist rushed out at her, taking shape . . . taking flesh . . . and she saw it had a face. Red hair, a beautiful girl, glittering fangs . . . a vampire. She stank of old blood and bitter oils and dead flowers. Her face and arms were a labyrinth of sigils, tattooed into her skin with ancient dyes made from Chaldean earth. Navalica knew those sigils; they spoke of a magic long forgotten, a sorcery that had been old when she had first set foot upon the soil of this plane.

Navalica screamed with a terrible fury. She reached for the vampire but her hands could not touch the bitch; the sigils and oils had seen to that. The chaos storm was her heart, the mad churning of her mind, and a dozen bolts of lightning lanced down and struck the vampire girl, who did not flinch away, but grabbed hold of Navalica's head, her fiery hair burning the bitch's hand.

Eye to eye, Navalica stared at her, full of hate and rage.

She grunted, and looked down just in time to see the vampire's fist dragging her bright blue heart out through the ruin of her chest.

No! she thought. *Not again!*

The goddess fell to her knees as the vampire flew away. The flesh of her chest knitted itself quickly, but already she felt the storm begin to wane, so much of her strength lost to her. But she was still strong enough to kill the vampire, she thought. To destroy her.

With a gesture, she had the attention of her Reapers. She pointed, and they swarmed, filling the sky, blotting out the storm for a moment, and then flying in pursuit of the vampire.

Weakened, but drawing strength from her rage and the chaos she herself had created, she tried to stand and failed. The Reapers would bring her more of the bright, sweet human sustenance that had sped her awakening, but without her heart, the storm would slowly die. The chaos would fade.

She could not allow it. The vampire could not be allowed to complete the ritual.

Again she struggled to stand, staggering to her feet, her heel bumping something. Metal scraped against the stone of the clock tower's ledge. Navalica looked down and saw the iron box still there, left behind in the vampire's haste, and she began to laugh.

Fool. The vampire had weakened her, had taken her heart, but she could not complete the ritual without something within which to trap it. To cage Navalica's essence.

The goddess laughed, glancing around, and then she saw them, just outside the town square—the vampire and three others, one of them the sorcerer she thought she had already killed. These were the forces arrayed against her?

She stepped off the clock tower, riding the wind, mind awhirl with murder.

These four were nothing.

Miles opened his eyes. He felt strangely at ease, cradled in a warm softness that gently rocked him. Someone played piano in a room nearby, and he realized that he knew the song, but only when the voice began to sing in lovely, melodic French, did he recognize the voice as his mother's. He went completely still, not even breathing, listening with a melancholy heart that brought the sting of tears to his eyes.

In the quiet between notes, the rest between one line and the next, he heard the silence inside his chest. It occurred to him that he had not yet started to breathe again, and that he felt no particular yearning to do so.

Sitting up, he found himself in bed—his own bed, in his home, where he had grown up, where his mother had taken care of him and where he, eventually, had taken care of her. A golden glow suffused the room, a persuasive light that might have been twilight or the last moment before dawn. The music made him ache with longing, but he felt it only the way he had felt the keenest emotions all his life.

"Mother," he said, testing his voice in the room. He could hear it inside his head, but it made no echo, did nothing to fill the empty corners.

He slid off the bed and frowned, for he did not hear the shush of his skin against the sheets. A trickle of icy dread ran down his spine and made him shiver. He swallowed hard, but thought the feeling might only be the memory of swallowing. The weight of dread upon his shoulders was terrible, but he forced himself to reach out and touch the sheets. He smiled, for he could feel their softness, but when he tried to press down on the fabric, to muss the sheets, to grab a snatch of the fabric in his fist, his fingers passed through as if the bed were an illusion.

Miles bit his lip, took a long, shuddering breath, and stared at his hand. He closed his eyes and hung his head and let himself relax into utter stillness. A stillness only possible for the dead.

He remembered now. The red-haired vampire. Her black eyes with the tiny red pinpricks for irises. Her teeth like razors in his throat. Pain and sorrow, as he felt life leave him. And hope, as he gazed at Keomany as she tried to use her elemental magic to remove the taint of chaos upon his soul, so that he could go to his natural rest.

The singing in the other room ceased abruptly, the last piano notes lingering in the air. He opened his eyes and his breath caught in his chest. *No breath,* he thought. *No chest.* But he could still feel. His body no longer had the weight it once had, but the memory of its uses stayed with him like that last note of music hanging in the air.

The house moaned, buffeted by the storm. His surroundings had changed. Whatever ethereal place he'd been in when he first awoke to his new awareness, he had moved from there and back into the world of the living. The rain still beat on the windows, blue lightning arcing outside, lighting up the room, turning his outstretched hand into even more of a phantom limb. Transparent blue light washed right through him.

It isn't over, he thought. *The evil is still here.*

"Miles?" a voice said, from the doorway.

Hope fluttering in his ghost heart, he turned to see his mother standing in the hall outside his room. For a moment he thought Tim McConville might be with her, but whatever message Tim's ghost had been trying to send him earlier, it must have been delivered. Or perhaps it no longer mattered, now that Miles himself was dead.

"Ma," he said.

He hurried to her, and if his feet did not exactly touch the floor, they certainly felt like they had. His mother's ghost embraced him, and he felt her arms around him, and he took solace from the knowledge that they were together.

After several long minutes, he asked the only question that seemed to mean anything to him.

"What now?"

His mother stepped back and looked up at him. He had been taller than her since the year he turned twelve, and she had joked about him being able to eat beans off her head, whatever that meant. It had always made him laugh.

"I don't know," she said. "I think . . . I think we wait here until we're not scared anymore."

Scared. Miles felt a painful hollow in his gut. Yes, he was scared. Frightened of what came next. He wondered if that was why Tim McConville had come to see him all those times, searching for someone to tell him not to be afraid . . . or that it was all right to be afraid. He wondered if the little boy who had never gotten to grow up was still afraid, or if he'd been able to finally put his fear to rest.

"We'll be all right," he told his mother.

She smiled. "I know, sweetheart. We have a piano."

Miles laughed, thinking of all of the songs she had taught him. Her students at the high school had called their French and music teacher Mrs. Varick, but in her heart she had never stopped being Toni Pelletier, whose parents had come to America from Saint Paul de Vence, in France. She had been a good mother.

"That's all we need now, is it?" he asked. "Music?"

His mother smiled and hugged him again. "It's all we ever needed."

Miles smiled, still confused and afraid but a little less of both. He kissed his mother's hair. He opened his mouth to make a joke about eating beans off the top of her head, but the joke never came out.

A sharp pain stabbed him in the gut. He grunted, clutching at his abdomen as he stepped back from her.

"Miles, what is it, darling?" His mother's fear pervaded the room.

Another pain twisted inside him and he shook his head. Was this supposed to happen? He knew this pain, this pang.

"I don't . . ." he began, but then he faltered and looked at her and a fresh pang stabbed at him. A chilling rush of horror swept through him.

"Are you . . . Mom, are you *hungry*?" he asked.

Octavian burned with embarrassment and regret. He could still feel Keomany's mouth and hands on his skin, and he hated Navalica for the chaos that had undone them both and forever stained their friendship.

He wiped the searing chaos rain out of his eyes and stared, trying to make sense of the figure flying toward him through the storm. The wind screamed in his ears, merging with the shriek of Navalica's rage that filled the square, but Octavian ignored it all. What flew toward him might have been an angel, if he thought such things still existed in this world. Enormous eagle wings spread and caught the air, dipped and sliced the current, and she soared directly toward him.

"That's new!" Keomany called, as she and Amber ran up beside him.

Octavian stared at the red-haired angel that dove toward them, and he shook his head.

"No," he said. "It's very, very old."

In his time as a vampire, with the ability to alter his shape on a molecular level, he had never taken this form. He had seen it only a handful of times, a shadow not changing its fundamental flesh, but adding to it. It took more than imagination; it took irreverence, and righteousness and a supreme effort of will to tap into the structure of the universe and steal some of its substance.

Charlotte alighted beside him, wings furling toward her back and diminishing to nothing, like the claws of a cat returning to their sheaths. With the tattoos all over her flesh, she had a fierce glory about her, like some ancient barbarian queen. In her hands she held the dripping, pulsing, pustulent indigo heart of the goddess of chaos.

"How did you do that?" Octavian demanded.

"I did what you wanted!" Charlotte roared over the storm.

"Not that!" he snapped.

Amber darted into the air in front of them, hanging there five feet off the pavement, though the rain still touched her skin, still beaded on her new flesh.

"Where's the chest?" she demanded, glaring at Charlotte. "You left it there!"

Charlotte snarled at her. "I got her fucking heart and I'm back here alive. I didn't see you up there!"

Keomany shouted, pointing, and Octavian looked up at the clock tower in time to see Navalica step off the edge, descending toward the square. Charlotte had bought them precious seconds, and they were squandering them. How a rogue vampire girl with little experience shapeshifting beyond the sinister forms—bat, rat, wolf—could manifest angel wings . . . that would have to wait.

"Give me the heart," Octavian snapped.

Charlotte hesitated, and he saw a flicker of something dark in her eyes, as though she might have some other plan for the goddess's heart, but then she handed it over. *Were you going to try to eat it?* he thought, but did not say. More questions for another day.

Rage bristled inside him. He opened his arms wide, summoning a fierce magic from within him. His chest had begun to heal from the wounds Amber had slashed there, but not completely, and he smeared his palms with his own blood, flicked his fingers so that droplets flew into the air, and then spoke a single word that froze the blood and the air around it. Muttering a short enchantment, a spell of the ancient Hittites, lost to time but not to him, he reached out to grab the frozen droplets of blood and a silver light burst from both of his palms and blossomed into a cage of light around those blood drops.

"Now," he said, thrusting the cage-sphere toward Charlotte. "Put it inside."

Fearless, she did not hesitate, thrusting both of her hands into the silver light and placing the heart within. She pulled her hands out and turned to face the first wave of Navalica's wraiths, which dropped down out of the sky to attack them.

"Bring it, bitches!" Charlotte screamed, and a fresh set of wings burst from her back. These were not angel wings, however. Webbed, leathery things, they belonged on a dragon, or a demon.

She launched herself into the air, slashing at two of the wraiths, and the battle was joined.

Octavian looked toward the square and saw people scurrying out of the way as Navalica stalked toward them. Blue lightning arced from the sky, striking her again and again. Wraiths dipped down to her out of the storm, bringing squirming blobs of color, bits of human joy, the stolen chaos of human hearts, to replenish her.

"Here!" he shouted, turning to Keomany and Amber.

He thrust the Hittite soul cage out to Keomany, who flinched away.

"I don't do that kind of magic!" she insisted.

"You're a witch, elemental or not," Octavian shouted, wiping the rain again from his face. "All you have to do is hold on to it until we get the high priests' damn box back. You know the feel of magic. You can do it!"

Hands shaking, Keomany took it.

Octavian turned to Amber. "Prep her for the spell, like we planned. Keep the Reapers off her."

Then he looked up at the savage air war taking place above him, Charlotte and the wraiths clawing each other to shreds.

"Charlotte!"

The vampire spun in midair, red hair spilling wetly across her face, slick with rain.

"Go back and get that chest!" he roared.

She sneered and shot him the finger, but she beat those demon wings and flew off, speeding toward the clock tower again. Some of the wraiths gave chase, but others dove toward Octavian, Keomany, and Amber.

Teeth gritted, Octavian summoned arcane fire and burned them out of the sky.

Amber let out a cry. He turned toward her and saw the confusion and regret in her eyes.

"They're not your family anymore," he told her. "Now get Keomany ready. And keep her alive."

Amber nodded, and Octavian turned to see Navalica striding toward him, arrogant in her rage. Without her heart, her magic had weakened.

Her control of the storm would falter. She would lose control. But she was a goddess of chaos and darkness and she had waited thousands of years to taste freedom and human pain again. She would never surrender.

Octavian ran toward her, summoning magic learned in Hell, sorcery that had no place in this world. His hair whipped around him as that sorcerous energy crackled, burning away the chaos rain before it could touch him, raw power with which he could have slain angels. He willed it to take shape, holding his hands in front of him, and forged the blazing golden aura around him into a single blade, a sword of Hell's fire.

Navalica paused, cocked her head, and laughed, the blue fire of her hair falling around her face. Lightning struck the pavement around her, cracking the street open. Steam shot up from the sewers below.

"Little magician, you inconvenience me," the goddess said.

"No," Octavian replied. "I bring you order."

Navalica narrowed her eyes with hatred, and in that moment, he saw her uncertainty. Without her heart, she weakened. He knew, then, that he could defeat her.

If she didn't kill him first.

Are you hungry? Miles had asked his mother.

Her mystified expression was all the answer he required. That, and the way his hunger had begun to focus on his mother, on the pale expanse of her throat. No blood ran beneath that ethereal skin. Like him, she had no substance except for spirit. And yet as the hunger gnawed at him, he knew that she wasn't like him at all.

"This can't be," he said, backing away, ghost tears sliding from his phantom eyes.

Were his teeth sharper now? He ran his tongue over them, all of it only a manifestation of his spirit, nothing but a ghost, nothing that should be able to be altered on such a level. What were ghosts? Spirits? Ectoplasm? Energy?

This is impossible, he thought.

But wasn't that the true terror of chaos magic, that it made the impossible possible? His body had been tainted by Navalica's chaos, and then savaged by a vampire. He had been impaled on the table, and those wooden shafts had thrust up through her body as well, and her blood had run down into his wounds, inside him . . . and then Keomany had touched him with her magic, made certain that his soul maintained contact with the earthly plane.

All those different strains of magic working on him at once, even as death took his flesh and his spirit slipped away, contaminated.

"Miles, please, you're scaring me," his mother said, reaching for him.

"Don't touch me!" he snapped, jerking away from her, though all he wanted was to embrace her again. It was what the hunger in him demanded.

"Miles?"

"I'm hungry, Mother," he said, running his tongue over the spectral fangs in his mouth.

Anguish clutched at his heart. He looked at the window and saw the rain running like thick syrup down the glass. Blue lightning flashed, and hate filled him so completely that for a moment his hunger faded.

"Chaos," he whispered.

Charlotte had been driven mad with bloodlust she could not control. Keomany had only tried to save his soul. Miles understood that he had become a monster, a pit of ravenous gnawing where a soul ought to be, and he knew who was responsible.

If Octavian and his friends were out there now, trying to kill Navalica, he wanted to see it happen.

"I'll be back," he told his mother.

"Sweetheart, please," she begged, reaching for him.

Miles skittered away from her. "No. Not now. I'm hungry now. But I'll come back."

"When?"

He shot her a look that he knew would haunt her, but he could not stop himself.

"When I've eaten."

As he walked toward the door his thoughts were focused entirely on Keomany. She had tried to help him. Whatever Octavian had in mind to fight Navalica, Keomany would be a part of it. Miles had to find her.

He went through the door, and for a moment the house shimmered around him, becoming once again that soft gray twilight realm in which he had awoken. *No,* he thought. *I need to be with Keomany. I need to go to her.*

For a second or two, all became gauzy mist around him, and then he blinked in surprise as the world resolved again. He stood in the town square in the midst of the storm, rain passing through him, wind not touching him at all. Wraiths darted overheard, diving in and out of the churning clouds. People fought and fornicated in the street.

A shout of rage came to him, and he turned.

Keomany Shaw stood only a few feet away under the awning of the Black Rose Grille, her hands on either side of a sphere of gleaming silver light. She looked as if she were in pain, struggling with intense concentration. Beside her stood a wraith unlike all of the others, the ones Amber had called Reapers. This creature had a sensual female body, nothing like the withered skeletal piping of the others. Its skin was a dark, bruised purple. The wraith had some kind of needle in her hand and was hastily tattooing arcane symbols on Keomany's face.

Miles darted toward them. Keomany saw him first. The wraith noticed the way she stiffened and turned, and he realized he knew her.

Hunger clawed at him, but he forced himself to be calm.

"Professor?" the wraith said. "Miles?"

Anger filled him. "Amber," he said. "God help us, what have we become?"

18

Amber didn't have an answer for him. In truth, she felt good. Better than she had ever felt when she was flesh and blood. She would miss her friends—because how could they accept her like this?—but she would not miss the weakness and the worry that came with fragile humanity. Octavian had told her she was beautiful, and now that the shock of metamorphosis had begun to wear off, she felt a constant stirring inside her that had nothing to do with the carnal desires prompted by chaos. She felt as though her life had been a dream and now she was at last awake. *Alive.*

But Miles . . . Miles was dead.

"Are you a ghost?" she asked.

The rain fell through him. The wind did not rustle his clothing. When the blue lightning cracked the sky, she could see through him. But even as some grave specter, he seemed gaunt and hollow and she took a step back from him.

"What am I?" Miles asked. He pointed at Keomany. "Ask her! Ask Charlotte!"

Amber turned to Keomany, who stared at Miles with curiosity and uncertainty.

"What's he talking about?" Amber asked, returning to her work, finishing the sigils she had begun to tattoo on Keomany's face.

They had all been prepared for this spell. The oils, the tattoos, the memorization of the ritual, words in ancient Chaldean that should not have been simple for her mouth to form, but Octavian had done something to them, almost like a posthypnotic suggestion, putting the spell into their brains like loading bullets into a gun, and all any of them—Keomany, Amber, or Charlotte—would have to do was pull the trigger.

But it required the final sigils, the last two, which could only be done in the presence of the goddess's heart.

Amber jabbed Keomany with the bone needle. "What is he talking about?"

Keomany flinched as if waking. She had been watching the Reapers that circled above them, diving in and out of clouds, attacking people in the square and stripping some of their essence, then flying to Navalica to keep her fed even as the goddess and Octavian fought, magic splintering the sky above them.

"Charlotte lost it," Keomany said, almost robotic, the soul cage holding Navalica's heart crackling in her hands. "The chaos took her over. She killed him. She murdered Miles."

Amber shrank back from her, cringing with sadness. She turned to Miles's ghost.

"I'm so sorry."

"What am I?" Miles demanded, staring at Keomany.

"I don't know."

Miles laughed at that. "I sure as hell do. I'm a goddamn vampire."

"That's not possible," Keomany said. "You're a ghost."

"This whole universe came out of chaos," Miles said, looking at Amber now, reaching for her, caressing her skin. "Chaos is where new things are born."

Ghost or not, she could feel his touch, and she yearned toward him, wanting that comfort. But then his ghostly lips peeled back and she saw his fangs, long, sharp, shadowy things.

"I'm hungry," Miles told her, and his sorrow was more than she could bear.

Something black swept by at the edges of her vision, and she turned. The wraiths had come for them. Octavian and Navalica fought, their magic tearing apart the storm itself. Charlotte had gone for the iron chest. The Reapers had come for their goddess's heart, and Keomany held the soul cage, had to keep it safe.

"Amber?" Keomany said, her voice pleading. With the soul cage in her hands, she could not fight back.

"I'm here," Amber said. These horrid things with their curved blades and their bodies like black piping . . . once they had been her family, her ancestors. But now they were monsters. She turned to Miles and pointed at the Reapers. "If you're hungry, see what *they* taste like."

Miles turned toward the Reapers, opening his mouth impossibly wide, and his face took on a monstrous countenance. His spectral form rippling, he rushed at them, and Amber wondered if he would be able to make contact . . . but only for a moment, before he collided with the nearest Reaper. It swung its sickle daggers into his ghostflesh, but the blades sliced harmlessly through him. Miles wrapped a hand in its tattered clothing, grabbed it by the throat, and drove his fangs toward its narrow chest. The wraith cried out in an unearthly shriek of pain, and Miles tilted back his head and swallowed a piece of it down. Black mist jetted from its chest like blood.

The hungry ghost tore out the Reaper's throat and sucked away more of whatever her ancestors had become. Not blood, and not ghostly ectoplasm, but maybe some combination of the two. Amber wondered what Miles truly hungered for, what would sate a vampire ghost. Could he drink blood? Eat the flesh of the living? Would it fill him?

The wraiths fell on her then.

Grimly determined, Amber fought them. Sickle blades glanced off her burgundy skin, scratching but not cutting. Two of them grabbed hold of her, but she twisted around, breaking their limbs, and she knew they had no chance against her. They could not cut her and her strength was so much greater. And she had Miles on her side, whatever he was.

"They're weaker now!" Keomany called to her. "Navalica's fading. Just keep them away until . . . until Charlotte comes."

Amber glanced at her, but Keomany's focus was entirely on the crackling silver magic of the Hittite soul cage she held between her hands, as though it might at any moment explode and kill her.

Three other Reapers dropped down from the roiling storm clouds.

Miles caught one as it tried to dart past him, and Amber cringed at the sound of its unholy, inhuman screams as the hungry ghost devoured it.

She grabbed one of the Reapers by the throat and crushed it, even as it tried to cut her, blades slashing her clothes to ribbons, leaving her all but naked. Purple sparks shot out where the curved knives scraped her skin.

Would she have been able to stop them so easily before Charlotte took Navalica's heart? She thought not. It had all hinged on that . . . on Octavian's plan. She had to trust him. She glanced over and saw him fighting the goddess. The moment she caught sight of them, Navalica gestured and turned the air in front of Octavian into swarms of bees, which made a cloud around him until a blast of tainted orange light erupted from their midst, turning the bees to glass. They fell, shattering on the rain-swept street, and Octavian leaped at Navalica, flaming sword raised.

Keomany screamed.

Amber turned, saw a wraith going for the earthwitch, and flitted toward her, flying at such speed that Keomany's scream had not yet finished before Amber had torn the wraith away from her.

She raised a fist, about to smash the Reaper's skull, when it cocked its head and drew back, its smooth carapace face wrinkling in a strange recognition. Its mouth opened and it tried to speak. The word came out a whisper. Two syllables. Her name.

And she knew. This was her Nana. Her mother's mother. In her mind, this woman had been dead and buried seven years ago, but she understood the complexity of the magic used to hide Navalica in her family's midst, and knew that there had never been a funeral. That there had never been a body. God, the scope of such enchantments! At least they didn't have to do that again. All they had to do was cage the goddess's heart and reduce her to a withered old woman again.

"Amber," the Reaper said, her voice like a gust of wind. And it faltered.

She could not destroy this wraith. Couldn't allow Miles to do it, either. But she needn't have worried. The thing that had once been her grandmother backed away, drifting into the air, and turned toward other wraiths that were flying down at them. It flew around them in a circle, gesturing, imploring.

And the wraiths began to drift away.

Miles alighted beside her. Somehow, he seemed more solid than before. The rain still passed through him, he was still a ghost, but he had substance and dimension and his face had new definition.

"Are you still hungry?" she asked.

The ghost reached out and took her hand. At first his fingers passed through hers, but then he seemed to focus and he tried again, and this time he grasped her hand, gave her a comforting squeeze.

"No," he said. "I'm all right, for now."

That *for now* unnerved her, but it seemed they both had much to learn about their new lives.

Amber had dropped the bone needle. Now she ran back underneath the awning where she had left Keomany and picked it up. Drying it on Keomany's shirt, she reached into the earthwitch's pocket and brought out the jar of dye she needed. And then she began to complete the last tattoo on Keomany's face, the final element of the ritual.

"Charlotte," Keomany said, her voice a rasp, still staring at the soul cage.

"No, it's me . . ." Amber said, worried.

Keomany raised her head and stared past Amber, toward the clock tower. "I know. And thank you for your protection. I only meant that she's coming."

Amber turned, saw Miles a few feet away, guarding them. And then she saw the pale figure flying toward them through the rain, the red hair and broad wings, and for the first time, she believed that they might actually see the sunlight again. That the storm might be almost over.

Octavian staggered but managed not to fall. Welts and gashes and burns covered his body. His clothes were scorched and torn. The ritual tattoos on his arms had been almost completely seared away and provided little protection from Navalica's chaos magic now. But if anyone could stand against her without such defenses, it must be him. He knew he flattered himself to think he might have still stood a chance against her at her most powerful. Even without her heart, her core essence, Navalica had nearly killed him a dozen times in just a handful of minutes. The blue lightning had struck him twice before he had managed to cast a spell that would shield him, and now each bolt glanced away, striking the street a few feet from where he stood.

Octavian held up the flaming sword he had forged of pure magic. He had inspired the goddess. As the storm above them weakened and her influence waned, she had crafted a sword of her own. He didn't understand its purpose, but it foamed with rust that dripped from the blade and hit the street, eating through the pavement like acid.

Navalica gathered herself up to her full height, at least a foot taller than Octavian.

"You're a fool to believe you might destroy me," she said. "You are mortal. I am a goddess. Your small mind cannot comprehend eternity."

Her hair blazed with indigo fire. Despite her dwindling power, she had a terrible beauty, and her imperious gaze made something inside Octavian cringe. But he had faced devils and refused to kneel before them; he would not give this bitch his throat.

"Perhaps I am more than I seem," Octavian said, knowing that she was using this momentary respite to muster her strength.

"You are a gnat."

Octavian rarely surrendered to pride. It was foolhardy to reveal too much to one's enemies. But he burned with embarrassment and guilt over the way the goddess's magic had undone him, had turned him and Keomany into animals rutting in the street.

"I am a prince of Byzantium," he said. "I have brought down warlords and tyrants and popes and stood against the demon lords of seven Hells. I have tasted mead with the fallen in Valhalla and broken the hearts of angels. I have been reborn from vampirism to humanity, and if I have learned anything in my long life, it is that even gods can die."

"You will not kill me," Navalica sneered, but she seemed diminished now. Her hesitation had worked against her. The longer she went without her heart, the less control she had over chaos.

"I don't need to kill you," Octavian replied.

Her eyes narrowed. "I will not be caged in dreams. Not again."

Navalica roared and leaped at him. Ordinary lightning began on the ground and arced into the sky, but the blue lightning she wielded came from above. It could no longer hurt him, but as it glanced off the defensive spell he had cast, it struck the ground, breaking pavement and sending up showers of cerulean sparks, and through the veil of that distraction came the goddess.

Her sword sliced the air, flickers of acid rust flying. Octavian had learned the mastery of the sword as a boy, and trained with samurai in his years as an immortal. He caught her attack on his flaming blade, sidestepped as fire and acid sprayed from the collision, and parried her with such strength that she stumbled and her blade twisted downward, its point hitting the street.

Where it touched, the pavement aged instantly, crumbling and falling inward, so that Octavian had to leap away. He stared in dawning unease as he realized what she had done, what magic she had put into the blade. Her sword was entropy. It sped up the natural deterioration of whatever it touched.

Navalica staggered back, hurling herself away from the hole that opened up in the street.

Hatred burning in her eyes, she turned on him, and then screamed skyward.

"Kill him! Tear him open! Devour his heart!"

From the diminishing storm came no reply. No wraiths dropped down from the thinning clouds to obey her commands. Octavian saw Amber flit through the clouds with some kind of apparition beside her, and several of the wraiths moved away from them instead of trying to kill them. More than any attack Octavian could muster, that seemed to shake the goddess.

Navalica faced him, holding the rusting sword in front of her, and stalked toward him. She began to chant loudly, and a wave of sickly yellow energy flowed out from her, rolling like ocean surf along the ground. Octavian wondered what she would try to set against him now, but he did not have to wonder very long.

He heard the barking and glanced toward the base of the clock tower, where the dead dogs had been scattered. Now those dogs were up and moving again, but just as dead. They had torn each other apart in a frenzy of violence and now they came at him with their throats hanging open, fur matted with blood, skin hanging in flaps.

Reanimating dead dogs. It showed how little she had left to fight him with.

He spoke the words of the spell in ancient Chaldean, so she would hear him and know that such things were no more than parlor tricks. Then, with a gesture, he returned them to death. The dogs collapsed all at once, flopping to the wet pavement without so much as a whimper.

Navalica screamed. Sword held at her side, she thrust out a hand and chaos swirled around her fingers, exploding toward him. Octavian felt the magic coming at him, so fierce, so powerful that it took him off guard. It would turn him inside out, reversing his entire body, blood and organs bursting. Instinct, and the magic at his core, saved him. He let go of the flaming sword and it vanished as he dropped to one knee and splayed his fingers out in front of him, creating a shield of sizzling emerald light that deflected her attack.

Stupid, he thought. He'd been arrogant, and such overconfidence could get him killed.

He did not have to defeat her, only keep her occupied until the others finished the spell to entrap her. It had been his plan all along, take her heart, weaken her enough to confine her anew, then put the iron chest into some parallel dimension instead of at the bottom of the ocean, so that even if it were ever opened again, Navalica could never be reunited with her heart.

All he had to do was fight her, and stay alive.

And the best way to fight chaos was with order. Navalica came at him again, still wielding that entropic sword, edging her way around the hole she had created in the street. Broken sewer pipes gushed water below. Octavian did not bother forging a new blade of his own. Instead, he struck her with a blast of concussive magic that knocked her back several yards. She landed hard, but sprang up instantly, a new confidence glinting in her eyes. Brute force would not destroy her; they both knew that. And he knew she would think he had run out of ideas.

But even as he had attacked her, Octavian had been crafting another spell. He reached deep within himself for the strength, and into his memories of Hell for the words, for he had learned them from a fellow prisoner, a Chinese sorcerer who subscribed to philosophies of simplicity and synchronicity . . . of Order.

The air around Navalica shimmered. A round hole appeared in the fabric of the world, and sunlight shone through it. Navalica cried out and turned toward that purity in surprise, but she was no vampire. It would not kill her. Confusion made her blade falter, even as a second circle appeared opposite the first, this one a window into winter night, snow blowing in from another part of the world. A third window opened, and then a fourth, one revealing a spring morning and the other a windy autumn afternoon, leaves dancing on a gust of wind.

The four seasons of the natural world in perfect symmetry. Order.

Navalica tried to slip between these openings, but they moved with her. The clean air of a world of order, untouched by her chaos, surrounded her. The goddess screamed in rage and rushed at him, but again the spell kept her boxed by those windows, poisoning her with order. She was already weak; confusion and frustration made her falter anew.

In the sky above Hawthorne, the storm had diminished enough that the first gleam of sunshine and blue sky broke through the gray and the rain.

"I told you I didn't have to kill you," Octavian reminded her. "Submit now. Your time in this world is over."

With a roar, Navalica swung her entropy blade. It struck the autumn window, cleaving the magic in half. The spell deteriorated instantly, unraveling so quickly that the backlash stunned Octavian, hitting him like the scorching blast of an explosion. He threw up his hands to protect himself and his flesh seared anew.

Weakened and unsteady, he looked up to see that the windows were gone. Navalica seemed withered now, aging, diminishing. The radiant power of a goddess had faded like the storm above.

"I will not be caged!" she shouted at him.

The goddess looked around, searching for something. He thought she hoped to find wraiths that would come to her aid, or worshippers still under her control. With the rain now nothing more than a light drizzle and the daylight glowing behind the clouds, filtering through and breaking up the storm, nothing could be hidden in darkness.

Navalica froze, gaze locked on something off to Octavian's right. He turned and saw them, standing under the awning half a block away, where he'd left them. Keomany and Charlotte and Amber. A ghost stood with them, wavering in and out of existence.

Charlotte held the box. Amber and the ghost stood back as Keomany closed the latches, the soul cage no longer in her hands. Navalica's heart had been returned to the chest where her high priests had trapped it millennia before. All that remained of the ritual was the enchantment that went along with it, the words of which he had implanted in their minds so they could not be forgotten. As he watched, Keomany raised her hands and began to speak.

Navalica shrieked. She leaped at Octavian. Weak and distracted, he avoided the killing blow of her blade only by throwing himself backward and deflecting her with a hasty defensive shield. But the goddess kept moving, rolling away from his shield and leaping through the air, magic carrying her forty feet or more.

She came down beside the awning. Amber attacked her, but Navalica threw her aside. The goddess might not be able to control the strange hybrid wraith that Amber had become, but Amber could not stop her.

Charlotte cried out a warning, tried to move the chest around, to hold it against her with one hand, but she was too late.

Keomany's eyes went wide as the entropic blade plunged between her breasts.

Octavian screamed, running toward them, knowing he was too late.

Charlotte dropped the iron chest, which struck the pavement and tipped over, but remained latched. Shapeshifting, she grew in the space between heartbeats, becoming an enormous black bear. One paw on Navalica's head; with the other she tore the goddess's right arm off. The entropic sword hit the sidewalk, but its magic had vanished without connection to Navalica, and with an acidic hiss it bubbled away to nothing.

Shifting back to her human form, Charlotte fought the ruined goddess, tearing at her, refusing to let her rise from the ground.

When Octavian reached Keomany, Amber was already at her side. They knelt on either side of her, but Keomany looked only at him. The hole in her chest had begun to sink inward and her skin wrinkled and sagged. Her hair whitened as entropy took hold.

"Peter," Keomany said, wearing a mask of sorrow and embarrassment. "I'm sorry."

He knew what she meant. She burned with the same guilt and humiliation he felt for the way Navalica's magic had made them behave.

"Nothing to be sorry about," he said, and found that he meant it. He regretted succumbing to chaos, but not what they had done under that influence.

Keomany smiled, but it did not erase the sadness in her eyes. She died with that expression on her face, her flesh continuing to wither and flake so rapidly that only half a minute passed before her body crumbled to dust and yellowed bone.

"Oh, my God," Amber whispered.

Octavian looked at her inhuman beauty, saw the ghost standing behind her and recognized Professor Varick, and thought about how much they had all lost to chaos.

"A little help here?" Charlotte snapped.

But a glance told him that she didn't really need help. A fresh wind was blowing the storm away, revealing more of the blue sky. The goddess no longer had the strength to fight them.

Octavian rose and retrieved the chest. He sat on the sidewalk and held it in his lap and he spoke the words. He could feel the seal on the iron chest tighten, and heard a small shushing noise as it expelled what air had been inside.

As they watched, the blue faded from the skin of the goddess Navalica. Her burning indigo fire became ordinary hair, thin and gray. Charlotte held the one-armed old woman in her arms, and for the first time, Octavian saw the vampire girl's eyes turn soft and kind.

"Gran," Amber whispered.

Octavian held the chest tightly and they all watched as the last of the storm cleared away, sunlight glinting off the towers of the church and city hall, the bell and the clock. Against the bright blue sky, he saw sparrows flying in formation.

Order had been restored. But it felt nothing like victory.

---------------------------- ✳ ----------------------------

Epilogue

Miles knew he could not haunt his own house, or remain in his child-hood home. As far as the rest of the world knew, he and his mother were both among the eighty-seven people who had died in the chaos storm that had cut Hawthorne off from the rest of the world.

As far as the world knows? he thought. *You* are *among the dead.*

He had to remind himself of this constantly. It was strange to be aware and awake, to have a sense of reality, to be able—under certain circumstances—to touch the living, solid world, while being neither solid nor alive himself.

"Miles?"

He turned to see his mother standing in the entrance to the living room. Miles himself sat—as much as a phantom could be said to sit—on the piano bench where she had taught him how to play. They had shared real joy there, a contentment that parent and child rarely experienced together. In school, Miles had often been called a mama's boy, but he had never seen any sin in loving his mother, she who had been kinder to him than anyone else in his life. His wife had broken his heart and then broken their marriage, and though he had returned to Hawthorne with deep regrets, he had never regretted being able to spend more time visiting with his mother.

Now, though, he had one last regret.

"I'm sorry," he said.

His mother's ghost drifted toward him, almost walking, though each stride covered more distance than it ought to have. She settled beside him on the piano bench and played a few notes of "Hit That Jive Jack," which had always made him laugh.

"What are you sorry for?" she asked.

Miles turned to her, felt the vague stirring of hunger inside him and pushed it away. He had sated his hunger with Navalica's wraiths, but already it had begun to return. When he looked at ghosts—and there were many new ones in Hawthorne, getting their bearings before they moved on to whatever came next—he felt that hunger. But he felt it when he looked at humans, too, and his spectral fangs were sharp indeed when he ran his tongue over them. He felt sure that he could drink blood to satisfy his hunger, just as easily as he could feed off a ghost, and if he had to choose, he would take from the living. The dead had suffered enough.

"You know we can't stay here," he said, running his fingers over the keys and then playing the opening run of "Devil May Care."

His mother joined in, her fingers dancing over the keys, but she did not reply.

Miles stopped playing and turned to her. "The house will be sold. New people will move in. Our things will be removed. I don't want to see all of that. I don't want to haunt my own house."

"This hasn't been your house in years," his mother said, but lightly. They both knew it had always been his home just as much as it had been hers, no matter where he lived.

"It might be fun," she added, lifting her hands from the keys and making absurd spooky-ghost noises.

The joke fell flat and the two of them sat there, side by side at the piano, for what might have been a minute or an hour—Miles had found that it was sometimes difficult to gauge the passage of time now that he was dead.

"What do you have in mind?" she asked, at last, playing with the keys again, mischief turning into a snatch of Mozart.

"You don't have to wait for me."

She stopped playing and turned to look at him, anger flaring in her eyes. They had talked about this already. Whatever he was, Miles did not feel the lure of the other side the way other ghosts seemed to. His mother described it as a yearning, but he did not share that yearning. Only hunger. Whatever final rest awaited the soul, he feared that he would never find it. But she could go. She could have that peace.

"I'm not going anywhere until we know more about what's happened to you. God will have to drag me screaming to Heaven if he wants me. At least until I can be sure that you'll be able to follow someday."

Miles smiled. It had been worth a try.

"Plan B, then, I guess," he said.

"Which is?"

"My student, Amber Morrissey—"

"The purple girl."

He nodded. "She's not . . ." He almost said *human*. "She's also been changed. But she's alive. Octavian—the sorcerer? He's helping her."

"Aren't her parents ill?" his mother asked.

Miles thought about that. They had been in the process of being transformed into Reapers before Octavian had frozen time around them. Last night he had woven spells around them that seemed to be slowly restoring their humanity.

"It looks like they're getting better," he said. "Amber has offered to let us live with her."

His mother stared at him. "She's got that demon in her house. The thing that killed us. That caused all of this."

Navalica was not a demon, but Miles knew better than to correct her.

"She's there, yes. But she's barely alive. She will never wake up again. Octavian has seen to that. She might as well be dead."

"But she isn't dead. We are."

Miles flinched at her bitterness. They fell into silence again, until at last her fingers strayed to the piano yet again. She couldn't help it.

"Mom . . ." he began.

She played through an old Charles Trenet song, singing softly in French. It had always been one of her favorites, one that she played to cheer herself up when she was feeling blue. He watched her translucent fingers moving across the keys and wondered what the new owners of the house might think when the piano began to play by itself in the middle of the night.

When she had played the final notes of the song, she turned to him. "Do they have a piano?" she asked.

"We could ask Amber to take this one. I'm sure she would move it over there. Maybe even tonight."

She considered for a moment and then gave him a nod. Then she nudged him and began to play. Miles joined in, accompanying her, though he would never play as well as she did.

Not even if he practiced forever.

Octavian and Charlotte had both spent the night at Amber's. He had done all he could for her parents and hoped that time would do the rest, but it remained to be seen if they would ever be completely cleansed of Navalica's influence. In addition to the ritual they had done to hide the goddess behind the guise of a withered old woman, Octavian had cast further enchantments on the creature Amber would have to pretend was her great-grandmother—spells that would keep Navalica essentially comatose.

The Morrissey family, as descendants of her ancient Chaldean high priests, had been her caretakers for thousands of years, and Amber vowed to continue to fulfill that duty. Abandoned, the old woman would not die. They could bury her in a hole in the ground and she would continue just as she was, perhaps for eternity, as long as the iron chest remained hidden in the dead, lifeless parallel dimension where Octavian had placed it. But Amber did not like the idea of burying Navalica where she might be forgotten. Someone had to keep watch, to make certain, and she was determined to be that person.

Octavian had tried to reverse the effects of long-term exposure to Navalica's anarchic magic on Amber, to make her human again, but whatever she had become, there would be no returning from it. Instead, he had cast a glamour upon her. She would be able to walk among ordinary humans and they would see her as they always had . . . as a pretty college girl, a good daughter, a hard-working student. Only other supernaturals would be able to see through the glamour. But Octavian had no illusions about Amber being able to return to her old life—that time for her was over.

Amber and Charlotte walked him to his car, the Morrissey house looming quietly behind them. It looked empty, but it would never be empty again. Chaos slept there. Soon ghosts would haunt its halls. Octavian wondered if people passing on the street would quicken their pace without knowing why. Such houses always gave passersby the shivers.

Amber carried a wine bottle that held what they had managed to collect of Keomany's ashes. Octavian had wanted something he could seal, and the Santa's Workshop cookie tin had seemed too disrespectful, though he thought it would have amused Keomany.

Thoughts of her weighed on him. Her life had been full of lightness and contentment before her home in Vermont had been destroyed by a demon called the Tatterdemalion. A demon that never would have been able to come into this world if the Vatican sorcerers were still alive to continually restore the magic keeping the forces of darkness out. Octavian had helped to destroy them in order to save himself and his kind, but the cost had been so much higher than he could ever have known.

He had liked Keomany very much, and perhaps he had felt something more for her. But he refused to allow himself to dwell on what might have been, and what should never have been, though he still burned with guilt and embarrassment about what Navalica's influence had caused them to do.

Charlotte squirmed as they walked the front path to the street, where his car was parked. She wore a thin, hooded sweatshirt with the hood up, hiding as much of herself from the sun as she could manage. Objectively, she knew it would not burn her, but Cortez—the vampire who had made her—had instilled the vampire traditions in her so deeply that the sun made her profoundly uneasy.

Octavian set his bags down behind the car.

"I want to thank you," Amber said.

"Nothing to thank me for," he replied.

She laughed. "Other than my life, you mean? And my parents' lives?"

Such as they are, Octavian thought, but he did not want to cast a pall over the bright spark of her hope.

He opened the trunk and loaded Keomany's suitcase and then his own.

"Just remember you can call me any time," he said. "And practice that glamour. You'll need to refresh it at least once a month to keep it from slipping."

"It seems weird," she said. "I'm no magician."

Octavian smiled. "I've done the hard part. The rest is small magic. You'll do fine."

Amber hesitated a moment, sadness touching her eyes, and then she handed him the wine bottle. The depth of her regret made her new features even more lovely, and Octavian thought he understood for the first time what it meant to say one was tragically beautiful.

"I prayed for her," Amber said.

Octavian took the wine bottle. "She would have liked that."

Charlotte shifted, anxious to be out of the sun. "What are you going to do with her? With the ashes, I mean?"

"I'm taking her back to the orchard where she lived. There are other witches there, her friends. I thought they'd want to scatter her ashes into the soil there, around the roots of the trees. She would have liked that."

An awkward moment passed among them as they all realized this was farewell.

"I want to thank you, too," Charlotte said. "For giving me a chance."

Octavian nodded, but he studied her closely. She wore sunglasses, but he couldn't escape the feeling that she didn't want to meet his gaze. Was it really just the sun that made her squirm?

"When are you leaving?" he asked.

"Tonight," Charlotte said. "When it's full dark. Until I get used to it, I'd rather travel at night."

"You've got enough money to get you to New York?" he asked.

"I'll be fine," she said, perking up as though she sensed his doubts. "I'll go straight to the shadow registration office, like I promised. I don't want to be a rogue, Peter. I don't want anyone hunting me."

Octavian narrowed his eyes. "Cortez is going to be hunting you," he said. "You know that. But we'll help you. I've got to take care of Keomany's ashes and then reconnect with Nikki, but give me a week and I'll meet you in New York. The UN Security Council and Task Force Victor are going to want to know everything you can tell them about Cortez. We can't afford to have him building some kind of secret vampire underground. We've worked too hard to establish peace."

Charlotte nodded. "Cortez killed me. I didn't want this life. I'll help in any way I can."

"Good. I'll see you there," Octavian replied.

He thought he should say something more, tell them that he hoped they did not end up like Keomany, but he knew it would serve no purpose. They were no longer human, but they did not have to share the earthwitch's fate. If they worked at it, they could both have some semblance of ordinary lives. It would be a pretense, but many people lived their lives behind masks. It could be done.

For a while, at least.

The wave of chaos that had spread out from Hawthorne would draw even more attentions from the demons and monsters and forgotten gods that had been banished into other realms, the forces of darkness that had been kept out of this plane for over a thousand years. There had been a number of incursions in the time since the Tatterdemalion, with Navalica only the latest. More would be coming, and he knew now that he had to be in the thick of the fight against them. If they were lucky, Amber and Charlotte would not be a part of that fight. But he feared that one day the whole world would have to take up arms against the darkness. It was a war he prayed would never come.

"Take care of yourselves," he said.

He climbed into his car and set the bottle of Keomany's ashes on the seat beside him, plumping a faded Sorbonne sweatshirt around it to keep it from rolling onto the floor. Then he started up the car, gave Amber and Charlotte a wave, and drove away.

Octavian thought that his spirits would lift when he crossed the town line and left Hawthorne behind him, but instead, his mood darkened. He had talked to Nikki twice yesterday and once this morning. She had taken the news of Keomany's death even harder than he would have expected. They had been good friends in college but off and on since. This morning, her tone had been different, as though she sensed something in his voice, suspected that there were things he was not telling her.

For an ordinary woman, she had always had excellent intuition. He needed to see her. To spend time in her arms and try to sort out what he really felt. He wondered about what he had felt for Keomany—if there had been anything real there at all—and what it might mean for him and Nikki. Of late he had begun to question more and more if it was possible for him to sustain a real relationship with an ordinary woman, with all of the threats lurking in the shadowed corners of the world.

It was a question they would have to answer together.

Exhausted and worried about Peter, Nikki rode the elevator to the twelfth floor of the Loews Hotel. She hadn't slept well the night before, woken too early, and then fallen back to sleep after her wake-up call, which had made her late for her sound check at the World Café. She always enjoyed playing Philadelphia and seeing the hope and enthusiasm in the faces of the college kids who came out to hear her. She wanted to give them a good show tonight, which meant getting something to eat, taking a nap, and trying not to think about Keomany's death, or the tension between her and Peter before he had gone off to save the world again.

Listen to you, she thought. *"Save the world." What a bitch.*

She knew she was being a bitch. Peter had obligations that were much greater than whatever he owed her and their relationship. But knowing that and fully accepting it were two different things. Some days it was all right, but right now she just wanted him with her . . . wanted him to put his arms around her and tell her that he loved her, and that everything would be all right.

"Could you be more selfish?" she said aloud in the lonely confines of the elevator. Keomany was dead, and all she could think about was the growing distance that she felt between herself and her boyfriend.

Peter had promised to catch up with her by Atlanta, at the latest.

That was four days from now. Four days was nothing. They had been apart from each other much longer in the past. All she had to do was pour herself into her music, sing her heart out, give her audiences the performance they deserved for shelling out their hard-earned cash.

"Get it together, woman," she whispered.

The elevator slid to a stop on the twelfth floor. Stepping off, she went the wrong way and then laughed at herself. She really did need to focus.

Wondering whether she might find something edible on the room service menu, she let herself into the mini-suite the club management had provided. The maid had been in, and the citrus-chemical scent of her cleansers filled the suite.

Nikki put her key card on the little coffee table in front of the love seat and kicked off her shoes. The room service menu waited on the desk over by the window, next to her laptop, but first she needed to peel off her clothes and slide into the cotton pajama pants and Boston Celtics T-shirt she had worn to bed last night.

As she walked into the bedroom, its curtains still drawn from the morning, she dragged her clingy black top over her head. A sliver of sunlight sliced into the darkened room between the curtains, enough for her to seek out the sleepwear she'd shed in such a hurry.

Only as she slipped off her bra did she recognize that something was not right. The maid had been in. She had cleaned the bathroom. Made the bed. There would be mint chocolate candies on the pillow.

A figure coalesced in the deeply shadowed corner.

"You *are* lovely," he said, in a rasping Spanish accent. "What a pity."

Nikki froze, flushing with the heat of fear.

"Who the hell are you?" she breathed.

Though he was all in darkness, somehow she knew he smiled then. "I am Cortez," he replied.

His fangs tore into her throat before she could scream.

She wept as she died.

Wondering why.

SIMON &
SCHUSTER

Christopher Golden

Of Saints and Shadows

Book One of *The Shadow Saga*

An epic tale of vampires, sorcery and war

Armed with an ancient book called tPhe Gospel of
Shadows, a secret sect has been slowly destroying
vampires for centuries. Now the book has been stolen, and
the sect races to retrieve it before their purpose is
discovered: a final purge of all vampires. As the line
between saints and shadows grows ominously faint, private
eye Peter Octavian is drawn into the search. And he'll do
anything to find the book . . . for Peter Octavian is also a
vampire.

In a deadly game with a driven, sadistic assassin, the trail
leads to Venice at the time of carnival, where the Defiant
Ones are engaged in a savage battle for their lives. Filled
with plot twists, mystery, sex and violent death, *Of Saints
and Shadows* is a spine-tingling thriller which opens the
door to the world of *The Shadow Saga*.

ISBN: 978-1-84739-924-3
PRICE £7.99

SIMON &
SCHUSTER

Christopher Golden

Angel Souls and Devil Hearts

Book Two of *The Shadow Saga*

An epic tale of vampires, sorcery and war

The Shadows have been revealed as living among us, and
now the ancient vampiric race must confront the most
powerful monster of all: human prejudice. In a world
where the good are no longer distinguishable from the bad
and where Shadows are indeed the saints, a holy war is
about to begin, pitting human and vampire together against
the darkest demons of Hell.

As they fight for their survival in the face of betrayal by
one of their own, the Shadows begin to discover at last the
astonising, long-hidden truth of what they are. What they
learn about their mysterious origins is more
extraordinary – and more explosive – than they could
possibly have imagined.

ISBN: 978-1-84739-925-0
PRICE £7.99

SIMON &
SCHUSTER

Christopher Golden

Of Masques and Martyrs

Book Three of *The Shadow Saga*

Vampires at war with the world, and with themselves

For the Shadows, nothing will ever be the same again.
Their existence revealed to the world in *Of Saints and
Shadows*, the truth of their divided heritage revealed to
themselves in *Angel Souls and Devil Hearts*, they must
now fight the hardest battle of all – against their own kind.
Within each of them there is a battle between the demonic
and the divine. Now that battle will be played out to the
death between those like Hannibal, who thirst only for
blood and power, and those like Octavian, who recognise
in themselves a different legacy.

The future of humanity will depend on who is victorious,
as the conflict tears the world of *The Shadow Saga* apart.

ISBN: 978-1-84739-926-7
PRICE £7.99

SIMON &
SCHUSTER

Christopher Golden

The Gathering Dark

Book Four of *The Shadow Saga*

An epic tale of vampires, sorcery and war

The Gospel of Shadows enabled the Catholic church to control supernatural beings for centuries. When the book was destroyed, it enabled the Shadows, the vampires of legend, to learn the hidden truth of their triple nature: part human, part demonic, part divine. It weakened the barriers that exist between the worlds, and now beings of pure evil are breaking through – creatures from other dimensions for which Hell is just a name.

Peter Octavian, once a powerful Shadow, now restored to humanity, is the only man with sufficient knowledge to stop them. Aided by an earthwitch, a vampire and a priest, and calling on the magical forces of mother nature herself, Octavian stands between the Earth and apocalypse, as entire cities are plunged into the abyss . . .

ISBN: 978-1-84739-927-4
PRICE £7.99